Damaged Mogul

Scarlett Avery

Edited by John Hudspith

Proofread by Lisa Fearday, Chrissy Becker, Melody Fuhrman, and Jamie Betts

Cover designed by Murphy Rae

Damaged Mogul © Scarlett Avery

The Moguls series

ISBN 978-1-77498-142-9

Dedication

This book is dedicated to all my readers who melt when the grumpy hero smiles only for her. And for those who yearn to be told you're a 'good girl' by a brooding man who keeps everyone at arm's length, but you.

Gage is waiting to break you and ruin you for all others.

Chapter 1

Lily

My eyes bounce around the space as I follow the maître d'.

The pale white walls, sheer drapes, soaring ceiling, and large windows contribute to the airiness of this gourmet New York restaurant. Unlike so many expensive eateries in the city, it doesn't have that harsh modern edge that can be quite off-putting. On the contrary, the décor at Jean-Georges is welcoming.

The coveted restaurant, located near Central Park, is packed.

Men in impeccable bespoke suits and women in their finest couture eat, drink, and laugh.

Your average Tuesday evening in New York City.

This is my first time at the three Michelin starred restaurant. If the wonderful aroma floating in the air and the glimpse of mouthwatering food I caught along the way are any indication, I'm in for a treat.

My father is sitting at a table near the large windows.

He isn't alone.

My face sours a bit when I spot who he's with.

Oh, God, not her.

Is it too late to run?

My father's eyes lock onto mine and he lifts a hand.

Crap.

He gets to his feet. So does his irritable side piece, towering over him.

Fisher Edgington thinks big, talks big, deals big, plays big, and lives big. Perhaps God knew his massive ego would be too much to bear for us mere mortals if it were accompanied by soaring height. To my father's irritation, he only stands five-feet-eight—much taller than me, but significantly shorter than his model-tall girlfriend who has a penchant for wearing five-inch heels.

We reach my father's table.

"Mr. Edgington, your guest has arrived," the maître d' says. "I'll send a waiter over."

"Thank you," my father says.

With that, the maître d' excuses himself with a bow, and moves his attention to another table.

We stare at each other for a long beat, my eyes bouncing from my father's icy blue gaze to the brunette forty years his junior who's draped around his arm like a poison ivy vine.

My father clears his throat. "I'll meet you at your place when I'm done with Lily." He dismisses his girlfriend.

Thank you, God.

In the six weeks I've been back to New York, I've had to see too much of her for my liking.

"Nom nom, I can't wait." Her voice drips with a suggestive tone.

Yuck.

"Be good." My father winks.

She runs her fingers through his salt and pepper hair. "I'll try, but I can't promise."

If this continues, I'm going to have to excuse myself to go to the bathroom and barf.

"*Tourelou* and toodles, Lily," she says, wiggling her fingers.

One would suffice. No need to double up on the idiocy. "See you." I keep it brief.

And... she's off.

The scent of my father's girlfriend's overpowering perfume still lingers in the air when a waiter materializes at our table. "May I take your drink order?"

"A Godfather for me and a Perrier pink grapefruit on ice for her." My father orders on my behalf before I even have time to open my mouth.

God forbid I'd make my own choice.

The waiter's eyes shift in my direction.

I respond with an imperceptible nod.

"That's her usual drink." My father snaps at the waiter.

The man nods. "Very well, sir."

In no time, he returns with our drinks.

Before I even have time to wrap my fingers around the highball, my father drains half of his drink.

I dip my lips in my Perrier, ready to quench my thirst.

"Thanks for joining me," my father says. "We have so much to celebrate today."

I drop my highball on the table and sit a little straighter in my seat.

For a second there, I thought he had forgotten.

"It's official as of today. Chandler is taking his BHAG by the balls."

"Which of Chandler's *big hairy audacious goals* are we talking about?"

"My first born is stepping into politics. I've been grooming him for long enough." He claps before rubbing his hands together. "He'll be running for mayor of New York City. That's the first step on his upward trajectory towards the big seat—the presidency."

My shoulders sag in disappointment.

This isn't why I thought we were meeting tonight.

"His decision is going to have a monumental impact on the family."

The family I'm ostracized from.

"You heading the publicity firm is more important now than ever before," he says. "We need someone we can trust to craft Chandler's image."

His comment about me heading anything is laughable. Fisher Edgington is the ultimate puppet master. He pretends to give you control, but he's the one pulling the strings.

I narrow my eyes. "According to Chandler, I don't exist. He and my three other half-brothers feel the same way." *After all, I'm the villainess.* "Need I remind you, your sons have treated me like a pariah since you became my guardian after Mama's death. So, why on earth would Chandler want me to craft his political image when he can't stand the sight of me?"

"A bit dramatic don't you think?"

Keep sticking your head in the sand, Father. You excel at it. "Prove me wrong." I cross my arms over my chest. "When was the last time any of your sons acknowledged me?"

My father averts his gaze as he pretends to adjust his tie.

"Speaking of your future career as the head of a successful PR company, I found someone who will accompany you to the event in LA."

"I don't need a chaperone," I say.

"You're not attending that event alone. You've never been to Los Angeles—"

"The last time you assigned me a chaperone for Emerson

College's meet-and-greet evening event in Boston, your contact was caught in a closet with his pants down as a waiter sucked his manhood." I roll my stiff shoulders, but they refuse to ease. "When you forced me to attend the University of Texas's open house, you assigned a chaperone who kept asking me—in not-so-subtle ways—if I'd consider deflowering his eighteen-year-old son, and would it be okay if he watched us in the throes of passion so he could coach his virgin teenage offspring on how to properly satisfy a woman. He also wanted to know if I was open to the idea of a threesome with him and his son after I was done deflowering junior to celebrate the joyous occasion."

"We're walking down memory lane."

I ignore his jab and soldier on. "The chaperone you selected for the Florida State University's evening had a disturbing flatulence problem." I thought I was going to suffocate from the foul smell. "Still, that didn't stop him from suggesting we swing by his favorite Cuban restaurant after the event for some *Pollo con Arroz Congri* with an extra side of beans, before we ended the evening at his place for a nightcap so we could get to *know* each other better. I've had it up to here"—I gesture a hand over my head—"with your crappy chaperones."

"Granted, those men had shortcomings I wasn't aware of—"

"You could say that again." I scoff. "I'm sure chaperone number four must have a long list of shortcomings you're unaware of."

"I've cut ties with those *former* friends," he says, "because their shortcomings reflect poorly on me."

It's all about image with Fisher Edgington. Although, in these cases, I can't blame him for distancing himself.

"Gage Hollingsworth isn't a flake and he knows how to conduct himself at an event," he says. "The man has a reputation to uphold. And to my knowledge, he doesn't pass wind in public. Also, at his size, he's more of a bodyguard than a chaper-one. The man is built like a brick wall."

"The answer is still no."

"Lily, this isn't up for discussion." His firm answer has the same effect as a judge slamming his gavel on a desk.

Any other day I'd move onto another topic, one that wouldn't put me on his bad side. But today isn't any other day.

I let out an exasperated sigh. "When you said you wanted to meet tonight because we had so much to celebrate, I never suspected we'd be discussing Chandler's political career, and you forcing, yet again, another dirty old man down my throat. I was expecting something else."

He frowns.

I throw him a bone. "Something pertaining to me."

He straightens the sleeves of his impeccable, bespoke navy-blue suit before adjusting his yellow tie, again. "What are you talking about?"

"You can't think of anything else worth celebrating today?"

The furrow between his neatly groomed brows remains. "No."

A world of emotion swirls inside me like filth floating over the waters of a polluted swamp.

Flabbergasted, I gape at him.

He has no clue what I'm talking about.

A lump the size of my fist rises in my throat. "Think harder."

The blank stare on his face speaks volumes.

The lump grows, threatening to choke me.

I search the restaurant for our waiter.

He catches my gaze and rushes towards our table. "What can I get you, miss?"

"What's going on, Lily?"

I focus my attention on the expectant waiter. I swallow past the lump. "Two glasses of your best champagne, please."

"What the hell are you doing?" My father's tone is sharp. "This isn't Europe. You're not of drinking age yet."

Confusion flashes in the waiter's eyes.

I rummage through my bag, pull out my driver's license, and hand it to the waiter.

He checks it with care.

"Happy Birthday!" he says, meeting my gaze. "I get to serve you your first drink."

From the corner of my eyes, I notice my father flinch.

He opens his mouth. He closes it.

He does that a few times.

No comments from the peanut gallery.

Still, the unvoiced criticism comes out loud and clear.

"My first drink *in the US.*"

The waiter hands me my driver's license. "Our best champagne coming right up."

"Thank you."

The waiter scurries off.

Aware of my father's stare, I take my sweet time placing my driver's license in the inside pocket of my bag.

"What the hell was that about?"

I meet his angry, icy blue eyes, reproach shines bright in them.

A war of glares ensues.

He forgot.

I'm dumbfounded.

"It's my birthday today," I say after a long beat. "I'm twenty-one."

Sparks of outrage shoot from his eyes. "Why not come out and announce it's your damn birthday instead of playing your silly little games? Your childish theatrics are unnecessary."

Ouch.

I'm stunned, humiliated, and hurt by his vitriolic comment.

"Why didn't you remind me?"

I let out a self-deprecating laugh. "Did you forget your sons' twenty-first birthdays?"

The corner of his upper lip pulls up, his discontentment evident.

It's dangerous to poke the bear, especially when you depend financially on said bear.

Fuck it.

I catch sight of the waiter approaching our table, balancing two champagne flutes on a tray, and lift a hand to stop him from taking another step.

He freezes in place.

Reaching for the dignity I too often suppress in the hopes this man who I share DNA with would recognize me as his daughter instead of a mistake, I get to my feet.

My father's eyes fly up to meet mine. "Where the hell are you going?"

For a man who's so in-tune when it comes to business, he's dumb as a rock when it comes to people.

"I get you'd rather I was never born." I bite down tears. "I thought after so many years, you'd find it in your heart to accept me." *Even love me.*

"Lily—"

"Don't Lily me." All eyes are on us. I can feel it. I hate calling attention to myself, but fuck it if I'm making a spectacle. "It's your turn to listen." I point at him. "I'm not expecting you to"—my voice cracks—"love me like you love your sons, but at the very least, respect me. You have two executive assistants *and* one personal assistant who takes care of your social calendar—"

"You know full well—"

"Don't you dare use the convenient excuse of them being new hires."

His propensity for always finding a scapegoat is baffling.

Working for my father isn't all rainbows and sunshine. Employee turnover is as common as huge profit in his world.

He pinches his lips.

Yeah, I saw you coming a mile away.

He averts his gaze for the briefest moment, no doubt racking his brain for a clever retort.

He returns his attention to me, his expression more annoyed than ever.

I dig deep. "Your assistants *aren't* my parents. *You* are." I point an accusatory finger at him. "They shouldn't be the ones managing that part of your life. If you can't remember my birthday without someone you pay reminding you, it tells me you value me less than gum under your shoe." I've never seen my father speechless. "My best friend is the only one who acknowledged my birthday—and she lives an ocean away. I didn't get so much as a text from the people I'm related to by blood, aka you or your sons."

"You should've—"

"Own up to the egregious error, Father." I throw one of his favorite big words in his face.

His expression turns baffled, as though he doesn't know what to make of me or my tirade. "Enough with the Broadway act." He has the audacity to chastise me. "Sit down, and let's have dinner like civilized people."

I don't give a damn about the warning in his voice. I stare him down, mustering up my courage. "In your world, I have little to no importance. When business isn't consuming you, your sons are deserving of your attention, care, and pride." *And love.* "You've made it clear over and over again, but never as cruelly as today." I snatch my bag off the table and tuck it underneath my arm.

He lets out an audible sigh.

He doesn't approve of my little performance.

I don't approve of his indifference.

I square my shoulders and stare straight into my father's eyes. "Enjoy the rest of your evening with your girlfriend. Even she gets to make it on your list of priorities."

I get the hell out of the restaurant like the building is on fire. I refuse to give Fisher Edgington the satisfaction of seeing me cry.

I should've kept my expectations low for tonight—I knew it from experience. And yet, my stupid heart had hoped. And now my stupid heart is broken. Again.

Chapter 2

Lily

A week and a half later

"Lily Schuyler!" As I head to the hotel's elevators, someone calls out my name.

I halt my step, forcing the bellboy walking alongside me to do the same.

I turn around.

A smiling woman impeccably dressed in a stunning fuchsia dress, with hair as jet black as mine, comes rushing my way, balancing beautifully on killer white high heels.

"Yes?"

"I'm Michaela König. Phoenix's wife."

Phoenix, the CEO, and Gage Hollingsworth's friend. Got it.

Wait a minute.

I frown. "How did you know who I was?"

"I asked the driver of the chauffeured car I put at your disposal to text me when you were approaching the hotel. He told me you were the woman wearing a light purple sweatshirt, white jeans, and white high-top Converse." She looks around the lobby. "Lucky for me, you're the only one who matches that description."

The service here is out of this world. "It's a pleasure to meet you."

"Likewise. Welcome to the Pompadour Hotel." She extends a hand.

"Thank you." I shake it.

"I'm sorry I wasn't able to greet you when you arrived earlier, but I was stuck on a call with our Paris hotel."

"Don't worry about it. You're the hotel's queen bee. I'm just another guest."

She shakes her head. "No, you're not. Gage asked me to look after you."

"I'm sure he had more important things to deal with than pick me up at the airport."

"He planned on picking you up, but he's dealing with a DEFCON crisis."

"I hope he's okay."

"He is. He's... having a rough day."

"Sounds like his day is shittier than mine."

Her eyes shift to my luggage cart. "Not that shitty."

"As much as I like this outfit, the airline's mistake forced me to go shopping for a new wardrobe before I was able to do any sightseeing," I say. "When life throws you lemons—"

"Make French lemon tart."

"Good one."

She winks.

Michaela turns her attention to the bellboy. "Can you please wait for Miss Schuyler near the elevators? We're going to have a little chat."

"Absolutely, Mrs. König." With a bow, bellboy moves away, rolling my new wardrobe with him.

Michaela's phone rings. She checks her screen and ignores

the call. Her eyes are on me again. "Did you check your luggage tracker app?"

"I did. My luggage is in Hawaii."

"Crap."

"My arrival in LA was epic. Not only did I lose my luggage, but while I was looking for it, I lost my phone somewhere in LAX."

Her lips pull down in a frown. "LA hasn't been welcoming to you."

"Not at all."

"Did you buy a new phone?"

"Yes. That was my first stop."

"I'm glad that's settled. Let me input my phone number."

We exchange phones.

"I'll also put Gage's in," she says. "I'll add Phoenix's. You're only here for a few days, but this way, you'll have a solid list of emergency contacts. You never know."

"Thanks, Michaela."

"Now that we're friends, you have to call me Mikki."

Friends?

I've always had a hard time making friends—never quite fitting in. I've never known this sort of unwavering welcome from anyone before.

"Thanks, Mikki."

"You and Gage aren't together, but since you'll be hanging out with him for the rest of your stay in the City of Angels, and he's asked me to take you under my wing, you'll get a chance to meet the sisterhood."

I frown my confusion.

"Phoenix's brothers are still holding on to their bachelorhood VIP cards with no intentions of ever settling down. However, most of Phoenix's inner circle of close guy friends all have girlfriends, fiancées, or wives. Most of us gals don't have siblings. Over time, we've formed a sisterhood."

I don't dare tell her this arrangement with Gage is only for one night. I doubt he'll be hanging out with me after tonight.

"That would be lovely."

"You'll love the girls," she says. "Rhys—my best friend Keira's man, also an only child—is celebrating his birthday tomorrow night."

Lucky Rhys, he has someone in life who gives a damn about his birthday.

"You have to come as Gage's plus one."

I flinch at her suggestion. "Shouldn't we discuss that with Gage first?"

"If you insist on being difficult, you'll come as my friend."

I laugh. "I can handle that."

"It's much easier to agree with me."

"Noted."

"Speaking of events, did you find the perfect dress for tonight?"

"I did," I say. "I asked the chauffeur to stop at a secondhand shop in Beverly Hills with great reviews. As I was approaching the entrance, a woman with arms weighed down with clothing was fighting her way inside. I helped her with the door. Fast forward, she was bringing in tons of designer clothing, including a Dior Haute Couture dress—with certification of authentication. It has an old Hollywood design to it, complete with a fit-and-flare cut that's plucked straight from the 1950s. It might be a bit too much—"

"Honey, this is LA. You can be as too much as you want."

I smile. "As luck would have it, the woman had a Dior off-the-shoulder pale pink dress altered from a ballgown length to a midi-length to fit her. The perils of being short..."

"I hear you."

"In any case, she insisted I try it on. I couldn't refuse. It fit me like a glove."

"I'm sure Dior Haute Couture isn't cheap, but you'll make a statement tonight."

"My father forgot my twenty-first birthday a week and a half ago, the dress is retribution."

Michaela's jaw drops, her eyes widening in shock.

Shit.

That overshare slipped my lips without my permission.

She frowns. "How is that even possible?"

"That conversation requires half a dozen martinis, and I won't have time. It's five o'clock now, and Gage will be here in an hour."

"Please tell me your father made up for it."

I hesitate for a moment, and decide to trust this woman with my humiliating secret. "He's giving me the silent treatment." I bite the inside of my cheek. "We haven't spoken to each other or exchanged texts in a week and a half. I sent him a quick text at five a.m. this morning before I left my place. No response."

Myriad emotions flash in Michaela's eyes.

The last one being the most heart-wrenching one. Few people know the story of my life because I don't want to be pitied.

And now, I regret opening up.

"I'll survive." I'm lying to myself.

Since it was two-thirty in the morning in Paris by the time I returned to my place after I left my father sitting at the restaurant, I couldn't call my best friend to lament. I had to suck it up.

One of the best things about New York is that it's the city that never sleeps. I asked the taxi driver to drop me off at one of my favorite spots. Sorrow curled my stomach when I walked through the doors of the bakery, but it dissipated when I inhaled the sweet sugary aroma floating around me.

I bought a pink champagne cake with pink champagne frosting before swinging by a liquor store to purchase a bottle of Dom Pérignon rosé. In the multi-million-dollar brownstone my father bought me to atone for his sins, I licked my wounds.

I celebrated the big 2-1. Alone.

As I numbed my pain with too much champagne, only the poignant vocals of my favorite blue-eyed soul songstress kept me company.

I didn't choose how I came into this world.

How long will I have to pay the price for being Fisher Edgington's illegitimate child?

Drunk on Dom Pérignon and high on sugar with my expertly applied makeup a mess because of the river of tears streaming down my face, I cried myself to sleep.

Yeah, Happy Twenty-First Birthday to me—

Michaela is still staring, dumbfounded.

Blink.

Blink.

Blink.

I grow more and more uncomfortable each time she bats her long, dark eyelashes.

She reaches out and runs a hand up and down my arm. "Twenty-one is a big deal," she says in a soft voice. "A big fucking deal, if you ask me." The expression on her face transforms into something menacing. "I don't know your father—and I might be out of line—but his behavior is appalling."

A wave of sadness washes over me. "I'm nothing but a footnote in his manuscript."

Chapter 3

Gage

This day steamrolled me.

I was so consumed by today's drama, I toyed with the idea of asking my receptionist to accompany Lily at tonight's event. Even in my pissed-off state, I recognized it was a bad idea. It's one thing to justify not being able to meet her at the airport, it's another to ditch her altogether.

As I stroll through the Pompadour Hotel's lobby, I pull out my phone and shoot off a text to Michaela and Phoenix to let them know I've arrived. I also send one to Lily to let her know where to find me. All three of them respond.

Done.

I head towards the Baudelaire Bar for a much-needed drink. Since I won't be here long, I refuse the hostess's invitation for a booth, preferring a spot at one of the high tables offering an unobstructed view to the entrance. I'm too restless to sit down.

After placing my drink order, I begin the countdown until I'm able to inject my veins with alcohol. When the bartender drops a gin martini on ice in front of me, I lift my eyes to the ceiling and let out a silent prayer. After the hellish day I've had to endure, I need to deep dive to the bottom of this glass, and never reemerge.

I drain half my drink in one go.

I drop the glass on the table, and realization hits me.

Lily and I never exchanged photos, and I didn't stalk her online.

Since Fisher connected us, our few exchanges have been brief. Not that I'm complaining. I'd rather that than her texting me incessantly. On the downside, I have no idea who I'm supposed to meet.

I'm about to shoot her another text and attach a photo, when Mr. and Mrs. König appear at the threshold.

Phoenix lifts a hand in salute.

I respond in kind.

He and his beautiful wife head my way.

"Hey," Phoenix says, patting my shoulder. "Did you survive the day?"

"Barely." I lift my martini glass. "That's why this is the first of many."

"I saw the screaming headlines," Michaela says. "Is any of it true?"

"Fifteen-year-old violinist Snow Hyman's aggravating, loudmouth mom is convinced her daughter is the next in line for her own Vegas headline show."

Michaela frowns. "Is her daughter that talented?"

"Snow has potential, but her bratty attitude is insupportable," I say. "In the end, the public voted her off the show. Her fame-hungry mom has been vocal in expressing her outrage, but I never thought it would amount to her accusing my show host of sexual harassment." My jaw ticks. "To add insult to injury, loud mouths on the internet are going apeshit crazy, chanting, '*Nail the motherfucker*' without knowing the facts."

"Is there any truth to the accusations?"

I shake my head. "No, Phoenix. Not a shred of truth."

"You're certain?"

"I am. Matthew would never do that."

Phoenix frowns.

I lean into him. "There are certain things I can't reveal right now."

He nods. "Got it."

I take another swig of my drink.

Michaela places a hand on my arm. "I'm sorry you have to deal with the ordeal and chaos that comes with these types of accusations. Again."

If someone doesn't want a piece of me, they're trying to get a piece of someone I know. "This time around, my head isn't on the chopping block, but I'm the executive producer of the show, so my name is dragged through the mud, alongside Matthew's. This drama has had a negative impact on my other companies." I rub my tired face with the palm of my hand and let out an audible breath. "Blanche Hyman gives stage moms a bad rap." *Fucking fame-hungry bitch.*

"She does," Michaela says. "And she's setting an appalling example for her daughter."

"Are things still in limbo for your host?" Phoenix arches a brow.

I check my watch. "Within an hour, the publicity team will push out a press release. My show host is going to hold a press conference tomorrow to clear his name."

"That's tough, putting yourself out there like that," Phoenix says.

"At least he'll be able to shut up that horrible woman and her prima donna daughter," Michaela says.

"That's the plan." I change the subject. "Thanks again for taking care of Lily."

The Pompadour Hotel has an irreproachable reputation, which is why I booked a room here for Lily. I don't want her to complain about anything.

"It's my pleasure," she says. "Not long ago, I was a newcomer in LA. Without my best friend, I would've been lost."

"So, I had no part in making your transition from the Big Apple to the City of Angels a smooth one, wife?"

Michaela swats Phoenix's arm.

He chuckles.

I never thought I'd see the day when bachelor forever Phoenix settled down. Then again, there was a lot on the line for him.

"Poor Lily, there's nothing worse than losing your luggage," Michaela says. "It's the most frustrating experience."

That must've been a nightmare. "Was she able to get everything she needed?"

Michaela grins wide. "She's a happy camper."

"That's good news," I say. "I'm surprised Fisher hasn't called me to either micromanage her arrival or voice his concerns over the media shit storm."

Michaela tilts her head to the side. "He's pissed off at Lily. That's probably why he hasn't called."

I frown. "What makes you say that?"

Michaela leans into me. "A father who doesn't acknowledge his daughter's twenty-first birthday? It doesn't make any sense."

"What?" I'm dumbfounded.

I'm equally surprised by Michaela's comment and the fact I didn't even know Lily's age. She wasn't forthcoming during our text messages, and I wasn't interested in knowing more than what she was willing to share.

"I had the same reaction when my wife told me," Phoenix says.

Michaela shares the highlights of her earlier conversation with Lily.

"Unbelievable," I say.

"I don't know Fisher Edgington, but I don't like him," Michaela says. "If it wasn't for poor customer service, I'd make sure Phoenix refuses him entry at any of our hotels."

Michaela's protectiveness of a mere stranger doesn't go unnoticed.

I tolerate Fisher because I have to. I'd never peg the guy as warm and fuzzy, but what Michaela described makes me lose all respect for the man. I may have the reputation of being prickly, but I'm not a heartless son of a bitch.

"And, by the way, you had her last name wrong," Michaela says.

"How so?"

She leans into me. "She goes by Lily Schuyler. Not Lily Edgington."

My eyes widen in surprise.

The plot thickens...

I'm about to respond, but words escape me when, from my peripheral vision, a spot of soft pink catches my attention. My gaze moves to the entrance, where a bombshell breezes into the bar.

Holy fuck.

"Speaking of the beautiful swan... she appears," Michaela says.

For the first time since entering the bar, I take note of the music playing in the background—*La Vie en Rose.*

Chapter 4

Lily

Sharing details about the worst birthday ever submerged me in a wave of melancholy. Even though my mom has passed away, I can't consider myself an orphan since one of my parents is still alive. My reality shatters that fact. Based on my nonexistent relationship with my half-brothers and my frosty relationship with my father—people I share DNA with—I am an orphan.

The selfless way Michaela—a stranger—welcomed me into her circle, left me unsettled for several long minutes after retreating to my hotel room.

It's only when Mikki texted me to let me know she'd be at the bar with Gage, it hit me. We never exchanged photos.

This topsy-turvy day is preventing me from thinking straight.

When I enter the Baudelaire Bar, I suppress a laugh.

My Parisian-born best friend has so many issues *with La Vie en Rose*—including the contemporary versions of Edith Piaf's iconic song. I don't have time to dwell on the song, because Mikki is waving me over.

Her and her husband flank a man—

Scratch that.

He's a gorgeous demigod.

Sweet mercy.

My previous chaperones weren't male models, but I didn't expect them to be. Gage Hollingsworth *is* male model material.

That handsome face.

That sculpted jaw, dusted with a 5 o'clock shadow.

That Grecian nose.

That slick haircut that accentuates his chiseled cheekbones.

Those lips...

I was so pissed off at my father, I didn't bother doing a search to find out more about Gage. I kept our communications brief, sharing the bare minimum, since I was going to hang out with him for only a few hours. I didn't even bother asking for a photo. Now, I see the error of my ways.

I would've much preferred being prepared for our first encounter.

When I approach the trio, Gage gets to his feet.

My eyes move up, and up, and up.

He circles the high table and reaches me with a long stride. He moves with the self-assurance of a man who holds the world in the palms of his hands. Compared to my father and half-brothers' short statures, his height, plays in his favor.

My father was right. At his size, Gage is more of a body-guard than a chaperone.

Michaela and Phoenix are right on his heels.

Holy hotness.

The man is clad in an impeccable black suit that hugs his bulky male lines. Even this late in the day, his white shirt is crisp and his silk tie isn't askew. Confidence radiates off him in waves.

Gage's tailor has been touched by God himself, and he's doing all women a favor.

Given I've lived in Switzerland, Paris, and now New York, a man in a suit shouldn't have this effect on me. Maybe it's the towering height, or the broad shoulders that stretch his suit jacket, or the pocket handkerchief—a touch of elegance that never goes out of style—but Gage Hollingsworth is suit porn personified.

I met Phoenix when Mikki and I were chatting in the lobby. He's tall, but Gage towers over him by a good two inches. Even in my four-inch heels, I'm tiny compared to this man. He's several years older than me. Closer to Phoenix's age—thirty-something.

Being in his presence is sensory overload.

"You're Lily."

Dear God. His voice is a husky, sultry rasp. The rich timbre reverberates straight down through my body, stopping right between my legs. On his tongue, my name is as soft as silk, sliding over my skin.

He extends a hand.

I slide mine into his massive one. His touch causes my heart to stop.

My breath hitches.

For a beat, I can only stare at our joined hands.

Mikki places a hand on my shoulder. "Lily?"

Huh?

I meet her eyes, which are emerald-green compared to Gage's translucent seafoam ones.

I've never seen eyes that color before.

He studies me like a fine piece of art he plans on buying.

I blush.

"Are you okay?" Mikki interrupts my gawk fest.

Oh, God, I'm making a fool out of myself.

Pick your jaw off the floor.

I snap out of it. "Sorry, it's been a trying day. It's a pleasure to meet you, Gage."

"Likewise." He gives my hand a good shake before letting go. The movement is a bit jerky.

He stares at his hand for a beat before returning his focus on me.

His dark brows meet in the middle. His eyes crinkle in the corners as he studies me. It's as if his lush lips frown as much as his brows. "You're not what I expected."

His bluntness catches me off guard, his words hitting me with a swift kick to the belly.

Another man who thinks I don't measure up.

"Gage, be good." Mikki elbows him.

"You might want to try that again," Phoenix says.

Gage's pale gaze flickers to me, burning into my skin.

He shifts his weight from one foot to the other.

The movement forces my eyes to his feet—his very long feet.

And those shoes. I'm willing to bet the brownstone I live in, they're bespoke.

"That dress..." He waves a finger my way.

I expect him to elaborate, but he doesn't.

He crosses his beefy arms over his chest, a brow rises as he studies me.

Or is it eats me alive? I can't tell.

His gaze travels up and down the length of my body, before settling on my face. He stares at me long and hard, as if all my secrets are stamped on my forehead.

His presence is magnetic.

Am I overdressed? "Did I commit a fashion faux-pas?" Embarrassment uncoils in my belly. My worried gaze meets Mikki's. "Is it too much? I can go change—"

"The dress is perfect on you," she says. "Gage, Lily looks pretty. Doesn't she?"

His expression pinches, and he responds with a grunt, followed by a scowl.

Do I offend him?

Perhaps I'm guilty by association. After all, our only contact is my father, and Fisher Edgington masters the art of pissing people off.

"You'll have to excuse my friend," Phoenix says. "He's normally disagreeable, moody, surly, and brusque, but he had a bitch of a day, so he's more irascible than usual."

A grumpy bodyguard. Fun times ahead.

Gage's eyes shift to the side. "Love you too, bro."

"If you get past the gruff exterior, he's *somewhat* tolerable," Phoenix says.

Unable to help myself, I laugh.

Gage's eyes widen and the scowl returns to his face.

This guy can't stand me.

If his opinion of me is based on whatever relationship he has with my father, I have zero interest in proving him wrong. I didn't even want to contact him in the first place. I should've stuck to my guns.

"If your day bitch-slapped you, I wouldn't be offended if you bowed out." I purse my lips. "You don't have to accompany me. I'm a big girl. I'll go alone." There, I gave him a way out.

Mikki flinches.

Phoenix cocks an eyebrow.

Gage sucks in a sharp breath, his nostrils flaring.

Good God, the man's eyes are showstoppers. The unique shade of green is arresting. They're stunning—almond-shaped under the frowning slashes of his brows and framed by long lashes. Men shouldn't have lashes that pretty.

When wintergreen eyes narrow in on me, I brace myself for what's about to come out of his mouth.

"No, I'm coming." That comes out like a dark rumble.

You don't have to be so happy about it. "Gage, I know you're doing this as a favor for my father. Don't strain yourself. I understand if—"

"I said, I'm coming." His tone brooks no argument.

"Are you going to be this sunny all evening?"

The expressions on Phoenix and Mikki's faces are priceless.

Gage's lips pull up in a forced grin. "Is this better?"

I make a face. "Much."

"Oh, you kids are going to have fun tonight." Phoenix pokes the bear.

"Shut up, König."

And the bear growls.

Chapter 5

Gage

From Fisher never mentioning a word of his daughter until he asked me to be her bodyguard for tonight, to Michaela's revelation about how he forgot his daughter's milestone birthday—*how the hell did he manage that idiotic tour de force?*—to a last name he doesn't share with Lily, the pieces of the puzzle were coming together. But seeing Lily drove the point home.

Fisher says his attractiveness lies in his wallet.

When it comes to his four sons, the apple doesn't fall far from the tree.

Lily is a peach from an orchard in a different state.

Her pale, luminous, porcelain skin is a contrast to the perma-tanned women I'm used to.

Her hair is as dark as Michaela's. My fingers itch to fuck up her hair, so neatly pulled back, to find out how long it is. I'm willing to bet she has a curtain of raven-black hair.

All that hair wrapped around my fist...

Fuck.

Her lickable, pouty lips, painted in a pale pink, complement her dress to perfection.

Her subdued makeup brings out her best feature—utterly gorgeous, huge blue eyes.

I'm not sure if it's the lights from the bar or the shade of her precisely applied eyeshadow, but there's a purple tinge to them—a mesmerizing color that renders me stupid. The same for her mile long, thick, black lashes that keep sweeping her cheeks each time she blinks.

My response to her was unsettling. Unnerving, even.

Electric tingles ran through my body when we shook hands. My cock wanted to jump out of my pants to say, *Welcome to LA,* when she stepped into the bar. It's as if all the blood in my body flowed to my crotch in one sweeping rush.

I wasn't prepared for Lily Schuyler.

And now, I'm trapped with her in the back of my chauffeured Rolls Royce Phantom.

The exquisite, delicate scent of her perfume permeates the car, making it impossible for me to pretend she isn't sitting mere inches away from me. It's a bewitching combination of flowers, sunshine, and diamonds—if that's even a thing. I'm certain long after she leaves the city, the vehicle will still be imbued with her cock-hardening fragrance.

Letting out a breath, I roll a crick out of my stiff neck. I'm no longer certain if the discomfort is from this hellish day or from this woman. Not wanting to take a chance, I lift my eyes to the ceiling, asking God for strength.

It's my only salvation.

There's not much space between us in the back seat, but you'd think it was an ocean from the way I'm hugging the passenger door. It's my weak attempt to be as far away as humanly possible from this temptress. It's as if I fear that physical contact with this woman, would screw up my wires. That earlier encounter is proof I can't be trusted around her.

Speaking has never been an issue. Until today.

I blame her.

Her striking beauty left me tongue-tied.

Like a cunning thief, I observe her with a side gaze, as she takes in LA, her nose pressed to the window. Her profile is as stunning as her face. From this angle I can't help but be mesmerized by the flutter of her long, dark lashes.

My cock was at full mast the moment Lily walked into that bar. After a long stretch of being disinterested in sex, the fucker decides to take a particular interest in a woman that's forbidden.

She drops her head against the headrest, her gaze still glued to the window.

I shift in my seat, adjusting my hard-on.

Great timing, buddy.

Dammit.

I need to snuff this tug of hot attraction before it gets me in trouble.

Lily Schuyler is Fisher Edgington's daughter.

He enlisted me as a companion for an event to ward off assholes. Not to be the asshole entertaining improper thoughts about his twenty-one-year-old daughter.

Jesus Christ.

She's only twenty-one.

By Hollywood and LA standards, eleven years difference is nothing. That should bring me solace, but it doesn't.

Lily is a walking distraction.

Rein it in, Hollingsworth.

Lily turns her head my way. "It must be something else to have an ocean at your front door. Do you ever get tired of living in LA?"

"LA isn't for everyone," I say. "But I couldn't see myself living anywhere else."

She nods.

"Do you ever get tired of living in New York?" I throw her question back at her.

"New York is a new adventure for me."

I flinch in surprise.

"For the past eight years, I've lived in Europe," she says, "I went to boarding school in Switzerland, followed by a degree at the American University in Paris. I returned stateside not long ago. So, in essence, this is my first time living in New York."

"You didn't come back for holidays or to spend time with your family?"

She stares at me for a long beat.

I'm about to retract my question, when she speaks. "I lived with my mom in Alabama until she died a few months before I turned thirteen——"

"I'm sorry——"

"Don't be, you didn't know."

I nod.

"It's a long—and not particularly cheery—story, but I'll give you the Cliffs notes. Until my mom died, I didn't know who my father was. Since I'm the result of an affair, Fisher Edgington kept me hidden in Europe until seven and a half weeks ago."

Whoa.

A glint of emotion flashes in her eyes, but she recovers with a forced smile. "End of story."

Her confession drops like a stone in my gut.

Before I can respond, she pulls those beautiful eyes away from me, returning her focus to the window.

An unreasonable desire to shield this woman from threats—

even in the form of her own father—washes over me. I might not know the full story, but Fisher is a callous asshole.

A foreign twinge within me makes me want to take her hand into mine and comfort her. Soothe the pain she was trying to disguise. But I don't. When I shook her hand earlier, the contact was electrifying, a high voltage zapping to my core. Touching her again would be too dangerous.

Silence falls between us for several miles. Her, admiring Los Angeles. Me, computing what she shared, while admiring her heavenly form.

"How close are you to my father?" Her gaze meets mine. "I'm late to the game. I should've found that out before landing at LAX. I ask because my father and I aren't on speaking terms right now—"

"Michaela told me."

"You know all my dirty secrets."

Man, her terse tone does something to me.

I clear my throat. "I doubt that."

That seems to appease her.

"Not that I want to badmouth your father, but how could he forget your birthday?"

"His eldest son's political ascension to the White House is top priority in his life."

I don't even know what to say to that.

I get that Fisher is all business, all the time, but this is wrong on so many levels.

"I should've asked earlier," she says, looking me up and down, "but what do you do for a living?"

She didn't look me up?

This isn't a question I get asked every day.

"I'm StreamTunes's CEO. I'm also the producer of Jam Sessions and StreamTunes Awards."

Those gorgeous big blue eyes are so damn incredible when they go wide.

"I'm a StreamTunes customer." She points a frantic finger at her chest.

"It's always a pleasure to meet satisfied customers."

"Who said I was satisfied?"

Don't make it sexual.

Don't make it sexual.

Don't make it sexual.

And... I make it sexual.

Images of ramming Lily's sweet pussy flash in front of my eyes.

Oh, honey, I can guarantee you'd be satisfied.

"To answer your earlier question," I say after a long beat, my voice gravelly, "your father is one of my big advertisers."

A little wrinkle of alarm knits her brow. "I had no clue. My father prefers to keep me in the dark."

"My headquarters are located on the fourteenth floor of a glass building on Sunset Boulevard in West Hollywood, aka the Sunset Strip. But I have another office in New York. When I work on the East Coast, I meet up with him for lunch, a drink, or dinner when our schedules coordinate. I've also met your..."

"Half-brothers."

"Yes." I nod. "Fisher didn't say much about you when he asked me for the favor."

"I'm not surprised." Bitterness coats her words.

"I assume you're single or else your boyfriend would've doubled as your bodyguard."

"That's funny." She scoffs. "Yes, I'm single."

An unreasonable sense of satisfaction washes over me.

"What about you?" She arches a brow. "Are you single?"

I flash her my left hand. "I'm a certified bachelor."

"You adhere to the same mentality as my half-brothers—if

you're rich enough to be offered a Black American Express, why settle down? It's futile. The divorce from hell that surely will come out of the marriage isn't worth it. It's far less expensive to play the field—plenty of gorgeous, available women who are more than happy with a one-night fling."

There's so much in that statement.

"I'm nothing like your half-brothers." That comes out a little harsher than intended. "I'm not in a place where I can commit."

"Got it."

A long awkward silence passes between us.

"You and my father aren't close friends?"

"We aren't."

"What about my half-brothers?"

"Same."

From the few times I've rubbed shoulders with the Edgington spawn, I wouldn't willingly hang out with them. The Edgington men are an acquired taste.

She narrows her eyes, considering me whilst licking her bottom lip with a tongue that's too damn cute. "Gage... can I ask for a favor?"

I swallow. "Sure."

"Is it possible not to mention my father while I'm here?"

I nod like a puppy. "Your wish is my command."

I'm rewarded with a smile more brilliant than the California sun.

Fuck, she's gorgeous.

Her smile fades and she returns her gaze to the window.

An unfamiliar urge to return her smile to her beautiful face rises up within me.

"You're staring," she says and glances my way.

"I didn't mean to." *Lies.*

She huffs and returns to watching the world go by.

And I return to her heavenly form.

By LA standards, Lily's dress covers a lot. From the cinched waist to the flared lower part that hits her mid-calf, the silhouette is reminiscent of old Hollywood. The top part is embellished with a chiffon fabric that drapes over her shoulders for that added touch of femininity. And the demure neckline reveals her delicate neck.

It's official. That neck will be featured in my erotic dreams tonight.

I continue my inspection.

Her jewelry is tasteful and eye-catching.

Her large diamond studs catch the light, illuminating her face. She's wearing a necklace with a statement medallion pendant. It's an old coin surrounded by brilliant stones.

Who's the fucker who gave it to her?

It's on the tip of my tongue to ask, but I brush off the thought and the wave of jealousy. I don't want to creep her out.

I suppress the growl that's about to leave my chest. I have no reason to be this possessive. She's a stranger.

My stare must weigh heavy on her, because her eyes find mine again.

"I was worried at the bar that you'd end up being a grunter—"

"Is that even a word?"

"If it isn't, it should be, and your photo should be featured right beside it in the search results. After all, a photo is worth a thousand words." Her lush, kissable lips slant with amusement.

My eyes are glued to them.

I'm overtaken by the urge to fucking own them—

I'm in trouble.

I grunt.

I guess I am a grunter.

"It's too late now to put the genie back in the bottle, Mr. Hollingsworth."

Why the fuck does my last name sound so sexy on her lips?

"You can hold a conversation when you put your mind to it," she says.

"You know everything there is to know about me now?" My voice comes out hoarse.

"No offense—"

"Which means you're about to offend me."

"You're not what I expected either."

I cock an eyebrow. "What were you expecting?"

She shakes her head. "You go first," she says. "Why did you tell me that at the bar?"

I weigh my words. "I expected you to be the female version of your half-brothers—"

"Bratty, snooty, spoiled, arrogant, and entitled?"

"That's a good beginning to the list."

She laughs.

The timbre of that laugh travels all the way to my balls.

"If you were expecting a prima donna, I'm sorry, but you'll be thoroughly disappointed."

That statement right there heightens her attractiveness a millionfold.

"Good to know," I say. "Now, it's your turn."

"I expected you to be like my other chaperones."

"Other chaperones? I thought this was your first time in LA."

"It is, but my father has been shopping around colleges."

She tells me all about the loser chaperones.

"I'm straight, but you'd never catch me in such a compromising situation with a woman," I say. "I don't have children, so you don't have to worry about me being a perverted old man with incestuous tendencies. And I'm not even going to touch that last one." I shake my head. "The guy wanted to pump his stomach with beans before inviting you to get down and dirty in the hopes of killing you with flatulence? The nerve."

Lily laughs, and laughs, and laughs.

She places a hand on my arm, as if bracing herself for a second bout of laughter.

The contact is ten times worse than before.

A tremor of awareness reverberates up my arm, traveling at light speed to my cock. For a moment, I can't concentrate past her touch. The urge to lean in and kiss her is overwhelming.

Scratch that.

The need to claim her mouth is all-consuming.

Fisher's face flashes in front of my eyes.

I chastise myself and force myself to remember who this woman is, but she's making it easy to forget she isn't a woman I can conquer.

Stay the fuck away, Hollingsworth.

Lily Schuyler is untouchable.

Chapter 6

Gage

Lucky for me, Lily kept her focus on the streets of LA for the duration of the ride. We didn't have far to go at that point, but it was enough time for me to find my composure and coax my cock to behave. I thought for sure the spell was broken until I helped her out of the car. When she glanced up to thank me, I lost myself in her stunning eyes.

There's no such thing as purple eyes. I know that, but gazing into this woman's eyes, I'm not so convinced. Her eyes have the same gem-like beauty as amethyst under sunlight.

I swear, God is testing my resolve.

Since I'm so used to walking the red carpet, it felt strange not to be blinded by flashlights or bombarded by questions from the press.

Making our way through the crowd took longer than expected.

Each season, Jam Session hires a fair number of camera people from different film schools for internships, so I'm a recognizable face at the event. Too many handshakes and introductions later, we head towards the bar. I'm about to inquire about her drink of choice, when someone shouts my name.

I turn around.

A smiling woman wearing a red, flowy dress with matching long flowy sleeves, waves. The stunning blonde makes her way towards us, arms outstretched.

"Hey, Dom." I encircle her in a hug, careful not to press my body against her belly. "I didn't expect to see you here tonight." I break our embrace.

"Neither did I, but Michaela sent a group text to the sisterhood, telling us all about how you'll be doubling as a bodyguard tonight. I didn't bother texting you. I figured I'd run into you." Dom's blue eyes shift to the woman standing next to me. "You must be Lily." She extends a hand.

"Where are my manners? Lily Schuyler, this is Dominika Wolfe, videographer extraordinaire and beautiful wife of the great Hall of Fame drummer turned badass music video production company CEO, Rod Wolfe—"

"Wife, and soon-to-be baby mama." She rubs her baby bump with her free hand, a proud grin stretching her lips.

"Congratulations," Lily says, shaking her hand. "It's a pleasure to meet you, Dominika."

"Please call me Dom," the petite blonde says. "You're part of the sisterhood now."

What the fuck?

Lily landed in LA a few hours ago, and Michaela and Dominika have taken her under their wings like big sisters in a blink of an eye?

"Okay." Lily's cheeks turn a beautiful shade of pink. "Dom, it is."

"Good," Dom says with a firm nod. "You don't want to upset a pregnant woman."

"Is that bribery?" Lily's tone is colored with amusement.

Dom's eyes shine bright with mischief. "Call it whatever you want, as long as I get my way."

Lily laughs and I swear my balls do a happy dance.

I focus my attention on Dom. "How's your little fighter?"

"Baby Wolfe is growing. From the strong kicks, he or she will come out like the heavyweight champion of the world." She cups her belly. "I'm only four months pregnant, and I'm counting the days to hold my little peanut in my arms."

"Five more months to go," Lily says.

"Given the size of my belly"—Dom rubs said belly—"I shouldn't have that many months to wait." She lets out a heavy sigh. "The perils of being short."

"I hear you," Lily says. "We're more or less the same height."

"Fair warning. Your pregnant belly will be huge compared to taller women."

"I don't have to worry about that for a long time," Lily says. "I'm not dating anyone, so babies aren't in my immediate future."

"The night is still young." Dom winks. "There are plenty single men in the house."

Jealousy and indignation wash over me. No way am I allowing any fucker to make a move on Lily. She came here with me. She's leaving with me. Not to mention, I'm standing next to Lily, and Dom bypasses me as a candidate—

It's because you swore up-and-down you'd remain single for the rest of your natural life after that last dramatic episode with your ex-fling.

I need to change the subject. "Are you here alone, Dom?" My eyes scour the room. "Or is Rod rubbing elbows with industry people?"

"Nope. Hubby and his business partner are wining and dining a record company. The University of Southern California invited me as a special guest speaker to share my experience with Brawn Impulse. I'm incredibly honored. Joel and his bandmates are floating around somewhere. They're also guest speakers and my dates for tonight—with my husband's blessings, of course."

"Got it." I nod.

"Who are we talking about?"

I glance down at Lily. "Joel Banner."

Perfectly groomed eyebrows knit together in confusion. "Who?"

When you spend most of your life surrounded by industry people, you forget not everyone is in the know.

"He's the lead singer of Brawn Impulse—a British rock band that's been making waves on this side of the pond for a couple years now. Dominika shot 'Shattered Windows'—an award-winning behind the scenes music documentary, tracing the band's journey from their humble roots to their rise to fame."

"I've never heard their music." Lily grimaces. "I'm not that much into rock music. Pop music is my jam."

"Don't ever let my husband hear you say that," Dom says with the upmost seriousness. "He'll lock you in a room and force you to listen to rock music until you change your mind."

Lily giggles. "Note to self."

"Rod is hardcore at everything he does," I say.

"That could be said of all the guys in your inner circle," Dom says.

I rub a hand behind my neck. "Good point."

"Speaking of the inner circle..." Dom turns her attention to Lily, "Michaela told us you'll be present tomorrow night for Rhys's birthday."

My eyebrows hit my forehead. "That's news to me," I say, meeting Lily's gaze.

"Um... Michaela invited me. But if that makes you uncomfortable or if I'm stepping on anyone's toes, I don't have to—"

"Hush. You're coming," Dom says.

Great. I don't have a say in the matter.

I grunt.

"He's grunting." There's a touch of panic in Lily's voice. "Since I can't make out his grunts, I'm not sure how upset he is with me."

"Grunts are tolerable." Dom brushes it off with a hand wave. "If he growls and shows fangs, that's when you need to run for your life. After all, paranormal romance is nothing more than a fantasy."

The two women laugh.

Glad to see someone's having fun at my expense.

When she finds her composure, Dom laces her hands around my arm. "He's a big teddy bear."

My ears burn hot.

I squint my eyes at Dom. "I. Am. Not."

The two women laugh again.

"You're going to fit right in with the sisterhood, Lily," Dom says.

"I appreciate the warm welcome, but that's too much fussing about for a stranger who isn't going to be in the city for more than a few days," Lily says.

Dom readies herself to answer, but a man approaches her.

After a round of introductions, the gentleman pulls Dominika away.

With a wave and a huge smile, she promises she'll be back.

Lily turns to face me. "I'm sorry about that. I don't have to come tomorrow night—"

"Dom made it pretty clear. You're part of the sisterhood."

"I'm touched, but these are your friends. I'm passing through town—"

"The decision is out of my hands."

"If you don't want me there, I won't go."

I work my jaw, pondering.

I didn't plan on spending a minute longer than I had to with Lily.

But the powers that be, aka, the sisterhood, would have my balls on a platter if I showed up tomorrow night without her.

Silence stretches between us, taken up by the laughter, chatter, and commotion of the event around us.

My nostrils flare.

The angel sitting on one shoulder cautions me to tread carefully, but the devil sitting on the other is taunting me.

She's waiting with bated breath for my verdict, her ridiculously long lashes fluttering.

My fingers twitch to caress those damn lashes.

And my dick twitches to a whole other tune.

I stick my hands inside my pockets. "You're coming."

Chapter 7

Lily

Holy testosterone.

Gage Hollingsworth is a force of nature.

Mikki invited me to Rhys's birthday party.

Dom insisted I come.

Gage *ordered* me to come.

I hate when my father abuses the power-play between us—he holds the purse strings—as a way to order me around, so I'm confused as to why I find the command so darn sexy coming from this brooding stranger.

The man is unsettling.

Even the way he walks. So much swagger.

After a much-needed drink to cool down because I was burning up like a wildfire from the proximity to my hunky chaperone-slash-bodyguard, Gage suggested I work the room.

So, here I am, making friends.

After an animated conversation with two video producers, I was chatting with a forty-something cinematographer agent with a flamboyant dress sense. Bless her for pulling off a red vinyl strapless floor-length gown which she wore over a white turtleneck, embellished with a cascade of bold necklaces, her wrist circled with wide silver cuffs.

As I was stuffing a Manchego cheese and chorizo sausage puff into my mouth, she lost her shit. I was so caught off guard, I almost choked. Freaked out, my eyes bounced around the room, searching for the eminent danger. There was no bogeyman and the roof wasn't falling in.

Joel Banner was in the house.

The woman has a thing for younger men with British accents, especially when they talk dirty to her in bed while they drive into her like military tanks. That was way more than I needed to know about her. Getting drilled by Joel is on her bucket list, so she left me standing there, as she chased after him.

Great.

Before I put myself out there again, I need to fill my belly. After piling delicious appetizers on a small plate, I find a little alcove, removed from the event's hustle and bustle, where I can eat in peace.

As I savor succulent angus beef meatballs stuffed with blue cheese, a man who's much older than my father—if the salt and pepper hair and wrinkles on his over tanned face are any indication—clad in a purple suit, lavender shirt unbuttoned enough to show chest hair, and wearing a pair of gold loafers, approaches.

"You're hired," the stranger says, pointing a finger at me.

I frown, a half-eaten meatball speared with a toothpick frozen in the air.

Smiling brown eyes stare down at me.

I drop the appetizer on the plate and place a hand in front of my mouth, chewing. I swallow. "I'm sorry?"

"You're hired." As if it makes more sense the second time around.

"I don't remember applying for a job."

"You're considering the videographer program?"

"Yes."

"You're going to graduate at the top of your class." He smiles wide, revealing a row of too white veneered teeth.

"Don't tell me, you're a psychic."

The man lets out a booming, fake laugh. "You're beautiful, funny, charming, and sexy as hell."

Eeew. And you're an annoying old man.

"I'd extend a hand, but you're eating," he says. "My name is Cadoc Cork Phallusburg."

"Hi, I'm Lily."

"No last name?"

"Nope." The quicker I wrap this up, the quicker I can go back to stuffing my face.

"It's your lucky day, Lily. I can make *all* your dreams come true."

My eyebrows rise. "That's quite the promise."

"One I can keep."

You're full of it. "You don't even know me. You don't know what I strive for in life."

"If you're here"—he gestures to the room—"I've got what you need in spades."

I try hard not to roll my eyes.

"I'm the CEO of Gennadius Records," he says, "and I have a long list of new talent in need of music videos. I want to hire you."

"I haven't even started the program yet. And it's not due to kick off until next year."

He takes a step closer, crowding my space.

I take a step back, but my back hits a wall.

"You're going to ace the program and you'll be one hot commodity."

"Your unwavering faith in me is... creepy."

He laughs.

My statement wasn't meant to be funny.

"I've been in this business long enough to know talent when I see it. Why wait until a competitor snatches you away? I want you all to myself."

"I'm sorry, but—"

"If I had to rate you from one to ten, I'd give you a nine, because *I'm* the one you're missing to make you a perfect ten."

God, that was lame.

This time, I don't suppress the eye roll.

"You're lucky to be in the right place, at the right time."

I want to tell this guy off, but making an enemy on day one of arriving in a new city, might not be wise.

"I've been watching you since you were talking to the dean —who holds me in high regard, by the way"—this man's inflated ego matches my father's—"out of all the girls—"

"I'm a *woman*."

He gives me a onceover that makes my skin crawl. "Indeed. All that to say, I choose you. I want to mentor you."

Stranger danger. "Mr. Phallusburg, I'm not—"

He places a finger over my lips, silencing me.

I lower my gaze, going cross-eyed.

Is he touching me?

Yuck.

I'll have to wash my mouth out with soap a million times. I might also need disinfectant. And bleach.

"Perhaps you could come back to my place so I can show you why my last name is *Phallus*-burg." He winks.

Gross.

A deep growl resonates, and a large hand clamps hard on the creep's shoulder.

The dirty old man squeals like a wounded animal, his face contorting in pain, as he folds over.

Chapter 8

Gage

I couldn't keep my eyes off my date—
She's not my date.
This woman is fucking with my head. That explains why I couldn't stop staring at her as she floated around the venue with the grace of a ballerina.

In an effort not to be rude, I allowed my peers to pull me into different circles of conversation.

Lily was engaged in an animated conversation with two guys—a Puerto Rican-video-producer-duo. Afterwards, she was talking with a blonde wearing an outrageous outfit I wouldn't even attempt to describe. The next thing I knew, she was gone.

Worried, I'd set off to find her.

She was nowhere to be found.

It's like she vanished into thin air.

I lucked out when I stopped a waiter who had noticed her whereabouts.

And now, I turn the corner and arrive at a quiet area of the building. I spot a flash of soft pink and shoes in the same soft shade I've committed to memory, and a man hovering over Lily.

Fucking Cadoc Cork Phallusburg.

No other man at the event is walking around in a purple suit, so spotting him is as easy as spotting an elephant in a swimming pool.

He can't be taller than five-nine, short compared to my own six-four, but a giant intimidating Lily, who's probably no more than five-two.

My hackles raise so fast, it's a miracle I don't bare my claws and fangs like a damn werewolf. The thought of Lily being harassed by a man with the reputation for preying on women young enough to be his granddaughters, makes me want to tear the asshole's head off his shoulders.

I march on up to the sordid old creep, clamp a strong hand on his shoulder and yank him away from Lily, forcing him to take several steps back.

His orange complexion turns dark purple as he winces.

I've made my point.

I let go of my vice grip on his shoulder, and approach Lily.

"There you are." I lace a possessive arm around her slender waist, pulling her body into the shelter of mine. The heat emanating from her seeps through me and it's so good, I want to—

"You found me." Her voice is higher by several octaves.

"I did." My words come out in a rough rumble.

We stare at each other for a long beat.

"Gage, I didn't know you were here tonight." The bumbling idiot reminds us of his presence.

I swing my gaze in his direction.

Cadoc massages his shoulder, his face contorted in pain.

"I see you've met my girl."

Where did that come from?

What the fuck am I doing claiming her?

You're delusional, Hollingsworth.

A pulse of surprise goes through her body and into mine. Her head whips up in my direction and she almost drops the plate she's holding.

From my peripheral vision, I catch her beguiling eyes widening so much, they practically take over her beautiful face.

I keep my focus on the predator standing in front of me instead of fixating on where our bodies join.

The closeness screams, *I claim you. You're mine. End of story.*

It's ridiculous.

We met a minute ago.

Yet, I could get used to the press of her heavenly body against mine.

Snap out of it.

I let go of the beauty whose eyes are still the size of dinner plates.

I clear my throat. "You've met Lily," I say in an attempt to backtrack.

Creepy Phallusburg lifts his chubby hands in surrender. "Oh, man, I—I didn't know she was spoken for."

"Now, you know."

"I was giving her some industry insight," he says.

I lock eyes with Lily. "Is that so?"

She places her free hand on my chest.

Fuck.

The contact is like I've been tasered.

"Cadoc kindly offered a private session at his place, so he could impart more of his wisdom about the industry," Lily says.

"You were about to cheat on me?" Mock indignation colors my words.

She gives me a solemn head shake. "Never, baby." Her response is priceless.

Oh, she's good.

This is pretend, but hearing the possessive moniker on her lips hardens my cock.

"Thank God," I say. "Or else you'd break my heart."

"I wouldn't be able to live with myself." Lily's gaze grows... hazy?

No way.

Not only am I losing my mind, but I'm seeing things.

"I was going to turn him down," she says. "I have enough daddy issues as is. Jumping in bed with a man who's *at least* three times my age is way up there on my list of stupid things to *never* do."

Mic drop.

"And not to mention, I'm a one-guy kind of gal."

Good girl.

I turn to face the dirty old man. "So, you were hitting on my girl?"

Cadoc's over tanned skin is now the color of a white sheet. "Gage, I can assure you, it was a little misunderstanding—"

I take a threatening step forward.

His hands fly to his face, shielding him. "Please don't hurt me."

"You use your title and position to get laid. Dickbags like you give our industry a bad rap." I jab an accusatory finger at him. Matthew's good name is being slandered in the press, while this guy consistently abuses his power. The sense of injustice makes me want to drive my fist into his smarmy gut. "Get the fuck out of my face."

I don't have to repeat myself.

With his tail between his legs, the record company executive cowers away.

Lily lets out a sigh of relief.

"You okay? He didn't touch you?"

She bites her lower lip.

"Lily."

"He silenced me by placing a finger on my lips—"

"The motherfucker put his filthy hands on you? He needs someone to teach him a lesson. I'm going to track down the degenerate asswipe and rearrange his face."

Lily places a hand on my arm. "Let it go, Gage."

I take in deep breaths to control my racing heart, as rage and fury threaten to make me do something I might regret.

Lily's lips part into a warm smile.

I frown. "What?"

"You."

My frown deepens.

"No one's ever stepped up for me like that."

I didn't see that coming.

She tilts her head back to meet my gaze, her eyes shimmering under the light. "Thank you, Gage." She gets on the tip of her toes and drops a soft kiss on my jaw. I'm guessing she was aiming for my cheek, but she's this little thing.

The unexpected move causes my wires to crisscross.

Goddammit.

Chapter 9

Lily

We're cruising down LA's animated streets in the back of Gage's Rolls Royce.

After my unpleasant encounter with Cadoc Cork Phallusburg, and Gage coming to my rescue like a white-hot knight in bespoke suited armor, we schmoozed for another hour. He introduced me to a parade of industry peers I've forgotten. Still, being introduced to his world was exhilarating.

"My girl."

My mind tripped over those words as my heart banged against my chest like a drum. My mind is still tripping since he uttered them. When he pulled my body against a wall of muscles, the flutters in my belly were so powerful, it took my breath away. The imprint of Gage's strong hand around my waist will haunt me with lust for days. Weeks, even.

My hero.

He may be grumpy, but Dom is right, there's a big teddy bear hidden deep inside.

I'm being ridiculous.

I'm crushing over a guy because he stepped up to the plate, literally.

I chance a glance his way, but I only catch a glimpse of his strong profile.

My chaperone-slash-bodyguard has gone back to wearing his trademark scowl. He's determined to ignore me, choosing to focus on whatever is happening on the other side of the window.

Sigh.

I mourn the great conversationalist.

My eyes fall to the seat where his hand is resting, and I have to resist the urge to snake mine into his. To avoid making a fool of myself, I join my hands together and place them on my lap. Taking a page from his book, I face the window and lose myself in the scenery, pretending I'm not a little hurt.

I chance another glance his way.

His throat works on a swallow, his jaw tightening.

He runs a hand through his thick brown hair, messing it up.

Tension radiates off him. Every fibre in his body screams, *leave me alone.*

Fine.

It stings, but I have some pride.

We're strangers, and he promised me only one night.

Who cares if I come alive when I'm near him? In a matter of days, I'll fly back to Manhattan, and we'll go our separate ways.

It's for the best.

I'm here to scout schools because that fits in with my father's grand plan for my life. Not to lust over a brooding man, even if he's sexy as sin.

Chapter 10

Gage

I struggle to understand how a woman who was a stranger a few hours ago managed to unravel my world in the blink of an eye.

I shouldn't have grabbed her in my arms.

Fuck you, Cadoc Cork Phallusburg.

I blame the dirty old man for my predicament.

Had I not entered a pissing contest, I would still be blissfully ignorant.

Now that I know what it's like to have Lily in my arms, I'm hooked.

Like a lock and key, she fits in my arms so perfectly.

The warmth of her body felt like salvation.

I still can't shake off the jolt that sizzled through me.

A lady in pink swept into town and turned me inside out.

Her eyes, her laugh— No. Everything about her is irresistible.

Her enchanting voice is a seductive melody. Shutting her out during the ride back to the hotel was self-preservation. It was the only way to avoid getting trapped in her web.

Thank God, my punishment is over. We're back at her hotel.

As much as I'd like to bid her goodnight and let her make her way up to her room, the gentleman in me, protests. I refuse to cower to bad manners. I'm willing to suffer for a few more minutes in her presence.

What doesn't kill you, makes you stronger, an' all.

After asking my chauffeur to wait, I slide out of the car and circle it. I compose myself before opening the door.

Keep it together.

When I open it, I extend a hand to help Lily out. When her feet are firmly on the ground, I let go of her hand. She's a bit surprised by the brusque movement, but she doesn't comment.

Good.

I'd only be capable of answering with a grunt.

Chaos greets us when we enter the Pompadour Hotel.

Crowds of tourists huddle around groupings of luggage.

Based on the conversations taking place around us, it's safe to say, these people are Italian. From the unmistakable flair in their fashion selection, I'm guessing they're from the motherland.

I follow Lily across the busy lobby to the elevators. At this time of the night, there are no chances of me bumping into Mr. and Mrs. König or any of the König brothers.

We turn the corner.

There's a long line at the elevator area.

Neither Lily or I speak as we wait our turn.

Not that we have to.

Between haphazard conversations, bellboys rushing up and down the hallway, and hotel staff fussing about, it's enough commotion to fill our silence.

I let out a sigh of relief when a vacant car arrives at the lobby. I invite Lily to enter first.

With a polite *thank you*, she steps inside.

I follow behind her.

She punches the button to her floor.

As the doors are about to close, a hand slams against the rubber padding, forcing the doors to open.

"*Buona serata*. Good evening," a man says in a heavy accent.

"Good evening," Lily says.

I nod.

The man lifts a finger. Then, he waves to someone outside of the elevator.

Footsteps echo against the floor before a group of travelers appear. It's a flurry of commotion as they crowd the car.

Between the people and the luggage, it's a tight fit.

Shit.

It's an excruciating ascension to Lily's floor, which happens to be one of the top floors.

"*Mi scusi*," a man says, and a bunch of people shift around, forcing Lily to shuffle back. Her body presses against mine. My cock is on alert.

Fuck.

Apologetic blue eyes meet mine. "Sorry."

Damn those kissable lips.

"It's okay." *Lies.*

The elevator stops at a floor. A bunch of people file out, but another group enters. An animated conversation in Italian ensues. I can only assume they got off on the wrong floor. The problem is, the elevator is so packed, Lily's body is still brushing against my unruly cock.

Heaven help me.

God must've heard my prayer, because the Italians exit on the next floor. Lily takes a long step forwards and hangs out close to the dashboard. The distance is a blessing and a curse. I now have an unobstructed view of her fine ass.

Why are you putting me through this, God? Why?

We reach her floor.

I let her step out first. Readjusting myself, I follow her down the corridor.

She stops in front of a door. "This is me."

Mission accomplished.

I should be sprinting towards the elevator, but I remain rooted in place.

An awkward moment passes between us.

She pulls the straps of her bag over her shoulder, and dances from one foot to the other. "Thank you again for accompanying me tonight."

Her lips are now absent of the nude lipstick with a hint of pink she was wearing earlier in the evening, making her mouth even more tempting now. The need to claim that pretty mouth nearly topples me over.

"I'm glad I was there," I say. "Cadoc is a handful."

Her stunning purple-blue eyes stare up at me. Several beats go by before she blinks. "Is that the only reason you're happy you accompanied me?" Her voice trembles.

No, your beguiling self was a joy to be with.

I let out a sigh, rubbing the back of my neck with my hand.

"If this CEO gig doesn't work out for you," she says, "bodyguard is an option."

"Thanks, I'll keep that in mind."

She bites her lower lip. "I enjoyed hanging out with you tonight, Gage."

"Unlike your other chaperones?"

Her lips part in a huge smile. "Yes. You're still okay with me coming out tomorrow night to Rhys's birthday party?"

I arch a brow. "We already talked about that."

"I can't read your moods. Are you pissed off at me?"

I'm pissed off at you because you weren't supposed to be this beautiful.

I'm pissed off at you because you're eliciting emotions in me I don't even understand.

I'm pissed off at you because you flare foreign desires in me. Goddammit.

"You got it all wrong, princess."

She studies me.

"This princess should say goodnight to her knight in shining armor." She gazes up at me, glassy eyes wide and wanting, lips parted and waiting.

Those damn bewitching eyes.

I suppress a groan.

The message registers in my brain to get away from the temptation, but my feet won't move.

Behind a curtain of black lashes, she fixes her gaze onto me. There's no mistaking the lust I read there.

I breathe deep through my nose, controlling the mounting need to do dirty things to her.

"I missed earlier because you're so tall." She places a hand on my arm, and gets on her toes. "I was aiming for your cheek, not your chin." Her voice is husky and low.

Thump.

Thump.

Thump.

My heart is beating so hard, and so is my cock.

The burning urge to claim that mouth is overwhelming.

I'm dying to kiss my way along her neck, lick her alabaster skin, and sink my teeth into her gorgeous, slender neck.

An assault of illicit thoughts flicker through my brain at the sight of this woman.

My cock—that's been nonchalant about women for years—throbs for release, aching for it.

Her breath hitches, and that's my demise.

I need to feast on this angel.

I'm about to say dammit to hell, when Fisher's face flashes in front of my eyes, sloshing a bucket of ice-cold water over my head.

I blink to pull myself out from under her spell.

Mayday! Mayday!

Abort mission.

Do not engage.

Move away from the temptation.

I repeat, abort mission.

I swallow, my throat working.

Cock blocked by the client. Her father.

I straighten. "I have to go." My voice is gruff.

The lust that was coloring her pretty eyes a moment ago, dissipates.

I curse myself, but stay the course. "Have a good day tomorrow. I'll text you late afternoon so we can make plans for tomorrow night. I'll pick you up."

A resigned smile plays on her luscious lips. "Okay."

I ignore the disappointment in her eyes and voice.

It's in her best interests and mine.

"Good night, Lily."

With an audible inhale, she squares her shoulders, as though gathering herself. "Good night, Gage."

I get the hell out of there before I hoist her over my shoulder—fireman style—kick open the door to her hotel suite, fling her sinful body on the bed, and have my way with her all night long.

I hustle toward the elevator and press the button in rapid succession.

In an effort to breathe again, I loosen my tie. It doesn't help. I'm still struggling for air.

How the fuck did I end up here?

Chapter 11

Gage

Instead of heading back to my place, I ask my chauffeur to drop me off at the Quintus Hotel. My home is stocked with some of the finest top-shelf selections, but sometimes a guy needs to sit at a bar and drink his worries away.

Since I was on bodyguard duty earlier, I kept it to one Manhattan.

As I drain my third drink in one gulp, the buzz of alcohol hits.

I lift my empty tumbler to catch the bartender's attention.

"More Macallan, please."

The bartender hesitates for a beat, but nods.

In no time, he's back.

I thank him and polish off half of the amber liquid. "Don't go too far, I'll need another one soon."

He cocks an eyebrow.

"What? This is a bar. I'm supposed to drink."

His eyes are glued on me.

"Stop staring me down. I'm not getting behind the wheel. I have a driver."

A few patrons glance my way.

I glare at them.

Mind your own business.

I return my focus to the bartender. "And I have the good sense not to mix drinks. Top-shelf whiskey all the way, baby."

"Of course, Mr. Hollingsworth. Let me see what I can do about your drink." He steps away.

You're not my fucking nanny.

I'm a grown ass man. I'm thirty-two and I'll get plastered if I want to.

I gulp down the rest of my drink and drop my tumbler with a little too much force on the countertop.

I have a nice buzz going on, enough to help me forget why I came here in the first place instead of going to bed.

Lily who?

Her angelic face flashes in front of my eyes.

Fuuuuck.

I'm screwed ten ways to Sunday.

I should sit it out tomorrow night. Lily can go to Rhys's birthday party with Mikki or Dom.

I swallow the last gulp of my drink.

It goes down easy.

Time for another one—

"Rough day, Mr. Hollingsworth?"

I turn my head.

A tall, sharply dressed man stands behind me.

Larkin Gallagher.

"If it isn't the owner of the Quintus Hotel." I greet him by lifting my tumbler. "How you doin'?"

"We haven't seen you in a while."

"Care to join me?" My words slur.

"Why not?" He pats me on the shoulder before unbuttoning his suit jacket. He takes a seat on the stool next to mine.

My eyes shift to the beefy bodyguards standing near the door, their eyes scanning the room for threats.

Larkin lifts a hand.

The bartender rushes over.

"Miguel, Perrier on ice for both of us—"

"I don't want Perrier."

Larkin stares at me long and hard, as if assessing my state of drunkenness. "Make that a glass for me and a bottle for Mr. Hollingsworth."

My eyebrows lift in surprise. *What the fuck?*

"Also, bring him an espresso."

Miguel nods and scurries off.

"I'd prefer something stronger than fizzy water and coffee."

"You've had enough for the evening."

Patronizing much?

I glare at him. "I'm not getting behind the wheel of a car."

"Perhaps, but there's nothing pleasant about a brooding, disruptive patron who barks at my staff. It's bad for business."

Larkin can never be accused of sugarcoating.

"I need this." I point a finger at the empty tumbler.

I sound like a petulant child—like a brooding, disruptive patron.

I blame you, Lily Schuyler.

To mock me, the bartender chooses that moment to return with our sparkling waters and my coffee.

Larkin nods his appreciation.

I shoot daggers at Miguel.

I bet you're the whistleblower.

Larkin lifts his glass.

I shake my head.

"I'm not your parent, so I can't force you to drink up," he says. "If you thought Monday was a bitch, try Tuesday with a mighty hangover."

He has a point.

I drain the sparkling water. Without asking, he pours me another glass.

Fucker.

I drink up.

He points to the espresso.

I purse my lips.

He arches a brow.

Fine, Dad.

I dip my lips in the hot liquid.

"You can do better than that," he says.

I roll my eyes.

Since I'm in no mood to prolong this stupid game, I sweeten the coffee.

Under his watchful gaze, I take a long sip.

"I get it," Larkin says, "this must've been a long, excruciating day. After all, the media frenzy surrounding your show host is keeping rag trade publications and websites in business. I'm sure I don't have to tell you, drinking won't make the problem go away."

I drop my cup on the saucer. "You're right, this has been a headache-inducing day. Lucky for me, I have a great team preparing Matthew to retaliate."

"So why are you here?"

I let out a long sigh, rubbing my hand over my face.

"Whatever it is, it must be serious," he says.

"Women." I shake my head.

"It can't be a club member since you haven't been at the club in months."

"You're right, I haven't been to Dark Compulsion in a while."

"Who turned your world upside down?"

My jaw ticks. "I was at another function."

His attention drops to the tumbler that contained amber liquid that matches his eyes. "And you're drowning your sorrows?"

"Funny."

"I wasn't trying to be."

You'll be pressed to catch Larkin crack a smile. I don't know his demons—he's never shared them. Anyone with half a brain knows not to ask.

In my case, tragedy stripped me of the ability to smile and let anyone who isn't in my inner circle get too close. When you trust the wrong people, they can destroy your life.

"What about this woman you met tonight has you finding solace in top-shelf whiskey, Mr. Hollingsworth?"

I consider him.

Larkin holds my gaze.

I should shut my mouth, close my tab, and seek the sanctuary of my home. Instead, I spill my guts.

"This bodyguard gig was supposed to be a walk in the park," I say, concluding my story. "My job was to accompany a spoiled princess at an event and be done with it."

"But she isn't a spoiled princess—"

"And that's part of the problem." I point a finger at Larkin as if all this is his fault. "Had she been demanding as fuck, that would've sent me running." I jab my fingers in my hair and pull so hard, my scalp tingles. "I understand why Adam and Eve got kicked out of Heaven. Sometimes, resisting temptation is an impossible feat."

"Who says you have to resist her?" Larkin's question causes me to flinch.

"I don't mix business with pleasure."

"You have no business dealings with the woman."

"She's the daughter of one of my biggest advertisers." I'm caught between a rock and a hard place.

"So?"

"Are you playing devil's advocate?" My patience is running thin.

"She's an adult, not a child." He straightens the sleeves of his jacket. "There's an attraction between the two of you. It's clear as day."

"She's forbidden."

Larkin cocks a brow. "Says who?"

Chapter 12

Lily

After closing the door, I lean against it with my eyes shut for so long, I lose track of time. I'm consumed by that near-kiss, reliving the memory in my head. I might not be experienced, but even I know, Gage Hollingsworth was going to kiss me.

And I would've let him.

I bet Gage's relationship with my father caused him to change his mind.

At least, I hope that's the reason.

It's as if I can't go far enough from my father without him still pulling the strings to my life. Even if I were to fly to the moon, he'd still be my puppet master.

Argh.

That brief bit of attention from Gage lit me up like a firecracker.

My skin is still tingling.

I'm used to a man with power. I'm not used to a *hot* man with power.

With a groan, I push off the door, drop my bag on the console, and kick off my heels, as I stride through the elegantly appointed suite. I enter the bedroom, flip the light switch with my elbow, and stroll to the full-length mirror to remove my pretty dress.

Before I do, I admire myself.

This expensive dress makes up for him being so callous about forgetting another milestone in my life.

I was never brave enough to confront my father about not acknowledging my sixteenth and eighteenth birthdays. This is my act of defiance. He'll get the message loud and clear when he receives the credit card statement.

With a sigh, I unzip the dress, let it pool at my feet, bend to pick it up, walk to the wardrobe and hang it. As I walk by the mirror again, I stop.

I'm in nothing but bra, panties, and necklace. The soft pink French Appliqué lingerie showcases my body in such a way. I've never felt prettier.

Scratch that.

I've never felt sexier.

Is Gage a legs man?

An ass man?

A boob man?

Does a short girl with raven hair have a chance with Gage Hollingsworth?

I shake my head.

He must only date tall, leggy, blonde-supermodel-types with double D's. God knows a whole army of them walk the streets of LA. A bunch of them were at tonight's event.

I shouldn't even be entertaining these questions that cloud my mind like a new obsession.

But that doesn't stop me.

I run my fingers along the bra's lace detailing, eliciting a throb between my legs.

Would he love this lingerie on me?

The expression on his handsome face as he held my gaze had me hot and bothered. His eyes were veiled with something I couldn't pinpoint. They were much darker than I'd seen them earlier. More menacing. Dangerous, even.

Myriad emotions run through me, all laced with lust.

A heart-thumping rush courses through my body at the thought of sexy Gage.

I'm drenched.

As I stare at myself, one hand travels down my stomach, until my fingers flirt with my pussy hair. The contact is enough to cause my pussy to clench.

God.

I take several steps back and lower myself to the king size bed.

I stare at myself in the mirror as I spread my legs, pull the fabric of my panties to the side, and glide a finger between my wet pussy. Remembering how my body felt nestled in Gage's protective embrace, I stroke a languorous finger over my hard clit.

Urgency slams through me.

Fuck.

I wiggle against the mattress until I remove my panties, throwing them somewhere in the room. I unclasp my bra, releasing my breasts. It goes flying across the room. Then, I work my chignon with impatient hands until I pull out the pins, letting my long cascade of hair fall over my shoulders.

Better.

My nipples are so hard, they hurt.

I flick at my peaks and groan, surprised by how sensitive they are.

I hitch back a little and spread my legs wide with my feet

flat on the edge of the mattress, stretching my pussy open, exposing my swollen pink lips.

What a provocative sight.

I imagine it's Gage looking back at me and my breath hitches, my heart racing.

The desire in my eyes is unmistakable. Desire for him.

Under heavy lidded eyes and with my lower lip trapped between my teeth, I examine the woman I don't recognize in the mirror.

She's brazen.

Bold.

Unafraid.

Assertive.

Unwilling to bend to other's will.

Uninterested in compromising.

This badass came to life when I landed in Los Angeles.

This is the first time I've touched myself in front of a mirror. I blame Gage Hollingsworth for pushing me outside my comfort zone.

I follow the trail of hair until my finger slides between my pussy lips, lodging deep inside me.

I don't allow my head to loll back and I don't close my eyes. For the first time ever, I want to watch myself come.

The thought makes me wetter, hotter, and I insert another finger and pump a few times, sending tingles to my needy clit.

I'd much rather if it were him.

Down there.

Sucking me.

Kissing me.

Licking me...

I pull my fingers out of my slick warmth and use my juices to take care of my clit.

Brushing against his unmistakable erection was so hot.

I pick up the tempo, my pace frantic.

Life is unfair.

My previous chaperones set the bar low, so there was zero chance I'd be attracted to them. Perhaps if I'd done my homework, I wouldn't have such a visceral reaction to the devastatingly gorgeous grump. A quick search would've given me ammunition. I wouldn't have been consumed at first sight.

My body shivers as I flashback to his hands. His strong hands.

I bet the man has magical fingers.

My pulse quickens.

And a magical cock...

I push two fingers inside my yearning pussy, pumping them in and out of my wetness, as the digits of my other hand skate over my clit.

Dear God.

I'm so turned on.

I'm so slippery wet, it's ridiculous.

My insides clench hard.

My breaths grow ragged with every thrust of my fingers.

I can't believe it when the girl in the mirror slaps her pussy and gasps at the blissful sensation.

Good God. This is too good.

My fingers are practically sucked back into my pussy and I pump them like crazy, my horniness jacked up to another level, the orgasm starting to burn from somewhere deep.

I yank my fingers free and bring them to my breast, circling my nipple and coating it with my slickness. Needing more, I close my fingers around my other nipple, squeezing hard as my other hand teases my engorged clit.

There's only one man occupying my thoughts right now.

A tall, brooding, mountain of a man.

I was desperate for his sexy mouth to kiss me.

I imagine his mouth, sucking on a nipple while he pounds my pussy with his big cock.

I stroke my clit faster, taken over by the desperate need to climax, gyrating my hips in a circular motion to intensify the sensation.

I'm delirious with pleasure.

A familiar hot sensation blooms at my core.

I stop with a groan and then gasp when I slap my pussy once, twice, and three times is more than enough as I pick up my pace, back to rubbing my clit like crazy.

And then...

Holy shit. Time stands still. The girl in the mirror seems to lift from the bed. How I manage not to throw my head back as the orgasm bursts through me, I'll never know. But I keep my astonished eyes on the girl in the mirror as she bucks and squirms.

Still panting for breath, I stare down at my trembling body.

My eyes shift to the mirror again. I don't recognize myself.

My hair is disheveled.

My skin is flushed pink.

My pose is indecent.

All signs of a woman who's come undone and enjoyed every toe-curling second.

I've never had such a strong orgasm in my life.

All thanks to one man.

A wicked thought enters my mind.

I can't.

Yes, you can.

There's a tug of war taking place inside me.

Should I?

Should I not?

The hell with it.

I channel the badass that embodies me now. "You only live once."

I rush to the console where I left my handbag to retrieve my phone. I don't even bother putting on a robe. Naked as the day I was born, I compose a message.

With my lower lip pulled between my teeth, I reread it.

Nope.

I jab a finger on my screen, erasing my paltry first attempt.

"*Sans vergogne, ma vieille,*" as my best friend Nadine would say.

Translation: *Without fear, dear friend.*

> Lily: You were going to kiss me earlier—

Too desperate. And too lame.

I erase it.

I compose another message.

I erase it.

I do this song and dance another ten times.

I grumble, frustrated with myself.

The brazen courage coursing through me earlier is fizzing faster than day-old champagne left in a flute.

"Just do it."

> Lily: I'm looking forward to tomorrow night.
> And it's not only because of the birthday
> party and the chance to meet your friends.
> Hanging out with you tonight was fun, and I
> wouldn't mind a repeat. Sweet dreams, Gage.

You'll be the star feature of mine.

It's a subtle invitation. I hope it doesn't end up causing him to retreat further in his cave. I can't handle the silent treatment two evenings in a row.

With my heart beating in my throat, and the post-orgasm buzz fueling me, I press the send button before I can change my mind.

There goes nothing.

My phone rings, making me yelp.

Oh my God, is he calling?

Panicked, I check my screen.

Disappointment prickles at me for a nanosecond.

It's not Gage, but it's one of my favorite people. With a huge smile splitting my face, I accept the video call. "Nads!"

"*Salut toi—*" My best friend's greeting is cut short, and her brown eyes grow wide. "What's going on in Los Angeles?"

"Huh?"

"Why are you accepting a video call naked?"

"Oh, shit."

Chapter 13

Gage

Two bottles of Perrier and several trips to the bathroom later, it's unlikely there's a trace of alcohol left in my system. To play it safe, I asked my driver to stop by Tonics + Elixirs. It's the go-to stop to score much-needed liquid medicine food for late-night partiers. Their well-crafted hangover smoothies are godsend lifesavers.

I allowed the girl manning the counter to come up with a concoction to ensure I wake up tomorrow ready to take on the day. It was a complicated mix. With the amount of seaweed juice she poured in there, I'm lucky it didn't taste—and smell—like sewage.

My driver leaves me at my door.

I enter my home, disable the alarm, and turn on the lights, dimming them low.

From the lofty living room, the heels of my shoes click hard on the granite floors as I head to the back of my gated home.

I enter my bedroom, remove my tie and suit jacket, and place them on the chair situated in the corner, near the floor to ceiling window.

I trail to the bathroom, but freeze.

I should charge my phone.

I walk to my jacket to retrieve it from my pocket. I'm about to ignore the text notification that pops on my screen, when I read the name of the sender. My curiosity wins over.

I unlock my phone and read the message.

My eyebrows shoot to my forehead.

I reread the message.

I read it a third time.

I thought I had the situation under control, and now she throws a curve ball my way.

Goddammit.

This woman is determined to unravel me stitch by stitch.

She deserves a lesson, and I have half a mind to administer it right the fuck now.

I pace the length of my bedroom, talking myself out of doing something stupid. My head gets it, my little head... not so much.

My cock is hard as a steel rod, making it difficult to walk.

My nostrils flare.

Down, boy.

Don't do it.

Complicated isn't your thing.

Do not fucking think about it. About her.

The helpless way Lily stared up at me—pouty lips eager for a kiss—flashes in front of my eyes.

Fuck.

My pep talk doesn't quell my desire. On the contrary, it intensifies it. I want to run downstairs, slide behind the wheel of my car, make my way back to the Pompadour Hotel, bang on Lily's door until she opens it, yank her over my shoulder, and march to the bed where I'd place her little, sexy body over my knee, and redden her fine ass for taunting me.

How dare she?

I get where Larkin is coming from, but he's never had to deal with Fisher Edgington. The last thing I need is for the man to ride my ass because I had to ride his daughter.

I stop my pacing.

With a frustrated huff, I throw my phone on my bed.

I need to purge these impure thoughts out of my system.

In a flash, I strip out of my clothes, leaving them on the floor in an expensive pile. A man on a horny as hell mission, I head to the bathroom and hit the shower, stepping straight in under the initial cold blast, gripping my cock as the icy thrill hardens my nipples and wakes up my eager balls.

As the hot water hits and steam billows around me, all I can see in the mist are those mesmerizing purple-blue eyes, that slender and so suckable neck.

Fisting my cock and jerking hard, thumping my gut with every stroke, I imagine the mist clearing, revealing her naked form. Perfect tits. Flawless, porcelain skin. Long legs, so pale as she spreads them, biting her lip, her gaze full of lust as she spreads her perfect pussy.

I turn the water off, panting into the steam, gritting my teeth and gripping my cock, so desperate to take her, to fuck her until she's crying out my name.

But no... the dirty girl slides two fingers into her pussy and moans before finger-fucking herself fast and furious.

I'm done.

I jerk my solid cock like a madman and it's me that cries out as I come, one leg trembling, the other braced against the wall.

Thick streams of hot cum mark the sweet angel. Cum hits her tits, her stomach, and with one final jerk, a satisfying ribbon of cum lands right on her pussy.

Dirty angel.

Lily doesn't stop, keeps fingering herself, my cum

squelching into her. And I keep trembling and jerking until I've got nothing left.

Through the clearing steam, puddles of cum glisten back at me from the tile floor.

Fuck.

What a fucking waste.

I should be shooting my cum inside her pussy.

At the very least, I should be christening her tits.

Fuck... those pretty nipples would be so beautiful painted with my release.

I smear a trail of my cum across my stomach.

Dammit.

With ragged breaths and my chest rising and falling, realization sets in.

It will be impossible to be in Lily's presence without filthy thoughts dancing in my head.

I need to get my shit together before I see her again.

Chapter 14

Lily

A few hours in Gage's presence, and I'm a mess.

How did I forget I was naked?

When Nads pointed that out, I freaked out and ended the video call.

She's seen me in my birthday suit before, but not after I had pleasured myself. That's a little too intimate.

I jump into a pair of shorts and pull a t-shirt over my head, before calling her back.

"*Bonsoir, Nads,*" I say.

Translation: *Good evening, Nads.*

"*Bonjour à toi,*" Nads says.

Translation: *Good morning to you.*

I frown. "It's eleven p.m. LA time, what time is it in Paris?"

"It's eight in the morning."

"Oh, you're right."

She laughs. "Glad to see you're more presentable."

"Sorry, I lost my head there for a minute."

"No one can blame you. You've had a cruel day. It's a girl's worst nightmare to arrive at her destination *sans* luggage." She shakes her head and makes a tsking sound. "What's the point of paying a premium to be seated in First Class if the airline company can't even get their act together so that your luggage makes it?"

I roll my eyes. "Exactly."

"On the plus side, it was an excuse to go shopping."

"It was."

"Please tell me LA isn't sunny all the time," she says, "because it's been raining cats and dogs here in Paris for the last week or so. Hence why I'm wearing this"—she pulls at her white sweatshirt—"instead of a cute little top like yours."

The sweatshirts were gag gifts from last Christmas. We exchanged personalized Vogue cover sweatshirts. Hers has my face. Mine has hers.

"Okay, I'll lie and tell you, LA isn't sunny all the time."

"God, I hate you," she says, mustering a menacing stare.

"Muah!" I send her a Hollywood kiss. "Love you, too, babe."

"Moving right along." She rolls her eyes. "How was shopping in LA, versus New York, London, or Paris?"

"Different cities, different experiences," I say. "Beverly Hills is the height of opulence."

"If you end up going to school in Los Angeles, I'm visiting for sure," she says.

"You better."

She grins.

"Speaking of which, how was tonight's event?" I'm about to respond, but she lifts a hand. "Bravo on the couture."

"You didn't mind the dozen selfies I sent?"

She shakes her head. "I was able to admire the dress from every angle."

"You're such a good friend."

"And you—" she points a finger at me—"were as glam as a Hollywood movie star."

I beam. "I felt like one."

"You were totally giving off vibes of a blue-eyed Jane Russell."

"Oh, stop it."

"I'm serious."

More beaming on my part.

"You wore the necklace."

My hands touch it. "I wanted to show it off."

"Did anyone ask you about it?"

"A flamboyant blonde agent I was talking to inquired about the name and address of my jeweler in Paris."

"Did you tell her who designed it?"

"No. It's still my secret to keep."

"*Oh là là.*" Nadine huffs in exasperation. "That's what you should be focusing on now that you're back in America. Not fulfilling your father's self-serving wishes. Instead of buying a PR agency and putting you 'in charge'"—the fingers of one hand form air quotes—"why not place a lackey he can control in the top position and call it a day?"

I bite the inside of my cheek.

"You're willing to go that far so your own father accepts you? That's fucked up. Your insensitive older brother goes out of his way to ignore you. You think he's going to warm up to you when you start working for him?"

My shoulders slump.

"Lily, these people don't care about you. They're going to use you and break your heart."

"I keep hoping things will change," I say.

"The mighty Fisher Edgington couldn't be bothered remembering his only daughter's twenty-first birthday, Lily."

I shrug.

"My father has his cross to bear, but he was there when I hit that milestone four months ago."

I know. I was there, envying your good fortune.

She soldiers on. "You're more than *une bâtarde*. You're his daughter. His blood runs through your veins."

I keep hoping he'll stop treating me like his bastard child, but so far, my wish hasn't been granted.

"I'm being harsh," she says, "but I'm the only person who cares about you, and we're not even related by blood."

I don't have a comeback because she's right.

Nadine Whelan and I are both *bâtardes*—the product of an affair. Our fathers and their families have treated us as such. The nonexistent relationship she was accustomed to with her dad has been transforming into a something civil. She still isn't sure what happened, but it's as if one day, he had a change of heart.

I was hoping my father would wake up to an epiphany, but it looks like that'll never happen. I'm still the dirty little secret that allowed his ex-wife to walk out with half his fortune thanks to an ironclad prenup.

Je suis la bête noire.

Translation: *I'm the black sheep.*

"Until I agree to a school, there's still time for me to change my mind about heading the PR company my father wants to buy," I say.

"Why not put your foot down now? Do what you were born to do."

She's been adamant about this since I discovered my father's real agenda in summoning me back to New York. He had my future mapped out, including schools I should check out. He never once asked if I had other aspirations for myself. Knowing that none of my father's dreams for me include anything I remotely want, cuts deep. It's as if he's cashing in his chips, requesting payback for supporting me financially since my mom died. Putting my foot down, could mean him turning his back on me.

"I was hoping my return to New York would be the beginning of a father-daughter relationship and the opportunity to form a closer bond with my half-brothers."

Nads stares at me long and hard.

Her lips part in a sad smile. "If anyone on this planet understands your desperate need to be accepted by someone you share DNA with, it's me. Had my father not had his come-to-Jesus moment, I was done begging for him to give me the time of the day. He might not shower me with love—I'll never get that from him—but he no longer ignores my existence. I don't care if my half-sisters and half-brothers still lift their noses at me. *Papa* and I have a weekly standing lunch date. He's making an effort. It's the beginning of something. I'm more than an expense line on his ledger his Champs Élysées accountant has to finesse to camouflage an oopsie baby the President was supporting." She brushes a strand of hair behind her ear. Her gaze darts over my face, and something passes over her brown eyes.

I brace myself.

"I'm not going to even bother to bring your half-brothers into the equation, because they're morons. But you have to decide when you're no longer willing to grovel for your father's love."

Chapter 15

Gage

I could blame today's foul mood on a few unexpected bombs Blanche Hyman dropped this morning in an interview on the East Coast. The fame monger is still wreaking havoc on my show host's life—and now mine.

I choked when the headline to the video clip my PR point person sent me landed in my inbox.

'GAGE HOLLINSGWORTH AIDING AND ABETTING A CHILD MOLESTER'

I was so enraged, I was about to burn this motherfucking city down.

The moment her lies hit the internet, Blanche came to her senses. She retracted her vile accusation.

Smart move.

She was going down a slippery slope.

With me out of the picture, she focused her vitriolic campaign on Matthew.

The way she keeps layering preposterous accusation upon preposterous accusation, forced the PR team to revise Matthew's attack strategy. Given this shitty day, no one would blame me for walking around with a chip on my shoulder, but I'd be lying to myself.

I have Lily Schuyler to blame for my surly mood.

I promised I'd text her to pick her up, but it's a quarter past four and I haven't.

I didn't even respond to the text she sent me last night.

I must've reread that blatant invitation a hundred times.

As the day comes to an end, I have a big decision to make.

I pace the length of my office, both hands tucked inside my pants pockets.

Back and forth.

Back and forth.

Fuck.

I post myself in front of the floor-to-ceiling window. With my eyes lost in the clouds, I beg the big guy upstairs to put an end to my misery.

How the hell did you let this woman sneak up on me, God?

My body has a weird, visceral reaction whenever I'm near her.

I'm so obsessed with her, I've committed her delicate floral scent to memory. It's so ingrained in me, I recalled it this morning as I jerked off twice—once in bed and again in the shower—in my attempt to exorcise this woman from my system but with zero success because I want her so damn much. I would've jerked off a third time, but I have an international company to run.

None of that changes the facts.

Her father remains Fisher Edgington.

Lily Schuyler is off-limits.

The only way to successfully resist temptation is to spend the least amount of time with said temptation.

I walk to my desk, snatch my phone off it, and send off a text.

Done.

Chapter 16

Lily

This morning, I was back at the University of Southern California.

Unlike yesterday's event, today was devoted to visiting the campus, and spending more time with the teachers. Since it's an intense and expensive program, the school wants to make sure we know what we're getting into.

In the afternoon, I visited UCLA.

After that, I stopped by the American Film Institute. It's not on the list of my father's approved schools, but curiosity won. That, and defiance.

Once that was done, I played tourist in Beverly Hills since I couldn't yesterday, given I was on a tight schedule.

LA is so different from New York, London, or Paris. The city has its own unique vibrancy—one I'm warming up to. I won't lie, this sunshine is making me drunk with giddiness.

Conscious of the time, I cut my stroll short. There's still time for me to get ready for Rhys's birthday party, but Michaela sold me on the orange blossom and honey body scrub treatment at the Pompadour Spa. She said it's a must to shake off the jetlag blues.

Sign. Me. Up.

I stroll across the lobby of the hotel on my way to the elevators, when Michaela approaches me, her trademark warm smile stretching her lips. "Perfect timing."

I pull my oversized designer diva sunglasses off my face. "Perfect timing for what?" She's about to respond, but I interrupt her. "I love your dress. You have impeccable style." My eyes drop to her feet. "And you're rocking those heels. Bravo for going with a bold color."

"Thank you." She beams. "I could've gone for white high heels, but these yellow ones make a statement."

"And black would be so predictable."

"I was thinking along the same lines." Mikki winks. "You decided not to wear your beautiful Dior Couture secondhand shop find two days in a row."

"Trust me, I considered it long and hard, but I thought it was a little much for afternoon visits at colleges. Not to mention, the couture would be over the top for the understated hairstyle." I pull at my long braid.

She laughs.

I opted for something less showy—a white sleeveless top with a pair of slim fitted raw silk three-quarter pants in fuchsia, which I paired with black satin Manolo Blahnik Hangisi heels.

"I love this on you." Her eyes are riveted on my necklace.

"Thank you."

"What a versatile piece of jewelry. It pairs perfectly with couture or a more subdued outfit. Where did you buy it?"

I bite the inside of my cheek, unsure if I should tell her the truth or not.

I decide to play it safe. "It's one of those lucky finds."

"If you find another one, buy it, and I'll reimburse you."

I contain my excitement. "Will do."

Praise from a woman with impeccable taste stirs something in me.

Mikki checks her watch. "Our table should be ready."

I frown.

"It's four-thirty. *Le goûter* is being served right about now in the *La Belle Époque* Room."

"Afternoon tea French style?"

"I made reservations for two." Mikki winks. "Care to join me?"

"*Absolument!*"

Translation: *Absolutely*.

"With each passing day, I like you more and more, Lily."

"Ditto, Mikki."

"As Marie Antoinette would say, *let them eat cake*. I love that expression. It's so joyous."

That comment angered the French and caused the Queen's death by guillotine. I don't correct Mikki. She said cake. I'm there.

Lacing her arms with mine, she drags me to the over-the-top elegant café.

The space is spectacular.

The décor at the hotel is quite modern, but the elegant tea salon is a perfect blend of modern and a touch of *je ne sais quoi* that hints at olde-worlde charm.

As we trail across the room, Mikki nods here and there at patrons who wave as she strolls past tables.

She's a formidable hostess.

Instead of sitting at one of the unoccupied tables, she keeps walking all the way to a private area located at the back of the restaurant.

We come to stand in front of a table set with an extravagant flair, including tiered cake stands, floral mismatched tea cups, cloth napkins, and a crisp white tablecloth that reaches the floor.

Nice.

"This is where upper management eats," she says.

I nod.

My eyes lift to the large candelabra chandeliers dripping with crystals dangling from the ceiling.

If I could whistle, I would.

I meet her gaze. "You don't do things halfway."

"At the Pompadour? Never. Not to mention, afternoon tea is an experience. You can't enjoy it sitting at your desk, stuffing your face, while poring over spreadsheets."

"I agree."

Right on cue the song changes to *C'est si Bon.*

I point to the ceiling. "It's a kitschy song, but a classic."

The sound of the accordion gives a Parisian atmosphere and complements the songbird's vocals.

"I agree, but it sets the mood, and guests love the oldies," Michaela says. "The newer French songs don't have the same cachet."

I bob my head to the guitar solo.

"Oh, it's a bilingual version," I say when the female singer sings the next verse.

"*Mais, bien sûr.*" Mikki winks. "Let's sit."

Translation: *But of course.*

Before I have time to blink, a parade of waiters fuss at our table, setting plates of desserts for a delightful afternoon snack. With irreproachable care, they serve tea and serve us a beautiful assortment of bite-size options.

With a solemn bow, they scurry off.

My mouth waters as I take in the display of scrumptious desserts set on beautiful ornate Limoges style porcelain plates.

"Madeleine cakes, *tartes au citron*, tarte Tatin, gâteau

opéra, Saint Honoré, and Paris-Brest," I say. "You're even serving baguette and chocolate squares." This is one of the most quintessential after-school treats for kids in France.

"I discovered how delicious that combo is the first time I visited France."

"Life is short. I love how the French bypass savory options and strictly focus on dessert."

"Got to love how the French think."

"Oh, I love *pain au chocolat*?" I point to the golden chocolate croissants.

She cocks a perfectly groomed eyebrow. "Try *pain au chocolat blanc.*"

"Mother of God. Croissants stuffed with white chocolate?"

She nods.

Sweet baby Jesus.

She points to another plate. "And these are *petits pains au chocolat blanc.*"

"White chocolate bread?"

"Yup!"

She says that as if it was no big deal.

Carbs *and* white chocolate? Angels are singing.

"Phoenix's youngest brother, Roman, doesn't like milk chocolate," she says.

"He doesn't?"

"He doesn't enjoy the taste."

That guy must be a Martian.

"Our pastry chef came up with the white chocolate alternatives to classic French pastries. Roman loves them. So does our guests. They're a crowd pleaser."

"You people know how to live," I say. "What about this?" I point to a small smooth caramel-colored cake.

"*Gâteau à la confiture de lait*, aka, dulce de leche cake. We're talking about moist and fluffy brown butter layers covered in sinful dulce de leche buttercream, topped with a braid of vanilla buttercream."

"You're killing me."

Mikki laughs. "Dulce de leche is heavenly."

#Fact.

"There are a few spots in New York that serve a French afternoon tea, but none rival what we serve at the Pompadour Hotel, which is why we had to open a separate afternoon tea salon that serves *le goûter* because the *La Belle Époque* Room at the New York location had a one-month wait list."

"Impressive."

"We keep the experience as traditional as possible, even going so far as choosing *Marriages Frères* instead of British tea." She points to the teapot. "As I'm sure you know, unlike the British high tea, the French only serve sweet. Some restaurants in Paris break with tradition, but we decided not to."

"It's like being in Paris."

"Minus the Eiffel Tower and the Arc de Triomphe, it's a close second," she says.

"You forgot the moody Parisians on a rainy day."

"Angelenos are darn right grouchy when it drizzles, and plain bitchy when it rains."

We laugh.

"I hope it's okay with you, but I asked the bar to hold on the booze since the champagne will be flowing tonight," she says.

"Not a problem."

"Please." Mikki invites me to dig in.

"You don't have to tell me twice."

I bite into the *pain au chocolat blanc*. I moan. "Oh my God, I may never leave this hotel."

"You don't have to. We can keep charging your credit card."

"My father would fly into town, throw a hissy fit, and demand an explanation."

Concern colors her green eyes and her lips flatten in a straight line.

Shit. "There I go ruining our time together by talking about my father."

"I don't know the man, but I'm not one of his biggest fans," Mikki says. "As for an explanation on the charges on his credit card…" She shrugs. "Too many film schools, not enough time. You *had* to extend your trip."

"Oh, you're good." I laugh. "I like having you as my accomplice."

"Anytime."

"I'll hold you to it."

For a few long minutes, we're far too consumed by our desserts to speak.

Once I'm done devouring the white chocolate croissant, I move my attention to the tempting dulce the leche cake. I'm unprepared for the burst of flavor gushing into my mouth. I close my eyes for a beat, as if I'm in a communion with God. "This is exquisite, incredibly moist, and not too sweet."

"I'm quite partial, but we have the best pastry chefs in the country."

"I believe it."

As we enjoy our afternoon tea, I answer Mikki's questions about the two schools I visited. It was nothing earth-shattering. Still, I'm touched she cares.

When it comes to the colleges, I'm going through the motions. In the end, since my father is footing the bill, he'll select the school of his choice. It's all part of the grand plan.

Whatever.

I should be offended the puppet master hasn't been in touch yet, but my father continues to ignore me. Ironic, considering he's the one who insisted I make the trip.

"My second visit to Beverly Hills saved the day," I say.

"Fingers crossed Rhys's birthday party will make up for a fairly boring day."

"No need to wish upon a star, dear friend. You're going to have a blast. Phoenix's inner circle know how to party. Same goes for the sisterhood."

"I can't wait."

Speaking of people who haven't been in touch...

"I wonder what time Gage is going to pick me up," I say. "I booked a spa treatment, and don't want to make him wait. He was supposed to text—"

"He won't be able to pick you up."

My brows wing in surprise. "Oh." I school my expression not to show my disappointment. "I see."

"He sent me a text and asked me to take you to the party."

Her words hit me in the gut.

I drop my fork on the plate and rummage through my bag for my phone. I pull it out and check my messages.

Nothing.

A pang of something I can't describe hits me dead in the chest.

"He didn't text me to tell me." I hate the complaint in my voice.

The deep-seated fear of rejection that's plagued me since my mom died, kicks in.

"He's having a hell of a day." Her expression is apologetic, but it does nothing to lessen the blow.

He couldn't text me or at least copy me on the message he sent Michaela?

Don't take it personally, Lily.

I'm being overly sensitive.

He's a virtual stranger.

No need to get bent out of shape because he changed his

plans at the last minute. The man has a business to run. I'm passing through town.

I pull in a breath and let it out. "Okay."

"Since yesterday, he's been dealing with a public relations nightmare, involving Jam Session's show host. It's a mess."

"I didn't know."

She adjusts herself on the seat. "I should warn you."

Uh, oh.

"Gage can be a bit... abrasive."

"Given his position, I'm sure everyone wants a piece of him."

"It's more than that." She lets out a long exhale. "People who were close to him, betrayed him in the worst possible way."

"Oh, no."

"It's not my story to tell, so I won't say more, but..." She falls silent for a beat. "I will say this, Gage tends to keep people at arm's length. It took him a long time to warm up to me, but my husband warned me, so I didn't take it personally. He also allows himself to be consumed by his business. In all fairness, most billionaires do, but Gage uses work as a protective shield." She brushes a hand in front of her face, as if to sweep everything she just said under a rug. "Anyway, you shouldn't be disappointed if he doesn't show up tonight."

A lump swells in my throat.

"But don't worry, the sisterhood has your back," she says. "Plus, you're absolutely gorgeous. I'm no psychic, but I can predict the single guys in our inner circle will fight over you. Men will fall at your feet."

There's only one man I want to fall at my feet.

Chapter 17

Lily

The star power at the private affair at Club SIX10 is ridiculous.

I'm partying with *the* Keira Knightley and kickass Stasia van Gameren. I didn't put two and two together when Mikki mentioned her bestie's name.

Oh, my freaking God.

When Keira arrived at Rod and Dom's house, where the sisterhood was getting primped for tonight, I was starstruck for a full minute before I thought I was going to lose my shit. I had to control myself not to fuss all over her like a fan girl or beg for an autograph.

I'm a huge Lucky Break fan. So is Nadine. She's going to die.

Even if the group is no longer active due to tragedy, I still shake my hips to their upbeat tunes.

As for Stasia—any woman who can bring the house down with her mad guitar skills while balancing on five-inch heels earns my respect.

I nearly fainted when Mikki suggested a selfie with the four of us. I guess my poker face wasn't as stoic as I thought. Maybe it's because I kept shooting glances filled with admiration Keira's way.

When Mikki talked about the sisterhood and the inner circle, she wasn't joking.

While the girls were primping at Dom's house, the men were kicking off the evening at Rhys's business partner's house. I was overwhelmed by all this girl power, but when we arrived at the club, I was hit with another wave of awestruck-worthy celebrities.

Cello2Cello's talented duo are here.

I'm not into rock music, so I didn't know Rod, Rhys's business partner Beckett, Beckett's older brother, and cousin were part of Random Misconception—one of the best rock bands of our time. The birthday boy also has superstar status as a former rap star.

Little ol' me is rubbing elbows with some pretty big names.

I'm nothing special.

I can't sing.

I can't compose music.

I'm not that great at faking it, so acting is out of the question.

God knows after a long string of music lessons, I still suck at piano and violin.

Despite my father's colossal wealth, I can't even call myself a socialite, because he's kept me a secret for most of my life, so I've always kept a low profile, for fearing of calling too much attention to myself.

Yet, here I am.

I'm a fish out of water, but I'm loving this new adventure. The people in my father's circle might be wealthy, but none of them have Hollywood star power.

I was having an incredible time until I went and ruined it for myself.

Arianne, Beckett's better half, introduced me to Cesar Navarro and his wife Diana. I'm not on top of my Latin music, so I didn't go into fan girl mode like I had with Keira and Stasia. Still, these two are mega music stars.

I was chatting up a storm—too many French martinis in a row tend to do that—when my mouth ran away from me. I made the mistake of saying I've always wanted to learn how to dance salsa. Diana promptly enlisted her husband as my dance teacher.

My cheeks warm, not because of the martinis, but because I'm injuring Cesar. The former King of Reggaetón turned successful businessman has been teaching me the basics for the past half hour. I wouldn't say I have two left feet, but salsa is hard. On *Dancing with The Stars, Strictly Come Dancing,* and *Danse avec les stars* everyone dances with such ease and grace.

I'm sure Cesar must be regretting he accepted to step up to the challenge. By the time this lesson is done, I'll have scuffed up his expensive looking shoes.

I stare up at him. "I'm sorry." I cringe when I step on his foot. Again.

"Don't worry about it," he says, his dark brown eyes filled with understanding. "Let's take it from the top."

"I'm a lost cause," I say.

The music isn't too loud to prevent easy conversation. Or in this case, easy complaining.

"Nonsense. Practice makes perfect."

If you say so.

"*Chica muévelo.*"

Cesar has been saying that on repeat since this torture began. I do as I'm told, and shake my hips.

"One, two. Three, four."

I follow my dance partner's instructions.

All these names to remember and me trying hard not to cause Cesar grievous bodily harm have kept my mind occupied.

No time to think about Gage.

"May I cut in," a man says, tapping Cesar's shoulder.

I lift my eyes.

A tall man towers over Cesar and me.

Wow, another guy who could double as a fitness model.

This group of attractive people is a little intimidating, to be honest.

"*¡Ay, caramba!* Go away, Collin, you're bothering us," Cesar says.

Translation: *Damn it.*

I laugh.

"Hello." The newcomer ignores Cesar's jab and focuses his attention on me. "I'm Collin Dennison." He flashes me a dazzling smile. "I'm sorry I'm late. Had I known you'd be here tonight, I would've arrived sooner... but I'm here now."

If he wasn't this gorgeous, that pickup line would have cheesy written all over it.

Cesar lets out an exasperated sigh and stops dancing, forcing me to do the same.

Cesar hooks a hand on his hip, adopting an impatient stance. "Can't you see we're busy, Dennison?"

"Don't be rude, *amigo,*" Collin says. "There's a gorgeous new face in our inner circle and we haven't been introduced yet. That right there, is a crime."

Cesar rolls his eyes hard.

Collin Denison is a blue-eyed hunk who has a face—and body—that should be gracing a men's magazine cover. He's adorned in a dark blue linen shirt that molds his muscular torso. His sleeves are rolled up, revealing a peek of tattooed forearms. The white linen pants and navy-blue shoes complement the shirt to perfection. The newcomer oozes as much style, confidence, and charisma as all the men at this private party.

"Pleased to meet you." Collin extends a hand. "You know my name, but I don't know yours. That means, I'm at a disadvantage."

Smooth talker.

I shake his hand. "Pleased to meet you, I'm Lily Schuyler."

"Lovely Lily, you're wasting your time with this guy. He's happily married."

"She knows." Cesar flashes his left hand. "My wife is here."

"My point exactly."

Cesar narrows his eyes at Collin.

He ignores the warning in my teacher's gaze and points his charm-laser at me. "I'm *very* single, and unlike him"—he crooks a thumb in Cesar's direction— "I'm an excellent salsa dancer."

He does a few suave moves to demonstrate.

Oh yeah, he's cocky all right.

"And which one of your parents is Latino?" Cesar purses his lips.

"Please." Collin rolls his eyes. "Being Latino isn't a prerequisite to having the right moves. You either have it or you don't, and I have it in spades." Mr. Casanova's gaze travels the length of my body. "Your outfit... could stop traffic."

"Thank you."

To Mikki's credit, I've received a lot of attention from men tonight. More than I expected.

Even if my luggage had arrived when I did, I wouldn't have anything remotely close to this in it. This outfit screams LA. I had an outfit selected for tonight, but the sisterhood vetoed it, stating it was too *good girl* for the City of Angels. Since Dom and I are the same size, she shoved an outfit she bought, but never wore, in my hands, pushed me in the bathroom, and ordered me to change.

After staring at myself in the mirror for an eternity, uncertain if I had the courage to pull off the daring outfit, I stepped out of the bathroom.

The sisterhood approved with cheers and thumbs up. Their reaction gave me wings.

"That outfit"—another onceover—"requires a bodyguard," Collin says. "Allow me to post my candidature for the job."

"Everyone is so friendly here." I smile. "I'm sure I don't have to worry."

"These guys are my buddies, but make no mistake about it, lovely Lily, they can be wolves. It's best if I stay close by."

"Lily has a bodyguard," Cesar says.

"You?" Collin scoffs.

An evil smile splits Cesar's lips. "Gage is watching over her while she's in Los Angeles."

Since he isn't here at present, that's not accurate.

Collin's head jerks back. "Gage?"

Cesar nods. "Yes."

All color drains from Collin's face. "You know what, I should go and wish Rhys a Happy Birthday again," he says. "Catch you later, Lily."

"Catch you—" The rest of my sentence dies on my lips.

Mr. Casanova bolts to the other side of the club so fast, I swear I saw cartoon puffs of smoke coming off his feet.

"Collin couldn't stay away from a gorgeous woman even if his life depended on it," my dance instructor says.

"I'm flattered. I think."

Cesar laughs. "He's a little bit much, but he's harmless."

"Noted."

The music changes to another sexy salsa beat.

Thank God I had the good sense to pull my curtain of raven-black hair into an updo. Had I not, I'd be blinded right now. My eyes are trained to the floor to avoid stepping on Cesar's polished shoes, as I'm so determined to get it right.

"You should hold your dance partner's eyes," Cesar says.

"I will." My eyes remain glued to my feet.

He chuckles.

With my attention focused on my feet, I repeat the steps in my head.

"Collin, I thought you got the message the first— Gage, *hermano*, you're here."

My eyes shoot up.

I stare Gage up and down as if he's a figment of my imagination.

My heart flips over in my chest.

"Hey, Cesar, I didn't know you were giving private dancing lessons," Gage says. "Trying to fund your retirement?"

"Nah, I'm in the business of making dreams come true," he says. "Salsa dancing was on Lily's bucket list, so I obliged." Cesar scours the dance floor before meeting Gage's gaze. "My wife pushed me into it, but that's between you and me."

Cesar laughs.

My brain registered his joke, but I'm too shellshocked to crack a smile.

He's here.

Gage moves his attention to me.

Holy hotness on legs.

For a second, I go stupid, gawking at him.

Those green eyes have the ability to make me weak in the knees.

Yesterday, he was the definition of suit porn, but today... the man is a walking Adonis.

Dear God, save me.

I'm not sure how that's even possible, but he looks more

badass than he did yesterday even though he ditched the bespoke suit. He's dressed down in a gray Burberry shirt with the first two buttons undone, revealing a glimpse of his chest and—

Gage has tattoos?

Visible colorful tattoos also peek from the folded cuffs, flashing the brand's trademark nova check fabric.

Gage was hiding a badass secret.

He's so out of my league.

My father doesn't rub shoulders with men who sport tattoos— I guess I can't say that. A suit and buttoned up shirt do a smashing job at hiding a man's edgier side.

My father turns his nose up at the entertainment industry and people who choose to sully their skin by marking it with vulgar ink.

My closed off bodyguard is becoming an even bigger enigma.

I wonder if the tattoos only run along his arms, or does he also have them on his back and chest.

I continue my inspection.

The shirt is snug around his wide chest and huge arms.

Gage completes the casual-but-oh-so-hot look with black jeans and kickass black shoes.

He's gorgeous. And he exudes such raw masculinity, it's bewildering.

It's unfair how beautiful this man is to me.

He might not have Beckett's or Phoenix's perfect features, but that's what makes him so hot.

"Hey," he says.

A blush creeps from the tip of my toes to the top of my head.

I'm so glad to see him—more than I should be considering he's been ignoring me—but I'm determined not to show it.

You're not a prepubescent teenage girl, so play it cool. "Hey." Okay not exactly cool, but at least I didn't come across like an overexcited puppy.

My heart thuds in erratic beats making it impossible to string a sentence together.

He takes me in, his gaze traveling down to my feet, up my legs, hips, brushing up my body to my breasts, before returning to my face, which I'm sure is a violent shade of crimson.

"May I cut in?" The question should be addressed to Cesar, but Gage's green eyes are still fixed on me.

I answer with a shy nod.

"Of course," Cesar says, before breaking out of our dance position and taking a step back. "It was a pleasure."

"Thank you for being so courageous." I grimace.

"You're selling yourself short, Lily."

"I doubt it." I scoff.

Cesar's eyes shift to Gage's. "A few more lessons, and this one"—he points at me—"will dance like a pro."

"I got it from here."

The two men exchange a silent conversation I'm not privy to.

"I'm sure you do," Cesar says. "I'll go give my sexy Dominican wife some salsa lessons." He laughs his head off. "Catch you kids later." He pats the tall mountain of a man standing in front of me on the shoulder.

For a beat, we stare at each other.

Even in my skyscraper heels, our height difference is laughable.

He takes me in his arms.

Wild flutters go off in my belly at the contact.

I hitch a breath, as my mind goes a bit hazy.

He takes a sharp one, and lets it out in a swift exhale.

I'm not sure if my inexperience is causing me to see things that are only a mirage, but I swear, there's something between us.

I felt safe in Cesar's arms—like you would in your older brother's embrace. Gage's proximity is dizzying. And intoxicating. And all-encompassing.

Our bodies move to the rhythm of the beat.

Needing to dump a bucket of cold water over my body to ebb the burning flames of desire, I speak, "Cesar is building me up. I can dance to pop music, but no one will confuse me for a ballroom dancer."

"That makes two of us," he says.

"You don't salsa?"

"I get by, but you won't catch me doing any crazy moves." He jerks his chin in Arianne and Beckett's direction. Other than those two, there are a few couples showing off their best salsa moves on the dance floor.

Gage gives me a twirl. Nothing crazy.

When he catches me in his arms, I lose my breath.

My happy martini induced buzz from earlier is nothing compared to how lightheaded I am right now.

"So, I don't have to worry I'll break an ankle?" My tone is teasing.

He pulls away from me, his gaze traveling down the length of my body. "Your outfit..." His nostrils flare. "Hmph..."

Not that again.

I'm wearing a pair of gold designer embroidered shorts with a sleeveless blouse in pale pink. The high neck hides my necklace. Lucky for me, Dom's outfit matches my designer peep-toe ankle strap heels in a metallic gold sheen animal pattern.

Dom let me borrow her Chanel gold crocodile embossed calfskin clutch. My jaw dropped when she offered. My half-brothers would never allow me to borrow a cup of sugar, let alone something they cherish.

"What's wrong with what I'm wearing?"

His mouth is pinched as he gives me another onceover. "It's a good thing I'm here to act as a buffer between you and all the single guys here tonight." He meets my gaze. "Especially, Collin Dennison."

How did he know?

And why does he care?

Something snaps inside me.

I halt my step, and twist out of his grasp. "That's it? You're here because you think I need a babysitter?"

Gage's expression is tight and intense, his ice-green eyes almost mystical under the low lights. He crosses his muscular arms over his wide chest. The authoritative stance makes me swoon in sheer lust.

"You're showing a mile long of legs." His tone is accusatory.

My head jerks back as if he slapped me across the face.

This is where I'd swallow my response, bite my tongue, suppress the need to retort to avoid causing waves.

Not going to happen.

"Yesterday, you had a problem with my dress. Today, you have a problem with my shorts. I don't need another man disapproving of me." I'm on a roll. "As per your message to Mikki—a message you conveniently forgot to include me on—you weren't going to show up. You should've stayed away. I don't need you on babysitting duty."

With that, I'm ready to distance myself from him, but I don't go far.

A large hand clamps around my wrist. "You're not going anywhere."

His commanding voice suggests I have no choice in the

matter, but fuck if that doesn't stop me from putting my foot down. "Let go." I try to free my arm from his vicelike grip.

It's in vain.

The man is too strong.

"Sounds like you have a lot to get off your chest, princess."

"I said, let go, you brute."

"Let's get it all out in the open." He pulls me off the dance floor.

"Gage, where are we going?"

He ignores me, and keeps eating the floor with his long strides, forcing my step to speed up to a stomping-jog to keep up without tripping in my sky-high heels. Each rapid step matches the pounding of my heart.

As if we're now the entertainment, the DJ lowers the music to background levels.

The sisterhood and the inner circle stare, but no one attempts to stop this beast.

Thanks for the support, guys.

My humiliation clutching for something to grab onto, I snap at him. "You're walking too fast."

Gage stops.

Unprepared, I practically bump into him.

He turns around, his eyes dropping to my strappy high heels.

Narrowed green eyes meet mine.

A foreign surge of fear, anticipation, and excitement swirl within me.

With a growl, he sweeps me off my feet, throws me over his shoulder, firefighter-style, and Tarzan, Lord of the Jungle, kidnaps me.

I screech.

Is someone going to stop this madman?

To my shock, the inner circle wolf whistles and catcalls, fists pumping in encouragement.

Ugh.

Struggling with the beast is pointless. I stand zero chance against this gladiator.

With my head dangling near Gage's fine ass, he resumes his mission.

I lift my head long enough to scour the room.

Judging by Mikki's stunned expression and that of many members of the sisterhood, Gage is stealing the show. And I am an unwilling participant. The men on the other end, are pumping their fists in the air.

Figures.

Given the difference in size, I can't fight him off. I'm pretty sure drumming my fists against his back in outrage would only tickle him.

I only have one recourse.

"You better—"

My protest fades on my lips when his hand tightens around my calves, while the other rests around my thigh, right below my ass. The intimate touch sends a ripple of sensation coursing through my body.

Good God.

I don't have time to linger in that blissful state for too long.

Gage walks us out of the private room and down a corridor.

In this position, I can't tell where we're going.

Another turn, and he comes to a stop.

He slides me down his body until my feet touch the ground.

I hook my fist at my waist. "What's your problem?"

His eyes roam over my face before his gaze lingers on my mouth. His nostrils flare like a bull ready to charge and the wide expanse of his chest hitches.

"Your heels aren't made for walking," he says.

He's so distracting that for a moment, I forgot my question.

My jaw drops, but fury prompts me to recover. "That's your lame explanation?"

He grunts.

"Let me get this straight," I say. "You operate on two settings—you either grunt like Mr. Grumpy Pants or revert to this... this..."—I wave a frantic finger up and down the length of his body—"primal, feral caveman? Can't you talk like a normal human being?"

He opens a door behind him. "Get in."

"Stop bossing me around."

He works his jaw. "You want to talk? Get inside, Lily."

Not bothering to wait, he pulls me by the hand, hauling me inside a dark room.

Cardboard boxes, wood crates, extra chairs and tables, a high-back office chair, and a desk, line the walls of the neat storage space.

I turn around to face him.

I cross my arms over my chest, steadfast in my stubbornness.

I expect him to turn on the lights, but he doesn't.

"Are we supposed to talk in the dark?"

The space basks under city lights coming through the large windows, but I'd welcome a more brilliant light so I can better keep my eyes on the beast.

He takes a step closer.

I unfold my arms and take one back.

We do this dance a few times as he backs me further into the room, his wide shoulders blocking the view to the door—the exit to safety.

A stuttering breath leaves me.

This close, under the faint luminosity pouring into the

space, his wintergreen eyes shine like pale gemstones, the fierceness unmistakable on his handsome face. The scent of his cologne wafting around me, is intoxicating. No doubt it's called *Eau de Scorching Hot.*

A little frisson of pleasure runs down my spine.

I snap out of my lust-filled stupor and remember how incensed I am by his over-the-top display of masculine power.

"You're taking this bodyguard role way too seriously," I say, coating my words with an extra layer of annoyance.

"You're right."

That isn't the answer I expected.

His big body is standing right in front of me, vibrating with... with... with... I'm not sure with what.

Argh.

"I was supposed to stay away from you—"

"Why didn't you?"

He steps up to me, clamps a hand behind my neck and pulls me towards him, and I stumble on my heels.

My breath catches.

My flight or fight mode kicks into high gear.

"Because I couldn't."

My brain doesn't have time to compute his admission. Gage's mouth crashes against mine.

Oh.

My.

God.

I moan into the kiss.

My insides flutter as if a swarm of butterflies were taking flight.

My hand lands on his muscular chest.

His lips grow more demanding by the second. He forces his tongue inside my mouth. I welcome the intrusion. His tongue swirls with mine in a passionate dance—you'd think I've never been kissed before. I match his ardor, tongue stroke for tongue stroke. The taste of strong liquor indicates he's been drinking tonight.

How long was he at the club before approaching Cesar and me?

With each heartbeat, the fieriness of the kiss creeps up to dangerous levels, threatening to scorch my body.

I lose my balance, as my legs go wobbly, heat swelling between my pussy lips.

He tightens his grip around my waist, fusing our bodies together as he deepens the kiss.

An intoxicating charge shoots straight to my clit.

"Fuck, Lily." The gruff voice I'm used to is as soft as a caress. "Do you feel how hard you make me?" He tilts his hips up, pressing his impressive bulge into me.

Mother Mary.

The man is huge.

"Oh." That's the most I can muster up right now. My mind is racing, trying to piece together how we went from duking it out to him pressing his cock against me.

He's unrepentant when he takes possession of my lips again.

His first kiss was intense, but this smoldering-hot make-out session threatens to make me lose my freaking mind.

What a departure from what I'm used to.

Our tongues tangle and swirl, intertwined in a sexy tango.

It's as if his mouth is savoring mine.

It's hot as fuck.

I hold onto his arms to avoid drowning in his kiss.

With a hand pressing against the small of my back, he brings my body flush to his. With a feral grunt, he grinds his rock-hard cock against me.

Heated lust rushes through my veins.

My clit tingles with need.

I tilt my hips, seeking salvation.

The height difference makes it awkward, but that doesn't stop me.

Gage's lips flirt with mine. "What do you want?"

His voice is a drug.

"I—"*I want you to make me come.*

It's on the tip of my tongue, but I can't bring myself to let the words leave my lips. Too many years walking a straight and narrow line will do that to a girl.

Unwilling to admit I can't find my lady balls, I shake my head.

The last thing I want is for him to see I'm a little wet behind the ears.

"No, that's not an answer," he says.

I clench my fingers around the fabric of his shirt, bunching it into my fist.

"What do you want from me?" The gruff undertone in his voice returns.

"Gage..." His name comes out in a breathless plea.

He leans into me until his lips are flirting with my earlobe. "These shorts will haunt my dirty wet dreams for years to come."

Me? His dirty wet dream?

His admission has the same effect as a bush fire blazing across its path.

He reaches out and brushes his knuckles over my breasts, eliciting a shiver that runs from the top of my head all the way down to my painted toes. Since the design of the silk top doesn't allow for a padded bra, my lacy bra does a shit job at hiding my arousal. Even a blind man could see my hard nipples scratching against the fabric, puckering with need.

"Fuck, those protruding peaks are so fucking beautiful." His fingers caress my swollen nipple over my top, and tweak it.

I let out a high-pitched sound.

"Shhh," he says.

I nod, my head bobbing in a jerky movement.

"Good girl." His eyes are hooded beneath his thick, dark eyelashes.

His hands travel down my body until his fingers close around my thighs.

I gasp.

With a feathered touch, his fingers caress my thighs until they're nestled between my legs.

I hitch a breath, but I don't ask him to stop.

"You make it impossible for me to stop thinking of you, Lily."

I'm so turned on, I'm dripping.

He leans close, his hot breath feathering across my lips. "Tell me if this is one-sided?"

"I thought you didn't like me."

He removes his hand from between my legs and presses his hard cock against me. "Does it feel like I don't like you?"

Holy shit, he's even harder now.

This man is impressive all over.

I'm glad it's dark because my face is on fire.

His hands travel down my back before cupping my ass cheeks and squeezing hard.

My eyes roll into the back of my head.

The sensory stimulation is dizzying.

"Fuck, your ass feels so good in my hands."

Granted, this is a little Jekyll and Hyde, but holy fuck is it ever hot. "You—you're confusing me."

"You took me by surprise last night, when I dropped you off and again with that text," he says.

"The one you never answered?"

He takes a step forwards, forcing me back against a wall, pinning me there.

Shit.

He places two fingers underneath my chin, forcing my attention to him. He leans into me, his mouth flirting with mine, sending my pulse leaping at the base of my neck.

"I can assure you, I wanted to do a hell of a lot more than answer your text. I wanted to get behind the wheel of my car and drive to your hotel, bust down the door, and wish you sweet dreams in person with my mouth on your pussy."

"Oh."

"I jerked off in the shower with that blatant invitation on my mind and visions of doing dirty things to you as punishment for taunting me. I came so fucking hard, I thought I was going to pass out."

I'm so shellshocked by his lewd admission, I can only stare in disbelief.

"Am I still confusing you, angel?"

"Err..."

"What was that?"

I open and close my mouth like a fish.

He ducks his head, locking his eyes with mine. "That text was a tease. You know it. I know it."

Answering would incriminate me.

"You wanted to poke the bear, Goldilocks? Game on. Now you're going to live with the consequences."

With his gaze fixed on me, he unbuttons my shorts

He waits for a beat, as if waiting for me to protest.

When I don't, he proceeds to lower the zipper.

In the emptiness of the room, I can hear the illicit sound over my ragged breathing.

His hand snakes inside my panties until it's nestled

between my pussy lips. Long fingers explore my wetness, teasing my clit, causing my core to clench, and my thighs to tremble.

My mouth drops open, my eyelashes flutter, and my fingernails bite into his forearms, as if that's all it takes to contain this blissful sensation.

This is so lewd.

So wrong.

So unlike me.

Yet, it's so, so good.

He growls in a low, deep voice. The rich timbre is enough to make me shudder.

"You're so fucking wet for me."

It's not a question.

Not that I'd waste my time denying how my body is reacting to him.

I added a new chapter to my LA adventure by being here tonight, surrounded by all the celebrities. Getting down and dirty with Gage Hollingsworth in a storage room when his friends are only a few feet away, is a finale I never saw coming.

Evidently, I'm tapping into the badass that materialized herself yesterday in my hotel room. The one that pushed me out of my comfort zone when I was giving myself pleasure, thinking of Gage. And now, she's the one taking over as this gorgeous man does naughty things to me.

I've never been this promiscuous. Ever.

I'm the girl who colors inside the lines.

I'm engulfed in a hedonistic bubble of his making and I have no intention fighting it. That, and the excruciating ache between my legs is unbearable.

I give myself to him without an ounce of shame.

The giant of a man towering over me makes it impossible to want to put an end to a good thing.

His masterful fingers never stop teasing me, taking me higher and higher.

A freaking tsunami of pleasure washes over me.

Gage is working my clit with the same dexterity as a talented musician plays an instrument.

A throaty, pleading sound I don't recognize leaves my lips. "You're going to make me come."

"That's the plan."

In an attempt to slow things down, I reach for his cock.

"Tsk." He brushes my hand away. "Did I give you permission to touch my cock?"

Holy shit.

I'm taken aback by the question. And the authoritative tone.

I'm an unruly student, being chastised by the principal.

I hesitate. "No."

"This is about you. I want to make you come and I want my name on your lips when you do. Got it?"

I nod.

"I'm not a mind reader. Words. I want words."

"Yes," I say in a faint voice.

"We're on the same page." His fingers keep moving on me, rubbing circles around my clit before he sinks them deep inside me.

My eyes slam shut, as an explosive sensation of pleasure bursts through me.

"No, angel. I want your eyes on me."

Mr. Grumpy Pants is commanding as fuck.

I open them, meeting his gaze.

"Good girl," he says.

I'm no match for this man.

"You're going to be fucking beautiful when you come for me."

His words detonate something in me.

His fingers alternate between teasing my clit and filling my pulsing pussy.

I'm so close to the edge, I can't think straight. Let alone breathe.

My core clenches with such force, I swear, I see stars.

"You're close."

"Yes."

He picks up the pace.

Goosebumps pebble up and down my body as shockwaves of heat zip through me, threatening to make me dizzy.

"Don't stop."

My legs are wobbly as he skates over my clit again, and again, and again.

My hips tremble.

I'm there. I'm so there.

"Give it to me, Lily."

There's no going back now. "I will."

"You're going to come hard for me?"

"Yes." With a single word, I pledge my promise.

The good girl in me feels so depraved for admitting that, but the badass is high-fiving me for riding this man's fingers like a slut.

"Oh, God. Oh, God. Oh, God—"

"That's not my name. What did I tell you?"

"You're making it hard to think straight."

All movement ceases.

A grunt of complaint leaves me.

"Is that a reproach?"

I shake my head. "Please don't stop."

"How can I refuse you? You beg so beautifully."

He resumes his mission.

Thank you, God.

My ex-boyfriend could get me off with his fingers, but I never felt like the orgasm was building from the tip of my toes.

I knew Gage's fingers would turn out to be magical.

"I— Oh— God—" All the blood in my body has congregated around my clit.

"Lily, if I have to remind you how the game is played, I'll hold back your orgasm."

A bulldozer wouldn't be able to hold back my orgasm, but under the city lights streaming through the window, the menacing threat shines bright in his eyes.

No way am I going to give him ammunition. "Gage, I'm on the verge of losing my mind."

"Now you know how I felt about you since I saw you yesterday."

I don't have time to process his words.

His fingers are doing mind-blowing things to me.

A few strokes, and I'm diving off the cliff.

"Oh, Gage." I chant his name over and over again.

The force of my orgasm causes my vision to blur.

I grip his forearm, as my rubbery legs are incapable of supporting my weight.

Smoldering heat burns in my core as I come all over this gorgeous man's hand in an epic climax.

Every cell in my body lights up like firecrackers.

Spent, I drop my head on his strong chest.

He kisses the top of my head.

I purr like a satisfied kitten.

We stay like this for a while, him cradling me in the safety of his big body, me caught in the warm aftermath still buzzing in the background.

After several heartbeats, I lift my gaze to meet his.

He pulls his fingers from my pulsating pussy and brings them to his mouth. With his eyes locked onto mine, he cleans his digits dripping with my juices with his tongue. It's perverted and sensual at the same time.

My mouth falls open.

Holy dirty.

I'm still struggling to catch my breath, caught in a haze of arousal, and my thighs are still shaking from the strength of the spasm, but watching him do that, nearly causes me to come again.

A jarring thought crashes into me. "Did you lock the door?"

"No."

Panic grips me by the neck. "Oh my God. Anyone could've walked in on us while we were doing raunchy things."

No answer.

"Gage?"

"Possibly."

I wait for him to elaborate, but he doesn't.

"That's it?"

"Angel, none of my friends were going to come after us. I made it pretty clear I needed some alone time with you."

Yes, you did, Tarzan.

"As for the staff... I guess there was a chance we might've had an audience."

Wait. What?

My eyes widen in shock.

"If that was such a concern, you would've told me earlier, but you were too eager to ride my fingers and come your head off to care if anyone walked in on us while I took good care of your sweet pussy."

This man's mouth is a weapon, capable of causing instant combustion.

"You can thank me for introducing you to the kinky world of public sex."

"That wasn't an item on my bucket list."

"Trust me, you'll be glad I'm a forward-thinker. The risk of getting caught is half the fun—"

"Gage—"

He cuts me off by cupping my face with one hand. "You sexy little thing. On the outside, you're a good girl, but that taunting text message from last night suggests you were waiting for the right person to corrupt you."

Those words cause a thrill of excitement to run through me.

"Lucky for you, I'm your man." He slams his mouth over mine.

I'm drowning.

And damn anyone who tries to save me.

This man...

I'm still levitating from his intoxicating words.

I clasp his cheek with my palm to deepen the kiss, as I drink him in, like this is my last drop of water before a long journey across the desert.

He responds with fervor.

I lose all concept of time until he breaks our embrace.

"My fingers are itching to fuck up your hairdo so I can fist your hair while I devour your mouth, but I don't want us to be that obvious."

I let out a little laugh. "I must look like a hot mess."

He shakes his head. "You look hot. Period."

I blush.

"I'm not done with you yet, angel."

A rush of heat blooms between my legs, causing my clit to tingle with anticipation.

"As much as I'd love to push you onto your back, splay you on that desk"—he points to the corner of the room—"tear off your shorts and scrap of lacy panties you're wearing so I can get my mouth on your sweet pussy, I won't."

Holy. Hell.

I'm positively dripping.

"It's best if we keep that for a more private setting. Because I intend on eating you out like a glutton until you come writhing all over my fucking face, screaming so loud they hear you all the way in your Swiss boarding school."

I blink.

I'm a deer caught in headlights.

"You're okay with that?"

More than okay. I want it all, and more.

I nod.

"Words. I want words."

I suck in a breath. "Yes."

He regards me for a beat. "You're sure about that?"

I nod again.

He arches a brow.

"Yes."

"Good. We're on the same wavelength."

Gage zips up my shorts before fastening the button. And then, he plays around with my top, readjusting it.

"There."

The hunger in his eyes is unsettling.

It shouldn't stir my insides like this.

I brush a hand over my hair.

This will have to do.

"Let's get out of here." He pulls me towards the door.

"Wait!"

He turns around and gives my body a quick inspection. "What?"

"I left my handbag behind." My teeth snag my bottom lip, and I eye him with hesitation. "I'm not courageous enough to face your friends. I'm sure it's written all over my face we've been..."

"Misbehaving?"

My cheeks burst into flames. "Yes." I lower my gaze.

I can't handle having a spotlight shining bright on me. That's what would happen if I were to step back into the club's main room with Gage by my side.

He drops a chaste kiss against my lips. "Let me take you to the car and I'll come back to fetch it."

Chapter 18

Gage

Lily is all mine, and the single guys at Rhys's party know it now.

It wasn't my plan to mark my territory, but fucking Phoenix and Michaela König played me like a violin. Shame on me for walking into their trap.

Phoenix must have repressed desires to be an entertainment TV reporter. My so-called friend texted me a minute-by-minute account of Lily's time at Rhys's party.

I ignored him at first, unwilling to fall for his obvious taunting.

He upped the ante.

He sent me photos of Lily, angling his camera so I couldn't miss her kickass gold heels or her dainty toes painted in a lovely shade of pink.

My desire for her ratchetted at rocket speed.

My cock approved, but I didn't fall for the bait.

When I didn't answer, he kept at it.

The next photo showed more of her slender legs.

The following one zoomed in on her shapely calves.

He kept inching up her legs and stopped right at the edge of her short-shorts.

The fucker knew what game he was playing.

When Michaela sent me a photo of Collin Dennison hovering over Lily, three things became clear.

One, Mr. and Mrs. König were in connivance, pushing their agendas with the same zeal as fucking politicians.

Two, with so many of our buddies in relationships, Collin Dennison remains a certified manwhore. I love him like a brother, but the man is like a dog after a bone when a woman catches his eye. A fresh face in our group is enough to send him into a tizzy.

Three, staying away from Rhys's party was no longer an option.

For three years, my security system has been tighter than Fort Knox's. I don't let anyone in who isn't part of my small circle of trusted friends. Not after the betrayal that shattered my world. I'm not sure what sorcery this woman possesses, but Lily Schuyler managed to cross all my wires last night.

Security has been breached.

The steel doors are open.

An invasion is imminent.

I should be calling the calvary for backup. Or better yet, the US Army. Instead, I got behind the wheel of my Wiesmann GT MF4, and drove my sports car like I stole it, a hot spear of jealousy tearing through me.

I'm surprised the LAPD didn't pull me over and slap my ass with a speeding ticket. Lucky for me, the club isn't too far from my Beverly Hills mansion.

I cut the engine, jumped out of my car, flung my keys to the valet, and headed to the front door, nodding at the bouncers posted at the entrance.

I busted inside Club SIX10 with the same urgency as a

man entering a bar after being in jail for a decade. Sometimes a guy needs to piss around a woman like a fucking dog to ward off others.

I take my role seriously.

I'm guarding her. *All of her.*

When I caught sight of her clad in that cock-hardening outfit, I froze.

The photos Phoenix sent me paled in comparison to seeing her in the flesh.

For a long minute, I stood there, mouth gaping open, all rational thought flying out the window because all the blood in my body was traveling at warp speed to my cock.

Holy goddess.

The flames of desire were burning so blistering hot, so urgent, so all-compassing, I couldn't breathe. Being in her presence caused parts of me to stretch and flex to life inside me. Parts that have been dormant for so long.

I blame Lily for making me drag her off the dance floor, find a secluded place, and do unspeakable things to her.

I had no chance against the oozing sexuality emitting from her. None whatsoever.

This is LA. Women flash skin.

Lily went from demure to sex bomb overnight.

I came here to watch over her, lurk in the shadows, and make sure no one bothered her. Ravishing her mouth while making her come all over my fingers wasn't part of the plan.

The heady smell of her arousal tickles my nostrils and hardens my cock.

No Rough Roger for me tonight. Lily's pussy is my only salvation.

An elegant woman approaches me, jarring me back to the moment.

Here comes the traitress.

I used to like Phoenix and Michaela.

Not so much anymore.

"Here you go." Michaela extends a bejeweled arm, flashing a stalk of gold bracelets, and hands me a gold clutch.

After guiding Lily to my car, I texted Michaela and asked her for her help.

Going back inside the party room would've elicited a barrage of questions from my friends.

I don't have time. I'd rather lose myself inside Lily's sweet pussy.

I grab the small bag. "Thank you."

Her green eyes, which are several shades deeper than mine, stare up at me.

Her lips devoid of lipstick purse together.

My gaze narrows. "Whatever's on your mind, say it."

She hesitates, which is unlike her. Michaela is a straight shooter.

"Let's hear it," I say.

"Don't hurt her."

I huff out a laugh that ends up a self-deprecating grunt. "You think so little of me, Mikki?"

She thrusts her chin up and out in that dogged, determined way she does when she's dead-set on standing her ground. "I'm sure I'm overstepping my boundaries, but she's like a younger sister to me."

If she was hoping to appease me with her words, she failed.

"And what makes you think I'd hurt her?"

"She's a sweet girl——"

"She's a woman."

"You're right. She is." She bites the inside of her lower lip.

"Get it off your chest."

"You're..."

"A blunt object with rough edges? A brooding beast? A

grumpy asshole? Short? Brusque? All of the above?" I scoff. "That's what people say about me behind my back." I arch a brow. "I'm sure many of my friends say I'm stubborn. Obstinate, even."

She stares up at me through narrowed eyes.

I glare back.

"I was going to say intense."

"If that's how you feel about me, Michaela, why did you and your husband taunt me until I showed up here? I texted you earlier and told you, chances were, I wasn't going to come. I made sure to call the birthday boy with my good wishes and even told him as much."

"Gage, you should've seen the way you were devouring Lily with your eyes yesterday when you first met."

My feral reaction to this woman was written all over my face?

Fuck.

I rub the back of my neck.

"It was as if Phoenix and I were witness to two people falling in lust with each other."

I roll my eyes. "You're layering it on a bit thick."

A smug smile stretches Michaela's lips as she studies me.

"What?"

"The chemistry between you was bouncing off the walls," she says. "For years, you've been immune, but yesterday... a young woman sparked something in you."

A strange sensation I can't quite label fills my chest, but I don't let on. "So now you're playing matchmaker?"

She tilts her head way back, cockiness shining bright from her eyes. "Are you going to tell me you guys have been *talking* since you dragged her off the dance floor?"

I flare my nostrils in lieu of an answer.

"My point exactly," she says. "Why do you think my

husband and I have been torturing you with teasing text messages? Collin is Collin, but he would never make a move on another man's girl—"

"She isn't my—" I stop midsentence.

What's the point?

Michaela grins from ear to ear.

"I'm watching over her," I say.

"Whatever you wanna call it, big guy."

I shake my head.

"It wasn't my intention to lecture you. I'm protective of Lily. So, don't overwhelm her with your brute force."

"I'll keep that in mind, Mom."

She pats my forearm. "Good boy."

Damn her for dishing it right back.

Chapter 19

Lily

My eyes are glued to the window, pretending to be mesmerized by Los Angeles's busy streets. In reality, I'm utterly engulfed by the man sitting next to me. Not only because his masculine scent surrounds me, but because I'm a mess of nerves and desire.

All that brooding force...

I'm scared shitless of what I've agreed to.

Changing my mind now would be embarrassing for both of us. And I'd be punishing myself by cutting my time short with this gorgeous beast of a man.

I chance a glance in his direction.

His eyes are riveted on the road in front of him.

Without an ounce of shame, I admire his profile. It has the same grace as a beautiful sculpture a master sculptor would carve from fine Italian marble. The sharpness of his cheekbones plays off the pale green of his eyes.

His jaw works.

I felt the light scruff of his chin against my cheek.

That would feel wicked between my thighs.

The ride to the hotel is quiet, the lounge music seeping from the speakers of his sports car fills the charged silence between us.

My gaze drops to his strong hand.

Watching him maneuver his speeding bullet is such a turn on.

Gage Hollingsworth drives like he kisses. With purpose.

He controls the vehicle with as much dexterity as he controlled my body.

God, for as long as I live, I'll never forget that naughty encounter.

And to think, it's the tip of the iceberg for tonight.

My stomach clenches.

As I was waiting for Gage to arrive with my clutch, I cursed the fact my phone was in it. Alone in his car, I was unable to call or text my best friend for support.

Now that he's retrieved my bag, I can't make the call.

I have to deal with this one on my own.

My fingers fidget with the clasp of the clutch on my lap.

"You're having second thoughts?"

I flinch. "No, I'm not."

He shoots me a side-gaze. "You're sure about that, angel?"

I love the nickname he has for me. "Are you having second thoughts?"

"One thing you should know about me, when I make up my mind about something, shy of a catastrophe that's out of my control, it's game on."

"Noted."

"I meant what I said earlier. I want more of you, Lily. Nothing could change my mind about that."

An eruption that could rival any Fourth of July firework explodes inside me.

He's not promising to pick the moon for me, but that declaration does something to me. Maybe I'm a silly girl, but I sense he's not the type to bullshit. No political verbal prowess to get me to bed.

He's not using me as leverage to get something out of my father.

What a change.

He wants me for me.

Me.

A cloud of sexual tension floats inside the car, so palpable, I could reach out and hug it.

Until yesterday, I didn't know what it meant to have chemistry with someone.

As it stands, Gage Hollingsworth is the sun, and I'm a planet floating around his orbit.

I'm wet again.

I've never been this aware of my body's reaction to a man in my life.

I want this man beyond reason.

His car pulls up in front of the Pompadour Hotel.

We're here.

My stomach bounces with nerves.

"Wait for me. I'll come around."

I shift in my seat. "Okay."

He climbs out of the car, hands his keys to the valet, and rounds the front of the vehicle. He opens the door and extends a hand.

The man is unfairly hot, smoldering with swagger, style, and sexiness.

A beast *and* a gentleman.

He helps me out.

Gage places a hand on the small of my back and guides me towards the entrance. It's a struggle to keep up with him. His gait is so much longer and faster than mine, I have to run on my tippytoes to keep up.

"Sorry," he says. "I'm walking too fast."

"Short legs and all," I say. "And skyscraper heels."

His eyes lower to my legs.

When they meet mine, the same hunger I saw earlier in the storage room returns in full force.

Oh boy.

"I can carry you," he says.

"We are not making another scene." My tone is firm.

He regards me for a beat.

Gage has that sullen, yet oh-so-scorching-hot *je ne sais quoi* thing going on right now.

He nods. "Okay."

That's all it took for the beast to back down?

I give myself an internal high five.

He sweeps me off my feet, bride-style. "You said not to make a scene. I'm not making a scene. This way, you can keep up with me... short legs, sky-high heels, and all."

I roll my eyes.

I lace my arms around his neck for stability.

I love being this close to him.

"I'm eager to get you behind closed doors."

My hormones ricochet through my body like the balls in a pinball machine.

I don't understand this magnetic pull between us.

Gage drops me to my feet when we reach the door. He does it with so much care. It's not what I would expect from this gruff, grumpy giant.

I adjust my outfit that's gone askew.

"I wouldn't worry too much about that if I were you," he says. "As sexy as it is, you won't be wearing that outfit for much longer. The sooner I have my mouth on your pussy, the happier I'll be."

Blink.

Blink.

Blink.

He's a serious as a heart attack.

My heart is pounding against my chest way too hard for me to respond, so I stare at him.

"I'm not one to pussyfoot, Lily."

I guess not.

He grabs me by the hand, and pulls me inside the hotel, forcing me out of my stupor.

The lobby is animated with travelers coming and going.

I don't know why, but I search the crowd, expecting to see Michaela's friendly face. It's stupid, since we left her at the party.

God knows, I could use some sisterly advice right now.

A set of doors opens as we approach the elevator hall.

Gage extends a hand, inviting me in.

I enter and position myself against the wall.

He presses the button to my floor and comes to stand next to me.

The doors close.

We're alone.

My eyes are glued on the dashboard as if it's the most fascinating thing in the world.

Am I going to let him have his wicked way with me?

The higher the elevator rises, the more I'm a jumble of nerves.

Breathe.

"I know I can be a little intimidating, but do I make you that nervous?"

A little intimidating?

More like a lot.

"I'm not nervous." My voice croaks, stressing the obvious lie.

He pushes off the wall and comes to stand in front of me.

He cups my face in between his large hands and leans into me.

I breathe him in. The expensive scent of his cologne. The warmth of his skin. The mesmerizing green eyes studying me from behind those long lashes.

A slow roll of heat eases its way through me like the warmth of a summer breeze. Goosebumps prickle along my arms.

Will my body ever stop reacting to this man's touch or proximity?

"Liar, liar," he says. "Your nervous energy is going to screw up the electrical wiring and cause this elevator to stop."

"Okay, I'm a little nervous." My heart is beating in my throat.

He brushes his lips along the underside of my jaw. "Let me help."

His mouth comes down on mine, hard and hungry. The contact is potent. When my hand travels along his arm and grips the hair at his nape, he lets out a string of curses.

If I thought he was kissing me before, now he's ravishing my mouth.

The scorching hot kiss sends shockwaves coursing through my system.

We're fused together so close, I'm certain he can hear the erratic beating of my heart.

My nipples scratch against the inside of my bra, wishing they were pressed against his bare chest. My pussy pulsates so hard, I swear I'm doing Kegel exercises.

This man is turning me into someone I don't even recognize.

He pulls away from me for a shuddering breath.

His enchanting wintergreen eyes darken to inky black orbs, his wide chest rising and falling, his nostrils flaring.

He's the Big Bad Wolf staring at Little Red Riding Hood.

"Fuck, I love your mouth." His voice is as delightful as buttered toast sprinkled with sugar and cinnamon. "I can't stop kissing you."

I'm fifty shades of turned on right now, so much so, I don't know what to do with myself. "Then, don't stop kissing me."

Fire ignites in his eyes, making me wetter.

He picks me up in his arms, and I wrap my legs around his waist, climbing him like a tree. Gage takes a step until my back is pressed against the wall. I moan when he pushes against me. A sharp ache pulses between my thighs.

I'm desperate for relief.

I use the hardness pressing against my damp shorts and grind.

"You dirty girl." His hands sneak underneath my shorts, groping my bare ass.

I gasp.

"Let me help with that," he says.

I don't have time to figure out what he means.

The hands groping my ass knead relentlessly, keeping me moving against his erection with intensifying friction.

All my nerve endings are lit up like fire torches.

This is so inappropriate.

So lewd.

So debauched.

Knowing I affect him in this way is such an aphrodisiac.

One large hand leaves my ass cheek to travel up, over my hip and rib cage, stopping under my breast. The back of his fingers brush over my nipples and my eyes roll into the back of my head.

"Fuck, these are so nice," he says.

"I don't have huge breasts." The words fly out of my mouth. *Crap.*

Great timing for my insecurities to rear their ugly head.

There are so many women in LA walking around with DDs.

"Your tits are perfect," he says before devouring my mouth. When his palm cups over my breast before squeezing hard, my eyelids flutter closed at the onslaught of blissful sensations.

He breaks our kiss, meeting my heavy-lidded eyes. "Fuck, you're so wet." When his mouth finds mine, he bites my lower lip.

A whimper escapes me.

Good God, this man needs to come with a warning.

He devours my mouth on a loud grunt, sucking my tongue until I writhe against him, his hips pressing upward, hitting me right where I desperately need it.

I'm going to come.

The elevator jerks to a stop.

Shit.

Panic slams through me.

We abruptly cease our naughty play, and Gage lowers me to my feet. With trembling hands, I struggle to adjust my clothing to hide what was happening between us.

The doors open and a wave of animated and chatty Italians crowd the elevator.

Chapter 20

Gage

I'm not sure how I made it through our first encounter without slamming my cock inside of Lily, but I'm not going to make that same mistake tonight. Not when this wild beast is howling inside of me, commanding me to stake a claim.

After three years without fucking, I'm going to make this woman mine.

The hold she has on my resolve is unsettling.

If I was gifted with the superpower to teleport, I wouldn't be in this predicament. Since I'm only human, I had to rely on my wheels to get us to her hotel.

It turns out, you can drive a car with a cock so hard, it's like a third leg.

That would explain why I burned rubber to get to the Pompadour in record time. That, and because I was losing my goddamn mind. The arousing combination of the floral note of Lily's perfume and her heady scent lingered in the car during the drive.

It was excruciating.

The longer it takes me to get inside of her sweet pussy, the more feral I become. I wanted to pull over, unzip her shorts, and dive between her legs to eat her out like a famished man. My only consolation was knowing with each mile, I was getting closer to the hotel.

As hot and sinful as that make-out session in the storage room was, I need more.

Finger-fucking her pussy wasn't enough. I need my mouth on the woman who consumed my dreams last night. I'm desperate to feel the swell of her clit against my tongue and taste the sweetness of her slick juices.

I didn't expect the dirty action in the elevator.

The fact she was willing to let me make her come in public made that little episode hotter than hell.

I didn't peg Lily as an exhibitionist.

She may come across as sweet and innocent, but she's open to me corrupting her.

I like her even more.

When we reach her floor, I grab her hand, and exit the packed elevator. I grasp her around the waist and drag her with a determined step to her room.

We come to a stop in front of her door.

I extend a hand. "Your card key."

She rummages through her clutch, produces it, and drops it in my expectant palm.

I swipe it, and let her in, following right behind her.

She drops her clutch on the console near the door, turns the light on, and dims them low.

Good girl.

I scan the room. "Where's the bathroom?"

Confused blue eyes stare up at me. "You need to use the bathroom?"

"That wasn't my question."

"There's a small bathroom in the corridor, but there's a larger one with a hot tub near the bedroom."

"That'll do." I sweep her off her feet.

"Gage, I can walk."

"I know, but this is much faster."

"I can remove my heels and walk barefoot."

Hell no. "The heels stay on."

I march us through the dimly lit suite and into the bathroom, kick the door shut, and set Lily down on her feet.

She turns on the light. "You have something against beds?"

I do.

Opening that can of worms would kill the mood.

I busy myself undressing, avoiding her questioning gaze.

"You're not going to answer?"

She's not going to let this go. "Why be predictable? I don't do vanilla. Not to mention, you deserve so much better than boring."

She doesn't have a comeback.

End of discussion.

I unbutton my shirt. I'm about to remove it, but the way she's eating me up pushes me to put on a show for her. Slow and easy, I peel it off my body.

Her breathing roughens as her eyes roam over my naked chest.

Under her lustful gaze, my cock hardens.

"Good God. Your body..."

"You like what you see?"

She approaches me.

"It's one thing to have a handsome face, but when you combine that with..."—she waves a manicured finger up and down the length of my body—"wow."

Her reaction is amusing.

"Are you buttering me up, Miss Schuyler, so I make you come again?"

She shakes her head. "You have that rugged gorgeousness I've never seen before. And you're built like an Olympian god."

My brows hike up to my forehead, surprised by her compliment.

"The tattoos..." Her eyes move around my chest and arms. "The muscles..." Her gaze bounces from my biceps to my legs, before settling on my stomach. "I've heard of a six-pack, but you're sporting an eight-pack, or is it a ten-pack?" She's on a roll. "You're even more intimidating half-naked than you are all dressed-up in a power suit."

"Are you done objectifying me?"

Her eyes grow wide.

I wink. "I'm pulling your leg. You can drool as much as you want... as long as I get to cast my eyes on your heavenly body."

A beautiful rosy shade creeps up her cheeks. "You want me naked?"

"How else am I going to get my mouth on your pussy?"

The crimson shade coloring her cheeks deepens.

"Strip for me." My tone brooks no argument.

She does as she's told.

She reaches around and unzips her top, before pulling it over her head, exposing beautiful creamy, pale skin.

Fuck, she's gorgeous.

I should remove my jeans, but I'm so fascinated, I can only admire the show.

She's about to toss her top on the floor, but I take it from her and hang it along with my shirt on a hook on the back of the door.

She unzips her shorts, shimmies them past her ass, and bends over to push them down her legs. In doing so, she flashes me in the mirror.

My exhale comes out hard, thanks to all the blood in my body rushing south to my cock. The arousing wet spot between her legs makes my mouth water, eager to taste her.

She straightens and steps out of the shorts to pool at her feet, kicking them to the side.

A carefree move that surprises me.

I don't have time to dwell on it.

She's down to her underwear.

I almost swallow my damn tongue at the sight of the sexy blush-colored bra and panties combo.

God knew what he was doing when he created this woman.

Lily's natural beauty is arresting.

Her eyes drop to her feet, forcing my gaze to her dainty toes painted in a bright pink shade.

She bends over.

"What are you doing?"

"Removing my heels."

"I said, those stay on."

"Oh—okay." She blinks. "I've never done anything like this before."

"You mean, take a hookup back to your place—in this case your hotel—keeping your heels on while you're naked, or forfeiting the bed for something less vanilla?"

"All of the above."

I nod.

Welcome to the jungle, princess.

She pulls her lower lip between her teeth and stares up at me from underneath her long, dark lashes. She's vulnerable, sweet, and feisty. A trifecta that's irresistible.

"Aren't you going to remove your jeans?" she says.

"You want me naked?" I borrow her words.

She laughs.

The most wonderful sound in the world.

Without breaking my gaze with hers, I toe off my shoes and remove my socks. I unbuckle my belt, unzip my jeans, and push them down my legs. Stepping out of them, I snatch them from the floor and place them on the hook behind me. I keep my boxers on because I need to ease her into this.

Lily's eyes drop to my crotch before bouncing up to meet my gaze.

She does that a few times.

I'm sure the outline of my hungry bulge can be seen from Pluto.

She blinks. "Wh—what about your boxer briefs?"

"You show me yours, and I'll show you mine, princess."

"Tit for tat?"

I shake my head. "I'm being a gentleman. Ladies first."

I'm rewarded with a cocky smile.

She unhooks her bra, slides it down her arms, and tosses it at me.

I catch it.

She wiggles her sexy little body out of her panties and throws them at me.

I catch them as well, but I'm too distracted by the vision in front of me to bring them to my nose to enjoy her heady scent.

I suck in a shallow breath before a rough sound drops from my lips.

Feeling her well-groomed pussy hair as I played with her is one thing. Seeing the neat landing strip of dark pubic hair is another. Her breasts are a work of art. They're not enormous, but they're perfect.

And those taut, pink nipples...

Damn.

"Christ, you're beautiful," I say as if in a daze.

She blushes.

"Your turn." She gestures a finger up and down my body.

"Not yet."

"Not fair."

"Remember what I said, ladies first."

I lift her off her feet, walk us to the counter, and drop her fine ass on the surface.

I place my hips between her parted legs.

Those beautiful sapphire eyes drop to my chest, taking in my tattoos before meeting my gaze.

Under the light, her eyes sparkle.

"Do your tattoos have a significance?"

Fuck. That subject is a guaranteed boner killer.

I fold my lip between my teeth.

"I'm sorry. I shouldn't have asked."

I exhale. "Most of my tattoos are intricate custom designs—art I like—but a few have a personal significance. Like the tattoo of the cross, rosary, and rose."

"What does it mean?"

"It's..." *...to remember someone I lost.* I let out a breath.

"I'm asking too many questions."

I can't handle the answer to your question.

She shrugs. "It doesn't matter. Your tattoos are pretty badass."

"None of the guys you've been with before have been inked?"

Her eyes widen. "No."

"You disapprove of tattoos?"

She shakes her head. "Not at all."

"You're stepping out of your comfort zone with me?"

"Way, way out."

"I'm good for you."

"That still remains to be determined."

I'll show you, little one.

My hand skims up and over her rib cage. Her skin is

smooth and baby-soft. I grope her tit, wedging her nipple between my fingers before pulling.

She shivers.

I hope you enjoyed the warmup.

I change things up.

I twist her nipple hard.

She lets out a sharp breath and folds over.

I sooth my sweet punishment by circling my open palm over her nipple.

"You're a cruel man."

"Let me make it better."

I lean forward, my tongue fondling her tits with avarice. I want these in my mouth every fucking day. Needing more, I pull her pretty little nipple between my lips and suck on it like I'm trying to draw milk.

She moans and her hand snakes in my hair.

Dammit.

It's been a long time. Too long. In the past few years, adulting and tragedy have done a damn good job at fucking with my desire for pussy.

My hand slides down her stomach and slips between her pussy lips, encountering her slick wetness.

She's so fucking ready for me.

I pull my fingers out of her pussy, and let her breast drop from my mouth.

"I think I've made my point."

She lets out a grunt of discontentment. "Message received, but you didn't have to stop."

"You want more?" I run my hands up her shapely calves and circle her knees, before gripping her bare thighs and parting them further.

Her breath hitches.

"You make big promises, but how's that going to happen if

you're unwilling to drop your boxer shorts. Not to mention, you pulled your fingers away just as it was getting good."

Tease.

I yank her body to the edge of the counter, startling a cry from her lips.

"Let's get one thing straight, Lily, *I* control this dance. You'll get my cock when I'm ready to give it to you."

She stares up at me with wide eyes.

"My cock is eager to be buried so deep inside you, but my tongue has first dibs."

I don't give her a chance to respond.

I drop to my knees, push open her legs further, and pull her pussy lips apart. Her heady scent hits me full force.

So fucking enticing.

I dip my head between her legs, poke my tongue out, and dip it inside her, keeping her legs wide with my hands.

My cock thumps in my boxer briefs when I take a long lick of her pussy.

Lily's soft sighs and moans are my reward.

My tongue skates around her clit, teasing her, careful to avoid skating where she needs it most. My cock is jealous, eager to plunge into her warmth, but not until I hear her scream out my name again.

Because I'm an asshole, I flick her clit with my tongue. Just once. I want to get her riled up.

She stares down at me.

I stare right back.

She scoots even further to the edge of the counter. "More."

"Do you deserve to lose your fucking mind all over my tongue?"

Her teeth work her lower lip.

Shy Lily is back.

"I do," she says.

"Good answer."

Her smile is radiant.

I dip my head between her legs.

She parts them wider for me.

I'm not done teasing her.

Lick.

She hitches a breath.

Lick.

She wiggles her hips.

Lick.

She does it again.

Lick.

She clamps her hands at the back of my head.

Now, we're talking.

"Please... this is too much." She squirms under the unyielding way my tongue teases her.

I stop my taunting. "I'm not in the business of mediocrity, Lily. When you're with me, you come hard or not at all. You hear me?"

She nods.

I'd normally demand words, but I'm sure she's a little overwhelmed.

"You take what I give you and thank me for honoring your pussy."

Huge eyes stare at me in shock.

"Can I go back to the program?"

"Yes, please."

I growl with satisfaction.

I close my mouth over her pussy, sucking on her hard clit with unrestrained abandonment.

"I... I..." Her words trail, giving way to heavy breathing. "Gage..."

I lift my eyes.

Fuck, I love my name on this woman's lips.

She throws her head back, gyrating her hips on the counter like a girl gone wild.

What a sight.

I plunge one finger inside her.

Her pussy clenches around it like a vice, so I slide a second one in.

With my digits pumping in and out of her, I focus on her clit, sucking on the tiny bud with fervor.

Her heavy breathing reverberates against the bathroom walls.

I curl my fingers inside her, stroking the right spot to send her flying.

"Oh, God, what are you doing to me?" She almost sounds panicked.

I lift my gaze.

Lidded eyes meet mine.

The pads of my fingers apply more pressure against the sensitive spot inside her, while my tongue toys with her hard clit.

She clenches around my intrusion as she writhes on the counter.

That's it. Come all over my face.

"Your mouth..." She arches her back, her hips lifting off the countertop. "Oh, Gage."

Use me, baby.

I rub and suck. Rub and suck.

She places her weight on her folded arms, lifts her legs, and hooks them over my shoulders.

Fuck, yeah.

Her angled hips allow me to finger-fuck her with more determination.

"Please, Gage. Please." Her hips jerk upwards with each word.

I don't disappoint.

Another rough jerk of her hips to the edge of the counter earns her a growl when the point of her heel digs into my back.

Christ.

She does it again.

Her heel digs deeper.

Fuck, that hurt so good.

I pin her hips down with one strong hand to hold her in place, and I growl into a series of long, languorous licks, dragging the tip of my tongue over her hard clit.

She grinds against my face without an ounce of shame. "Sweet baby Jesus..."

My eyes are on her, unwilling to miss a beat. I want to savor the expression on her face as she comes.

I close my lips around her clit, trapping all the blood there.

She rubs her pussy all over my face.

She's wild. Unleashed.

She throws her head back.

She's close.

I close my upper lip around her clit, my tongue teasing it. The feel of her swollen bud against my tongue is Nirvana.

"Oh— My— God—"

I apply more pressure.

"I—" She breathes in and out in heavy pants. "I'm— I'm —" Her second attempt doesn't fare much better than the first. "I'm— Com— Ga— Gage—" She stutters all over my name.

Her pussy clamps hard against my intruding fingers and her whole body convulses in strong spasms.

Lily detonates.

She shows me her appreciation in the best possible way.

Her abundant juices gush into my mouth with the force of a geyser.

Holy shit.

I lap it all up.

I don't alleviate the pressure from my tongue or fingers. I want to prolong her pleasure.

More of her sweet juices gush into my mouth as she chants. "Oh, oh, oh."

Holy fuck.

There's so much, it's ridiculous.

We're both soaked.

It takes her several long heartbeats before she comes down from her climax.

She moves.

I help her to sit up.

Her eyes are wide as she stares at me.

"Oh my God, my body has never done that before." The words tumble out of her mouth. "I'm so sorry. That was so embarrassing."

Pride swells inside me.

"On the contrary. That was hot as fuck."

"But... I gushed all over you."

Such innocence. "I fucking love how your body responds to me. Not every woman is capable of coming like that."

"So, it's not bad?"

"Did it feel bad?"

She shakes her head.

"You have your answer."

She offers me a shy smile.

I want to make her come like that every single—

What the fuck?

This is a fun fling.

She'll be gone in a few days.

I stand up.

I grab her by the waist and pull her body against mine, pressing my covered erection against her pussy, allowing her to feel how much I want her.

Naked thighs come up to circle my hips, as she grinds against me in a kinky way that sends a pulse of electricity to my aching balls.

I groan. "You're going to make me come in my boxers."

She doubles her efforts, her juices soaking through the fabric of my underwear.

"Naughty girl."

A slow, wicked smile stretches her lips.

Goddammit, it would be so sweet to lose myself inside her without any barrier.

Whoa.

Where the hell did that come from?

I've never fucked a woman without suiting up. Ever.

Lily is not only throwing me off my game, she's messing with my head.

Condom, Hollingsworth. Always a condom.

I take a step back from the sorceress with the magic pussy.

I push my boxer briefs down my legs, stepping out of them and kicking them to the side.

My cock is so hard, it points north.

From her freaked out expression, I expect her to call the whole thing off.

She doesn't.

She tilts her head side to side, admiring my cock from different angles.

The fucker grows impatient.

I walk over to my jeans.

Do I even have a condom?

I fish inside my wallet and find one.

I check the expiry date.

We're in business.

In no time, I'm sheathed—locked, loaded, and ready to shoot.

She's still staring at me, dumbfounded.

"I've never wanted a woman more in my life, but if you're having second thoughts—"

She places two fingers against my lips. "I want you, too, Gage."

That's all I needed to hear.

I reach for her hair. When I do, I catch my gaze in the mirror. My eyes are wild—veiled with lust.

This woman is unraveling me.

With impatient hands, I play around with her updo.

Her half-lidded eyes collide with mine. "Let me do it."

I don't argue. I'm in such a rush, I must be hurting her.

She removes several pins and places them on the countertop.

A cascade of raven hair tumbles down to her waist.

I'm mesmerized.

Fuck, this woman is a dream.

Still in a daze, I run my fingers through her thick mane. "It's so long."

"I know, I should cut it—"

"Don't you dare cut it." The words are out of my mouth before I can catch them.

I have no right to be this possessive.

Little fingers walk across my chest. "I won't."

The contact jolts my cock.

I let go of her hair and fist the fucker.

I step between her parted legs. "The first time is going to be fast and furious. I want you too much. Do you understand?"

She nods. "Yes."

"We'll do it again, still furious, but not as fast."

"Okay."

I guide my cock between her pussy lips, dragging the head through her wetness. Unable to help myself, I circle her clit with my engorged head.

Round and round.

"That feels so good," she says.

Too good.

I place my hands on her ass, pulling her close. "Wrap your legs around my waist."

She does as she's told, cradling my erection with her warmth.

I push inside her.

Lily hitches a breath.

She's so fucking tight.

I try again.

The second time around, I thrust into her with such force, an animalistic growl drops from my lips.

She clings onto my shoulders, digging her nails into my skin, and lets out an agonizing sound.

All movement stops, the muscles in my body stiffening.

She's in pain?

What the fuck?

Was I too rough?

Did I hurt her?

Her labored breathing echoes through the bathroom.

My chest heaves.

I pull away from her until our eyes meet.

I stare at her, an unspoken question burning my tongue.

She averts her gaze.

I grip her chin, forcing her attention on me.

"Talk to me."

Nothing.

"Are you a virgin?"

She answers with a one-shoulder shrug.

"Words, Lily."

"I'm not anymore."

My jaw comes unhinged.

That confirmation lands like a grenade.

For the love of God.

Regret washes over me.

"Oh, baby." My voice is strangled. "Why didn't you tell me?"

Blue eyes stare up at me from under long lashes.

"Answer me, Lily."

"I wanted you to be my first."

I let out an audible breath, raking my fingers through my messy hair.

I'm honored, but holy fuck, a little warning would've been nice.

"Please don't stop, Gage."

"I don't want to hurt you. Had I known..."

I would've been more careful.

Selected another position.

Heck, eased you into it.

My cock is huge for a virgin pussy.

Her fingers caress my neck and shoulders. "The worst is behind me."

"It would kill me to have to stop now."

She peppers kisses along my collarbone and neck. "Don't stop."

"You sure?"

"I want it to be you."

My cock swells.

My hips move.

She lets out a pained groan.

My body freezes.

She tightens her legs around my waist, urging me on.

I thrust in and out of her at a slow cadence at first, giving her time to adjust to my size. It doesn't take long for her body to relax.

"You okay?"

She nods. "Yes."

"Can I go faster?"

"Yes."

That's all the encouragement I need.

My hips drive into her in a powerful thrust.

I'm unprepared for the incredible sensation of a virgin pussy sinking down onto my cock. I'm not ready for the mind-blowing tight fit or the hot, pulsating walls that milk me.

I'm not going to last.

I glance down to where her virgin pussy swallows my cock.

This is too much.

The foreign sensation of extreme tightness brings a close-mouthed roar up from my chest.

Dear God, I won't survive this.

"I'm going to make it so good for you, angel."

"I know you will."

"Grind that little clit against me. Use your body to chase after your release."

I don't have to repeat myself twice.

She circles her hips over mine, moaning without restraint.

My hands grip her ass, my fingers digging into her flesh.

She works her lower body into a rhythm that matches mine.

"That's it." My voice is gruff.

"Oh, Gage."

Her head lolls back.

To my shock and delight, Lily brings her hand to her clit and rubs herself.

She lifts her head, locking her eyes with mine.

"Your tight little virgin pussy will be the end of me."

She smiles.

She knows she's holding me by the balls.

Two can play that game.

I dip my head and take her nipple into my mouth, drawing on it with avarice.

Her fingers move faster and faster.

My breathing escalates with each passing second.

After licking and sucking her nipple to a peak, I bite it.

She cries out, the sound traveling all the way to my balls.

That's the end of the line for me.

"Angel, you need to come. I'm holding on by a thread."

Lidded eyes stare at me.

"You're gonna come hard for me?"

"Yes."

My lips find hers, devouring her mouth in a passionate kiss.

She matches my ardor, tongue stroke for tongue stroke.

She slides against the countertop's smooth surface as I move her up and down my hard cock.

My pace grows frantic as the pressure builds inside me.

She breaks the kiss and screams out my name as she comes apart in my arms, riding my cock.

"You've ruined me, Lily." I'm not sure if it's an accusation or statement.

I'm entangled in her enchanting web.

I pump into her once.

Twice.

Three times.

With one final thrust of my hips, I release my cum into her.

My climatic roar is so loud, I bet they hear me all the way down in the lobby.

Chapter 21

Lily

I bite my cheek to stop from smiling.

Within twelve days of turning twenty-one—and within thirty-two hours of landing in LA—I'm officially a woman.

Sexy Gage Hollingsworth punched my V card.

He was the perfect man for mission *Bursting Lily's Cherry.*

Nads is going to die.

Gage made me feel so desired, and I wanted him so much, I didn't care if it was going to hurt. The burning lust in his eyes was my undoing.

I've had it bad for him since the first time I laid eyes on him.

I wasn't prepared for his massive cock. Long, thick, pulsing, and lined with veins. I guess I should've known from his impressive height, large hands, and long feet.

I'm not Lily the innocent virgin who'd never seen a cock in her life until an hour ago, but I've never gone all the way. The only other cock I've seen was half of Gage's size, and the man it belonged to wasn't a strapping hunk who stands at least six-four. Gage's cock is so eye-popping huge, I'm surprised I didn't run out of the bathroom when he dropped his boxer briefs.

Holy enormous appendage.

The first few thrusts were so painful, it was a struggle to breathe. It was like being impaled by a tree trunk, but in no time, pain gave into pleasure.

Ohmygod, sex is a beautiful thing.

After a shower in the luxurious spa-like bathroom, Gage and I are both draped in the hotel's silky-soft white bathrobes, sitting at the round table in the living area, enjoying a lip-smacking meal.

"On a scale from one to ten, that was a solid seven," I say, meeting wintergreen eyes.

His gaze drops to his sandwich before lifting to meet mine. His perplexed expression is priceless.

The midnight menu at the Pompadour is irreproachable. All the meals I've enjoyed since I arrived, have been. Gage recommended the lip-smacking pulled pork sandwich. It's out of this world phenomenal. He's devouring his second one. I'm still working on my first.

The trimmings are also commendable—frites with shaved grana Padano, drizzled with truffle oil and the hotel's signature Seriously Good Coleslaw. For dessert, I did a mental happy dance when I saw English raspberry trifle on the menu.

"This is one of the best pulled pork sandwiches I've ever eaten," Gage says. "Seven out of ten? The Königs will be disappointed. Heck, they might end up firing the chef."

Uh, oh. This game isn't going like I intended. "I wasn't talking about the food. I was talking about my first time."

His head jerks back. "A seven?"

"Yes." It's a struggle to keep a straight face.

He narrows his eyes. "I can put you flat on your back on this table and turn that failing grade into a ten in a New York minute."

"I was pulling your leg. That was a solid one hundred." Not that I have anything to compare it to, but I'm certain it was.

He drops his half-eaten sandwich on his plate, wipes his messy fingers with the napkin before lifting his eyes to meet mine. "Why didn't you tell me it was your first time?"

I let out along sigh and mimic him. "Why is that so important?"

"A bed would've been a good idea—"

"I thought you didn't do predictable."

"Lily." He purses his lips.

"What?" I feign innocence.

"That was a little intense for the first time."

I reach out for his hand. "It wouldn't have been as raunchy on a bed. It would've been like so many other first times. So boring. So *déjà vu*."

"How do you know, if it was your first time?"

I read a lot of spicy romance books. "Girls talk."

He nods. "Are you on the birth control?"

I grimace.

"I'm going to take that as a no."

"I would've requested we use a condom," I say.

He considers me for a thoughtful moment.

I can't read his expression.

How many women has he been with?

Has he been fucking half of LA?

I give myself a slap upside the head.

Silly Lily.

He's not a monk. No doubt, the drop-dead gorgeous, powerful, billionaire mogul has been with his fair share of women. Men like that wear condoms.

"I hope I didn't disappoint you." The words come flying out of my mouth before I can catch them.

His eyebrows knit together, his lips turning down into a frown.

I grow more and more worried under his stare, wiggling in my chair in discomfort. "I'm sure you're used to women with so much more experience than me. Being with a silly virgin must be a downgrade for you."

"I can't fake an erection. Neither can I fake coming."

I hope he's not surgarcoating it. "Okay."

"I'm not bullshitting you."

Is he telling me the truth?

My inexperience is shining brighter than a neon sign.

"I haven't been with anyone in a long time, and I wanted you so damn much from the moment I saw you yesterday."

My eyes grow wide. "Oh."

"What happened between us tonight wasn't about ending the evening with a woman, it was about ending the evening with *you*. Since yesterday, I've been obsessed with kissing you. I didn't expect I'd need to devour the rest of you. The thing is, once our lives crossed, I couldn't put the brakes on."

I blink.

Mother of God.

The man who spent most of our first encounter growling at me, just pulled the rug from under my feet. I'm not stupid enough to think it's a love declaration, but his confession tugs at something inside me. Gage Hollingsworth is a man of few words, but when he speaks, hold on to your fascinator.

"To answer your question," he says, "I'm not disappointed at all." He leans into me. Something dangerous veils his green eyes. "Not only are you a hot little thing, but now, your tight pussy has been perfectly molded for my cock."

Did the temperature in the room go up by a hundred degrees?

"Next time, I won't be as gentle."

Holy Jesus.

"But before I fuck you again, I need to know why you didn't warn me? What's your story, Lily Schuyler?"

He deserves an explanation.

"Dating is an interesting topic," I say. "After boarding school, I went to the University of Paris. When I arrived in the City of Light, my father had a long list of potential suitors—sons of his business connections. Some were Parisians. Others were like me, studying in Paris. I didn't connect with any of them, and the idea of dating someone my father dictated was unappealing. I told him I wanted to focus on my studies. Miracle of miracles, he didn't push."

"I'm surprised."

"That makes two of us. My father is a bulldozer when he's on a mission, which is often."

"Tell me about it."

"Is that how you ended up becoming my bodyguard?" Why else would a powerful mogul agree to be my babysitter?

"Yes." He nods. "But I'm glad I agreed."

I have to bite the inside of my cheek to prevent the smile threatening to part my lips in a huge grin.

"For once, hanging out with one of my father-imposed companions wasn't an excruciating exercise."

"Glad to be of service."

We stare at each other for a beat, the electricity crackling between us.

I discovered what sex was a New York minute ago. How can I crave it again so soon?

I shake my head, hoping to dissipate the hedonistic haze engulfing me.

Bad girl. Bad girl.

I continue my story. "I was having lunch at Les Deux Magots Café in the Saint-Germain-des-Prés neighborhood, when a distinguished Frenchman asked me if he could sit at my table. He had a short window for lunch, and all the tables were occupied. I accepted. My French wasn't great at the time—I'm still not fluent, but I speak it better now than I did back then— so, I didn't expect much conversation. My lunch companion surprised me. Jean-Philippe Dutronc had studied in London, so his English was decent. Lunch came and went, and we sat there talking, drinking coffee, and eating pastries. Eventually, he had to go. He asked to see me again. We had a great connection. He wasn't a pretty boy, and he wasn't tall—he was only five-seven. Yet, he had that irresistible *je ne sais quoi* so many Frenchmen have. He was twenty-six and one of the youngest literature professors at the Sorbonne University—"

"How old were you?"

"I was nineteen."

He nods.

"Jean-Philippe was well-traveled and a charmer. I was upfront about wanting to take things slow. He agreed. So, we dated, kissed, and fooled around. Eight months into our relationship, I felt I was ready. He'd been so patient. I figured going all the way would be the ultimate birthday gift for a guy. Well... that's what an article in a girly magazine told me."

"You got cold feet?"

"No." I close my eyes, reliving the humiliating events.

Gage places a hand on my knee, and my eyes pop open.

"What did the fucker do?"

"After we savored a catered meal at my place, Jean-Philippe suggested a sexy shower to ease me into it. As we were stepping out of the shower, his phone rang. He apologized, wrapped a towel around his waist, and rushed out of the bathroom to silence it. I was taking my time drying my body, thinking he'd come back to join me. After a while, I got worried. When I stepped into my bedroom, he was getting dressed."

"What happened?"

"He had to go."

"Why?"

"I inquired to find out if a family member got in an accident, had suffered from a heart attack, or worse, died."

"It was none of the above?"

"It was the last thing I ever imagined."

"I'm not even going to try to guess."

"His wife's waters broke—she went into labor early—"

"Wife?"

"Yup," I nod. "His sister-in-law was rushing her to the hospital. He had to scamper off so he could be present for the arrival of his son."

"What the fuck?"

"Yes. Jean-Philippe was married."

"He never told you?"

"No. I asked him if he had a girlfriend, and he assured me, I was his *only* girlfriend."

"He never wore a wedding ring?"

I shake my head. "No. That would've sent me running the other way."

"Motherfucker."

"To my horror and dismay, the guy I'd been seeing was leading a double life," I say. "Apparently, it's the French way."

"The French way? What the fuck?"

"Right before dumping my ass to run to his wife who was about to give birth to their first child, Jean-Philippe felt it necessary to mansplain how things worked in France. A little *vagabondage* while you're married is normal. The French aren't as uptight as us overly puritan Americans when it comes to affairs. And it's an equal opportunity thing. Both men and women have *petites aventures*, aka booty on the side. It's the best way to ensure a long-lasting marriage."

"Isn't that an oxymoron?"

"Not according to Jean-Philippe. Affairs prevent you from getting bored of your spouse and the day-to-day drudgery of married life."

"Why not be upfront about it from day one?"

"He assumed I knew how things 'worked' in France," I say with air quotes.

"Un-fucking-believable."

"As the door slammed behind him, I realized when he told me I was his only girlfriend, he meant I was his only side piece."

Gage shakes his head.

"Embarrassed, I called my best friend Nadine because I needed a shoulder to cry on. She came to the rescue in record time with booze and loads of desserts. As I was crying my eyes out, she consoled me by reminding me, although there are jerks and assholes in every country who cheat on their wives or partners, Frenchmen who stray are more prone to telling their mistress about their wife—and vice versa—when the situation calls for it. In her opinion, Jean-Philippe expected me to be okay with it."

"Were you?"

"Hell, no," I say. "Nadine also warned me Jean-Philippe would be the type to call me to pick up where we left off."

Gage's eyes bulge out of his skull.

"I thought she was lying. That's the only reason why I didn't block his number."

"He contacted you?"

"To my utter disbelief, he texted me to share photos of him holding his bundle of joy. He also wanted to know when we could pick up where we left off since his wife couldn't have sex for at least six weeks."

Gage's jaw drops.

"I was outraged and enraged. Not only for myself, but also for his wife."

"I hate drama."

"Trust me, it's not my MO."

"You were an unwilling participant."

"I was unknowingly the other woman. Same as Mom—"

"No shit."

"Yup." I nod. "She was also nineteen when my father seduced her. Granted, he was more than twice her age. Since I was born a bastard child, I promised myself I would never look at a married man. Worse, sleep with one. But there I was, about to make the biggest mistake of my life."

"Jean-Philippe is a fucking cheater."

"Given how I came into this world, that's one aspect of France's culture that would never sit well with me."

"Here in the US, cheaters are crucified. The higher your status, the more the public cries out for your balls."

"France tends to turn a blind eye to cheaters. My best friend being the exception to the rule."

"What do you mean?"

"My best friend's mom knew the older man who was overtly flirting with her was married. The whole world knew. She was so much younger than him and a subordinate, so it was easy for him to abuse his power. That's how she ended up as France's Monica Lewinsky—"

"Your best friend is Nadine Whelan?"

"Yes."

Gage's eyes widen in surprise. "Holy shit."

"Nadine's mom one upped Monica with a surprise baby. The fact Marciana was American didn't play in her favor. She was lynched in the media and in the court of public opinion."

"And you and Nadine ended up becoming friends."

"Isn't it ironic?" It's a rhetorical question because I keep talking. "Nads is like a blood sister to me."

"Doesn't the former French president have children?"

"Yes, Nads has half-siblings, but they've never warmed up to her."

"Like your half-brothers."

"Like my half-brothers." I bite down the bitterness. "We've struggled with imposter syndrome our whole lives. Our fathers are powerful and wealthy men, but we came out of the womb labeled as the undesirable progeny. We've spent our whole lives feeling less than. For my best friend, it's worse because her name is splattered all over French social media forever more."

"The American press didn't spare her."

"True, but she doesn't live here, so those opinions don't affect her everyday life. It's not the case in France. She'll never be able to escape the stigma. To this day, many circles in Paris give Marciana the cold shoulder, snubbing her, while singing the praises of former President Laurent Rocard de Villepin. It's an unfair double standard."

Gage shakes his head. "The onus is on the person doing the cheating to be on the up and up. In your case and Nadine's, we're talking about dirty old men, preying on young, vulnerable victims. Your mom was only nineteen—barely legal. Marciana Whelan was twenty-two—a woman, but still so young. As for you and Jean-Philippe, he's a royal douchebag. I don't care if it's the French way or not, he should've made sure you two were on the same fucking page."

The fire behind his words does something to me. So far in my life, I haven't had that many people in my corner.

I respond with a sad smile.

"Can I ask you a question about your dad?" Gage changes the subject.

I brace myself. "Sure."

"You always refer to Fisher as *Father*. Never as Dad or Daddy. There's no steadfast rule, but for some reason, I can't help but sense in your case, it's deliberate."

He's perceptive.

"If I could still get away with calling him Fisher, I would. He put an end to that when one of his business associates thought I was his flavor of the month, commenting how he liked them younger and younger, bordering on not quite legit. I was seventeen at the time, so that guy guessed right. My father always treated me like a dirty little secret, so other than close family, few people knew he had a daughter. That incident creeped him out. After that, he demanded I call him Dad. I settled for Father. It allows people to know the type of relationship we have, without pretending he's the doting dad figure you expect to see in a light-hearted romance movie of the week." *Warm and fuzzy are foreign words to Fisher Edgington.*

Gage nods.

The energy in the room has shifted. This conversation is a mood killer.

Delving into my past tends to do that. So far, this evening has been such a high, I'd hate for it to end on a depressing note.

"There are a thousand more interesting things to talk about than Jean-Philippe, the former President of France, or my dysfunctional relationship with my father."

"What do you want to talk about?"

I bite my lower lip, my cheeks flushing. "You know," I say.

His gaze drifts down to my chest. "Why don't you spell it out for me?"

Shit.

My bravado slips a little.

He cocks an eyebrow. "All talk, no action?"

He scoots his chair back.

A pole is tenting under his robe.

Adding fuel to the fire, he parts his legs. Unlike me, he isn't wearing any underwear. The fabric of the robe slides, revealing strong, muscular thighs, and...

Did his cock grow by several inches?

Oh, boy.

Old Lily would agree with him on the all talk, no action part, aware she's no match. LA Lily has a decisively more daring and bold approach.

Challenge accepted.

I lean forward and allow my hand to drift over his thigh, moving closer to his mighty erection.

My pulse quickens as my hand explores his body.

He moans.

God, I love that I do that to him.

His eager hands work on the tie holding the sash at his waist, pushing the robe fully open. I didn't think I could find tattoos attractive, but he's proved me wrong.

The man is unbelievably well-built and my mouth waters at the sight of him. It's a struggle to tear my gaze away from his tattooed chest, chiseled rippled eight-pack, and his happy trail that runs from below his bellybutton to the top of his pelvis. And there's the *pièce de resistance...* the V-muscle... it makes me want to drop to my knees between his legs and lick it.

God Almighty.

I reach out a hand.

"I haven't given you permission to touch me."

My eyes fly up.

I'm about to laugh, but his expression has me reconsidering.

He's serious.

"*I* give you permission to come and *I* give you permission to touch me."

I'm baffled.

He narrows his eyes. "I'm guessing that's not how it worked with Mr. Cheater Douchebag?"

Jean-Philippe was a puppy dog, always eager to roll over for a belly rub. Gage is an Italian mastiff. He's the indisputable top dog.

I can't explain it, but a frisson of excitement runs through me.

I shake my head.

"Words, Lily."

"No."

"Everything is different, angel, now that I've claimed you."

I'll have to thank Nads for introducing me to steamy romance novels.

I thought alpha males could only be found between the pages of a book. These men exist in real life?

Color me surprised.

"Are we clear?" The lust-filled gaze he levels me with causes my pussy to pulse. Nope. Not pulse. I'm doing Kegel exercises.

I nod. "Yes."

"Now you can touch me," he says. "My cock needs attention."

I run a finger along his chest, tracing tattooed music notes and stars in a languorous movement, before traveling down his body until I reach the prize. I curl my hand around his impressive length, and stroke him up and down.

"You have an eye-popping shaft—"

"Cock," he says. "Dick, is also acceptable." His eyes lower. "He's American. Not European."

I laugh. "Your American cock is cut."

"Mr. Cheater Douchebag wasn't?"

I shake my head. "No. And he wasn't as big as you. Not

that I ever pulled out a ruler, but it's like comparing a baby carrot to a zucchini."

"Which begs the question. Didn't you want a smaller cock for your first time?"

"I wanted *you* for my first time. Big dick, big balls, and all."

Gage Hollingsworth bursts out laughing, his broad shoulders shaking.

I stare at him, my mouth agape.

After several heartbeats, he finds his composure.

I'm still in a state of shock.

"What?"

"You know how to laugh?" I shake my head. "Wow. I didn't think it was part of a curmudgeon's DNA."

"What's a curmudgeon?"

"A bad-tempered geezer," I say. "Who are you, imposter?" And what have you done with the real Gage Hollingsworth?"

"Smart ass."

My grin is epic.

He lifts me from my seat, placing me between him and the table so I'm standing in the V of his thighs.

Okay, that was impressive.

God the man is strong.

With rough hands, he rips open the robe I'm wearing, leaving my body bare, save for my blush-colored panties.

I gasp.

His green eyes lift to meet mine before lowering to my body.

He growls, drinking me up. "Fuck, you're gorgeous."

I blush. "You keep saying that."

"Because it's true."

My blush deepens, turning my whole face as hot—and I'm sure as red—as a stove burner.

He reaches for my underwear and bunches the lacy fabric in a large fist.

I expect him to tug aside the strip of material that shields my pussy, but that's not what happens.

Rip.

Holy. Hell.

"Those were new."

He checks the label. "French Appliqué. Noted. Don't worry your pretty little head. I'll replace them so I can rip them off your sexy body again, and again, and again."

When he puts it that way, who am I to say no?

He run his finger down my slit until it glides between my pussy lips.

I gasp, folding over, using his broad shoulders for support.

"Since I'm the first cock you've ever had, I need to fuck you hard, in every position, multiple times so you never forget me. I want to ruin it for all the fuckers that will come after me."

His filthy promise resonates all the way to my clit.

"So far, it's been easy for me to put blinders on my needs—fucking my fist for salvation—that's until a sexy little thing with raven hair and big, beautiful blue eyes the color of gemstones, came crashing into my life. My cock wanted to come out and play with the sexiest woman on the fucking planet." He's not done rocking my world.

If I thought I was wet before, now, my inner thighs are turning slick with my own juices.

"So, we're gonna play some more?"

I nod, as if in a trance.

He leans forward and nips at my sensitive nipple with his teeth.

I let out a sound I've never heard slip from my lips before.

"Words. If I have to ask again, I'll have to bite harder."

"Yes."

"Yes, what?"

"I want to play some more."

"Better."

My whole body is buzzing.

As if things weren't too hot to handle, Gage wraps my shredded lacy panties around his cock. With his eyes on me, he strokes himself up and down in a tight fist.

Stunned, my mouth drops in an O.

Oh. My. God.

For a long moment, I forget to breathe as I stare wide-eyed at him working his cock.

When his other hand cups his big balls, I press my legs together, in the hopes of alleviating the aching need.

"Did I give you permission to do that?"

I stop all movement. "Err... No."

"Then, don't."

He lets go of his balls and swipes the tip of his fingers over the wet head of his cock.

My mind is blown into smithereens at the raunchy sight.

"Open up."

Huh?

"Don't make me repeat myself."

I open wide.

"Clean my fingers with your tongue."

My eyelashes flutter in surprise.

He cocks an eyebrow.

I hesitate at first, but stick my tongue out.

I run the tip along his fingers.

His saltiness hits my taste buds full force.

"Good girl." He brings my panties to his nose and inhales. "I can't wait for my face to smell like your tight little pussy. Have you ever sat on a man's face, Lily?"

I frown. "I don't understand."

"You sit on my face, and I gorge on your pussy. I might even reward you by finger fucking your ass. If you're a good girl, I'll let you ride my face reverse cowgirl style so I can stroke your G-spot and make your pussy gush like a fucking waterfall."

Blink.

Blink.

Blink.

My mind struggles to compute what he said, but my body reacts favorably to the possibilities.

"You've never tried that before?"

That would be a definite no. "Never."

"We'll have to try it..."

Yes, please.

He taps his thigh. "Straddle my legs."

I don't move.

I'm paralyzed.

His long legs are parted wide.

How the hell is this going to work with my short legs?

He brings his legs closer together, as if he's able to read my thoughts. "You'll use my shoulders for support."

I'm a little awkward, but I assume the position.

We're so close. I'm sure he can hear the frantic beating of my heart.

"Lower your hips for me. I want your pussy hovering over my cock."

"Aren't you going to use a condom?"

"I'm not going to fuck you yet. I want your clit to get acquainted with my tip."

Jesus Christ.

Jean-Philippe's bedroom vocabulary extended to a few go-to phrases.

"Tu me suces ma bite géante et tu me lèches mes couilles."

Translation: *Suck my enormous cock and my balls.*

His cock wasn't enormous, but I never pointed that out.

"Je veux une branlette espagnole ce soir."

Translation: *I want to fuck your boobs tonight.*

"J'aime jouer avec ta petite chatte."

Translation: *I love playing with your pussy.*

For that last one, he'd add disturbing meowing sounds.

Compared to the Frenchman, Gage holds a PhD degree in dirty talking.

Come to think about it, it was all about Jean-Philippe.

Selfish asshole cheater.

"Is that okay with you?"

Gage's question forces me back to the moment.

If my clit getting acquainted with his tip results in me having another core-shaking orgasm, I'm all in. "More than okay."

He places a hand on my hip, positioning me the way he wants.

When his slick tip glides over my clit, I let out a long moan.

Granted, his head is much wider than the tips of my fingers, I was unprepared for the flurry of new sensations.

I relish them all.

He does it again.

Good God.

My fingers claw their way into his thick, silky hair, and my head lolls back.

The lewd sound of his slickness circling my clit is so hot.

Round and round.

With each revolution, he takes me higher and higher.

I curl my arms around his head, plowing my fingers in his hair, drawing him closer. If I don't, I'm liable to tumble backwards.

This is too good. Too sinful. Too hedonistic.

All movement stops.

"What's wrong?"

"Do you want to come?"

I'm a bit taken aback by the question.

"Answer me."

"Yes." The word rushes out of my mouth.

"In that case, don't let me do all the work."

Holy hardball. "I didn't know I could be turned on by this level of dominance."

"You were waiting for me."

Horror washes over me. My inner voice wasn't as quiet as I would've hoped.

I blush from ear to ear.

"I wasn't supposed to hear that?"

I shake my head.

He drops a tender kiss on my lips. "I'm glad I did."

I smile.

I can't take it back. And even if I could, I'm not sure I would.

"That means we're on the same page," he says. "You surrendering so beautifully to me turns me on because you trust me enough to let go."

Slap!

"What was that for?"

"Back to work, dirty girl."

Gage picks up where he left off.

My hips rock back and forth as the tip of his cock grazes my clit.

This is beyond naughty.

"Please don't stop. *Please.* It's perfect. It's . . . oh God, oh God, oh my fucking God."

His lips split in a cocky grin. He knows I'm on the verge of delirium, and he's enjoying every sinful second of it.

He inserts a finger inside his mouth and licks it. Without

warning, he slides his digit inside my sacred place. A place where no man has ever been before.

I'm so stunned, I'm rendered speechless.

"Don't freeze up on me," he says. "Keep working your clit on my head."

My hips sway.

Back and forth.

Back and forth.

My whole body shakes as I chase after my orgasm.

The intrusion of his finger is foreign and pleasurable at the same time.

My pussy's practically weeping, desperate for release.

"Use my cock."

Dear God.

There are no words.

Gage alternates between dragging his swollen tip through my slickness and skating his head over my clit. His bare, tattooed chest heaves, a fine sheen of sweat coating his divine muscles.

What a sight.

My clit hums and it's a struggle to breathe.

"I want you to come so fucking hard all over my cock, you'll forget how to say anything but my name."

I'm nearly there.

He accelerates my climax when he gropes my breast before closing his mouth over my nipple and biting hard.

"Oh, Gage—"

I dive off the cliff into an abyss of pleasure.

I've traveled to a distant magical land where men are sworn to oath and face death if they don't always make their sexual partner come so hard, they momentarily black out.

I never want to leave this fairyland.

Heck, I don't even want to leave LA at this point.

When I go back to New York, this transcendental experience will only be a memory. What are the chances of finding a lover that matches Gage's prowess?

"You're still with me, angel?"

"I... I'm not sure."

He chuckles.

I untangle myself from his body so our eyes meet. Since my disheveled locks are obstructing my view, I brush my curtain of hair away from my face.

Gage's handsome face is almost unrecognizable.

The hunger I read in his eyes burns hot and wild and causes my pussy to pulsate. *Again?*

A horrible thought hits me. "You didn't come?"

His huge cock is still nestled between my pussy lips.

"I always take care of you first."

A warm smile splits my lips. "That's so considerate."

His expression changes.

"Let me guess. Mr. Cheater Douchebag made sure his needs were satisfied before yours."

I respond with a one-shoulder shrug.

"Not with me. You always come first."

I'm at a loss for words.

In case there weren't enough reasons to like this man, he gave me an extra one.

Gage Hollingsworth is setting the bar too high.

He's fucked me once so far, and he's ruined it for all others.

The realization smacks me hard in the face.

I'm so screwed.

A pang catches in my chest.

This attraction is ill advised. Dangerous, even.

I try to slide off him.

His eyes narrow as if he senses my mounting panic, his hands closing around my hips. "Where are you going?"

"I should reciprocate. You know... a blowjob."

"Baby, a blowjob is supposed to be pleasurable for you and for me. You're as tense as a politician on election day. What happened?"

I shake my head. "Nothing."

"What if I don't want a blowjob?"

I roll my eyes. "Every man wants a blowjob."

"How many guys have you been with to entitle you to make such a blanket generalization?"

Ouch.

"Don't you dare put me in the same category as Mr. Cheater Douchebag. I'm not a selfish asshole."

I'm stumped.

He brings a hand to my face, cradling my jaw, his winter-green eyes searching mine. "I can't wait to fuck your pretty little mouth, but only if you want to suck my cock, and not as a way of deflecting whatever it is you're hiding from me."

Busted.

A few long seconds tick by.

"You make me feel good." *You also make me feel good about myself. Men in my life tend to do the contrary.*

"And that's a bad thing?"

Yes, because our time together is limited. "No."

"I didn't think so."

Gage's hard mouth crashes over mine, his tongue delving deep, dancing with my own, quieting my mind with thorough strokes. I let go of my insecurities and give in to the kiss, matching his fervor.

A low groan of satisfaction simmers in his throat.

When he pulls back, he stares at me with half-lidded eyes. "I'm not done making you feel good, Lily. Not by a long shot."

Chapter 22

Gage

I wake up with a jolt, my eyes flying open.

Pre-dawn rays illuminate the room.

Shit.

I fell asleep?

I promised myself I'd leave within an hour after fucking Lily for the third time.

There was a breach of security in my internal Fort Knox.

Lily's virgin pussy is to blame.

I've never fucked a virgin before her. Some men get off popping a girl's cherry. I'm not one of them. Not until last night.

I want to plant a stake beside her that reads *Claimed. I'm the fucking king of this undiscovered land.*

She stirs next to me, pulling me out of my ridiculous thoughts.

Even princesses snore.

Her long black hair drapes in a curtain on the white pillowcase. The contrast with the cotton fabric and her milky skin is striking.

I don't have a hair color preference, I've never been with a woman with jet black hair. I reach out and caress the lush thickness of her silky mane.

Wrapping all this hair around my fist as I fuck her from behind with her on all fours...

She shifts, arching her back.

Her body is angled perfectly. I could spread her ass cheeks, and slide my morning wood right into her warmth.

Fuck.

My cock goes from hard to rock hard, veins popping like crazy.

After only one day, I'm addicted to her tight pussy.

I didn't spare her last night. Not until we both passed out, comatose from too many strong orgasms. The cherry on the sundae was playing with her clit bareback. That was so fucking hot. It took herculean effort not to slide inside her inviting pussy and fuck her raw until I spilled my cum deep inside her.

It's crazy and reckless, especially considering I have no intentions of becoming a father anytime soon. Yet, I was this close from sliding all the way to a home run.

A surge of lust travels through my veins, and my cock hardens, imagining how blissful it would be.

This is what this woman does to me.

My balls and abs are tender with a satisfied ache, but that doesn't prevent my cock from being greedy as fuck.

I want more of her.

I want to make her cry out for mercy.

I need to hear my name on her lips again.

I snake an arm around her waist, pulling her close, pressing her backside against my front. I brush her cascade of hair. Leaning forward, my mouth moves over the satin skin of the curve of her neck.

She tilts her head against the pillow to give me better access.

I cover her neck with kisses as my erect cock relishes the heat seeping from her body. I close a hand over her breast, her puckered nipple scratching my palm. My fingertips pinch the tight bud until she lets out a little pleading sound.

"Is your cock always on alert?" Her voice comes out sounding groggy.

"I can't control *him* when I'm around you."

"Oh my, Mr. Hollingsworth, do you intend on taking advantage of my sleepy, hazy state?"

"Abso-fucking-lutely."

"I don't know if I have the energy for another marathon. I haven't recovered from last night."

"You don't have to do a thing. Let me take care of you."

"How can I say no to that?" The laughter in her voice doesn't go unnoticed.

"You can't." Leaning in, I kiss her cheek. "You sore? I fucked you hard. And multiple times."

She scoots her body closer to mine, her ass cheeks flirting with my tip.

I groan under my breath. "Eager much?"

"You made big promises," she says. "All the benefits, without any of the work. I might have only lost my virginity yesterday, but I'm no fool. I know a good thing when I hear it."

"So, you're not sore?"

"Not enough to say no."

"You're sure?"

She tilts her hips back.

That's all the confirmation I need.

I fist my cock and angle it. I don't know why, but I hold my breath when my tip presses against her warm entrance. I slide my cock between her drenched pussy lips until my head skates over her clit.

Christ, she's ready for me.

I go at it nice and slow at first. Not for her benefit, but for mine. If I go any faster, it might give me a heart attack.

The mixture of the slickness of her arousal, her heady scent, and the lingering notes of her expensive perfume has me all riled up.

When I'm certain my heart won't give in, I heighten the pleasure for her and for me. I rub my tip against her clit, applying extra pressure.

She moans.

"You're so fucking wet."

She makes to turn around, but I stop her.

"Don't move. You're in the perfect position."

I skate my cock around her pussy, relishing her slick juices.

My head lolls back at the all-encompassing sensation. "Is it as good as it was last night?"

"No." She shakes her head against the pillow. "It's a million times better."

Music to my ears.

My naked cock has never been near a woman before. I didn't know what I was missing. I've done kinky things in my life, but this trumps them all.

For a few long breaths, I tease her soaking pussy in languid circles, stroking her engorged clit with my fat knob.

Greedy for more, I glide my cock down through her pussy lips to her ass, nudging the little puckered hole.

Her body tenses.

"I'm teasing you. I won't go all the way."

"Promise?"

"We'd make that decision together."

She relaxes.

I resume my mission.

I glide against her clit, her dripping pussy, and the bud of her tight asshole.

I grunt.

She hisses.

I do it again, and again, and again.

I reposition my cock, choking my head with my hand, and I pick up my pace, focusing on her pussy.

Lily's hips undulate back and forth, matching my cadence, accelerating my demise.

Dammit.

The sinful sound of our slickness reverberates throughout the room.

The need to slide my cock inside her pussy is overpowering, but I resist. Barely.

This woman will be the end of me.

I need to keep my head on my shoulders.

All movement stops.

With rough hands, I flip her so she's lying flat on her back.

I get on my knees and position myself between her legs.

"You look good enough to eat in this position."

She responds by spreading her legs wider.

I want to take her up on her invitation, but I have other plans in mind. "Make yourself come for me."

Her eyes go wide.

"You've touched yourself before?"

"Yes."

I cock an eyebrow. "So, what's the problem?"

Her expression is positively horrified. "I've never done that in front of someone else."

"If I'm going to be your first, we should aim for gold. I want you debauched. You play with yours and I'll play with mine."

Her lips form an O, and her long eyelashes flutter.

I pump my cock. "Play with your sweet pussy."

She doesn't join in.

I'm about to repeat my command, when her eyes meet mine. The lust I read in them threatens to make me come in the palm of my hand.

Game on.

I give myself a couple of vigorous tugs, swelling even larger in my hand.

I put on a show for her, stroking my cock like it's my job.

"When you play with your pussy, do you use toys or your fingers?"

"My fingers, or a pillow."

Lily's hooded blue eyes are riveted on my cock when she answers my question. The fucker jerks in my hand at the imagery of an innocent Lily riding her pillow as she chases after her orgasm.

"No toys?"

She shakes her head.

"Why not?"

"It sounds a bit perverted... sticking things up your private parts, seeking pleasure. I don't get it."

"Don't knock it 'till you try it."

"Do you put toys up your..." She can't even say the word.

"No, I don't put toys up my ass. I'd much prefer putting a toy up yours."

"Double standards?"

"Perhaps."

"Watching you do that is so hot," she says, changing the subject.

"Is this your first time watching a guy jerk off?"

"No," she says. "Granted, I only have one point of reference, but dare I say, the way you stroke your cock... it's so manly." She licks her lips. "The experience is vastly different from watching a guy jerking off his heirloom-carrot-size-cock versus enjoying the eye-popping show when a guy has a cock the size of a large zucchini." She flashes me a sassy grin.

I shake my head. "You've never watched porn?"

"No."

"Why not?"

"My father pays for my phone plan and internet connection. The man has ears—and eyes—everywhere. I'd be petrified if he were to find out."

"I see."

"I'm sure he indulges. Same for my half-brothers."

Those are visuals I didn't need.

"I'm also certain, I wouldn't be able to get away with it. My father is a big believer in double standards. I can't watch porn at Nads's place since her dad still foots the bill for most of her expenses. We make self-deprecating jokes about ourselves. We're part of a small group of women who don't watch porn."

Talking or thinking about Fisher Edgington or her half-brothers is a quick way to turn my rock-hard cock to a limp dick.

Time to end this conversation.

I pump my fist up and down my cock, forcing her attention on me. Under her gaze, my cock strains, my veins bulging thick.

I jack off harder, groaning with each stroke.

"Yesterday, you were begging to give me a blowjob," I say through gritted teeth. "Soon, your lips will be wrapped around my huge cock, my generous girth stretching your pretty mouth to the limits, my length hitting the back of your throat again, and again, and again."

Half-lidded eyes meet mine.

I squeeze out a pearl of pre-cum, scoop it up with a fingertip, and reach my hand out to her. "This is for you."

She props herself on her elbows and opens her mouth. She

cleans my finger with a few sensual licks, her heated gaze never leaving mine.

I could get lost in those blue eyes.

"You'll get more when I fuck your mouth."

Excitement and anticipation flash in her gaze.

Good girl.

"Join me. Show me how you make yourself come."

She settles back on the bed. Manicured fingers slide down her taut stomach until they're nestled between her pussy lips. "I feel so vulnerable."

"In no time, you'll feel so good, vulnerability will fly out the door. Trust me."

She smiles a little.

She strokes her clit.

This isn't the first time a woman has pleasured herself in front of me, but something about the way Lily does it and knowing this is her first time tugs at my balls.

I fist my cock and pump it as her fingers play with her pussy. The sinful expression on her face is one I'll never forget.

Fuck.

We're both in silent contemplation as we stare at each other's hands.

"The sound of your dripping pussy is pure filth."

"It feels better when it's your cock."

I didn't see that coming.

"You like when my cock teases your clit?"

"Yes."

Something must come over her because she bites hard against her lower lip and arches her back. "God, this is so filthy."

"Damn right."

When she picks up speed, it's my turn to bite my lower lip to avoid grunting.

My fist works up and down, sliding from base to tip.

"I'll never be able to do this again without thinking of you," she says.

I'm sure it's the lust talking, but fuck if her confession doesn't do something to me.

Her cadence becomes erratic and she rubs her pussy with determination as she chases after her orgasm. Her moans fill the room with each stroke.

My flared-out purple head turns dark with my vigorous thrusts. I cup my balls and squeeze tight, torturing myself a little before I give in to pleasure.

"Angel, there isn't much left to me." My voice is as rough as gravel. "Tell me you're close."

"Yes."

If I wasn't hovering over her, I would've missed her response.

She bucks her hips, and her head moves from side to side in violent jerks against the pillow. One hand flies up to her breast, and she twists her nipple hard.

I do a mental snapshot for later use. This will be a go-to favorite in my spank bank.

I choke my cock, stroking it back and forth with vigor.

She keeps working her pussy, writhing on the bed. She closes her eyes, but I won't have it.

"No. I want you watching when I come."

Her beautiful blue eyes are on me again.

Good.

She finger-fucks herself as she toys with her clit.

Jesus Christ.

Her fingers pump in and out of her pussy with slick velocity.

She throws her head back. "Oh, oh, oh, it's happening again. It's happening again."

The most beautiful thing ensues.

Lily's hands leave her pussy and find her nipples. She twists both at the same time, as her hips gyrate on the bed.

She's wild.

She lets out a keening cry of ecstasy that's so primal, you'd think I'm torturing her.

The vibrations travel to my balls.

And then, it happens.

Lily's pussy gushes.

I swear, it's even more abundant than before.

The sound of her hand slapping her wet pussy is pure sin.

Holy shit. She's a fucking geyser.

I might have to pay to replace this king bed, but damn, is it ever worth it.

The most intense sense of pleasure and satisfaction I've ever experienced washes over me as this gorgeous woman comes undone. And to think, she didn't even know her body could do that. Our time together will change the way she thinks of sex—and her body—forever. It's better than any drug.

My dirty girl.

As if that wasn't spectacular enough, her body convulses. I'm guessing it's from a second climactic wave.

Her juices are flowing like the dam to a river broke.

"Gage. Oh, Gage. Oh God—"

Her pleasure-filled whimpers are my undoing.

I walk on my knees until I'm hovering right on top of her.

I grip my cock hard.

One hard jerk.

Two.

Three.

A curse spews from my throat as my climax rips through me. "God, Lily." I point my cock and my release explodes and lands in hot white streaks across her creamy skin.

She glances down at her body.

I christened her stomach with a river of cum.

Damn.

I grab a few tissues from the box on the nightstand and clean her up. I take care of my cock next. When I'm done, I toss the dirty tissues over my shoulder, and drop on the bed next to her.

At this rate, this bed won't survive our passion.

I flip to my side, and pull her into my embrace. Although there's A/C in the room, she's sweating.

We stay interlaced for a long while, breathing heavy.

"I still can't believe what you do to my body," she says, against my chest.

"I didn't do a thing. I wasn't even touching you."

"You must've put a spell on me. There's no other explanation. I've touched myself many times before, and my body has never reacted that way. Never. Not even close. I blame you for turning me into... a waterfall."

I brush her damp hair from her forehead and drop a soft kiss against it. "It's a good thing we met."

"I'm not so sure."

I pull away from her, my gaze skeptic, brow cocked.

"It's... too much. Unsettling, even."

"Like I said, not every woman experiences that."

She opens her mouth to say something, but I precede her.

"Embrace it. Own it. It's sexy as fuck."

She smiles.

"If I wasn't as mesmerized by the sight, I would've been licking every drop," I say.

She hides her face in my chest, a reminder of her innocence. "For the record, that was the best wakeup call ever."

"I agree."

She nestles closer.

Her warm mouth moves to my neck, peppering soft kisses against my skin.

Goddammit.

She's making love to my neck.

The urge to cover this beautiful woman in diamonds and sapphires that match the violet hues in her eyes is overwhelming. This is unprecedented.

"I don't think anyone has ever kissed my neck like that before," I say, my tone deep and husky.

"So, I get to be your first."

I chuckle. "You do, angel."

"I suspect there aren't that many things you haven't experienced with a woman."

I take her chin in my hands, forcing her attention on me. "Whatever I experience with you, is a first. For instance, I've never rubbed my cock on another woman's bare pussy before."

Big blue eyes light up with glee. "Firsts must be rare instances for an *old* guy."

I bite her shoulder. "Who are you calling old, little girl?"

She giggles. "That was my not-so-subtle way of asking how old you are. It might be a little late in the game, but I might as well know now."

"How old do you think I am?"

"You're not as old as my father."

"That was a boner killer."

Her eyes widen. "Don't tell me you're ready to go another round?"

"Don't sound so shocked. With you, angel, I could go all day long."

She responds with a radiant smile.

I've known this woman for less than forty-eight hours, and I'd do anything to keep that smile on her face.

Whoa.

Where the hell did that come from?

You're out of your fucking mind, Hollingsworth.

"Are you going to tell me how old you are, or do I have to guess?" Her question brings me back to the moment.

"I'm thirty-two."

"Hmmm."

"Hmmm, what?"

"Nothing."

"Liar."

"You're still in great shape for a guy your age," she says.

"You're begging for me to pin you to this mattress and fuck you until you can't remember your name. Keep it up and you might get your wish."

She stares at me with innocent, angelic eyes. "Who says that wasn't the plan all along?"

"Good God. I've created a monster."

She grins wide.

We lie in silence for several breaths.

I should be itching to bolt out of this hotel room like the roof was on fire, but I'm not. On the contrary, I'm in no rush to let go of this gorgeous woman.

I've seen my fair share of fake eyelashes and extensions, and you can tell. I'm not sure what to make of Lily's eyelashes. "Your eyelashes are stunning."

"I was born with distichiasis."

I frown. "What's that?"

"It's a genetic disorder that produces an extra row of eyelashes. So, it looks like I'm wearing volumizing mascara twenty-four seven, even when my face is devoid of makeup."

"There's so much to know about you."

"I'm not that interesting."

"Tsk. Stop selling yourself short."

"Okay, Daddy—"

"First, I'm old. Now, I'm your daddy." I make a face. "Unless you're referring to a daddy/little girl kink, don't call me Daddy."

She giggles. "Let me rephrase that. My genetic disorder is one of the many fascinating things about *moi*," she says in a theatrical way.

I chuckle. "Speaking of Lily Schuyler's many riveting facets, do you have to visit any film schools today?"

"Yes, I do."

"What time?"

"Five. It's an hour-long visit."

"Are you free before that?"

"I was going to play tourist, but other than that, I am."

"What about a drive up to Malibu?"

I don't ever wake up in a woman's bed and I sure as hell don't tie myself to her for the day. Lily is the exception. I want more of this woman. I want to learn all her secrets.

Her eyes light up. "I'd love that. I didn't expect to spend the day with you. This is a treat."

You're the treat.

I kiss her pretty mouth.

Her hands tunnel into my hair as I deepen the passionate kiss.

I pull away from her before I drown in her warmth. "It's settled."

She nods. "I'm looking forward to discovering LA through your eyes."

"You're in for an unexpected day."

"Bring it on, Mr. Grumpy Pants."

Slap!

"What is it with you and spanking?"

"Oh, sweetheart, that wasn't spanking. That was a tap.

When I spank your ass, you'll know. In fact, I'll make you count."

Her eyes widen in shock.

"That'll be another first you can cross off your list."

She doesn't have a comeback.

"Come on, princess, we're going to take a shower to wash my cum off your heavenly body. Once you're all cleaned up, we'll have breakfast and hit the road."

Chapter 23

Lily

I went into this with my eyes wide open and kept my expectations low.

One night—and morning—of toe-curling pleasure would've sufficed. I'm so giddy with happiness Gage would want to spend the day with me, I'm floating.

Since Jean-Philippe was leading a double life, he kept our outings to restaurants in the area where I lived in Paris, never venturing too far. It's only when I found out he had a wife, it all made sense. The Frenchman kept me as his dirty little secret. Being seen with a man is a new experience for me.

I might've only gotten my V card punched yesterday, but I'm not delusional.

My drop-dead gorgeous bodyguard turned lover is a magician capable of turning my pussy into a waterfall, but the writing is on the wall.

I'm passing through town.

My father is one of his big advertisers.

And Gage Hollingsworth is a certified bachelor.

So that settles that.

I didn't even want to come to LA, and I was dreading spending time with one of my father's connections. But something tells me it's going to be impossible to forget Gage.

I sigh.

A strong hand closing over my thigh forces me out of my rumination.

"Earth to Lily."

My eyes fly up to meet Gage's.

"Where were you? I was talking, and the music is playing in the background. Still, you were a continent away."

"Sorry if I didn't hear what you said. I was swept away by the breathtaking scenery." It's a partial lie. "Photos and videos of the City of Angels don't do it justice. This is the polar opposite to New York's concrete jungle."

He shoots me a dubious gaze.

I respond with an innocent smile.

Gage has been playing the role of tour guide, pointing out landmarks and providing me with Travelocity-worthy facts as we drive around LA. I was a captive audience until we stopped at a traffic light and my eyes landed on a young couple waiting on the sidewalk, kissing with passion. Instantly, I was transported to last night. From there, my overactive mind unraveled.

"If there's something else you'd rather do, say the word."

"You mean something other than driving in a pricey navy-blue Wiesmann GT MF4—a sports car I had never heard of until I climbed into it—with the top down, on a spectacular and sunny day, zooming towards the Malibu coast with the most attractive chaperone I've ever had?" I shake my head. "Nah. This is good."

"I've been demoted to chaperone?"

"Chaperone. Bodyguard." I shrug "Same thing."

He swings those mesmerizing wintergreen eyes my way, an eyebrow cocked. "I've been demoted after I made you come your head off in the shower? If you need me to pull over right this minute so I can remind you I'm far more than a chaperone or bodyguard, I'm happy to oblige."

Shower sex when the guy is standing up and he's lifting you in his arms is so damn hot. Another feather in Gage's sexy cap and another reason for my euphoric Saturday morning.

A wave of lust sweeps through me, causing my nipples to pebble and goosebumps to raise on my arms.

Down, girl.

I just discovered sex, and now I can't live without it?

My face bursts into flames.

What's wrong with me?

"Your cheeks are flushing."

Busted.

"That's a little caveman-ish." My voice is weak.

"Doesn't mean I wouldn't do it."

In what parallel universe did I think I was a match for this man?

He has enough balls—literally and figuratively—to do it, too.

Best not to start something I can't finish. I keep quiet not to worsen my case.

A few orgasms, and I'm Superwoman.

"If you can't take it, don't dish it out," he says.

"Noted." I nod.

Gage shifts his attention to the road.

I pull my oversized designer sunglasses over my eyes and lose myself in the scenery.

Driving in LA is an indescribable experience. We left the bumper-to-bumper traffic behind, and now it's *ride, baby ride.* As the road leading to Malibu unfolds underneath the wheels of Gage's speeding bullet, I take it all in. Each time I blink, it's as if I'm trying to capture a snapshot of the city. If I come back to study in LA, it'll never be the same.

It's never as good as the first time.

I fight off a smile at the double entendre.

I pull out my phone to take photos and videos for Nadine.

Save for the horrendous traffic and a few other nightmarish things typical of megacities, I can see why people think this place is Paradise. Sun, sea, surf, sexy people, and the chance of spotting celebrities—unless you're partying with them at a private affair in a swanky club.

My eyes bounce to the majestic peaks.

I was expecting to see the Pacific Ocean, but I didn't expect to see mountains. A group of men saddled on motorcycles that look like they belong to another era zoom by. Some are alone, others have a woman clinging to their back.

Wicked.

Does Gage own a motorcycle?

Not that it matters. I'm way too much of a chicken to ride on the back of a motorcycle. I prefer to be encased in steel when I'm on the road.

I tap my foot and bob my head to the tune playing.

Catchy.

This is the perfect day.

There are plenty of sunny days in New York during the sweltering summers, but the sky is never this bright. As my eyes stretch to the horizon, I spot a group of surfers riding a wave.

So cool.

California sure is beautiful.

Unable to help myself, I steal a glance at another beautiful view.

Long gone is the morning stubble. He's clean shaven and hot as ever.

While I was getting ready, Gage drove back to his place for

a change of clothes. He traded what he was wearing yesterday for another casual yet smoking hot outfit—black jeans that mold his muscular thighs to perfection and a blue shirt with a purple undertone that makes his green eyes even more seductive. Not that I know how that's even possible.

My suitcase is still a no-show.

At this point, I'm certain it traveled to Australia. Thank God, I had something suitable for our outing. I opted for a cobalt-blue midi skirt and a white flowy sleeveless top with a sexy V-neck. When it comes to footwear, Gage and I match. I went with a pair of silver Converse I bought during my shopping spree. He's rocking a pair of cool high top custom designed ones.

He catches me ogling. "You like what you see, princess?"

Yes. I. Do.

I don't have a chance to incriminate myself.

The song changes to one of my favorites.

Excitement courses through my body. Before I can catch myself, my hands are over my head. I wiggle in my seat as I sing along.

I'm no songstress, but fuck if that stops me from going for it.

Gage's head jerks back at my impromptu show.

I move my upper body as if auditioning to be part of a video.

I don't hold back.

I belt the lyrics to the bridge of Ultra Nate's song *Free*.

Gage blinks.

I guess this is a departure from the quiet woman he met yesterday.

I've worn shackles my whole life.

This is the freest I've ever felt.

I'm going to blame the California sun—and the man sitting next to me—for yanking me out of my shell.

~

After a pit stop at O'Dwyer's Fine Ice Creams, we were back in Gage's Bond car, armed with a cooler bag filled with ice packs and pints of ice cream. I was dying for a scoop for the road, but my travel companion suggested I wait. He promised the perfect spot to enjoy our creamy desserts. I took the bait.

I didn't expect a rest stop along the Pacific Coast Highway to Malibu, but that's where we are.

He cuts the engine.

He unfastens his seatbelt, shifts in his seat, and pulls his leg up so his body is facing me.

I mimic him.

He pushes his sunglasses over his head.

There's nothing obstructing his handsome face.

Yesterday, his face was all granite. Gone are the sexy lips pressed in a grim line. Although, he isn't grinning ear to ear, the hint of softness is so attractive on him.

He brushes a strand of hair behind my ear.

I had it in a pulled back style, similar to what I had it at Rhys's party, but when Gage came back to get me, he insisted I wear it out. I'm obsessed about having it perfectly straight, but he loves the wave. Since I'm only wearing a touch of makeup, he says it adds to the fresh-faced look.

"I thought we'd enjoy this sunny day and some lunch before heading to Malibu," he says.

"You grabbed lunch on your way back to the hotel?"

He shakes his head. "I grabbed lunch *at* the hotel."

I furrow my brows.

"It's in the trunk," he says. "You're okay with that?"

"I am."

"Let me come around." He gets out of the car.

I sit pretty.

He opens the passenger door and extends a hand.

I take it.

A thrill runs through me at the contact. It's different from the five thousand volts of electricity that zapped through me when I shook his hand the first time we met, but it's still unsettling.

He helps me out of the car, and we walk to the trunk. He aims the key fob at the vehicle. We watch as the hood of the car retracts. He points the little device towards the trunk. It pops open, revealing a feast.

Wow.

The scrumptious spread makes my mouth water. Same for the aroma.

My surprised eyes fly up. "When did you have time to pick this up?"

"I grabbed the blankets from home," he says. "As for the food, Michaela suggested I place an order for the Pompadour Hotel's gourmet picnic basket with a few extra trimmings. Twenty-four-hour notice is appreciated, but the CEO and owner's wife connected me to the right person." He winks.

"You texted her?"

"I did," he says. "It's easier to go straight to the top. Also, she was happy to hear from me. I reassured her that I didn't fuck you to the point where you couldn't walk anymore. She appreciated the heads up."

I gasp, my hand landing on my chest. "Please tell me you didn't tell her that."

"I didn't go into that much detail, but I told her you were mine for the day. She was glad I didn't scare you so much, you ran out of town."

Something tugs at my heart. "I assume that's what it's like to have a big sister."

"She warned me she was protective of you, so yeah, she's taken on the role."

I don't know what to make of his admission. It's like being enveloped in a warm fuzzy blanket. Michaela and Gage care more about me than my own father and half-brothers.

Sigh.

"I'm touched," I say. "Both by her concern and your gesture."

Gage taps the tip of my nose. "It's only food."

But it's so much more than that.

It's the attention.

It's the care.

It's a small gesture that means the most.

He makes me feel like I matter.

My stomach grumbles.

"Good thing I brought lunch," Gage says.

Never mind the breakfast of champions I wolfed down. I'm starved.

Embarrassed, I place a hand on my tummy. "My body is getting used to..."

"Being sexed up?"

I blush. "I guess."

"That's why I planned ahead," he says. "I can't keep you all day and not feed you."

You can keep me forever.

"Fair warning. Make sure you eat enough... you'll need the energy for later."

I blink up at him.

The promise in that statement causes my pussy to flutter.

"I wouldn't want you not to have the stamina to sustain the half dozen orgasms I have planned for you when we get back to the Pompadour."

...And I'm wet.

That chocolatey voice and those dirty words could make a girl lose her head.

"It's your first time discovering LA," he says. "I was picky in my food selection because I wanted to make sure this day was memorable. I didn't want anything to taint the experience. You're used to the best—aka the exquisite cuisine at the Pompadour Hotel. I didn't want to shock your taste buds with a menu that didn't measure up."

Is this guy for real?

Dear God, Mr. Grumpy Pants—this big, beautiful man—has a heart of gold.

Another wave of attraction sweeps through me so strong, I want to press the back of my hand against my forehead to check if I don't have a fever. But I catch myself in time and shake it off.

Reality check, Lily.

No matter how smoking hot the man is, no matter the palpable energy between us, no matter how much he turns me on, and no matter how many orgasms he gives me, our time together is measured in days. Not weeks. Not months. When the clock runs out, I'm going back to the Big Apple.

I do my best to keep a neutral expression, so he doesn't know how much this affects me. "That's so thoughtful of you."

"Anything less would be a crime."

I'm in serious danger of swooning like a silly teenager. I would never have protested stopping at a random eatery in the city for a quick bite, but the fact he put so much thought into it, warms my heart.

Keep your feet firmly on the ground, Lily.

I beckon him with a crooked finger.

He obliges.

He's so tall, he has to dip his chin to meet my gaze.

Mesmerizing wintergreen eyes stare at me with such intensity, my body flushes with heat.

I have to shake my head to break from the spell.

"Between you and me"—I wave a finger between us—"I must admit that after only a few days, I'm addicted. So much so, I'm considering chaining myself to the pipes in the kitchen so I never have to leave the Pompadour."

"If we're sharing secrets..."—his eyes shift left to right before settling on me—"I've tried—and failed—to hire Phoenix's chefs from underneath him. Numerous times."

"I would've done the same." I play along, matching his faux-seriousness.

He winks. "Let's go find a spot so we can feed you." He pulls the bags and picnic baskets from the trunk. "Don't forget the ice cream."

"That's unlikely to happen." I grab the bag from the back seat. "I can't wait to deep-dive, headfirst."

He chuckles.

We aren't the only ones out today. The picnic tables are occupied with a heap of people enjoying a perfect Saturday under the California sun.

"Do you mind sitting on the ground, Lily?"

"Someone came prepared with blankets. So, no, I don't mind."

"You woke up on the sassy side of the bed."

"I remember waking up with something poking at my back."

He narrows his eyes in warning.

We find a free spot and drop everything to the ground.

In no time, Gage has the blankets and the food spread out.

He invites me to take a seat.

I lower myself to the blanket, fold my legs underneath me, and drop my new adorable mini blue leather Louis Vuitton bag to the side. It's part of the list of things I was forced to buy because of the situation with my luggage. With my hands free, I fan my midi skirt around me.

Gage sits cross-legged on the gray checkered blanket. His long legs resemble a giant pretzel.

He pushes his designer shades over his head.

Oh hell, those eyes.

Under the bright sun, they're almost translucent.

He winks.

Stop ogling at him. The man will end up with an inflated ego.

He shifts his attention, rummaging through the picnic basket. "We have three sandwich selections."

"Which ones?"

"Roast beef with caramelized onions and arugula cheese, chicken salad with homemade mayo and walnuts served on black olive rye bread, and fancy muffaletta."

"What's that last one? It sounds Italian."

"It is," he says. "It's two slices of focaccia bread slathered with a tangy olive spread and layered with mortadella, uncured salami, uncured ham, and provolone."

My stomach grumbles again.

"It's settled. The fancy muffaletta for the lady."

"Sorry, but that sounded delicious."

"I agree. That's why I grabbed three."

I frown.

"One for you, and two for me." He shrugs. "I'm a big boy."

"Don't I know it."

"You weren't complaining last night or this morning."

Damn, he always one-ups me.

He hands me a lunchbox, containing my sandwich, a small portion of vegetable sticks, and a favorite from last night I couldn't get enough of.

I meet his gaze. "Coleslaw?"

"You went on and on about it, so I made a special request. It's part of their midnight menu, but again, that's where knowing the owner pays off."

I flash him a warm smile. "Thank you." I'm overwhelmed.

"Don't mention it."

Does he treat all his hookups this way? Nonetheless, I'm touched.

He lifts his half sandwich.

I do the same.

He taps his sandwich against mine.

I laugh. "I didn't even know that was a thing."

"Stick with me, kiddo, and I'll be sure to cross many firsts off your list while you're here."

You're doing a bang-up job of it.

I bite into my sandwich, and moan.

Sweet baby Jesus.

The medley of flavors hits my taste buds.

Heaven in my mouth.

"This is ridiculous," I say around a bite, pointing at the sandwich.

Gage takes a bite of his. He nods while chewing. "You're right. This is delicious."

"I swear to God, I'm never going back to New York," I say. "I don't understand how Michaela isn't the size of a baby elephant."

Gage chuckles.

"I mean, seriously. She has access to these culinary delights anytime she's at the hotel, which means five times a week she's exposed to endless temptations. I don't know how she does it. The woman has some serious willpower. I'm not that strong. I'd crack under the pressure." I let out a suffering sigh. "My name is Lily Schuyler and I'm a glutton for great food."

He offers a genuine smile that lights up his face.

It's so rare, and I cherish the gift.

I respond with a small smile.

We stare at each other for a long beat.

I'm the first to break eye contact. If I don't, I'll melt—and not because of the heat.

For the next several minutes, we devour our sandwiches in silence.

Gage's eyes are on me.

The unabashed yearning I read in them is unsettling.

I do my best to hold his gaze, but I waver a few times. When I'm courageous enough to stare right back, the intensity emanating from his eyes is dizzying. It makes me feel like I'm the center of his universe.

As usual, my eyes are bigger than my stomach. It's because Gage is too distracting. I can only finish half of my sandwich. Gage on the other hand is blazing right through the food. After finishing two muffaletta sandwiches, his attention moves to the roast beef one.

"Do you want a bite?"

"Sure." I offer my plate.

"Unh-uh. I want you to crawl on your hands and knees."

My eyes widen. "Crawl?"

"Yes."

"Is this a joke?"

"Do I look like I'm joking?"

Nope. Your face is dead serious.

"You want a bite or not?"

This has nothing to do with the food.

"Um…"

My gaze shifts left to right.

People are minding their own business.

What to do?

What to do?

I drop my plate to the side, get on my hands and knees, making sure my skirt isn't in the way, before crawling to him.

"That's it." His eyes flash with something raw. Primal, even. "Crawl to daddy."

Those three little words spoken in his deep voice are so fucking hot.

This guy doesn't hold back. Forget about a hint of sensual teasing, he's dosing me with hedonism.

And fuck do I crave it.

Although I'm submitting to his command, I feel so powerful.

I sit back on my haunches next to him.

"You submit beautifully," he says. "Now, open wide."

I do as I'm told.

He feeds me, his eyes bouncing from my gaze to my mouth.

Holy hell.

This is hot.

Scratch that.

This is five-alarm scorching hot.

We're both dressed and we're in public, but this feels as intimate as when he was rubbing his cock against my clit this morning.

Coming to LA was about scouting film schools. I didn't expect I'd end up with a PhD in naughtiness. Talk about a crash course.

Gage Hollingsworth has a dirty mind and a penchant for debauchery.

Why is this such a turn on?

As I close my mouth around a bite, some of the melted cheese sticks to my chin. I'm about to scoop it up with my finger before it lands on my clothing, when he stops me. He leans into me and licks it off with his tongue.

Oh.

My.

Freaking.

God.

My panties are drenched.

I'm certain the wet spot between my legs is visible.

"You come across as all innocent, but deep down inside, there's an exhibitionist dying to come out and play."

My head jerks back at his bold statement.

"I'm not an exhibitionist."

"Do you think no one noticed you crawling to me?"

"Um..."

"Don't pretend that didn't cross your mind."

Maybe.

"My point exactly," he says. "If you were waiting for someone to corrupt you. Congratulations. You found him."

I open my mouth to retort, but nothing comes out.

With my crotch dripping wet and my legs wobbling from the onslaught of lust coursing through my body, I can only stare, dumbfounded.

"Sit closer." He taps the spot next to him.

Like an obedient girl, I do as I'm told.

"You sure you don't want anything else to eat?"

I shake my head. "No, thanks. I'm leaving room for dessert."

"You can eat your ice cream if you want."

"I'll wait for you."

He takes a bite of the sandwich, and winks.

My heart pitter patters.

How can a wink turn me to mush?

He polishes off half a sandwich in no time. "Ultra Nate's *Free?*" he says, circling back to the song that made me lose my mind earlier. "That's considered old school house music. True, house music will never die. Still, I didn't expect that from you."

"I create a playlist before any new adventure. That way, certain songs will always be linked to the memories of that trip. This new-to-me song is part of my California Love playlist."

"What else is on your playlist?

I rattle off a list of songs—a mixture of styles throughout different decades. "Oh, and a cool remix of *Ain't Nobody*."

"You should listen to the original song by Chaka Khan. Given what I do for a living, I'm all for a kickass remix. That said, sometimes, you have to go straight to the source."

"I'll add it to the list."

"Going back to *Free* and your reaction to the song, if you were free to do what you want to do, what would it be?"

The lyrics of the song are an anthem. I guess that's why it became an instant favorite. "If a fairy godmother granted me a wish, a spot in a prestigious film school wouldn't be my first choice."

"What would it be?"

"This."

His brows crash over his nose.

Chapter 24

Gage

Lily's fingers close around the pendant of the necklace she's wearing.

"You're a jewelry designer?"

"A closeted one."

So, it's not a guy or her douchebag ex who gave it to her. "Can I see?"

She lowers her hand.

I reach for it, turning the pendant around, examining it from different angles. I let it drop against her chest and trail a finger along the chain.

"This is well made," I say.

"Thank you." Shy Lily is back.

"Is it silver or white gold?"

"Neither, it's stainless steel."

"Why stainless steel?"

"Unlike silver, it doesn't tarnish, and unlike gold, it's affordable."

"You had it made? I assume it's not handmade."

"I outsourced the production. Italy and Spain are both top

exporters of stainless steel. However, manpower in Spain is much cheaper, and the Spaniards rival the Italians when it comes to master jewelers. Since I was living in Paris, traveling back and forth between the two countries was easy."

"Smart."

"I had two prototypes produced—one for me and one for my best friend for her twentieth birthday. We're the same age, but she was born four months before me. Nadine loved it. She insisted there was a successful business waiting to emerge from my creative concept. That gave me wings. The first design was plain. But I graduated to something with a little more bling—cubic zirconia surrounding the pendant. I was thrilled with the end result, but I wanted something that had more presence. I upped the ante by opting for Swarovski crystals."

"You're talented. I'm impressed."

"Thank you."

"Is Nadine your business partner?"

"No, she isn't. This is a solo venture."

This woman has more layers than I expected. She's interesting, gorgeous, smart, and far more daring than she gives herself credit for. There's also a sweet vulnerability to her that's so darn attractive.

"How did you and Nadine meet?"

"We met in boarding school in Switzerland. We shared a room with four other girls, but we fast became friends. She's a brunette to my jet-black hair. She stands three inches taller than me. I hate her for that." She laughs.

"So, your best friend's dad is France's former President Laurent Rocard de Villepin. That's wild."

She nods.

"Since she's half American, will she come and join you in the States?"

"No. Nads is too Parisian to ever leave Paris. Not to mention, she earned her right to stay in Paris the hard way."

"What do you mean?"

"For years the French referred to her mom, Marciana, as a modern-day Monica Lewinsky. The French don't tend to bat an eyelash when a husband or wife stray. Nads's father not only lied about having sexual relationships with an intern from the French PR company that oversaw the publicity for the charitable campaign his wife chaired, but said intern was an American. Three months after the scandal broke, a whistle-blower leaked she was pregnant to the French press, and then, outed him to a US newspaper for a big pay day. *Le President* claimed he didn't have any sexual relations with that woman. In fact, they never crossed paths. But his penis crossed paths with Nads's mom's vagina."

"Good one."

"Marciana's parting gift from that internship wasn't only a stained dress soiled with *le President*'s semen, it was also a bun in the oven. She never left France, dead-set in her determination to force *le President* to acknowledge her and her baby. She found a job with an American company with an office in Paris who was willing to sponsor her work visa. That opportunity allowed her to give birth in France. Five years later, she got her French residency. It took twenty years for the former President Laurent Rocard de Villepin to acknowledge his illegitimate daughter."

"Nadine's mom weathered that scandal like a champ," I say.

"She did. It took courage."

"What does Nadine do for a living?"

"She owns a flower shop in Paris called Blue Belle—it's a tiny shop with a pretty blue façade. It used to be called *La Boîte Fleurit,* but she changed the name when she inherited it. She'd been working there since she was sixteen. The owner didn't have children, and none of her nieces or nephews were interested in the business. Or the hours. Nads gets up at the crack of dawn Monday to Saturday to make it to the flower markets. Between her shop's colorful exterior, the evocative name, and the old school jazz music playing nonstop in the background, she's managed to create a timeless atmosphere in her shop that keeps her clients coming back. In the last year or so, since her father has recognized her as his daughter, he's used his connections to further her business. Blue Belle is now the go-to florist for many high-ranking French politicians."

"Good for her for making her mark instead of trying to shine in her father's shadow."

"I agree."

"Does your father know?" I point to her necklace.

Her hands fly to her neck to cover it. "No, he doesn't know I'm a jewelry designer."

"How do you manage to keep that a secret?"

"I pay cash," she says. "I never use up my monthly food allowance, so I squirrel away what I don't spend. That way, I don't leave any traces. He would disapprove of my project and belittle it." She wrinkles her nose. "The list of cons he has for me is long enough."

It pisses me off to hear her say that. Her idiot father should support her dreams instead of squashing them. Or worse, forcing her into a sentence of misery.

"Who's on the pendant?"

"This is an old French coin—the one Franc. The figure is Marianne. She's been the national personification of the French Republic since the French Revolution. She stands for liberty, equality, fraternity, and reason. She's also the portrayal of the Goddess of Liberty—"

"The one Statue of Liberty was modeled after Libertas—the Roman goddess of freedom."

She nods. "Yes."

"Again, the freedom theme—same as the song."

"Indeed," she says.

"How did you come up with the idea? French francs were replaced with Euros a long time ago, I can't imagine it's easy to find coins."

"I found an artist in Paris who does replicas of old franc coins. I was able to strike a deal with him because I would be buying them in multiples. I figured I had plenty of time to source something on a grander scale for when the project took off."

"Smart," I say. "What prompted the idea?"

"Mama's memory pushed me forward with this project."

"In what sense?"

"She struggled to make ends meet. She never sugarcoated our reality. We could only afford the basics. Sometimes, we'd have hotdogs for dinner for weeks on end. And I'm not talking about name brands. I'm talking about a generic brand of sausage sliced in half and wedged between one slice of white bread—whatever was on sale. The mustard and ketchup were packets from McDonald's. Mom would stuff her pockets with condiments and sugar when she stopped by for her weekly cup of coffee—one of the only luxuries she allowed herself. Watching QVC was her escape. She could shop to her heart's content, without spending a dime. She always commented on everything that flashed on the screen. Jewelry was her favorite. Especially the lines from celebrities who would create affordable versions of the pricey counterparts they wore in real life—"

"Or what they want the public to believe they wear in real life."

She works her lower lip. "I'm sure you're right."

"It's a great tribute to your mom."

"That was my goal," she says. "Although, I no longer live in a tiny, crappy, bordering on dilapidated apartment with rickety furniture in Escambia County, Alabama, and I get a colossal monthly allowance, none of it is mine. It's my father's. And he never misses a chance to remind me he holds the purse strings. As long as I toe the line and don't cause waves, my account is replenished on the first of each month, like clockwork." She averts her gaze.

I don't rush her.

"I guess in many ways, I'm still that little girl, sitting on a beat-up couch, next to Mama, watching QVC, and listening to her shopping advice." She returns her attention to me. "This"—she touches the pendant—"is the type of jewelry Mama would go crazy for. Especially because of the French connection—a country she would never have been able to afford to visit. We were too poor to afford a motel in a nearby state, let alone get on an airplane. I can hear her now, *'Lily, darlin', that fine piece of jewelry right there would be worth the monthly payments'.*" She laughs, but it's devoid of lightness.

The weight of her revelation stretches between us like the English toffee sauce Mom used to make at Christmas, pulling and clinging.

"Can I ask a personal question?"

She takes in a deep breath, and exhales on the word, "Sure."

"If Fisher never acknowledged you, how did you come to live with him?"

"I've never lived with my father. I still don't."

I level her with a quizzical stare.

"We've never lived under the same roof," she says.

I frown my confusion. "How is that even possible?"

"After Mama's passing, I lived in my father's Connecticut house."

"Alone?"

She shakes her head. "The house was fully staffed with a cook, a house cleaner, and a butler. Since it was too late for him to register me in a new school, my father hired a full-time governess of a sort to look over me and tutor me."

I incline my head, as if trying to discern if my ears are playing tricks on me.

She nods, answering my silent question. "You can't make that shit up."

"I suppose not." *Wow.* "How did you communicate?"

"Phone. Emails. Texts. Video chats."

"Who came for you after your mom's death?"

"Henry, the butler with the Australian accent."

"Fisher doesn't have siblings?" I've never cared to find out.

"He has two sisters and a brother. All younger."

"You don't know your aunts and uncle?"

"I know them as much as I know my half-brothers."

The most over-the-top soap opera doesn't measure up to this unbelievable story.

"The following school year, I was shipped to Switzerland," she says. "Once I graduated from boarding school, I moved to Paris to attend university. My father has an apartment in Paris, but he bought me another one because God forbid, we'd share a roof. Someone might learn of his dirty little secret and that would be so, so bad. Now, I live in New York, in a house my father bought me on the Upper East Side. He lives on the Upper West Side—the opposite side of Manhattan Island."

I'm incredulous.

"Fisher Edgington has gone out of his way to pretend I don't exist," she says. "He's done such a smashing job of it, he forgot my twenty-first birthday. He hasn't been keeping score of the milestones in my life—unlike my half-brothers. He's so obsessed with his sons, he knows how many times a day they burp." The statement is coated with bitterness.

"How did Fisher meet your mom? They're from different worlds."

"A few months after turning eighteen, armed with a high-school degree, Mama moved to Florida with her older sister. They set their sights on Miami. They figured working at a five-star hotel—even if it was as room service staff—was the closest they'd get to living a glamorous life."

"Your father was a guest at the hotel?"

"Yes. He was in Miami for an extended three-month business trip. He spotted Mom and he had to have her. My mother fell for him, not knowing he was married because he never told her and he wasn't wearing a wedding ring—there wasn't even a tan line."

Asshole cheater.

"It's only when she got pregnant, and told my father, she found out he was married and had another family in New York. She was devastated. He made promises to help her out financially, but made it clear, they'd never be together. Mama moved back home because Miami was too expensive for a single mom with insignificant job experience. Her sister stayed behind, because she was dating this guy and things were getting serious. Soon after returning to Alabama, Mama got another surprise after her first doctor's appointment. She was pregnant with twins—"

"You have a sister or a brother?"

"I *had*."

Past tense. "I'm sorry."

"I don't remember my sister. She died when we were five months old. She suffered from a birth defect. Identical twins get hit with the same health issues since we share the same DNA, but in this case, I was spared."

Jesus. "Where was your father in all of this?"

"He was in the picture until Mama announced she was carrying twins. It became a little too real and a little too overwhelming—he stopped coming down to visit her in Alabama."

"Your father never sent money?"

"He did for a while, but that dried up at some point."

"Was he aware of your mom's dire situation? After all, he knew she was a young single mom."

"He didn't care if I went to school on an empty stomach most days, or if Mom had bought my clothes from thrift stores because Walmart was too expensive, or if the landlord would look at me like I was a slice of chocolate cake when he'd come knock on our door, demanding the rent money that was always late. Nope. Those were none of my father's concerns."

Although not a billionaire, Fisher is extremely rich. He wouldn't have struggled financially. Why not step up to the plate?

Fucking deadbeat dad.

"At least your father manned up after your mother passed away."

She sneers. "Mama didn't leave him a choice."

"How come?"

"Mama didn't date for most of my life. Around the time I was about to turn twelve, she met this guy. He was good to her and to me. I was excited at the prospect of having a father figure. He wanted to rewrite Mama's story. On their one-year anniversary of dating, he planned a trip to Miami. I stayed behind with Mama's best friend and her kids. I remember waving them off before they hit the road. Then, a few days later, Mama's best friend is telling me Mama would never come back... because she was in Heaven." Her voice breaks. "Mom and her boyfriend died in an accident on their way back home."

I place a hand over hers. "If it hurts too much, you don't have to continue."

She offers a sad smile. "That's sweet of you to say, but it's only a wave of melancholy. It happens when I recount my story."

Been there. Done that.

I tuck a strand of long hair behind her ear. "Only if you're sure."

She nods.

"Okay," I say.

"A couple weeks after Mama's passing, her best friend announced I'd be moving to New York to live with my father. I assumed I'd be staying with her. I knew nothing about legal matters surrounding a parent's death and what that meant to the child."

"You had to deal with the death of your mother and a man who was going to step in as a father figure. On top of that, you found out you had to leave Alabama to live with a father you didn't know. That's a lot for a kid to handle."

"It was." She nods. "I asked Mama's best friend why I couldn't stay with her. She told me Mama made sure I'd be taken care of if anything were to happen to her. My grandfather was never in the picture and my grandma had passed away when I was a kid."

"What about your mom's older sister?"

"The boyfriend she stayed behind for in Miami turned out to have a side hustle for a drug lord. It's not clear what he did to piss off the kingpin, but he ended up with a bullet between his eyes. My aunt suffered the same fate."

My eyes widen in shock.

"Yeah, it's pretty gruesome," she says. "Mama made sure I had an insurance policy—one my father couldn't dispute."

"How did she manage that?"

"My aunt was ordinary looking, but Mom was incredibly pretty when she was young—"

"The apple doesn't fall far from the tree."

Lily blushes. "Thank you."

"Sorry I interrupted you."

"That's okay. Even after he fessed up about being married, my father couldn't stay away. He was taken with her. Mama wised up real fast. She pulled a soap opera stunt."

"A what?"

"DNA testing. She stole his toothbrush, hairbrush... and even underwear."

I whistle. "She wasn't leaving anything to chance."

"She took things one step further."

"Blood samples?"

She laughs a little. "She took photos of my father sleeping when they were together in bed. She kept the incriminating details in a small suitcase. When she died, her best friend knew what to do. Tracking down my father wasn't that complicated, given his status. A couple weeks after Mom passed away, Henry, the butler, came to take me to New York."

"Jesus, you didn't even know the guy."

"I didn't know my father either at the time. I had never met him. I only knew of him. In fact, I thought Henry was my father until he corrected me."

I shake my head. *Unbelievable.*

"We flew together to Connecticut—my first time on a plane." She continues. "I went from slumming it in a tiny apartment to living in a big, luxurious house similar to the ones I'd only seen on TV."

"Your father wasn't there to greet you?" She said as much, but I can't get over it.

"It took three months before my father came to visit." She lets out a breath, audible and sad. "He needed time to set things in motion so he could ship me to Switzerland, undetected. That ninja move didn't prevent his wife from finding out about me."

"One of your father's staff members blew the whistle?"

"I assume."

"Unless it was your mom's best friend."

"She swore it wasn't her."

I nod. "After the way Fisher has treated you, I don't understand why you're willing to go along with his idea of having you run a PR company you're obviously not interested in."

"My father pushes my half-brothers to play their part in furthering the Edgington name and fortune—"

"But you don't even have his last name."

She averts her gaze for a beat. "To this day, he still blames me for losing a significant chunk of his fortune in the divorce. Going along with his master plan is my way of making up for his loss."

Un-fucking-believable.

My jaw tightens to the point my teeth are about to shatter.

Everything about her story flares the protector in me.

"Jesus Christ, Lily, did you even hear what you said?" I don't give her time to answer. I'm irate on her behalf. "You're willing to suffer through a career to gain your father's acceptance? If he's not able to appreciate the woman you've become, fuck him."

She shouldn't be bending over backwards for the approval of a man who treats her with such disrespect. Regardless of the DNA connection.

"It's easy to say when you have both parents."

If you only knew, sweetheart.

"If I turn my back on my father and half-brothers, I'm essentially..."—her small hands twist in her lap—"an orphan."

"Your father and half-brothers don't acknowledge you and they don't respect you," I say. "Not to burst your bubble, but I lost both my parents."

Her surprise is broadcast upon her face.

"So, my siblings and I are orphans."

"I'm sorry." Guilt morphs her beautiful features.

I brush it off. "You didn't know."

"Did you lose them at a young age?"

"I lost my dad when I was eight—"

"You were only a boy."

"I was," I nod. "He died of a heart attack. I didn't understand much about death. All I knew was Dad would no longer be sitting at the dinner table with us, help me with my homework, or doing father and son things together. He was gone."

She places her hand against her heart.

I continue. "My father was twenty-seven years older than Mom. In fact, he was my grandfather's best friend."

Lily's eyes radiate with shock. "Oh, wow."

"Your mom's story and mine have parallels," I say. "Mom was in an unhealthy relationship for years until her loser of a boyfriend walked out on her for good, leaving her with a mountain of common-law debt. She had no choice but to move back with her parents with her two daughters. Dad always claimed he fell for Mom before she got involved with her asshole ex, but since he was much older and her father's best friend, he stayed away. When she returned home, he didn't miss out on his second chance. He played his cards right. He offered Mom a job at his construction company. Working together allowed them to get close. Soon, Mom was dating the boss. A year later, he proposed. I was born eighteen months after their wedding."

"What a story," she says. "You have two half-sisters?"

I nod. "And an adopted sister. She's also older. My half-sisters head a couple of my European offices. Lana is forty-four. She used to work for a leading TV network. She's posted in London, and oversees the London, Paris, Milan, and Madrid offices. Marika is forty-two. She's a former content director for MTV in LA and New York. She now oversees the Copenhagen, Amsterdam, and Berlin offices. She lives in Copenhagen. My adopted sister Sara is thirty-eight. She's whip smart, which is why she's a doctor. She's an anesthesiologist, who recently got promoted as a chief physician at Cedars-Sinai Medical Center here in LA. All three are married. Lana and Marika have kids. Sara is trying."

"From the sound of it, you get along with your sisters," Lily says.

"I do. I love them. Mom always joked that when I was a baby, I was *their* baby, not hers. They never allowed my tiny body to touch the floor. They would carry me around like a doll. They spoiled me rotten."

Lily laughs.

"I understand your half-brothers would resent your arrival," I say. "Eight years later, you're all adults. It's surely time to bury the hatchet."

She rolls her eyes. "I'm not holding my breath."

Which begs the question, why are you trying so hard?

"Did your mom also pass away from an illness?" Lily says, changing the subject.

I rub the back of my neck.

I knew the question was coming. It's a natural progression. It still doesn't prevent the familiar pang of guilt that hits me whenever I think of Mom.

"No, she didn't." I keep my answer brief.

Lily's expression suggests she's waiting for me to elaborate.

The topic of my mom's death is off the table.

She shifts on the blanket.

Her cheeks are flushed. No doubt she's embarrassed by my stoic reaction.

"I'm sure your mom is looking down at you from Heaven and she's proud of the man you've become."

"Right back at you," I say. "I'm sure your mom is beaming with pride at the woman you've become."

She moves her eyes to a spot over my shoulder. "Thank you for saying that."

"I'm not bullshitting you." I take hold of her chin, forcing her attention to me. "You're an incredible woman. Don't let the way Fisher and your half-brothers treat you dictate your self-worth. Don't give them that kind of power."

She shrugs. "It's hard to do."

"The more you do it, the easier it will become."

I lean forward and drop a soft kiss on her lips.

The gesture surprises me. I don't date anymore, so I'm never in a position to demonstrate PDA. Even when I dated, that was never my MO.

"You, mister, are a real Jekyll and Hyde," Lily says.

I humor her. "In what sense?"

"One minute, you're demanding as fuck. The next, you're so tender."

"Keeping you on your toes." I wink.

She shakes her head. "Tell me about StreamTunes? I could do a search, but it's more fun hearing it from the mastermind."

"Those who can't sing or play instruments, DJ. I took it one step further by launching a successful streaming service. The end."

Lily laughs.

Her lightheartedness is contagious.

"Talk about giving someone the Cliffs notes to your life story," she says, still laughing. "It took me forever to give you snippets of my life, and you summarized your existence in three clipped sentences. Sheesh. Way to go to make me feel like I suffer from verbal diarrhea."

"Is that your way of saying you want more?"

"I do."

"Sheesh." I borrow her word. "Tough crowd." I chuckle. "I wanted to be a rock star. That was instant bad ass factor and guaranteed chick magnet. Cliché, I know."

She giggles. "I doubt getting girls was ever a problem."

"I had my awkward years."

"That's a blatant lie. You?" She waves a finger up and down my body. "No way. I'm sure you were born with swagger."

"Thanks for the vote of confidence, but the swagger came much later."

"Do tell." She wiggles her ass on the blanket, getting in a more comfortable position.

"Unlike pretty boy Beckett—"

"Is that his nickname?"

"That's what we call him," I say. "You have to admit, it suits him to a T."

"Not that I want to badmouth him, because I like Beckett, but you're right. It's the perfect nickname."

"There you go." I wink. "Pretty boy Beckett is a natural born singer. I can't carry a tune to save my life. After many hours of practice and too much money thrown out the window in the form of lessons, I had to come to the conclusion, I wasn't much of a musician either. So, I decided to focus my energy on my hobbies, creating music playlists and tinkering with computer codes—"

"Creating music playlists? We share something in common."

"We do."

"Sorry, you were saying."

"During my senior year, I became obsessed with this new girl who transferred to our school. I overheard the blonde complain that her boyfriend spent too much time gaming. I wasn't much better, but her boyfriend didn't know it bothered her. I did. I also overheard her lament to her friends about inequalities in the gaming world. *There should be cool computer games for girls who didn't want to play bang 'em and shoot 'em down or sports games.* This girl was totally out of my league—pretty, rich, and unattainable. She even had a rich girl name—Blair Elizabeth Marie Collins. None of that stopped me from trying to catch her attention. I went home determined to win her over. For hours after I was done with my homework, I would tinker around with codes until I created a game I thought girls would love."

"What did you end up with?"

"RodeoDoll."

"What's that?"

"Mom's favorite movie was *Pretty Woman*. She must've watched that movie a thousand times. She always said every girl dreams of meeting a man who tells her she can shop to her heart's content on his dime. So that's what I did."

"You sent Blair on a shopping spree on Rodeo Drive?"

"I created a virtual experience."

"Oh."

"Hours of hard work paid off. I was so proud of myself when I created an online game that would answer her prayers. RodeoDoll allowed you to create your own doll avatar based on a photo you uploaded on the app or you could create a fantasy version of yourself, go virtual shopping in the most luxurious shopping areas around the world, dress up, decorate your deluxe virtual suite located in one of the best ZIP codes, and socialize with other like-minded fellow players. Basically, with RodeoDoll you could live large without the sticker shock."

"That's so cool."

I shrug. "I thought so."

Lily frowns. "Blair didn't like RodeoDoll?"

"I didn't have what it takes to get the girl."

"What do you mean?"

"I've always been tall, but awkward—my long legs were always in the way. I also had a bad experience with an overzealous coach who constantly pushed me so hard, I'd end up puking my guts out at football practice. That only made me the target of ridicule. My teammates didn't spare me. So, sports and I were distant cousins. On top of that, my social skills weren't sophisticated—some might say they still aren't. All that to say, the prissy princess lifted her nose at my game, and chose the mayor's son instead, who happened to be a star quarterback. To make matters worse, Blair didn't turn me down in private. She did it in the middle of the cafeteria during lunch."

"That's cruel."

"Yeah, my ego was crushed. I was certain I wouldn't survive, and if I did, I knew I wouldn't recover. I had nothing to offer compared to a rich, star quarterback."

"But you did. Her boyfriend ignored her. You listened and you created a video game for her." Lily shakes her head. "Blair was severely misguided."

"True, but revenge is so sweet."

"How so?"

"Blair turned her nose up at a game that came to be loved by hundreds of millions of users."

"Note to self, don't piss off Gage."

"Damn right."

"Details. I want details."

I'm happy to oblige. "Out of spite, I kept perfecting the codes. Eventually, I made the game public. I had invested so much time and sweat equity in it. Why not allow others to enjoy it? Given Blair's reaction, I didn't expect much. To my surprise, it became a hit, real fast. My half-sisters who were working in showbusiness at the time, connected me with the right people who helped me with trademarks and other legalese. I ended up forming a corporation at the tender age of eighteen, with my sisters and my mom as board members."

"So gifted at such a young age."

"I had the skills, but I owe the women in my life for believing in me. They were convinced I had something big on my hands. I decided to ride the wave. Lo and behold, a few years later, Mattel approached me, wanting to buy me out. We're talking about a life-changing offer. I took the money and moved on. I was twenty years old, and I was rich. My sisters and Mom benefitted handsomely as well. With my pockets lined with money, I set my sight on a new challenge."

"Your streaming music service?"

"No. DJing."

"Why DJing?"

"I wanted to travel the world, but I didn't want to rough it like a bohemian, and I didn't want to use all the money I earned from the sale of RodeoDoll. I learned from one of the best DJs in Los Angeles. Little by little, I was getting booked. I made a name for myself and became one of the most in demand DJs in LA and Vegas. When the international bookings poured in, I packed my bags and I was off traveling the world."

"Do DJs get paid well?"

"It was good money," I say, "but the perks were the wow factor."

"What kind of perks?"

"The most epic parties and the privilege of rubbing elbows with celebrities."

"Sweet."

"Although I was only spinning records in the club scene, I

was viewed as a rock star. I even had a Swedish heiress commission me to DJ her wedding to a Finnish billionaire—two dynasties merging as one. Not only did she fly me on a private jet, but she paid me a fortune for the wedding night reception and two nights of post-wedding parties, on top of putting me up in the most luxurious Stockholm hotel. It was wild."

"I feel a but coming."

I wink. "*But,* I was constantly jetlagged. Since I never stopped coding, I combined my love for music and my computer skills together to establish myself as a leader in the music streaming business. The concept behind StreamCloud was a natural progression. I poured my heart and soul into the project—much like I had with RodeoDoll. In no time it became the world's largest online community of artists, bands, DJs, and audio creators. In the process, it also became the number one platform to stream and listen to music online for free. It's still ads-free. With StreamTunes overshadowing it and competitors entering the market, it's no longer a leader in terms of platforms built for new artist discoverability, but it made its mark."

"I didn't know that belonged to you."

"It does. That's how I cut my teeth. StreamCloud acted as a springboard to StreamTunes."

"That explains why you're the brooding, grumpy type—I mean, so serious all the time—there are too many computer codes colliding in your head."

I stifle a chuckle.

"Watch it, little girl."

She laughs her head off.

Her exuberance is contagious—almost enough to thaw my frozen heart. Almost.

"The reason I'm a freaking ray of sunshine all the time"—the sarcasm is unmistakable in my voice"—is because everyone wants a piece of me."

Her expression turns somber. "Michaela alluded to that."

I'm not surprised.

I'm enjoying my time with her, I don't want to bring the mood down by talking shop.

"Going back to your assessment of my personality, I have a team of pro coders, so I don't touch that side of the business anymore. My job is to show up at the office in a suit and tie, and strike deals."

She shoots me a dubious glance. "I doubt it's that easy."

I let out a self-deprecating laugh. "You're right, it's not."

"But, you're a king among kings, so you must be doing something right," she says. "My father began his career as a low-level insurance salesman with a high-school degree and worked his way up to become a Wall Street Wolf and earning a part-time MBA. He bought out the company he was working for when the owner—who never got married and didn't have kids—was ready to retire. Sure, he's grown the company, but he took it over. He didn't build it from the ground up."

The way Fisher spins his tales, you'd think he was born with a silver spoon in his mouth and he had an Ivy League education. Shyster.

"Speaking of which, how did you find the money to fund StreamCloud? You have mad coding skills, but what about servers and such? Storing all of those songs can't be cheap."

With a cocked eyebrow, I study her.

She cringes. "Was that a dumb question?"

I shake my head. "Not at all. That was a smart one. Most people never ask the question, although servers are the lifeline of any streaming company."

She blushes.

"Allow me to repeat myself. You underestimate yourself, angel."

The rosiness coloring her cheeks deepens.

I cut her some slack. "I met pretty boy Beckett and the rest of Random Misconception when their record company hired me to DJ one of their parties."

"At Rhys's party, Cesar explained Beckett, his older brother Holt, their cousin Jace Halsey, and Hall of Famer drummer Rod Wolfe, aka Dom's baby daddy, were once rock gods."

Rod Wolfe is a soon-to-be father. What has the world come to?

Of all the guys in my inner circle, I was certain he would be the last one to cave in.

Like Mom always said, *"When you find the right person, it's because you were fated. The love gods rearranged the sky so you could be in the right place, at the right time, in the right situation—aka, you're both single. You owe it to yourself to grab that person by the hand and never, ever let go."* She held on to that belief decades after my dad passed away. Until a snake oil salesman came into her life and pretended to love her.

I stare at Lily a little too long.

I shake my head, breaking the spell I'm under.

Where were we?

Oh yeah.

"Random Misconception was on top of the world, so it made sense for them to party *on top of the world.*"

Lily furrows her brows. "Which means?"

"Mom was moonlighting as my booking agent and doing a fine job of it. I was in Bali when she sent me an email to let me know she had received a request for a gig at CÉ LA VI Marina Bay Sands in Singapore for VIP clients—"

"Oh, that's supposed to be an amazing party spot."

"You know of the place?"

"Nads and I have it on our bucket list after we saw the photos of a celebrity we follow on social media. We launched into a furious online search because we were certain the photos were Photoshopped."

"That's how I felt when I saw the photos."

"For good measure, we checked out videos of the venue. No Photoshop required."

"I had the same reaction. Still, I wasn't prepared. When I got there, I couldn't believe my eyes. Or my luck."

"Wow." She says that with stars in her eyes.

Why do I have the urge to make it my mission in life to take her there?

"CÉ LA VI is an open-air restaurant perched on the 57th floor of Marina Bay Sands with one of the most jaw-dropping panoramic views of the city skyline and Singapore," I say. "It's mind-blowing—the best rooftop bars on the planet."

"I believe you."

"As if the setting wasn't over the top, when I found out who the VIP clients were, I almost lost my shit."

"I hear you." Lily points a finger over her head. "That was me yesterday, when I met Keira Knightley. She's a huge star."

Never mind the rest of the star power at Rhys's birthday party.

"Multiply the starstruck effect by four. It was the equivalent of DJing from heaven for gods," I say. "It's was an unforgettable experience. After that, Random Misconception requested I DJ several of their parties and even some personal and family events. That's how we became close. When I needed funding for StreamCloud, my sisters helped me put together a kickass business plan, and I presented it to them. I had money, but not enough. The guys jumped onboard. I thought it was going to be a much harder sell, but I guess it's true what they say. Timing is everything. I had a project that had legs, and these guys' pockets were weighed down with money. It was a match made in heaven. When I wanted to take things to a grander scale with StreamTunes, they didn't even bat an eyelash."

"It must be amazing to have people who root for you."

I stroke her cheek with the back of my hand. "You have those people in your life, angel. Your best friend Nadine, your self-appointed big sister Michaela, and yours truly."

She responds with a shy smile. "So, you're the guy responsible for turning rock stars into billionaires?" She veers the conversation away from her.

I see what she's doing, but I let it slide. "Beckett is a self-made multibillionaire thanks to his partnership with Rhys. His shares in StreamTunes only served to make him obscenely rich. As for Rod, Holt, and Jace, you could say that. Jace's older brother Jagger also invested. Same for Lochlan Berkshire—Rod's business partner, the band's former roadie, and Jace and Jagger's cousin. So did Levi Aldridge, another buddy in the music industry. Their belief in my vision not only ensured my rapid success, it made them paper billionaires in record time. When the valuation of my company hit twenty billion dollars a couple years ago, I purchased their shares, making them bona fide billionaires. Without those guys and the blind faith they had in me, I wouldn't be where I am today."

"The moral of the story is, *not* getting the girl was the prize," she says. "Blair must be slapping herself upside the head. Unless she ended up marrying a prize winner. Who knows? Her husband might hold the Guinness World Record for the most eggs smashed on your head in one minute while yodeling. Sure, you make it in the history books, but it's not as sexy as being crowned a billionaire mogul. Don't get me wrong, an honorable mention is an honorable mention. However, I doubt it affords you the luxury of riding in style. A chauffeured Rolls Royce Phantom, a Wiesmann GT MF4, and God knows how many other pricey vehicles? Take that, Bitch Blair!"

I bark out a laugh, my whole body shaking.

My laughter is so boisterous, I'm aware of people glancing our way.

When I regain my composure, Lily is staring at me, almost in awe.

"What?"

"Can I make a confession?"

"Shoot."

"You're fucking sexy when you laugh."

The fact she swears when she says that, is such a turn on.

I'm fucking hard.

I'm on my feet. My need to corrupt her consumes me.

"Let's go back to the hotel." My voice is gravelly.

Her head jerks back. "But what about the ice cream?"

I extend a hand. "I intend on spreading it all over your heavenly body and licking every inch of you."

Taking my hand into hers, she shoots to her feet. "Time to go."

Not so innocent Lily.

My cock swells up even harder.

Chapter 25

Lily

For the umpteenth time, my attention drifts to Gage's lap and the growing bulge between his legs. I shift in my seat once more in an attempt to tame my pulsating clit.

It's not working.

My aroused state is preventing me from focusing on anything other than what's happening between Gage's legs.

He adjusts himself with a rough tug.

That thing is so big, it threatens to rip the zipper of his jeans.

I will myself to focus on something other than his cock, but it's not easy.

Who is this horny, insatiable woman?

I was a little bummed out when Gage cut our time short because it's such a perfect day, and I was enjoying getting to know him better, but the promise of misbehaving is too tantalizing to say no to.

Fuck the ice cream.

Fuck the sunshine.

Fuck the beautiful blue sea.

Let's get down and dirty.

Almost as if pulled by a magnet, my eyes shift to his bulge once again.

Holy erection.

"You can't wait to ride this," he says, groping his groin.

The hint of promised debauchery is strong in the air. I can practically taste it.

I bite my lower lip, squirming in my seat.

"You dirty girl. I've created a monster."

It's not like I'm going to deny it.

"I bet you're wet."

That would be a yes.

"Lift your skirt up so I can see your pretty pussy."

I do a double take. "You want me to do what?"

"I don't believe I stuttered, Lily."

For a few seconds, I'm so stunned, I don't know what to do.

"You either follow my command, or the only thing you're going to get when we get back to your hotel is ice cream. No cock. The decision is yours."

He made the decision for me with that ultimatum.

Yesterday, I would've selected ice cream over a cock. Then again, I only had my sexy times with Jean-Philippe as comparison. Now that I'm wiser, cock trumps. Specifically, Gage's.

I obey.

I grab the hem of my skirt and pull it up above my knees. My eyes shift to my right, and I worry my lower lip.

That car is mighty close.

Granted, the driver is focused on the traffic lights, but that doesn't mean he wouldn't be able to catch a glimpse of the dirty action happening in Gage's car.

"You're assessing if he can see you?"

Gage read my thoughts.

"Yes."

"It's highly unlikely at his eye-level."

I let out a sigh of relief.

"The driver of an SUV or truck on the other hand, would get a show."

My heart races.

Freaked out, I pull down my hem.

"Did I say you could do that?"

I stare at him.

"We're not too far from the hotel," I say, my voice pleading.

"I know that, but I want to see your pretty pussy right the fuck now."

He must have some magical powers because I pull my hem back up.

"Better," he says. "I want to know how wet you are."

My panicked eyes fly up to meet his calculating ones.

He's waiting.

"I punish bad girls who don't obey, but reward good girls who do what they're told."

His dirty promise ignites my whole body.

Still, my mind is a jumbled mess.

A voice inside my head is screaming at me. *"Don't do it, girl."* Another voice screams even louder. *"Pick the reward. Pick the damn reward."*

"Well?"

"Well, what?"

He sighs. "I want to know how wet you are."

"How am I supposed to do that?" My voice is quivering.

"You figure it out. You're a smart, intelligent woman."

Thanks for being a lifeline, buddy. Not.

My eyes swing to the right.

A handsome biracial black man in a convertible sportscar, wearing a white shirt, cuffed at the elbows, that showcases his bulging arms, bobs his head to the sound of music. His eyes swing my way and he flashes me dazzling white teeth.

I'm a little too freaked out to respond in kind.

He frowns, as if I've offended him.

Social graces kick in, and I pull my lips in an exaggerated smile, my eyes widening to the size of dinner plates. I'm sure I look like a loon.

He nods and gives me a salute.

My creepy smile widens further.

He leans forward and increases the volume to his music and resumes bobbing his head. His focus is no longer on me.

The lights change, and the man pumps the gas and speeds forward.

We follow right behind him.

My eyes are still trained to my right, so I'm unprepared when Gage's hand yanks my skirt higher up.

I yelp.

He slides a hand up my inner thigh and under my panties before his fingers plunge inside my dripping pussy.

I gasp.

His fingers skate over my clit.

My head falls back against the headrest, my eyes closing, my thighs quaking on either side of his intruding hand. My heart is beating so hard against my chest, I swear it's about to jump out of my rib cage and sprint down the streets of Los Angeles. If that wasn't an overwhelming concern, I'd be able to appreciate the seat's buttery soft leather beneath my ass.

"I want your eyes on me."

Gage's deep voice causes my eyes to pop open.

I meet green eyes the color of translucent sea glass and lose all the breath in me.

That intense gaze locks me in, making it impossible for me to avert my gaze.

He brings his fingers to his lips and licks off my juices.

Oh.

My.

God.

If I needed a visual representation of the word naughty, that was it.

Heat pounds between my legs, and my nipples strain against the fabric of my bra. I'm so turned on, I don't know what to do with myself.

"Since I need to keep my focus on the road, I want you to play with your pussy."

Huh?

My head is still spinning from his bold declaration, it takes me several breaths for his request to hit me full force.

Is there no end to this man's twisted mind?

"Didn't you hear what I said?"

I heard you, but this is way, way out of my comfort zone.

When his request fully sinks in, I have a big decision to make.

Am I daring enough?

He reaches out and tugs my skirt down, concealing my pussy, and covering my naked thighs. "You're not as exposed. This way, no one but us will know what you're doing. It's our little secret."

I still hesitate.

Gage's gaze moves over me, scorching a blazing path along my skin.

"If you don't play with your pussy, neither will I."

The axe falls.

That does it.

As if I'm under his spell, one hand moves to my inner thigh, caressing the skin with tentative fingertips.

"That's it."

Fueled by Gage's approval, my hand glides higher, until my fingers slide underneath my wet panties.

He lets out a feral grunt, his hand squeezing his bulge.

"You touching yourself will become my go to material in my spank bank. I'll jerk off, remembering how you pleasured yourself in front of me."

I pant.

This shouldn't feel this good.

I should be appalled. Insulted, even. Firecrackers shouldn't be going off inside me.

"Make it dirty for me."

Isn't this debauched enough?

"Take it up by ten notches," he says.

I can't believe I'm willingly doing unspeakable things in public.

I imagine Gage's long fingers, his wicked tongue, or the fat head of his cock, stroking my hard clit.

Mother of God.

My fingers are a little rougher than usual.

"I love when you use your cock to play with my clit." The confession drops from my lips without my permission.

"You and me both."

I stroke faster, relishing each revolution around my pulsating clit.

Gage stops at a red light.

I glance in the direction of the car stopped to my right.

Oh shit.

That alone should prompt me to put an end to this insanity, but on the contrary. It jacks things up.

Gage Hollingsworth is transforming me into a woman I don't even recognize.

With my free hand, I pull back my skirt, so he can see my fingers working my pussy.

A growl reverberates from him. "And I didn't even have to ask."

I can't help my smile.

"You come off all sweet and innocent, but that's a ruse. You get off playing with your pussy in front of others."

I'm too far gone to remind him he's the one who put me up to this.

"I want a taste."

Of course you do...

"Quick, angel, the light is going to change."

I remove my fingers from my dripping pussy and extend my hand.

Gage clamps his big hand around my wrist, pulling my hand to his mouth.

He licks my fingers clean in such a sensual way, the sight causes my eyes to roll to the back of my head.

The driver next to us honks his horn.

From my peripheral vision, I spot a blond man leaning against the door of a red convertible car.

"Fuck her real hard when you get her home, bro."

I can't believe he shouted that.

I doubt the man would recognize me, but that doesn't stop me from bowing my head, using my curtain of hair to hide my face.

"I intend on doing that." Gage is addressing the man, but his eyes are locked onto mine.

...And I'm fifty shades of red.

"Enjoy the ride," the man says. "Can't see her face but I'm sure she's a sweet little thing."

This is not happening.

"I will," Gage says. "And she is."

My mortification deepens.

The light must've changed to green because the driver next to me revs up his engine.

Gage lets go of my hand to shift gear, before accelerating.

"Keep going," he says, without pulling his attention away from the road.

He radiates pure dominance.

I submit.

With trembling hands, I resume my mission.

The vibration of the car's powerful engine is sublime.

"Good girl. Round and round."

My fingers follow his command.

His breathing roughens. "My dirty little slut."

Wh—what? "Did you call me a slut?"

"No. I called you *my* dirty little slut. Big difference."

I should be insulted. Heat shouldn't simmer low in my belly.

Gage's gaze drops to my lap. "I never told you to stop."

"You're bossy."

"Don't kid yourself, we both know you like me bossy."

"Even if you tortured me, I'd never admit to it." My voice is husky. I don't recognize the person who said that.

"Challenge. Accepted."

Dread washes over me.

Have I made a bet with the devil?

"Keep working that pussy."

His command jerks me out of my thoughts.

My fingers skate over my clit in fast strokes, bringing me higher and higher until my hips move restlessly on the seat.

I'm going to need holy water to save my soul after this.

A sweet blissful sensation builds at my core.

Considering the mess I made this morning, I'm a bit worried I might ruin Gage's car, but my orgasm is looming, taking over any and all logical thinking.

I glance at him—the man that's turned me into a dirty girl. *His* dirty girl.

He unleashes his deadliest weapon—his smile.

I'm all riled up.

I'm breathing so hard, my pants echo over the roaring of the engine.

Heck, I don't care about breathing at all, because I'm so desperate for relief.

God.

I've never felt more exposed, more vulnerable in my life. And I've never felt more turned on and more empowered.

This man...

The road and everything around me blurs. My body is flooded with ecstasy as I near the edge.

My muscles tighten, the trembling beginning in my upper thighs and moving higher.

I'm close.

"Stop!"

My heart is beating so hard, it's knocking against my eardrums. Surely, I misheard him.

"What?"

"I said, stop."

My breath shudders in and out. "I can't."

"Lily."

"But—"

"Don't you dare come."

I'm on the verge. My body needs this release.

"Lily."

Damn him.

All movement of my hand halts.

My hooded eyes drop to his lap.

The thick erection between his legs is ever so present.

Fuck that.

A defiance I didn't know I possessed kicks in. I squeeze my legs hard, bow my back against the seat, and I come.

In a car.

On a busy LA road.

With witnesses.

I come, and I come, and I come.

My body trembles in the seat as wave after wave of climactic pleasure courses through me.

"Did you disobey me, Lily?"

It's a struggle to find my composure and my voice. "I needed to come. I didn't have any other choice."

"Yes, you did."

"No, I didn't," I say. "You're cruel. You're playing my body like a fiddle. And you're fucking with my head."

He shoots me a side gaze.

"I'm a virgin. All of this is new to me. What do I know about these kinky games?"

No response.

I debate on pleading my case further, but decide to remain silent for the remainder of the ride, my gaze swinging in his direction from time to time, gauging the situation. Gauging if I'm in deep shit or not.

He doesn't grant me a glance, his focus is on the road.

Fine.

I pull down my skirt with an irritated tug and adjust it around me.

He's back to being a brooding grump.

Great.

I sink into my seat.

I've pissed him off.

He'll drop me at the hotel and dash off.

So much for him licking ice cream off my body.

Crap.

A few minutes later, the hotel comes into view, and he's pulling in front of it.

To my surprise, Gage cuts the ignition.

He unbuckles his seatbelt and angles his body on the seat.

I meet his eyes. They're... blazing with heat?

He's not pissed off?

"Fair warning," he says.

Oh shit.

I brace myself.

"You challenged me *and* you disobeyed my command." He pauses for a heartbeat, those long lashes sweeping when he blinks. "You're going to pay for that level of effrontery."

Can't we make a deal?

"I have an elevator ride to decide what kind of sweet torture I'll submit you to." His words are measured, calculated.

I swallow.

"One thing is certain, you'll come screaming my name so loud, the security guards will come barging in, busting down the door to find out what the fuck I did to you." A muscle ticks in his jaw. "Don't poke the bear, Lily... unless you want him to come out and play..."

I'm at a loss for words.

Chapter 26

Gage

I t's another excruciating ride up to Lily's suite, crammed in an elevator with a bunch of animated Italians.

I thought it was going to be the two of us, but at the last second, a hand slammed against the rubber, preventing the doors from closing. A flood of smiley faces poured into the car. I wasn't planning on fucking her in the elevator, but I was hoping for a repeat of yesterday—her in my arms, rubbing her pussy over my jeans covered cock.

Now, I have to wait.

It's only a few minutes, but even that is too long.

All the blood in my body has rushed south. To say my cock is rock hard would be an understatement. The fucker is so swollen, it's jammed up behind the zipper of my jeans, I have to grit my teeth during the ride up.

Jesus Christ, I have a pulsing trunk between my legs.

Lily is a sexy submissive.

She could've balked in protest at my demand, but she didn't.

Watching her finger-fuck her pussy in my car while we

were cruising down Santa Monica Boulevard nearly had me coming. I will never be able to drive down that major artery again without thinking of Lily. The sight of her stripped of all shame and willing to submit to my dominance was as mind altering as a drug. And I need another dose.

When we hit her floor, I thank all the angels up above.

I exit the elevator and drag her by the hand behind me as my long legs eat the carpeted floor.

Something potent surges in my blood with each step.

I'm horny as fuck. My balls are about to explode.

She's to blame, and she needs to fix it right the fuck now.

I've never felt this level of raw desire before, and it's driving me out of my damn mind. One dose of Lily Schuyler and I'm being led around by my dick.

When we arrive at her door, I extend a hand.

I don't even have to say a word.

My docile pet hands me her key card.

I swipe it over the keypad and open the door.

I let her in first and follow right behind her.

The door closes, locking us inside.

Let the games begin.

She drops her designer handbag and the freezer bag containing the ice cream on the console, and makes to enter the suite.

No, you don't, princess. "You stay where you are."

Her step halts.

She turns around.

A flash of worry gleams in her eyes.

"Bad girls who disobey, get what's coming to them."

Her pupils dilate, the blue darkening to an intense, dark sapphire shade.

"I want you naked."

Her eyes bounce around the entrance before fixing her gaze onto me. She wrinkles her adorable nose at me. "Here?"

"Here."

"Why don't we go to the bedroom?"

"You're in no position to make demands."

She bites her bottom lip, and it has my cock swelling.

I lean against the door and cross my arms, waiting.

She stares at me.

I stare right back.

I'm not standing down.

She lowers herself to the floor and undoes her shoelaces.

She steps out of her silver Converse, her bare feet touching the white tile floor. She wiggles her toes painted in a pretty shade of pink.

"I'm not a patient man, Lily."

Her eyes snap up to meet mine.

Her arms fold behind her and her mid-leg skirt drops to the floor, pooling around her ankles. Crossing her arms in front of her, she pulls off the white top that's obstructing the view of her delectable body.

I stop breathing.

I was expecting sexy lingerie. I wasn't expecting her to pull out the big guns.

Lily selected a mouth-watering combo in the same shade of vibrant blue as her skirt. The color against her milky skin is striking. The design is intentional, with a precise mission—bring a man to his knees. And goddammit if that's not what I want to do—drop to my knees and worship this woman. The bra is a bewitching combination of sheer mesh and lace under-wire cups with cutouts and bow details.

And there are the panties...

Be still my beating heart.

Lily is wearing a pair of all-lace high-waisted panties. I'm used to seeing women clad in thongs and bikini underwear. Many prefer to go commando. What she's wearing is a blatant invitation for misbehaving.

"I'm going to need the name and address of the shop where you bought that mouth-watering lingerie."

Her eyes drop down to her body before meeting my gaze. "Why?"

"Because I'm going to have to buy that combo in every fucking color."

She laughs. "You like it?"

"It looks fucking hot on you."

"It comes with a garter belt, but I thought it was a bit much for a picnic. Not to mention, stockings in this heat...? I'd melt. But if you want me to wear them for you..."

I narrow my eyes at her.

Before I have time to answer, she gives me a twirl.

Jesus Christ.

What she's wearing is as cock-hardening from the front as it is from the back.

She faces me again. "Are you still sure you want me to strip?"

I push off the door and stalk towards her, the beast inside me roaring to life.

To her credit, she doesn't back away.

"You're a feisty little one today. So defiant. So cocky. So brazen. The more sass you throw my way, the harder I'll fuck you."

Lust flashes in her eyes.

"To answer your question, either you remove the expensive lingerie, or I do. Fair warning, if I get my hands on what you're wearing, I'll tear it to shreds. The decision is yours."

It doesn't take her long to get naked, the underwear

discarded on the floor. She brushes her cascade of black, silky hair that hangs all the way to her waist behind her shoulders.

My heated gaze caresses her sensual, slender curves.

This woman is a goddess.

With my eyes holding hers, I unbutton my shirt, remove it, fold it, and drop it on the floor in front of me.

Puzzled eyes stare up at me.

"On your knees. Use my shirt as a cushion."

"My punishment is to give you a blowjob?"

"No. Your *first* punishment is me fucking your mouth."

"How many punishments do you plan on administering?"

"As many as I see fit."

"All because I came?"

"All because you disobeyed me."

"All this is new to me. Don't I get a pass for being an innocent virgin?"

"That was yesterday's news. You ceased being innocent when you came all over my cock. You don't get a pass anymore."

"Tyrant!"

I lean into her. "Do you want me to go?"

She tilts her chin up. "Whatever you have in store for me, I can take it." Blue eyes gleam with determination.

"You're not afraid I'll push you too far?"

She worries her lower lip. "I trust you."

Fuck, she's perfect.

I point to the floor.

She drops to her knees.

The hint of vulnerability I read in her eyes is intoxicating.

I've never seen anything more beautiful in my life.

"Seeing you on your knees... it's yet another image for my spank bank."

"You make me feel so sexy."

I shake my head. "I don't do shit. You *are* sexy. Own it."

She responds with a shy smile.

I reach for her face and glide a sensual finger along her jawline, letting my hand trail behind her neck, until I fist her hair and tug at it hard.

She gasps, staring up at me, her delicate throat exposed. Her eyes are glassy, her pupils dilated. She's so fucking turned on, the smell of her sweet pussy fills the space.

"I can smell how ready you are for me."

She lowers her eyes.

"No, Lily. Eyes on me."

She obeys.

"Your headiness is intoxicating."

Her perky pink nipples harden to pebbles under my heated gaze. Unable to contain myself, I pluck a peak between two fingers, flicking the tip with my thumb.

She groans.

Her hand cups her other tit, her pink nipple poking between her fingers. It's a mirror image of what I'm doing to her, which makes the visual even more erotic.

Fuck.

I pinch her nipple so hard, she squeals.

"That's your punishment for pulling the innocent card. You know what you're doing."

She flashes me a wide grin.

With my free hand, I stroke my lengthening cock through my jeans.

She reaches out, but I swat her hand away.

"I didn't give you permission to touch me."

She responds with a pout.

I have to hold back a chuckle.

Until last night, a woman kneeling at my feet was the only

pleasure and intimacy I'd allow myself with the opposite sex. Guilt has a way of souring pleasure.

"You've sucked off a guy before?"

"Yes, but it's the first time I'm on my knees."

My eyebrows hit my forehead.

"My ex had this weird fixation about blowjobs," she says. "He only wanted them in the morning, and it always happened in bed. Once he came, he'd rush us to the shower. He wanted to be certain I brushed my teeth and used mouthwash, citing he didn't want to taste himself on my tongue."

Fool.

Moving right along.

I let go of her hair. "Unbuckle my belt."

She does as she's told.

"Unzip me."

Her eyes are on me as she inches the zipper lower.

My cock throbs hard through my boxer briefs, begging to be freed of its confinement.

Soon.

"Pull my jeans down to my knees."

Her hands grip my jeans and with one swift movement, she lowers them.

My cock springs free of my boxers, snapping against my stomach.

A low growl escapes me.

Her eyes grow wide. "You're bigger than you were this morning. How is that even possible?"

"It's all your fault. I'm in a permanent state of arousal when I'm around you."

"You are?" She's unconvinced.

"I can't fake this." I wrap my hand around my cock and stroke it a few times. "This is all for you."

She licks her lips, her eyes fixed on my stroking hand.

"I don't know how much restraint I'll have, angel. If I'm too feral, tap out."

She frowns.

I demonstrate.

"Got it."

She's ready to play.

I present my cock to her like an offering.

She reaches out, but I angle my body so she can't touch me.

"I don't want your hands on me."

"How can I give you a blowjob if I can't hold your cock?"

"This isn't a lazy morning blowjob. I'm going to be fucking your mouth. No hands required. I need you to open wide, wrap your pretty little mouth around my big fat cock, suck me dry, and make me come so hard, I forget which coast I'm on. Then, and only then, will I allow you to come."

Her mouth opens in shock.

"That's it." I grin. "Arms behind your back and open wider for me."

She blinks.

"Stick out your tongue."

She obeys.

I angle my cock and stroke the tip across her tongue.

She sticks her tongue out further for more.

"You can't get enough of my taste?"

She shakes her head.

The veil of lust coating her eyes is almost enough to make me come.

I guide my cock into her eager mouth.

"Fuck." I exhale as it slides against her tongue. Her mouth is so inviting. And warm. And wet. And perfect. Her fluttering tongue dances along the underside of my cock, sending a flourish of tingles to my balls.

I let out a low groan when she swirls her tongue around the head of my cock.

Shit.

I expected Lily to be shy. Tentative, even. The woman sucking my cock is neither of those things. She knows what she's doing.

I grip her hair tight. "You have a wicked little tongue."

She smiles.

"Do it again."

She obeys my command.

Another wave of pleasure rips right through me.

Without being asked, she does it a third time.

My balls tug and I let out a guttural growl.

The moan that rises and floats out of her makes me harder. Not that I know how that's possible, considering I'm as hard as granite.

She swallows around my cock.

Fuck.

The confinement of my jeans around my legs feels like a noose.

I'm an idiot for not removing them all together.

But I don't have time to dwell on it.

"You look so beautiful with my cock in your mouth."

I expect a moan as a response. A smile, even.

She pulls back until she lets my cock drop from her lips.

I'm about to protest, but she pokes her tongue out and teases my tip, sliding between my slit.

Jesus. She's sucking my soul out of my cock.

She takes it one step further when she presses her lips hard around my tip.

My hand fists her thick, raven hair, keeping her right there.

My eyes roll into the back of my head.

Dammit.

How the hell did she turn the tables on me?

This was supposed to be *her* punishment. Why am I the one being tortured?

I take control back from her.

I grip her hair even tighter, forcing her attention to me.

"Clearly, I don't need to show you any mercy."

That's all the warning she gets.

I tilt my hips back before thrusting forwards, pushing my full length between her lips, cramming my cock into her mouth.

She closes her eyes at the impact.

I give her cheek a few taps. "Eyes on me. Don't make me repeat myself."

She opens them.

What an obedient little sub.

I fuck her mouth.

And I'm not gentle.

She doesn't protest.

Not even a whimper.

I keep up my shallow thrusts.

Her mouth is too sweet.

Her hands work their way up my thighs, and I choke when she gropes my ass cheeks and squeezes hard.

I didn't see that coming.

"You wanna play dirty?"

She smiles around my cock.

"I'm happy to oblige."

As I slide in and out between her lips, her body moves rhythmically to meet my next thrust. Her big, beautiful eyes are pinned to mine.

I lose myself in those violet sapphire gems as I pick up the pace.

My cadence is punishing, but she welcomes my thrusts.

She drools all over my cock.

I give her cheek a harder tap this time. "My dirty slut can still take it?"

She nods.

I let loose.

I hit the back of her throat.

Christ.

She gags, her eyes watering.

I cock an eyebrow, waiting for her reaction.

She responds by slapping my ass.

"Oh, you're going to get it now." I tighten my grip on her hair, exerting my dominance over her.

I swing my hips back before thrusting inside her mouth with force.

I do it again.

And again.

And again.

She has no choice but to take what I give her.

More tears stream down her face.

"Too much?"

She shakes her head, her watery eyes blinking up at me.

"Too much?"

She shakes her head again.

"Good girl."

Not that the training wheels were ever on, but now, I go for it.

I lose myself between her lips, pumping in and out of her with a hand holding her head down, so I can go real deep.

"Take every fucking inch of me."

I swear she's giddy as she sucks my cock.

"Jesus. That mouth of yours is going to be the death of me."

She sucks harder and deeper.

I hit the back of her throat again.

This is so fucking hot, it's a struggle to keep my thoughts from becoming scrambled.

Her mouth is stripping all the power out of me.

One of her hands slides off my ass and goes between her legs.

"Don't you fucking dare." My tone brooks no argument.

She whimpers around my cock, her eyes pleading.

I hold her gaze.

Her hand is back on my ass.

I tap her face. "Show me you deserve my cock down your throat."

She swallows around the head of my cock, and I fold over.

I regain my composure.

I thrust in and out of her mouth, and she takes it.

"You're perfect. Knelt in front of me, swallowing my cock. You're a good little slut."

She sobs.

"Suck me dry."

More sobbing.

Her hands come up to fist the length of my cock she can't get in her mouth.

If I could still think straight, I'd protest.

But the way she grips me, rubbing up and down as I fuck her mouth is so hedonistic, I let it slide.

I tighten my hold on her hair, controlling her movement as I thrust in and out of her mouth.

"Gorge on my thick cock."

She moans, the reverberation traveling to my balls.

In and out.

In and out.

I don't hold back.

She doesn't tap out.

I didn't expect this much from her.

Her saliva drips over my swollen balls.

Fuck, yeah.

"Oh, shit, Lily. You're gonna make me come hard." My voice is trembling.

Her hand lets go of my cock and cups around my balls, squeezing the right amount of pressure.

By the time I register it's too late.

"Oh God," I say. "Oh fuck."

With herculean effort, I pull my cock out of her mouth.

Confusion is painted all over her beautiful face. "I'm not doing it right?"

"You are."

She beams up at me.

"I intended on jetting my warm cum inside your wicked mouth, but there's a change of plan." My heart is beating so hard, I have to press a hand against it, willing it to slow down. "I need to get out of these jeans right the fuck now, but I need you to take care of my shoes first."

She unlaces my Converse.

I toe them off.

With rushed hands, I remove my socks.

I lower my jeans and boxer briefs and step out of them.

Not that I thought it was possible, but the sight of Lily naked, sitting on her haunches with her hands on her lap, staring up at me is even more arousing than her swallowing my cock between her lips.

I drop to my knees and cup her face with one hand. "Fuck punishment. I need absolution. And right now, your pussy is it."

I take her lips with mine. My tongue sweeps in, stroking

hers in a wild dance. Gripping her hair, I pull her head back, giving me a better angle to take her mouth. I relish her whimpering sobs.

I deepen the kiss as my hand slides down her body until my fingers are nestled between her pussy lips.

Her breath hitches.

I break the kiss. "You're so ready for me. Your sweet juices are dripping down my hand."

My mouth crashes onto hers.

I tease her with a languorous touch, skating around her clit unrushed, enjoying how she undulates her hips in the hopes I'll hit her clit. "What do you want?"

"I want to come."

"But you already did in the car when you disregarded my command."

"It's not the same when you touch me."

Fuck if those words don't do something to me.

"Why didn't you wait?"

She clamps a hand around my wrist, trapping my fingers there as she rocks her hips back and forth against my fingers, chasing her orgasm.

Through hooded lids, I take in the hedonistic scene.

"Your greedy clit is needy?"

"Yes."

In one swift movement, I unlock her hand from around my wrist. "I want you on all fours."

Her eyes dart around the foyer.

"Here?"

"Here."

I reach for my jeans, rummage through the pocket for my wallet, and pull out a condom.

I sheathe my aching cock in a flash.

Lily hasn't moved.

"On your hands and knees." My unwavering tone pushes her into action.

I kneel behind her on the floor.

It hits me.

With a brutal storm raging inside me, neither of us will be able to walk when I'm done with her if I fuck her in this position.

I scour the space, my eyes peering in the distance.

"This isn't going to work," I say. "I want you bent over with your hands gripping the high-back chair over there." I point in the direction of the living room area.

She's up on her feet and hurrying away on her tiptoes, her hips swinging left to right, her ass cheeks wiggling.

Damn, I want to bite right into that beautiful ass.

She assumes the position, legs spread apart.

Her dripping pussy is in full view, begging me to fuck her. I lick my lips at the invitation.

"You look so beautiful. You're ready and willing."

She wiggles her ass in response.

Two long steps and I'm standing behind her.

I caress her ass, my hands traveling up her back. I wind her long hair around my fist, tugging her head back so our eyes meet.

My other hand finds her hip. "Spread your legs wider for me."

She does.

"Hold on for the ride, baby."

She glances over her shoulder, her blue eyes darken with arousal.

I angle my hips and take my cock in my hand. I rub it back and forth over her eager hole before ramming inside her.

It's so rough, she screams.

I let out an animalistic growl.

Even though I fucked her real good this morning, you'd never know.

I can't get enough of her.

"Your pussy was made for me."

She mewls.

I grip her shoulder in one hand and go to town.

I ride her like a stallion.

"I need to fuck you harder."

"Please." That one word drops from her lips on a shaky breath.

I give it to her.

My thrusts punish her with relentless force.

She's dripping.

I fuck her harder.

Jesus, she's a fucking waterfall.

"Your wet pussy is making lewd noises. Is my dirty little slut going to come gushing all over my cock?"

Lily nods, sobbing, working her hips back and forth in a dizzying rhythm to meet my brutal thrusts.

"Words."

"More. More."

That's not the answer I was expecting, but to her credit, she gave me words.

I bury my cock deeper inside her, fucking her like a savage.

The wet sounds of her pussy intensify.

She gasps.

"That horny pussy of yours is going to make a big fat mess all over this floor."

"You—you do that to me."

My orgasm is looming.

I quicken my pace, my hips slapping roughly against her jiggling ass.

I lower my gaze to where we connect. "Your sweet little pussy is so tight."

More juices come gushing out of her dripping pussy, running down her legs and mine.

The sight is filthy as fuck.

"You're never going to find another man who fucks you the way I do."

"No. Never."

"No other man will make your pussy weep."

"Only you."

"Your pussy is molded to my cock now. You'll never feel this full with another."

"I won't."

I pound in and out of her.

"When I'm done with you, you'll never want another cock for the rest of your natural life."

"It'll never be this good with another."

"Fuck no, it won't."

I'm feverish, teetering on the edge. That's the only explanation for all this gibberish flying out of my mouth without my permission.

"You're dirty only for me." This primal sense of possessiveness is foreign.

"Only for you."

Damn right.

"No one else, Gage."

The addition of my name hits me in the gut.

I was pleased with her response, but she had to take it up by several notches.

"Don't you dare forget it."

"I'll never forget *you*."

Ditto that.

Her pussy clamps and release around my cock, signaling she's close.

Jesus.

"You're gonna come hard for me?"

She doesn't respond.

Her eyes shut closed.

"Lily—"

"Oh my God. Oh, Gage. Gage."

A strong gush of her juices runs down my legs.

Damn.

My brain takes a leave of absence as my body takes over.

I pump into her from behind like a madman, my cadence so erratic, my big balls slap against her pussy. The sensation is as potent as a shot of ecstasy, the sound is lewd and debauched. The way I'm fucking her is primal and barbaric, but I can't dial it down.

Lily's body convulses. "Gage—" She clamps hard against my cock, milking it, clenching, and releasing her pussy around me.

"God, Lily—"

The floodgates open.

Holy shit.

My body loses the battle.

I release the cum that's been building up in my balls since she was playing with her pussy in my car.

I give in to a climax so strong, I see stars.

The intensity knocks me over. It's something I've never felt before.

I've been starved for too many years.

Lily freed me of my self-imposed sentence.

Nothing compares to seeking pleasure inside a woman's pussy.

For several heartbeats, our panting takes over the suite.

How I manage to remain standing on my shaky legs is a mystery to me.

With every breath, the storm inside me simmers down.

I caress her back, coated with a sheen of sweat. "You're still with me?"

"I am." Her voice is faint. "I'll never have sex on a bed ever again."

"I've corrupted you?"

She shakes her head. "I'll ruin the sheets and bed."

I laugh.

"I'm serious."

I pull out of her and help her stand straight.

I turn her around so she's facing me. "That was hot as fuck."

"You say that because you're used to this."

I stroke her damp hair off her face. "I've never been with a woman who's reacted that way."

A veil of shyness covers her eyes. "You're not just saying that?"

"No. The way your body responds to me is so hedonistic. You're sexy when you come so hard your juices gush all over the place."

"I'm sure not all men like…"—her eyes lower for a beat—"such a reaction."

"You don't want to fuck an idiot who can't appreciate that. You want a man who gets turned on by it." *Like me.*

"Thanks for making me feel sexy about my intense reaction."

I tap the tip of her nose. "I fucking love your intense reaction."

I place two fingers underneath her chin and lift her face up to mine.

Something passes between us.

She gets on her tippytoes and offers me her lips.

I kiss her. Slow at first, but it soon turns ravenous.

She matches my passion with as much fervor.

I suck her tongue as if I'm trying to steal her sobs and whimpers. I'm not complaining about fucking her from behind, but I missed not having my mouth on hers.

I haven't kissed a woman in so many years that each time I lock lips with Lily's, the contact ignites my soul.

Something thunderous beats at my chest. A foreign sensation I can't quite describe.

What the fuck is this woman doing to me?

I pull away from her, freeing myself from the spell she has me under.

She grunts her dissatisfaction.

"I should warn you," I say. "Not every guy out there can turn you into a waterfall. I'm gifted."

She swats my chest. "Cocky much?"

"You bet." I wink.

Something flickers in her eyes.

"What is it?"

"I'm a day late and a dollar short if you're the only man my body reacts to like that since I'm going back to New York soon."

Ah. The elephant in the room.

She talked about her passion project, but she didn't mention anything about a job. If Fisher is grooming her to take over a PR company, perhaps she works for her father.

I cup her face in my hands and press our foreheads together, her soft exhale bathing my mouth. "Do you have anything pressing to deal with when you get home, or can you extend your trip?"

Her eyes sparkle as they fix on me. "You want me to stay longer?"

"Yes. We can spend more time together."

"Oh."

"If you have other plans, I understand—"

"No, I don't have anything urgent." The words come rushing out of her mouth.

"Stay."

"Okay. I will."

"Good." Warmth fills my chest. There's so much I want to say to her, but I've done such a bang-up job jailing my feelings for the past three years, I no longer know how to unlock them.

Her brilliant smile takes over her beautiful face.

"Let's go take a shower so I can enjoy some ice cream," I say.

"Oh, yeah, I forgot about that. Ice cream is a great idea."

"I wasn't talking about you."

She furrows her eyebrows.

"Remember my promise?"

That frown deepens.

"I'm going to clean you up before dirtying you again by spreading ice cream all over your heavenly body and licking it off you." If I keep things sexual, my mind will stop confusing me.

Big blue eyes widen. "You... We... You want me again so soon?"

"Damn right, I'm ready for another round."

"You're insatiable."

"Is that a complaint?"

She giggles. "No."

"Glad we're on the same page."

I don't give her time to respond, I bend and pick her up fireman style.

She squeals.

"Put me down, you beast."

"Behave, woman."

She wiggles her legs, thrashing over my shoulder.
"Keep it up, and I'll leave my handprint on your ass."
She goes still for a beat before wiggling again.
Slap!
Her breath hitches and then she lets out a low moan.
Well, hell.
"My little slut is begging for a good spanking."

Chapter 27

Lily

After spending a couple of hours by the pool, enjoying a good book while working on my tan, I head to my suite. As I step over the threshold, my phone rings in my tote bag. Giddy with happiness, I pull it out. It's not who I hoped it would be, but it's another one of my favorite people.

I accept the video call.

"Hey, you." Nads waves. Then, she squints. "Is it sunny again?"

I pull my Hollywood style designer sunglasses over my head and let out a theatrical sigh. "The temperature here is insufferable. All this bright sun and perfect weather. I've been told there's two hundred and sixty-three days of sunshine in the City of Angels. It's torture. I don't know for how much longer I can handle it." *Lies. All lies.*

My best friend narrows her eyes even more. "I hate you. It's raining in Paris. Again. At this rate, I won't remember what the sun looks like. Parisians are moody on a good day, but this past week, they've been positively bitchy." She sighs. "If it weren't for the flower shop, I would've headed to my father's house in Corsica, or better yet, I'd be with you in sunny LA."

"Sorry, sweets. I wish you could be here with me."

"So do I."

"You can't be a boss lady and a bum at the same time."

"You're not a bum."

"Okay, a vagabond."

She laughs. "In any case, enough about Paris's drab weather. How was that exclusive private party you went to Friday night?"

Oh yeah, Rhys's birthday party.

That was a lifetime ago.

"Since I can't bottle the California sun and send it to you overnight, why don't I take this conversation outside?"

"I like the way you think."

I turn my phone so she can catch a glimpse of my luxury suite as I head towards the large deck.

Oohs and aahs fall from my best friend's lips. "Nice hotel."

"The owners are amazing. Especially the wife. Michaela is sweet, warm, and caring. And so protective."

"You arrived in LA on Thursday. Today is Sunday, and you're chummy-chummy with the owners of the hotel? What gives?"

I slide open the glass door to the deck and step outside.

"Gage is friends with Michaela and her husband Phoenix." I tell Nads all about the Königs and Rhys's party up until the point my bodyguard showed up.

"Sounds like you had fun. And, a private salsa dancing lesson with a former Reggaeton chart-topper. It's good to be you."

"It was amazing, Nads. Our fathers are rich, but celebrities and Hollywood people live large at a different level."

"In other words, it wasn't a stuffy, stiff upper lip, yawn-inducing event?"

I laugh. "It was far from it."

"What about Gage? What's his last name again?"

"Hollingsworth."

"He wasn't at his friend's party?"

I bite against my lower lip, averting my gaze.

"Don't tell me he's another chaperone who turned out to be a jerk or a pervert? The men your father associates with are questionable."

"You're absolutely right on that last point," I say. "My father has questionable connections. Gage isn't one of them. Although he didn't come right out and say it, but it's clear, he likes my father and half-brothers as much as you do."

Nadine nods. "A man after my own heart."

Or after mine.

"So, things are going well between the two of you?"

"A lot... has happened."

"Fill me in."

I play with the tip of my long braid falling over one shoulder, pondering on how I'll drop the news on her.

"Lily, you're keeping something from me. Your blue eyes are twinkling with mischief."

I sigh. "Okay, I was the center of attention at Rhys's party."

"You?" Her head jerks back. "What happened?"

"Gage showed up out of the blue—"

"Wait? You texted that he was going to accompany you."

I give her the run down.

"Got it." She nods. "So, Gage showed up out of the blue... Please continue."

"He hoisted me over his shoulder like a warrior, dragged me to an empty storage room, stuck his fingers down my shorts, and played with my clit until I came all over his fingers while his inner circle was only a few feet away."

Shock registers on my best friend's face.

I keep talking. "We came back to my suite and he popped my cherry. I didn't tell him I was a virgin because I wanted him to be the one."

Nadine's mouth drops open.

"We spent all day yesterday together. Today, kicked off with a good, hard fuck, and ended the same way." I shake my head and let out an audible exhale. "Let's say *la petite mort* with Gage is a world apart from *la petite mort* with my ex."

"The orgasms were good?"

"Not good. Earth-shattering."

Nads's eyes are enormous.

I keep spilling my guts. "By the afternoon, Gage was like a savage beast. To my shock, I loved every minute of it."

Nadine cocks a brow.

"He spent the night fucking me to exhaustion and woke me up with his tongue between my legs. He needed a taste before leaving this morning."

Nadine is doing a great impression of a guppy.

"Oh—" I lift a finger—"every woman should be lucky enough to have a lover who knows how to give her a G-spot orgasm. Until you've had one—or several—you have no idea what you've been missing. You know when people say it's so good, your eyes roll to the back of your head? I can vouch for that."

Nads is now doing a bang-up job doubling as a marble statue.

"Aren't you going to comment?"

She blinks.

She blinks again.

She blinks a third time.

"*Ma grosse bite?* What a joke." I keep talking. "Jean-Philippe is delusional about the size of his cock. There's nothing dishonorable about an average size cock—I don't have double D's or E's—but please, wake up and smell the cappuccino. Don't label your penis as giant unless it is." I scoff. "And his isn't. Not even close."

"Ga—Gage has a giant cock?" Nads finds her voice.

"It's not grotesque. We're not talking Guinness World Records penis size, but it's way bigger than Jean-Philippe's."

The stupor vanishes from Nads's face as a beaming smile stretches her lips. "Aren't you happy I convinced you not to cancel your trip? Fuck the film schools. LA was about connecting with a man who could rock your world."

I'm about to agree with her, but she lets out an evil laugh.

"I'm afraid to ask what prompted that."

I pace around the deck. "It wasn't his plan, but your father gave you a birthday gift after all. Gage Hollingsworth is the ultimate milestone birthday gift."

I burst out laughing. "What a difference a few days make—"

"A few days that propelled you into womanhood."

I nod.

"A flower blooming in late spring..." Nadine's words trail.

"Only a florist would make that analogy."

Amusement dances in her eyes. She cocks an eyebrow, a wicked smile pulling at her lips.

Uh-oh. "What is it?"

"LA looks good on you. With a little luck—or a little more time spent with Gage—sweet Lily will become Voodoo Lily—"

"You're such a florist. You're hoping I leave LA like one of the most poisonous flowers on the planet?"

Her smile is sinister. "It's a colorful way of saying I hope you grow a protective skin that repels the shit spewing out of

Fisher's mouth and allows you not to give a flying fuck what his sons think of you."

I catch my reflection in the glass door. *Can I become that girl? Will there be a day I'll stop craving my father's and half-brothers' acceptance? Can I grow a tough enough skin to protect my heart from never earning my father's love?*

Chapter 28

Lily

Most of my friends from boarding school returned home once they graduated. Those girls are scattered across the planet. Some of us keep in touch, but unless you're living in the same city, virtual friendships are never the same.

The only reason Nadine and I are still besties is because we were two peas in a pod in boarding school, and she insisted on attending the University of Paris even though she could've selected any college in Paris because she speaks fluent French. She didn't want to break our bond.

A friendship is a special gift. I always thought it was years in the making.

LA changed that.

It's possible for strangers to become fast friends.

"The French afternoon tea I had with Michaela a few days ago was high up there on my list, but this..." I point to my dessert plate.

"I know, right?" Dominika digs in for another spoonful of lip-smacking Bakewell tart.

This new to me English dessert is heaven in my mouth.

"Stasia introduced the sisterhood to the Millennium Bilt-more's Rendezvous Court," Dominika says. "It's become one of our favorites."

It still blows my mind I rub elbows with Stasia van Gameren—rocker chick goddess.

"I can see why," I say. "It's a level of olde-worlde chicness I would've never associated with the City of Angels. The handful of historic buildings I've visited all had modern interiors. Not this one. It's old Hollywood. If I lived here, it would become a favorite as a brunch spot."

"It can be if you come to school here or when you come visit," Dominika says.

The prospect of spending more time with the sisterhood fills me with joy. That's the only silver lining in attending film school in LA. That, and seeing Gage.

My eyes land on an elegant couple sitting at a table behind Dominika.

I'm grateful I don't stick out like a sore thumb, given my missing suitcase. I would've preferred wearing a dress, but I wasn't about to buy more clothes. Since this brunch invitation was last minute, I'm wearing the same outfit I wore a couple days ago. Thank God the white sleeveless top with a pair of slim fitted raw silk three-quarter pants in fuchsia, which I paired with black satin Manolo Blahnik Hangisi heels are chic enough.

Dominika on the other hand is dressed for the occasion. The dress she selected has bell sleeves, similar to the one she wore the first time I met her. I never would've guessed a blonde could get away with wearing a yellow dress. The emerald-green high heel peep toe shoes are a bold choice. The woman wears pregnancy well.

Her wardrobe selection isn't the only surprise. I guess I was too overwhelmed the first time we met to take note of the tattoos peeking from her sleeve.

"This dessert is ridiculous," she says. "The baby loves it. That's my excuse for having a second slice." She smiles wide. "You can blame a baby for everything and get away with it."

She laughs.

I don't.

A foreign sensation washes over me.

She has it all—a gorgeous, sexy husband who loves her, the sisterhood to support her, a kick ass career, and a baby on the way that will allow her to step into the next phase of her life.

She's not a lost soul with a family that excels at ignoring her and giving her the cold shoulder.

That ruined my appetite.

I drop my spoon on the dessert plate and push it away.

"Are you okay?" Dominika is sporting a worried expression.

I force a smile. "I'm sure I sound like a broken record, but I'm humbled you'd give up spending Sunday with your husband and his family to be with me. I could've totally played tourist today." I skirt the issue.

She places a gentle hand on my forearm. "It's my turn to sound like a broken record. It's a pleasure for me to spend the day with you. Not to mention, I see my husband all the time." She waves a dismissive hand in front of her face. "We live together. We carpool together. We work together. A little distance only makes a marriage stronger." She winks.

"Noted."

"When Gage sent a group text to the sisterhood to find out who could hang out with you, I was first in line."

My cheeks burst into flames.

Gage was my alarm clock this morning again. I could get used to waking up in his arms. Even though last night was a sex marathon that left me spent and satiated, we got entangled in a round of passionate morning sex that left both of us breathless. I can still feel his massive cock inside me hours later.

After a shower that turned into another round of toe-curling sex, Gage announced we wouldn't have a repeat of yesterday. He had other plans. His brother-in-law is celebrating a milestone birthday and his adoptive sister is throwing a big bash for her husband.

I was okay spending the afternoon at the pool, working on my tan. I didn't expect he'd reach out to the sisterhood so I wouldn't spend the day alone.

It's chaos and confusion in my head. And in my heart.

He wasted no time bursting my bubble when he announced the festivities would last until late in the night, so I shouldn't expect to see him tonight.

I should be thrilled he was honest and upfront. I have no right to be this disappointed.

"I'm touched he did that," I say.

"If we were all tied up in family functions, he would've reached out further into the inner circle," Dominika says.

My eyebrows hit my forehead in surprise.

"Cesar and Diana are in San Diego today, but Collin and Shane Dennison are around. Gage wouldn't have hesitated to enlist them as your bodyguards for the day."

"He didn't have to go to that much trouble."

"He's made it his personal mission to look after you. Let him."

I open my mouth to say something, but there's so much to what she revealed.

Dominika studies me. "I haven't seen that side of Gage in a long time."

I'm not sure how to respond to that.

"I've known Gage well before he became a successful CEO," she says. "Three years ago, life served him a devastating blow, transforming him into the brooding man who can scare lesser men with a warning glare. Since the life-altering incident, he's retreated into a shell, only surfacing to manage his empire. He was no longer Gage."

"Does it have to do with his mom?"

Dominika places a hand against her chest. "It's not my story to tell—"

"That's what Mikki said."

"It's heavy."

"It must be for all of you to be so hush-hush about it."

She nods, her lips pursed.

I'm dying to know, but I'm only passing through town. These people don't owe me their life story. Still, my heart bleeds for Gage.

"I know too well how devastating it is to lose a mother," I say. "From the little he's told me about his parents, I don't think Gage lost his mom at a young age like I did." I swallow past the lump of emotions. "It doesn't mean it doesn't hurt like hell each time you're flooded with memories of the woman who loved you unconditionally, and who was taken away too soon."

Dominika's eyes hold mine. "We all have scars. Few of us are lucky enough to only have them on the outside. For most of us, our scars are buried deep—"

"For some deeper than others."

"Truer words have never been spoken." She lifts her sleeve, revealing the full effect of her colorful tattooed arm.

"Oh, wow, that's stunning. You're so brave. I'm way too chicken. That must've hurt."

"It hurts less than the actual scars." She traces a manicured finger along her arm.

Her skin is uneven.

My eyes fly up to meet hers. "You were hurt?"

"An evil man hurt me."

I bring both hands to my heart. "I'm so sorry a despicable person did that to you."

"The pain from the injury and the tattoo needle subside."

I shift on my seat.

This is heavy conversation for a light-hearted brunch.

"Physical scars, heal. The scars that are here"—she taps against her temple—"and here"—she taps against her heart—"can hurt for a lifetime."

"I don't have any physical scars, but I have plenty here." I tap against my heart.

"Welcome to the club."

This woman, who from the outside has it all, carries baggage?

"All that to say, Gage has his fair share of scars." She purses her lips. "For three years he's denied himself pleasure."

Is she talking about fun, or sex? It has to be the former.

"He's a stoic beast clad in bespoke suits with anguish swimming in his gorgeous green eyes," she says. "Anguish that runs so deep, no one could touch it. Heal it. That's until you came crashing into his life..."

My heart flutters like crazy.

I don't dare say a word.

"That was quite the statement he made at Rhys's party," she says.

A telltale flush spreads up to my hairline. "He wanted to talk in private."

Gage wasn't subtle that night. Damn caveman.

"Right." Dominika nods. "And I'm about to give birth to the heir of the British Crown"—she caresses her belly—"instead of the first born to a reformed bad boy."

Busted.

"You have a positive effect on our grumpy giant." She smiles.

I'm shellshocked.

Something foreign tugs low in my heart.

I shake off my stupor. "You're giving me too much credit."

"You're *not* giving yourself enough credit." She holds my gaze. "You're a unicorn, Lily—the woman who might have the superpower to fix Broken Gage Hollingsworth."

Chapter 29

Lily

After brunch, Dominika insisted on playing tour guide. I wasn't going to say no. I like her and the conversation flowed so easily, I didn't want to put an end to a good thing. It was a fun Sunday afternoon of sightseeing, shopping, and indulging in some of the best homemade ice cream I've ever had in my life.

She invited me to her brother-in-law's place for a barbecue. I was worried it would be awkward, but to my delight, it wasn't. On the ride back to the hotel, Rod took the wheel. Sitting in the back seat, I was able to witness what Nadine and I have coined #couplegoals.

Sigh.

During the ride to the Pompadour, I kept checking my phone, hoping for a text from Gage.

It was radio silence on his end.

Bummer.

Last night, I learned the hard way what addiction is all about. I tossed and turned, and couldn't fall asleep alone in the king size bed after two consecutive nights wrapped in Gage's big, strong arms.

Going back to New York will be a rude awakening.

After an afternoon spent evaluating another film school, I stroll through the lobby of the hotel towards my suite, humming The Bangles' *Manic Monday*.

A short elevator ride later and I enter my suite, still humming. I change into a bikini before slipping on a sundress. Some women have no problems walking around flaunting it all in the hotel, I'm not that brave. I'm about to head to the pool when my phone rings. I rummage for it inside my tote bag and cringe.

"Crap." I'm tempted to let it go to voicemail, but that's only delaying the inevitable. It could've been worse. It could've been a video call.

I accept the call. "Hello—"

"What the fuck is this about a new phone number?" My father barks a question in lieu of a polite greeting.

"Hello, Father. It's been a long time. Thanks so much for asking how I'm doing."

"Enough with the attitude. Why do you have a new phone number?"

He doesn't enquire about how I'm doing or about my stay in Los Angeles.

Typical.

I tell him all about my luggage drama and losing my phone somewhere at LAX.

"Why didn't you call me? I could've overnighted a phone to you."

"That's fine. I got a new iPhone. I'm good."

"I could've asked someone from the tech team to set up your phone."

"It wasn't that complicated."

"Make sure to get it checked out by the tech team when you return."

"Why?"

"Don't argue with me. Just do it."

I purse my lips together, suppressing a snappy remark from spilling out.

I hated all the bells and whistles his tech team added to my old phone. No way are they getting their hands on this one. I'll conveniently forget to do what he tells me.

"You should've told me sooner you had lost your phone," he says.

I was tempted not to tell him at all, but I had no choice when I decided to extend my stay in LA. Even though I hadn't heard a word from my father, I figured I'd warn him since he's footing the bill. Four extra nights at the Pompadour Hotel don't come cheap.

"You made no effort to text or call. You didn't even call the hotel to find out if I had landed safely and if I was still alive. I was the last thing on your mind. As usual."

"Things have been extremely busy." He booms his response in his don't fuck with me voice. "Chandler requires my attention. We're organizing a party at the house out East in the next few weeks."

"The Hamptons? You're pulling out the big guns."

"It's the perfect setting to fan excitement around your brother's candidature for the mayor's position and get people enthused at the idea of backing him up."

Funny how Chandler is my *brother* when it's convenient.

"In order to convince people to part with their money, it's best to warm them up in advance."

I roll my eyes. "Is that your way of confirming I was the last thing on your mind?"

"Consider yourself lucky, you're top of my mind now," he

says, turning my words against me. "What's this about you delaying your return?"

"There's a long list of great film schools in LA. I want to see what they have to offer."

"I've vetted the best schools. You're going to a school of my choosing. End of story."

I hate when he's high and mighty... which is most times.

Yes, Father, you hold the purse strings. No need to remind me.

I need to come up with a better lie. "I also want to explore the city to make sure I want to live here. It's a different vibe from New York."

"You're not going to be in Los Angeles for years. It's a six-month program. You can suck it up for that long. Your job is to soak in the knowledge and use it when you head your own PR company."

"You mean when I become *head puppet* at your public relations company."

"Lily."

"We both know that's exactly what's going to happen." I refuse to take back my words.

"So, you'll be back in New York on Friday?" He ignores my comment. Of course.

"Yes. Since it's a red-eye, I'll be back early Saturday morning New York time."

"Let's hope nothing or no one prompts you to change your plans."

My eyebrows drop. "What do you mean by that?"

"Your sudden interest in Los Angeles wouldn't be because of Gage Hollingsworth?"

I proceed with caution. "What makes you say that?"

"Someone I know saw you." He's being vague.

"Few of your friends and contacts know I exist—"

"You weren't walking hand-in-hand in Malibu with Gage on Saturday?"

Shock and confusion hit me in one hard blow.

"You have someone spying on me?"

"At least you're not denying it." That's his fucking answer?

"You can't be bothered to call to find out if I've been mugged in the streets of Los Angeles. Yet, you have time to hire a private investigator to follow me around?"

"I didn't have to resort to anything that dramatic," my father says. "Alder saw you."

"Alder is in LA?"

"Yes. He's seeing a semi-famous actress who's bicoastal. They're at her Malibu house for a few days."

His revelation lands me on my ass. "Let me get this straight." I lift a hand, as if he could see me. "Your youngest son, my half-brother, is in LA—in Malibu, to be precise—"

"I'm not a fan of his choice. Hollywood types are flaky at best. And actors are master performers. You never know when they're being genuine or playing for the camera. Whatever-her-name-is, is the flavor of the month. It'll die soon. It always does. Alder will find a new toy."

"Who cares about the stupid actress? Alder is in the same city as I am, but instead of coming up to me and saying, '*Hey, how you doin', Lily?*' he reported my whereabouts to you?" I'm enraged. Incensed. And hurt. This is beyond ridiculous. I'm tired of being *persona non grata*. "If he wants to pretend I don't exist, he should pretend he doesn't see me when we're in the same city."

"I sent you to LA to scope out schools, not to get sidetracked. Gage Hollingsworth?" He snorts. "He's a playboy, Lily."

His patronizing tone infuriates me.

"Don't fall for his act. He'll use you and disregard you like yesterday's news."

Like you did Mom?

"That's *your* MO. It doesn't mean every man on the planet operates the same way."

"All I'm saying is Gage has plenty of options." Fisher Edgington is Teflon. Insults bounce off his invisible shield. "He'll have forgotten about you before your plane takes off... if he hasn't already."

My blood boils. "You know nothing about——"

"There are certain gifts you can only offer once, Lily... choose wisely."

Huh?

He knows I was a virgin?

Impossible.

I've never had the birds and the bees talk with my father, let alone divulge anything about my sexual life.

He must be playing some sort of twisted mind game to get me to open up. I wouldn't put it past him.

Not happening.

I soldier on. "If you think so little of Gage, why did you enlist him as my bodyguard?"

"At the time, I thought he was a safe bet. I figured the brooding CEO with a chip on his shoulder wouldn't give you the time of the day. Rich California moguls tend to prefer blondes."

I'm not even sure how to decipher that insult.

Okay, there's an eye-popping number of blondes in Los Angeles. That doesn't justify his grotesque blanket statement or his putdown.

The fight leaves me, evaporating like a puddle of water under the hot California sun.

This conversation is a waste of my time.

This conversation is draining.

This conversation is killing my fucking soul.

Without so much as a goodbye, I end the call.

I should've expressed my anger at my father instead of letting it consume me, but as usual, I toe the line.

Nadine hates how I'm always the one to put water in my wine. I'm not conceding to my father's bullshit, but until I can stand on my own two feet financially, my hands are bound.

I'm still on the verge of blowing a gasket when a text from my father pops up on my screen.

> Puppet Master: Don't let a player play you. When you get back to New York on Saturday, let's have dinner.

"Jerk!"

Chapter 30

Gage

God should bestow on us humans only one hellish day per month.

There weren't enough extra tall cups of steaming latte, doped with a double shot of espresso or top-shelf whiskey to make Monday palatable. At least, Tuesday is looking like a day that won't cause my head to explode. After a morning at Wire News Network's Enews studios with the publicist and my show host, I eventually have the stomach to handle food.

"That was some outstanding PR work this morning," Rhys says, his eyes meeting mine. "I caught the highlights of Matthew's interview on WNN. He handled it with such composure."

After not eating all day yesterday, lunch at *Triple Crème* inside the Quintus Hotel is exactly what the doctor ordered.

I finish chewing the bite of my delicious prosciutto and grilled aubergine sandwich before answering him. "Snow and Blanche Hyman upped the drama factor by having Snow sit in the audience of the different talk shows Blanche selected for her media circus. Blanche's defamation campaign was well-crafted. Too bad her most damning piece of evidence had zero credibility."

He nods.

"The publicist was worth every penny," I say. "She masterminded the attack. She has high-ranking contacts at WNN, so she was able to secure Matthew a last-minute interview."

"It's baffling he had to expose that much of his private life to ward off those hounds."

"You mean, pariahs."

"That's a more accurate term. Blanche is nasty."

"And a fucking liar." My lips curl up in a snarl. "What kind of example is she setting for her daughter? What about working your way to the top instead of bullshitting your way to the top?"

Rhys nods. "I wonder if we'll ever find out whose cock that was."

"Whoever that was, thanks for taking one for the team." I sneer. "And thanks for clearing Matthew's name."

Rhys chuckles. "How did you find out Blanche was going to stoop that low?"

"Monday kicked off in a startling stir—"

"Isn't that typical of any Monday?"

"You're right." I let out an audible breath. "Had it not been for a publicist who has her ear to the ground, Blanche's new claims could've been the kiss of death for Matthew's and the show's reputation. Thank God the publicist caught wind Blanche had a breaking news interview lined up. We all congregated in a conference room at my office, waiting on tenterhooks. The interviewer's opening statement toppled me over. We all watched as Blanche cried wolf about appalling dick pics Matthew sent her daughter. One look at the blurred image, and Matthew exploded in laughter."

Rhys's brows furrow. "What was so funny?"

"Once Matthew found his composure, he explained his

baffling reaction. After hearing his explanation, I sighed in relief."

"Don't keep me waiting. Did Blanche have ammo or not?"

"That horrible stage mom's greediness was her demise." I lean into him. "What I'm about to tell you is between the two of us."

"Absolutely."

A smirk tilts my lips. "A tattooed chest and stomach, and a Prince Albert saved Matthew's ass."

Rhys frowns.

"The publicist tracked unblurred versions of the accusatory photos. The model—or asshole—on Blanche's dick pics had a bare stomach and no piercings on his cock."

Rhys rests back in his seat. "Well, I'll be damned. Matthew is clean cut on the outside, and a rebel on the inside."

"You can never judge a book by its cover. The saying is even truer in the City of Angels. Under his suits, Matthew hides a few secrets."

"Did he have to flash his abs as proof of his innocence and absolve him of any wrongdoing?"

"He didn't have to drop his pants and boxer briefs. The publicist had multiple photos of Matthew shirtless ready for his interview on WNN, poking a hole the size of the moon in Blanche's case. The publicist didn't want to leave anything to chance, so she had Matthew's tattoo artist and piercing artist on standby, in case date confirmations were needed."

"Smart move."

I nod. "At first, Matthew was dead set against using his sexual orientation as leverage, but Blanche's defamation campaign was fraying his resolve. If it came to that, he was willing to go down that road. He's never denied he was gay, but he's always been a private guy. Same for his partner. Some might say it's a dichotomy to be in the public eye and want to keep your private life private. Just because you're in the public eye doesn't make you a circus animal."

"He's entitled not to have every aspect of his life scrutinized."

"Damn right."

"Did Blanche's camp have a comeback?"

"It's been crickets." *The bitch is silent. It's about time.* "Even if she were to come up with a new attention-grabbing scheme, I doubt it would be enough. She's lost all credibility. From now on, any accusations that come out of her lying mouth will be received with a shovel of skepticism."

"She caused a good man anguish, and damaged your show's reputation."

"The nightmare is behind us now." I play with the collar of my shirt. "I can breathe again."

Rhys lifts his beer glass. "Here's to the next celebrity scandal that'll steal the spotlight from yours."

I clink my glass with his. "I can drink to that."

"Gentlemen," a tall, dark-haired man says, approaching us.

"Larkin," Rhys says.

"Hey," I say.

Larkin pulls out a chair. "May I?"

"You own the joint," I say.

"I do, but it doesn't hurt to ask."

He undoes the top button of his gray suit before taking a seat.

My eyes swing to the entrance of the restaurant, and sure enough, his shadows are standing guard. I don't recognize them. Larkin must've added to his team.

Rhys and I are both multibillionaires—same for most of the guys we hang out with. Without ever catching a glimpse of Larkin's bank account, it's clear, he trumps us all. The only guys who stand toe-to-toe with Larkin when it comes to wealth is Phoenix König and his brothers. Their international conglomerate of hotels and real estate is a force to be reckoned with. Phoenix's cousin Callum is another, via his father's empire and his own business dealings. But neither Phoenix or Callum walk around with bodyguards. That right there is quite telling. There's more to Larkin than meets the eye.

Larkin lifts a hand, and a waiter, carrying a tray, rushes over.

He drops a highball containing ice on the table and proceeds to fill it with Perrier.

"Thank you, Antonio," Larkin says.

How he remembers all of his employees' names, blows my mind. Staff comes and goes in the hospitality business, but Larkin does an impressive job at keeping track.

With a little head bow, Antonio scurries away, empty Perrier bottle in hand.

"Since I don't drink during the day, this will have to do," Larkin says, lifting his glass.

Rhys and I follow his lead.

"Blanche Hyman is determined to use her daughter's *hymen* like a lottery ticket," Larkin says. "Here's to shutting up the twat."

I didn't see that coming.

Thank God I didn't take a sip of my drink or else Larkin would be wearing it.

I roar in laughter.

Rhys joins me.

We're making a spectacle of ourselves, while Larkin remains cool as a cucumber, not even cracking a smile.

"I'll drink to that," I say when I regain my composure.

The three of us clink glasses before taking a long swig of our drinks.

"Now that the monkey is off your back, I hope I'll see you tonight," Larkin says.

I frown.

"The theme party," Larkin says.

"We didn't even bother asking if you were attending," Rhys says. "You've been avoiding those parties for a long time."

I nod.

"That's because he didn't have a good reason to show up. Now, he does." Larkin's eyes hold mine. "That was quite the Tarzan performance at Rhys's birthday party. Your Jane is still in town—"

"You were there?"

"I walked in as you were soldiering towards your victim," Larkin says.

My brows arch. "I didn't see you."

"You only had eyes for one person," Larkin says.

"He was so much under her spell, he didn't bother with me even though it was my birthday." Rhys takes a jab at me.

"Hence, the lunch invitation." I point to his plate. "And I apologized. Multiple times."

Rhys play-punches me. "I'm giving you a hard time."

I shake my head.

"Going back to what I was saying, Miss Schuyler would be the perfect date for our Angels and Demons party at Dark Compulsion tonight." Larkin holds my gaze.

I cock a brow.

"I wasn't planning on asking you," Rhys says, "but now that Larkin tabled the matter, you should bring Lily."

"I'm not sure that's her scene." I shift in my seat. "It might be a little over the top for her."

"How many times have I heard that before?" Larkin says. "Sometimes the shyest ones come alive once they step inside my club."

"The sisterhood will be there. They'll hold her hand," Rhys says. "Not to mention, you'll be there."

"If the raunchiness that takes place in the main party room is too much to handle, I'll give you my private room. All the rooms, lounge rooms, and mini lounge rooms are booked. I was planning on having a little fun tonight, but I'm willing to make the sacrifice for you. What are friends for?"

I consider Larkin.

I've been avoiding Lily since Sunday morning after leaving her hotel room. Asking her to be my date at an exclusive adult club where high rollers meet for an illicit night and all sorts of kinky stuff should make for a great conversation starter.

"Ask her," Rhys says.

"Had you not claimed her, I would've."

My eyes snap in Larkin's direction before narrowing, jealousy beating at my chest.

"Down, boy," he says. "You wouldn't be able to land a punch." He crooks a thumb over his shoulders to where his bodyguards are standing. "They're former Irish Army Ranger Wing."

I frown.

"Elite soldiers of the special operations force of the Irish Defence Forces," Larkin says. "You don't want to mess with that level of military training."

My nostrils flare.

"I wanted to rattle your cage, Mr. Hollingsworth. Mission accomplished."

I roll my eyes. "If you're trying to be funny, that was an epic fail."

"You saw her first," Larkin says. "A real man doesn't mess around with another man's girl."

My lips stretch into a thin line. "In that case, why poke the bear?"

"Because for the past three years, you've made it a point to use women for one specific thing."

"And you haven't deviated. Ever." Rhys piggybacks on Larkin's campaign. "Lily is the perfect candidate to help you break the curse."

My hands dive into my hair to tug at the strands.

Larkin and Rhys are aware of the demons I've been battling for the past three years. Fuck them for using that knowledge to manipulate me.

"Mr. Hartford is right. A beauty with raven hair, passing through the City of Angels, enticed you to break your self-imposed rule."

My eyes bounce to Larkin. "So, now you two are shrinks?"

Larkin shakes his head. "A blind man could see what was unfolding."

"My bad. You're a poet. Rhys is the shrink."

Larkin levels me with a threatening gaze.

I don't avert my eyes.

"It's your prerogative to keep your head stuck in the sand, Mr. Hollingsworth."

A long beat passes.

Me, stewing.

Rhys and Larkin alternate between staring at me and glancing at each other.

I cross my arms over my chest.

The walls around my heart have been reinforced with high security locks and chains. The plan was to never let anyone in.

Then came Lily...

"Own it, Gage," Rhys says. "You stole the spotlight away from me on my birthday by making a hell of a statement. Don't let it all go to waste."

I open my mouth to tell them to mind their own damn business, but a petite blonde with almond-shaped hazel-brown eyes, dressed in a chic, sky-blue double-breasted blazer and a white skirt, approaches our table.

"I'm sorry, Mr. Gallagher, you have an important call from the Cayman Islands. I have the call on hold in your office."

Larkin nods. "Thank you, Gloria," he says. He rises to his feet. "Gentlemen, if you'll excuse me, duty calls." He shifts his attention to me. "Text me if you want the room."

"Thank you," I say.

Larkin cocks an eyebrow. "You didn't flat out refuse my offer. Progress."

I don't have a comeback.

"I'll forward the details so your date is aware of the dress code," he says.

I nod.

"Oh, Mr. Hollingsworth, you're going to love the dress code," Larkin says.

"That theme party kicks ass in terms of dress code for the women," Rhys says. "We show up in a boring suit."

"It's a favorite among members," Larkin says. "It has to do with the good versus bad rhetoric that's been drilled into Catholics for centuries—"

"Same goes for Anglicans," Rhys says.

"Point taken." Larkin nods. "At Dark Compulsion you get to live out the good versus bad rhetoric in a far less dogmatic way. When you give a woman the permission to be bad, something switches in her brain... It's going to be a night of debauchery."

"I'm looking forward to it." Rhys lifts his glass in salute.

Theme parties are particularly kinky at the club. I have no doubt Angels and Demons will live up to its promise.

With a nod, Larkin turns on his heel, Gloria and his beefy Irish shadows following him.

Bringing Lily to Dark Compulsion is crazy. Even more so

on a theme night. Now that Larkin has planted the seed in my head, I'm dying to corrupt her at the club.

Needing time to digest it all, I pick up my sandwich and keep eating.

Rhys does the same.

It doesn't take long for us to finish our food and wash it down with craft beer.

"It's good you're coming out tonight," Rhys says, tucking his napkin underneath his empty plate.

"The jury is still out if I'm coming or not."

He considers me for a long beat.

"What? I didn't commit. I thanked Larkin for his willingness to give up his room," I say. "This is an intimate part of my life. Lily will be on a flight to New York on Friday."

"Not that I want to sound like a fucking motivational quote, but so much can happen in four days..."

I respond with a non-committal shrug.

"No one has the right to put a timestamp on grief," he says.

He should know.

"You're allowed to take as long as you need to make amends with the bleak reality of losing a parent." He glances over his shoulder before returning his attention to me. "The guilt you've been carrying would break your mom's heart."

I'll go to my grave with the guilt.

"I made a promise to my dad." A lump forms in my throat. "I swore to him I'd always look after Mom." Rhys has heard this story I can't break free from before. "The red flags were there. Mom said she was happy. I didn't want to be the selfish son who told her she wasn't allowed to love again. I should've been like a dog on a bone. I bear the responsibility of her death on my shoulders."

After losing my mom, it got to a point where diving to the

bottom of a top-shelf bottle of liquor was my only salvation. Grief almost cracked me wide open. Same for survivor guilt.

During that dark time in my life, I wasn't as close to Rhys as I am now, but that didn't stop him from being there for me when I needed it most.

I didn't slide into full-blown alcoholism. I suffered from alcohol-related bereavement. Hours of therapy confirmed that.

Work helped me to move on, even though I knew I'd never be fully absolved of the role I played in my mother's death.

"Aren't you tired of holding up all those walls?" Rhys lets out an audible sigh. "It's been three years, Gage..."

"I know it's been three years." *I've been trapped in hell for that long.*

"Let go of the guilt before it kills you."

Chapter 31

Gage

This morning's publicity win caused a ripple effect. Not that I was planning on an extended lunch, but right after Rhys dispensed his words of wisdom, my executive assistant texted to let me know the media was camping in front of our offices, requesting more from Matthew.

By the time I returned to HQ, our security guards and the publicist had everything under control.

One less headache.

I was planning on calling Lily earlier, but I had to take care of an avalanche of congratulatory phone calls. To my surprise, Fisher texted me. I kept my reply brief.

Despite the fact Lily doesn't get along with her father, responding to a man a few hours before you're about to corrupt his only daughter is unholy.

After a pitstop in the kitchen to shoot my veins with an afternoon double shot café macchiato, I stroll back to my office. I post myself in front of the floor-to-ceiling window and make a call that's long overdue.

"Gage, how are you?"

Damn, I've missed her melodic voice.

"Hey, angel. How are you?"

"I'm good, but not as good as you. I'm so glad that horrible ordeal is behind you."

I'm surprised by her comment. Other than to give her a bit of background on me, I've never talked shop with her.

"You saw the news?"

"No. I had lunch with Michaela. She told me all about it. When I returned to my suite, I searched for the full story. Blanche Hyman is a nasty human being."

"She is."

"I feel sorry for her daughter."

"Snow is the loser in this story," I say. "I'm sure this never crossed her mother's mind because she was motivated by greed, but her daughter's credibility also took a hit. She can pretty much kiss her chances of becoming a violin star goodbye. Industry people are going to stay far away. By running her mouth, Blanche put a red X on her daughter's forehead."

"I have a puppet master as a parent."

She does.

"Speaking of your father, he contacted me about the media drama."

"He called you?"

"No, he texted me."

"I see," she says. "If it's okay with you, I'd rather not talk about him. I'd rather forget all about my puppet master until I'm back in New York when I have no other choice but to face him."

Message received loud and clear. "No skin off my back since that's not why I called."

"Can I be honest?"

"Sure."

"Had Mikki not told me about the nightmare you and your

show host were going through, I would've thought you were avoiding me because of something I did."

"Why would you think you did something wrong?"

"You were sending mixed messages. One minute you ask me to extend my trip, the next, you forget I'm in LA. I understand you had prior commitments with your family—and I'd never expect you to put me in front of them—but it's been radio silence on your end for days. Not even a quick text message. It's almost as if you regretted asking me to stay. I thought I'd made a mistake by pushing back my departure."

Lily's frank talk is sobering.

I let out an audible sigh, raking my hands through my hair. "I was avoiding you."

"Oh." The disappointment in her voice is unmistakable.

"It's nothing you did and it's nothing you said. The onus falls squarely on my shoulders."

"What do you mean?"

"Five days ago, I didn't even know you. I was doing your father a solid. I figured I'd accompany you to the gala and that would be that. I was planning on having dinner on your last night before waving you goodbye—"

"At least you're not lying about it."

"I might've been a dick for not being in touch, but I'm not a liar," I say. "I stayed away because I needed time to sort things out in my head."

"Where do we stand?"

"That's a bold question."

"Sorry, I didn't mean to—"

"I like you bold."

She lets out a little giggle. "It's your fault."

"Are you saying I'm rubbing off on you?"

"I'm saying you don't try to manipulate me when I stand up

for myself... that gives me the courage to say what's on my mind without pussyfooting for fear of retribution."

I let out a whistle. "There's so much in that statement. But delving into it further would imply involving your puppet master... and we're not talking about him."

"We're not."

"Everything that's transpired between us since you landed in LA took me by surprise."

"It's the same for me. I was expecting an insufferable chaperone, instead I ended up with a brooding billionaire hottie."

I chuckle.

"Let me explain why I haven't been in touch," I say.

"Okay."

"I haven't allowed a woman to get this close in a long time. Things between us have been fast and furious. I struggled to make sense of it. After my brother-in-law's birthday party, I wanted to be with you so damn much. That raw need scared the shit out of me." I pause. "So, I didn't call. Yesterday was hell. Still, I could've texted or called to let you know what I was dealing with. But I was too busy wrapping my head around how you went from being a stranger to a woman I wanted to fall asleep with." I weigh my words. "I had a shit night's sleep and it wasn't because of Monday's media circus. It's because you weren't nestled in my arms. After Friday and Saturday night, it was a hard habit to break."

Silence stretches on the other end.

I pull the phone away from my ear to make sure the call didn't get disconnected.

"Lily?"

"I'm still here." Her voice comes out breathless. "If it's any consolation, Michaela noticed the bags under my eyes because I had a terrible night's sleep. Apparently, my body needs the closeness of a brooding hottie to fall asleep now. A few days ago, I could sleep alone in the hotel's king size bed the minute my head touched the pillow. I had a restless night, tossing, and turning."

"I fucking miss you."

"I missed you too."

Music to my ears.

"Do I get to see you tonight?" Her tone is bubbly and bright.

"I'll do you one better. We're going out. There's a theme party taking place at a club I'm a member of, and I'd love for you to accompany me."

"What's the theme?"

"Angels and demons."

"That sounds fun. Good girls and bad boys."

I'm about to burst her bubble.

"There's nothing nice about tonight's party," I say. "It's bad girls *and* bad boys."

"Oooh. What's the name of the club?"

"Dark Compulsion—"

"That sounds like fifty shades of mysterious."

"More like fifty shades of kinky."

"Kinky?"

"Yes, kinky."

"As in... lewd?"

"As in darn right depraved," I say. "Once you step over the threshold of the club, expect over-the-top, obscene, and indecent."

"Oh."

I keep talking. "Dark Compulsion is an exclusive high-end adult club. It's annexed to the Quintus Hotel. It's where the crème de la crème goes to play. Most of the people you met at Rhys's birthday party are members."

"Including the sisterhood?"

"Yes. The guys go with their girls—"

"Your friends are swingers?" Her voice goes up several octaves.

"None of the guys in my inner circle would allow another man to touch their woman. They don't hook up with other members. Some members are swingers, but you don't have to be into that lifestyle to be a Dark Compulsion member. There are so many other ways to have a fun evening without swapping partners."

"Toto, I have a feeling we're not in Kansas anymore."

I chuckle. "No, Dorothy, you aren't."

"What you describe... is so out of my comfort zone. I'm going to stick out like a sore thumb. I'm sure I'll embarrass you."

"You won't. There's a first time for all members and guests. There's a dress code—"

"Oh, gosh—"

"Calm down. I wanted to talk to you first, but I'll call Michaela and Keira so they can hold your hand. We can figure out if you'll ride with them or if I come and pick you up."

"Okay. That eases the pressure a little."

"You're going to step into a world you've never been in before. You can indulge in as little or as much as you want..."

Chapter 32

Lily

If someone had told me one day I'd step into an adult club, I would've laughed until I ran out of air. Yet, here I am, stepping into one of LA's most exclusive adult clubs, dressed like I'm about to audition for a spot as one of the entertainers at Crazy Horse Paris. Never in a million years did I imagine I'd have the guts to pull this off. It would've never happened without the sisterhood.

There's a long driveway from the security gate to the club, flanked by tall trees and high bushes. The landscaping is as immaculate as the palace of Versailles's gardens. My nose was glued to the window of the chauffeured Rolls-Royce Mikki hired for us girls as I took it all in.

This is like stepping into a magical land.

I spot a group of men, dressed in tuxedos or sharp suits, smoking cigars, drinks in hand. Women wearing not much strut around, winking and blowing kisses, hips swaying left to right in a tempting way.

I was certain that was enough to give me a taste of what's to come. That's until Michaela, Keira, and I enter the main party room.

I freeze at the threshold.

Holy. Shit.

Our surroundings scream influence, prestige, and misbehaving.

My puppet master would have a cardiac arrest if he knew I was here.

So, this is where LA's crème de la crème comes to play.

My wide eyes bounce around the room, my senses on overdrive.

I swallow my tongue when my gaze lands on a daring brunette with brown eyes, wearing a pink see-through mesh slip.

She isn't sporting wings or a halo. She's wearing a mask that covers her eyes. The upper part of her slip is pulled down to her waist and her breasts are exposed. Her gigantic, sagging boobs with huge areolas droop down to her waist.

As if that wasn't shocking enough, she's sucking on one of her breasts. She's so determined, it's as if she's trying to shove the whole thing into her mouth.

Mikki wraps an arm around my shoulders and pulls me forwards. "That's Shione. She's an exhibitionist. Sucking on her own breasts while masturbating or using toys on herself while seated on a couch is her thing. She never hooks up with anyone. She prefers going at it solo. That's why she's wearing a face mask. It lets members and guests know that she doesn't play with others."

I scrunch my nose. "Why bother paying the crazy membership fee?"

Mikki is about to answer when Shione slaps her enormous breast hard.

My head jerks back.

She pinches her nipples so hard, *I* feel it.

Dear God.

"She's an eccentric who divorced well. Twice," Mikki says. "She has the money and she loves being watched and watching others."

"Okay." I don't get it.

"The first time at the club is jaw-dropping," Mikki says.

"She's right." Keira nods. "In case you were wondering, it takes a while to stop being freaked out by people fucking each other or performing oral sex on each other on one of the oversized L-shape couches, up against a wall, in the staircase, or on the floor. And, don't be surprise if you smell the scent of sex for days to come."

What have I gotten myself into? "Noted."

Keira invited Michaela and I to her place for dinner, a scrumptious dessert, and some liquid courage. Phoenix, Rhys, and Gage are hanging out with Collin and his brother Shane.

Gage and his buddies arrived a little while ago. He's floating somewhere.

Dominika isn't coming because Rod refuses to let another man see her baby belly, so they're having a private Angel and Demon night at their place. Other people in Gage's inner circle will arrive later. I'm still trying to wrap my head around the fact I'm partying with this crowd.

In a matter of five days, I went from being a virgin to stepping into a private adult club.

I leapfrogged my way up the kinky ladder.

Unbelievable.

Nadine is going to freak out.

"Do you need a drink?" Keira says.

I shake my head. "I'm okay for now. I have enough liquid courage in my system as is."

"Don't forget, we're only allowed two drinks," Mikki says.

"I won't."

Security is no joke here. You don't waltz into Dark Compulsion, even if you're on the guest list. After signing the lengthy NDA and given a warning about the use of phones, a tall, leggy blonde secured a cuff around my wrist before giving me a club name—a computer generated Crayola color. Pretty original.

Michaela and Keira have proper club names and club rings.

When I enquired about the annual fees, my eyes doubled in size. That's some serious coin to get your freak on.

Keira scours the room before fixing Mikki and I with her hazel-green eyes. "I'm guessing our friends who've arrived are up in their rooms, involved in some kinkiness. I don't see anyone that's part of our inner circle," she says. "Let's go to the bar for some sparkling water. I'm thirsty."

"Lead the way," Mikki says.

I follow my two friends through the mass of bodies.

I can't help but wiggle my shoulders when I recognize the song playing.

Don't Call Me Angel.

The perfect theme party song.

The music is low enough not to drown out conversation, but loud enough to enjoy.

With a glass of Perrier in hand, we roam around the room.

Members are serious about dressing the part.

A man in a tailored suit always looks so fucking hot.

I have no doubt my man—

Whoa.

He's not my man. He's my date for tonight.

After a tour of the main party room, my friends and I come to stand near the bar. A tall man with brown hair, clad in a bespoke suit flanked by two human walls of muscle approaches our trio.

"Ladies, thank you for coming out to play tonight," the man says.

"Zeus," Keira says with a nod.

"Hey, Zeus," Mikki says.

Ah. Larkin Gallagher. The owner.

"Styx." The man nods at Keira before raking his eyes up and down her body. "Emeraude." Mikki receives the same treatment. "You ladies do tonight's theme justice."

Mikki's slender curves are clad in a sexy bling rhinestone bra that you'd expect to see on the runway. The nude padding prevents her from exposing her boobs to the world. An intricate crystal body chain circles her waist. She paired the bra with bling silver boy shorts and sky-high silver heels. She has silver wings strapped to her back.

Keira selected a sheer, shimmery white chemise that barely covers her ass. She has white wings strapped to her back.

Female members and guests either get to wear angel wings or an angel halo, depending if they're spoken for or not.

Beckett's fiancée, Arianne, is a blue angel with matching blue wings. The selfies she sent us rock.

Keira, Mikki, and Arianne owned their wings. Dominika dropped hers at Keira's place for me to wear.

Makeup and hair were a production.

After watching way too many tutorial videos, we went all out. The end results are pretty spectacular. Any Vegas show makeup artist would be proud.

I feel like a supermodel.

"Thank you, Zeus," Keira says.

"You're full of compliments, like always," Mikki says.

"I speak the truth." The owner of the club lasers his eyes on me. "Birds of a feather flock together." He gives me a onceover. "You're stunning."

I blush.

"Ladies"—Larkin's cognac-colored eyes bounce from Mikki to Keira—"bravo on guiding our first-timer. Wisteria, you could cause a man to suffer from a heart attack."

He knows my club name? "Thank you," I say from under my lashes.

"The wings send a clear message to members and guests who are unaccompanied to keep looking." He points to his pocket square.

Men without a red pocket square have a date for the evening.

Larkin is on the prowl.

"If you weren't spoken for, you'd be very popular tonight."

My blush deepens.

Larkin cocks a brow. "Lucius is one lucky club member."

Oh, yeah, Lucius is Gage's club name. I can't slip up. "I'm the lucky one."

"Gorgeous *and* modest." He nods. "Good on you for getting a tiger to change his stripes." Larkin holds my gaze. "Not an easy feat considering Lucius can be dead set in his ways. You've reformed him."

I'm so overwhelmed by his words, I don't know what to say.

His eyes move over my head for a brief moment before fixing on me. "I've been summoned. It was a pleasure to meet you, Wisteria."

"Zeus, it was a pleasure." I have no idea why I feel the need to curtsy and bow, but I do.

Way to show you're a newbie.

"I'm a mere mortal," Larkin says. "I don't have a drop of royal in me. No need to be that formal."

Keira and Mikki laugh.

I cringe. "I'm sorry."

The tall man leans into me. "Don't worry, I won't hold it against you as long as you promise me one thing."

I stare up into his amber eyes. "What?"

"You'll let Lucius push you outside your comfort zone, so you'll never forget your first time here."

He pulls away and studies me from his towering height.

Oh, don't worry, buddy, I'll never forget my first time here. "I will."

"A member in the making," he says. "I'm pleased."

There's a bit of commotion at the bar, which pulls my attention away from Larkin. When I catch sight of the action, my eyes bulge out of their sockets.

Jaw meet floor.

A plus size woman, wearing a purple wig cut in a bob style, and sporting tattoos on each arm, is the cause of the chaos. She isn't wearing wings, a halo, or a facemask. She's wearing a headband on her forehead.

I'm dumbfounded by the fact she's only wearing a G-string and platform high heels—both yellow. And she has one guy sucking on one of her giant boobs and another guy sucking on the other, and a third guy is knelt at her feet, fingering her pussy while jerking off at a furious pace.

That man's cock needs to come with a warning.

He can't close his hand around his shaft because he's huge.

And his balls are the size of... kiwis.

Oh.

My.

God.

I clamp my teeth together to prevent my mouth from gaping.

Keira leans in. "That's one kinky couple."

I blink at her.

My gaze moves towards Mikki.

She shrugs. The expression on her face says, '*This is an adult club. Not a theme park for kids*'.

Larkin jerks his chin towards the risqué woman. "That's Tetona." He points to a less than average height, muscular, dark-skinned man in a burgundy-color suit and an open black shirt. "The bald guy is her husband." The man is rubbing his cock over his pant suit.

His cock is running down his thigh?

Holy enormous.

"Since she's been a member, she's always showed up topless and wearing a G-string —regardless of the evening's theme." Larkin isn't done shocking me. "She loves getting her mammoth tits sucked by men or women. She was quite popular during the last trimester of her pregnancy when her breasts were eye-popping M-cups. She gave birth nine months ago. This is her second time back at the club. Her popularity has skyrocketed with members who have an adult breastfeeding kink."

Alrighty then.

"Tetona is a femdom."

What does that mean?

God. My innocence is glowing in the dark.

"She orders her husband to whip out his dick and rub one out, while he watches others give her pleasure, and shoot his load in the mouth of one of her willing playmates—man or woman. Whatever her husband lacks in height, he makes up for in dick size. Which is why Tetona doesn't allow any of her play-mates to suck off the hubby's dick. She's territorial like that." Larkin's explanation rattles every good girl fiber of my being.

Holy fuck.

"The guy knelt at Tetona's feet is Gilby. I've been told his superpower is his longer than average tongue and the fact he knows what to do with it. He's one of Tetona's favorite play-mates. She always comes, screaming, gushing all over his face. Gilby's fetish is eating out women who have the ability to come like water fountains. That man can eat pussy morning, day, and night. I'm sure it's only a matter of time before Tetona sits on his face. It's a pretty spectacular show."

Too much info.

"Those members take playtime at the club seriously."

No kidding.

"The headband lets members and guests know they can approach her even if she's married," Larkin says. "Anyone can suck on her tits and play with her pussy. However, she'll only suck her husband's cock and he's the only one allowed to fuck her."

I pick up my jaw from the floor.

Tetona's eyes meet mine and she waves me over with one hand, the other pointing at her boobs.

This isn't pushing me out of my comfort zone. This is jumping out of an airplane without a parachute.

Nope.

Not happening.

"Hard pass." The words rush out of my mouth. *I hope I didn't commit a faux pas.*

"One on one is more up your alley?"

I stare up at Larkin. "Yes."

"In that case, you're ready to go up to your room and play. Lucius wanted to give you time to soak in the... atmosphere." Larkin produces something from the inside of his suit jacket. "Your keycard. Lucius is waiting for you in your assigned room."

"Thank you." I pluck the card from his fingers.

"I assume, Styx and Emeraude explained how the keycard works?"

"Yes." I recite what my friends told me. "Once I scan the card against one of the iPads near the elevator, it will show my room number and the location of said room."

"Good girl," Larkin says. "You're ready to play."

Chapter 33

Gage

Phoenix and Rhys are in their rooms, waiting for their significant others. Collin and Shane Dennison are in the gardens, each searching for a willing soul to corrupt tonight. With Shane's good looks and Collin's cocksureness, angels sporting halos will trip all over themselves for a chance to catch their eye.

When I arrived at the club, there was a message from Larkin waiting for me. A security guard walked me to one of the control rooms where Larkin handed me the keycard to his private room. He also suggested I hang out.

There's something illicit and erotic about watching someone without their knowledge. Since Lily set foot inside the main party room, I've had my eyes on her. It killed the element of surprise, but at the same time it prevented me from having a heart attack.

Holy fuck, my angel is hot.

Lily is the most beautiful woman I've ever laid eyes on, but tonight, she's transformed into a breathtaking super model.

Even though she's sporting wings, men glanced her way as she sashayed behind Keira and Michaela. A fresh face at the club always gets members excited. Especially when it's a gorgeous face.

That's right, fuckers. She's mine.

Lily was oblivious to all the attention from male members.

I'm guessing her senses were on overload.

I was certain she was going to bolt out the door when her eyes landed on Tetona's giant exposed tits. Not all members require a room to get down and dirty. Her and her husband are among that group.

Watching Lily watch Tetona as three men brought her pleasure was priceless. Not even Gilby rubbing one off was enough for her to change her mind.

It wasn't my plan, but my little angel got a hell of a crash course.

Larkin made it his personal mission to ensure I never forget this night... neither will Lily.

It was his idea to hand her the keycard.

The second Lily plucked the card from his fingers, I was heading to the elevator to Larkin's private room.

It's been years since I've been in one of the rooms or lounge rooms. The level of luxury hasn't changed. If anything, it's increased.

Larkin's quarters are next level opulence. It's like sitting in a chic Parisian apartment.

I sit on the king size bed, waiting for Lily to show up, willing myself to be patient.

A door closing lets me know I'm no longer alone in the suite.

The click of her high heels against the herringbone pattern wooden floor alerts me she's nearby. That, and the lovely floral scent that reaches my nose.

An angel dressed in black, sporting the same color wings, appears in the threshold of the bedroom.

Jesus Christ.

The expanding bulge in my pants makes it hard to breathe.

My eyes roam over her body before settling on her face.

Her long black hair is pulled back, revealing her stunning features.

I can't wait to fuck up her hair, so I can run my fingers through her silky mane.

Lily's makeup is as dramatic as the outfit she's wearing.

She gravitates towards pale pink lipstick shades. Tonight, she's wearing a deep reddish shade that accentuates her lips.

Fuck, I want that color staining my cock when her luscious mouth wraps eagerly around it.

Big blue eyes roam around the room before settling on me.

"Hey," she says. The shyness in her voice is a stark contrast to the cock-hardening outfit she's wearing.

"You didn't want to stay downstairs and play with Tetona and her friends?"

"Good God, no." She scoffs. "Never. Not even for ten billion—" She frowns. "How did you know about Tetona? Were you downstairs?"

"I was watching you."

"You were?"

"I wanted to experience your first time at the club through your eyes. I didn't want to give you time to filter what you saw. I wanted it raw."

"Did you see Keira and Mikki?"

"I might have caught a glimpse of them, but I was way too focused on a beauty with raven hair to pay them too much attention."

She blushes.

"Did I look freaked out?"

"You did." No point in bullshitting her. In fact, at times, she looked terrified. "But you're still here."

"I'm still here." She punctuates her sentence with a firm nod. "Wait. If you were stalking me—"

"Stalking?" I feign being offended even though that's what I was doing. "I was checking you out."

"Sure." Her tone suggests she doesn't believe me. "That killed the element of surprise when I walked into the room."

"I beg to differ. Seeing you on a monitor is different than seeing you standing in front of me dressed like my fucking wet dream."

"Your wet dream?" Her eyes widen. "You're pulling my leg."

"No, I'm not. From the moment I caught sight of you, I was hard. I couldn't wait to get you all to myself."

"That's all I've been thinking about since you called me to invite me here tonight," she says.

"You've been counting the hours until you got down and dirty with me?"

She bites her lower lip. "Yes."

One word. So many possibilities.

I wave her over. "Come here."

Something veils her eyes.

I don't catch on, but when she struts towards me like she's working the runway, I get it.

She comes to stand in front of me and does a little twirl before adopting a seductive pose, glancing at me from over her shoulder.

Her beautiful ass is on display.

Be still my beating heart.

"I wasn't sure you'd go for it." I give her a onceover. "You're revealing a lot of skin."

She turns around. "You don't like the way I look?" Insecurity colors her words.

"I love the sexy lingerie. And I have no doubt, I'll love it even more when it's on the floor."

Relief washes over her.

She turns around again, shimmies her shoulders, and faces me. "Did you see the wings? So cool."

They're impossible to miss, but I play along. "I did. You wear them well. After all, you were born to fly."

Her joyful expression vanishes, replaced by... longing? Yearning? Regret? I can't quite put my finger on it.

Her eyes drop to the floor for a beat. "I'm still working up the courage to fly on my own."

I let her confession float between us.

"You'll get there," I say.

She responds with a warm smile.

"Tonight is quite the production." I change the subject. "The hours it took to find the perfect lingerie. The grooming, prepping, and primping. The angel wings." She lets out a dramatic exhale. "It's quite the production only to end up naked, but it wouldn't have been as fun if I didn't go all the way."

"I agree."

"Excuse me, Mr. Suit. It probably took you five minutes to slip into that"—she gestures to my black suit which I paired with a black shirt, sans tie—"and about thirty seconds to slide into those shoes." She points at my British bespoke black shoes. "This"—she waves a finger up and down the length of her body—"was hours of work. *Hours.*"

"And I appreciate it."

She flashes me a beaming smile.

Lily selected a black lace corset with garter belt, black stockings, and sky-high black heels. An intricate trail of crystals decorates the bodice and loops around her neck, giving the illusion of a necklace.

The padded cups accentuate her breasts. It's a form-fitting number that creates the ultimate hourglass silhouette. Six gold hook and eye snaps hold the corset together.

Six gold hook and eye snaps that are between me and the object of my desire.

I called French Appliqué and made sure the sales attendant helping her had my credit card to pay for the seven-hundred-dollar corset, a matching thong that set me back a hundred-fifty-dollars, and the other items she tried on.

Worth every damn penny.

"So..."—she dances from one foot to the other—"what happens now?"

I reach behind me, grab a red lacquered box, and hand it to her.

Her eyes light up. "A gift?"

"You could say that."

She opens the box and stares at the contents.

She brings a hand to her neck. "A necklace? Oh, my gosh, that's so sweet—"

"It's much more than a necklace. It's a vibrator designed to double as a necklace."

Her gaze snaps up to meet mine.

"The chain is removable," I say. "It's one of the most powerful clit stimulators on the market."

The vibrator resembles an elongated silver bullet with a rose gold flat top where the removable chain can be attached. Fashionable and pleasurable. Talk about a two for one deal.

Myriad emotions flash in her eyes. "A sex toy? You got me a sex toy?"

"The demon gets to select how he corrupts his angel."

She's staring at me, dumbfounded. "And you selected a sex toy?"

"There were other options."

"Which ones?" The question flies out of her mouth.

"Do you trust me, Lily?"

A wrinkle of concern forms between her brows.

"Without trust, this"—I wave a finger between us—"won't work for tonight."

"I trust you, but... a sex toy?"

"That's not trust. You either trust me implicitly or you don't."

Silence.

"Beckett reserved one of the Peek-a-boo rooms. It's a room set up to allow an exhibitionist couple to fuck, while an anonymous couple watches them from another room, separated by a glass wall. It's Arianne's first time in the Peek-a-boo room and her first time as a voyeur." Lily's eyes bulge out of her skull. "Phoenix selected a room with a suspended cage located near a window that overlooks a dance below where members will be partying. Michaela will be dancing naked for her husband." I don't tell her the windows in the room he reserved are tinted. Not even Michaela knows. Phoenix will be the only one to enjoy his wife's body. "Rhys also reserved a Peek-a-boo room. The couple he and Keira will be watching are particularly kinky. Holt—Beckett's older brother—has his girl all tied up for the night. The man is a master at rope bondage. His girl can only receive pleasure. She can't touch him."

Blink.

Blink.

Blink.

"I wanted to ease you into it, but if you prefer a cage or if you're up for watching another couple fuck, I have no problem changing our plans. If you want me to tie you up, I'm happy to oblige."

She shakes her head.

I couldn't fathom her agreeing to either of those options.

"You're sure about that?"

"I'm positive."

"Consider yourself lucky. As the demon, I could've asked for your soul or demanded you use the vibrator downstairs in the main party room—"

"In front of other people?" Her eyes are the size of saucers.

"It works for Tetona." I wink.

"You're a bad man."

"A demon is supposed to be evil."

She narrows her eyes at me.

"So, you're okay with the toys?"

"Toys? There's only one in here?"

I slide my hand behind my back and produce a gold lacquered box. "Here's the other one." I extend both hands and we trade boxes.

"What's the difference between the two?"

Such innocence. "One is for your pussy and the other one... is for your ass."

A second ticks by.

And another.

And another.

Her eyes drop to the box she's holding. "Will it hurt?"

If she had refused and requested plain vanilla sex, I would've granted her wish. I need to be with her tonight. The fact she's willing to trust me and submit so beautifully is fucking hot.

"We'll use lots of lube, and we'll take it nice and slow."

"What if I don't like it?"

"You'll have to be satisfied with riding my cock."

Her glassy eyes shine bright with desire. "You say that like it's a consolation prize. Your cock *is* the prize."

Fuck, there isn't a man on the planet who wouldn't want his girl to have such praise about his cock—

Whoa.

My girl?

This is crazy.

Lily lives on the other side of the country.

This is about tonight and the next few days before the fantasy vanishes into smoke.

"You're ready to play, angel?"

She flashes me a seductive smile. "I'm more than ready."

"Give me the box you're holding."

She does as she's told.

I place both boxes on the bed, so my hands are free.

"I want you to unclasp the garter belt, slide out of your panties, and throw your panties at me. Make sure to fasten the garter belt, so the stockings don't become a distraction."

She leans forward, hanging on my every word.

"Once done, I want you on the bed, on all fours, filling your pussy with the toy."

"What?"

"Did I stutter?"

"No, but..."—her eyes dart left to right—"but..."

"But, what?"

"Aren't you going to insert the toy?"

The corners of my lips tug upward. "You want me to do it?"

"Yes."

"That's not how the game is played, Lily. I give the orders. You"—I point at her—"submit."

"I've never done anything like that before."

"You had never played with your pussy in public until I came into the picture," I say. "I can't tell you how many times

I've jerked off to the memory of you being my dirty girl in my car."

Our gazes clash, and she squares her shoulders.

A battle of wills plays out in silence.

I'm a patient man.

Her lips twist. "Got it. You give the orders."

My good little submissive.

"Do I need a safe word?"

That's the last question I expected from her. "No."

"Isn't that how it works?"

"Isn't this your first time in an adult club? What do you know about safe words?"

She cringes. "The heroes in romance books often suggest one."

This isn't a fiction novel and I'm no knight in shining armor. "We're not going to do anything that would require a safe word." I set her mind at ease. "If something doesn't feel comfortable, tell me, and everything stops."

"Okay."

"Any other questions?"

"Can you help me with my wings?" She turns around. "It's a two-person job."

"My pleasure."

I slide the wings off her body before placing them on the floor. I make sure to place them out of the way. I don't want to have to explain to Rod how my kinky ways ruined his wife's wings. I reach for the two long sticks protruding from her hair like chopsticks, pull them out, and toss them so they land near the wings. Her long hair tumbles over her shoulders, down her back, the tips flirting with her ass cheeks. Unable to resist, I run my fingers through her thick, silky mane.

"You have the most beautiful hair."

Lily turns around. "Thanks."

I push the cascade of hair off her shoulders.

I don't want anything obstructing her beautiful body.

I grab her arm and pull her towards me.

She stares at me through hooded eyes.

Cupping the back of her head, I take her mouth in a heated kiss.

A part of me feels guilty for messing up her lipstick, but fuck it, I've missed her mouth so damn much. The kiss is a passionate storm—fervent, ardent, and intense. It sparks a foreign sensation in my chest I've never experienced before.

I pull away from her, so I don't end up drowning in the kiss. "Hand over your panties. I need to have a taste of your other lips."

She kicks off one shoe.

"What are you doing?"

Questioning eyes stare at me. "How else am I supposed to get undressed?"

"You're not. You remove *only* the panties. That's it."

She corrects her error, sliding back in her high heel.

Her lips curl up as her hands land on her body. She traces the contour of her figure until her hands land on the clasp that holds the stockings. Watching her unclasp the garter belt and shimmy out of her G-string is a vision far more erotic than anything I've seen at the Crazy Horse Paris or Vegas burlesque shows.

I expected her to follow my command without much fanfare, but that's not what I got.

Holy goddess.

I'm utterly captivated by the sexy-as-fuck strip show Lily grants me.

When she throws the scrap of black lace at me, I catch it with one hand and bring her panties to my nose.

I breathe her in.

"Fuck, I missed your heady smell." I growl, burying my nose into the fabric.

Her eyelashes flutter.

Poor little lamb. Let me be your shepherd. I tap the bed. "Hop on."

With hesitant steps, she approaches.

She gets on the bed.

She's about to crawl, but I stop her. "Don't go any further."

She freezes.

"Move down a little. I want your knees right at the edge."

She assumes the position.

I toss her panties aside and give her my full attention.

I reach for her ass, caress it, and drop a soft kiss on her cheek.

She glances over her shoulder.

With my eyes locked onto hers, I trace a finger between her pussy lips. "You're so fucking wet. Is all that for me?"

"Being around you turns me on so damn much."

I grope my hard cock and squeeze. "I feel the same about you."

Even though she can't see my hand, a wide smile stretches her lips.

I let go of my cock and hand her the vibrator. "Slide this little gem inside your dripping pussy."

She obeys.

"Slide it in and out."

She heaves in a breath and does as she's told.

Watching her fuck herself is so hot.

"Stop."

Her hand halts.

Feeling my way, I find the little button on the side of the toy and press it.

Lily pants. "Oh... it vibrates."

"Hence why they call it a vibrator."

"Hey, don't be so hard on me," she says. "This is my first sex toy."

"Speaking of which, I want you to place the tip of the vibrator against your clit."

As she obeys my command, I remove my jacket and toss it onto the chaise longue. I unbutton my shirt and do quick work at rolling up my sleeves to my elbows.

I crouch behind her, grip her ass cheeks with both hands, and open her wide.

She inhales a sharp breath, but her hand stays wedged between her legs.

I poke a finger between her pussy lips.

She clenches around it.

"Bad girl."

She relaxes.

"You still trust me?"

She nods.

"Words."

She glances over her shoulder. "Yes, I trust you."

I skate a languorous finger around her pussy.

"You like this. Being at my mercy. Being my dirty girl. Obeying my commands, unsure what I'm going to do to you, but still willing to go along with it."

She moans.

I coat my fingers with her pussy juices before moving them to her tight hole and tracing around the entrance.

Fuck, she doesn't even object.

I return my fingers to her pussy and plunge them in one hard thrust inside her slickness.

She gyrates her hips in a circle.

"You're a greedy, dirty girl. And to think, if our paths had never crossed, you might never have known that about yourself."

She rotates the vibrator around her clit.

With my free hand, I find the button, and bump up the vibration to the highest speed.

"Oh, oh, oh." She wiggles her ass.

I'm so hard, it's painful.

"You have me breaking all my rules."

"Which rules?"

I didn't mean for her to hear that.

Going down that road would be a mood killer.

"Don't worry about that," I say. "Keep working that beautiful pussy for me."

She doesn't disappoint.

I lean into her and drag my nose along her inner thigh, breathing in her scent.

She shudders.

I tease her entrance with a finger, her wetness dripping more and more before pushing it inside.

My lips curl up in satisfaction. "I'm going to feast on your greedy little pussy."

"God, yes."

My smile turns victorious.

I replace my fingers with my tongue, sticking it inside her warmth.

Lily lowers her body, as if to make sure my tongue goes as deep as possible.

She thinks she controls this.

I clasp both hands on her cheeks and squeeze hard.

"So good. That feels so good."

I tongue-fuck her, relishing how her abundant juices coat my tongue.

Change of plans.

I latch onto her pussy.

Lily cries out.

I devour her like a starved man.

"Oh, Gage."

I double my efforts.

I'm wild as I lose my goddamn mind eating her out.

"You're torturing me," she says.

I pull away from her. "You want me to stop?"

"Don't stop. Don't ever stop." Her words come out in a frantic rush.

I pull her pussy lips between my teeth and bite down gently.

She makes a choking sound.

I do it again. Harder.

She lets out a long exhale.

Sweet Lily enjoys a little pain.

I nip it again, this time tugging back so I can make it hurt real good.

Her legs close around my head.

That's it, angel, smother me.

That's my incentive to tongue-fuck her without restraint.

I lose myself in my mission, my tongue more and more demanding. My cock is so fucking hard, it's threatening to burst right through the zipper of my pants.

Lily takes it one step further.

She rubs the vibrator over her clit, chanting something that's a cross between a curse and a prayer.

Fuck the butt plug.

I use my thumb to scoop up her juices before inserting it inside her puckered hole. Easing it in to give her time to adjust to the new sensation.

She wiggles her ass, wanting more.

Your wish is my command.

I push my thumb in to the first knuckle, teasing her mercilessly.

More ass wiggling.

Okay. You asked for it.

I slide my thumb all the way in and fuck her pussy with my tongue as I fuck her ass with my thumb.

"Gage— God— I'm— I'm going— God, I'm going to come."

My tongue and thumb work in tandem.

A feral sound escapes from her lips, reverberating against the walls.

She's so loud, I wouldn't be surprised if they heard her in the main party room.

Lily comes, and comes, and comes.

I don't rush her.

As soon as her orgasm simmers, I slide my thumb out of her asshole, and stand up.

She glances over her shoulder, her blue eyes veiled with lust. "Please, fuck me."

I can no longer contain the bulging hard-on in my suit pants.

I undress at lightning speed.

My cock springs free.

I can't wait to lose myself between her legs.

I bend down, searching my pants pocket for a condom.

I rip the packet open with my teeth and make quick work of sheathing my raging cock.

Her eyes are glued to my mighty erection.

I give myself a hard tug and place the head of my cock at her opening.

"This is going to be fast and furious. I want you too damn much to last long."

"I don't care. As long as you fuck me."

Her response is my demise.

With a roar, I bury myself deep inside her pussy in one hard thrust.

Jesus Christ.

How did I survive two days without fucking this woman?

I drive into her.

In and out.

In and out.

I fist her hair and pull so our eyes meet.

She gasps.

"You're dripping because of me. Slick, sweet juices only for me."

"Yes, only for you."

"I'm the only one who can fuck you this well." Her pussy is so potent, I'm losing the grip on my sanity.

"Only you, Gage."

Goddammit, I love hearing my name on her lips in the throes of passion.

Sweat beads trickle down my face as I fuck her hard.

A burning urge takes over me, and all movement halts.

I let go of her hair and pull out of her.

"Wh—why did you stop?"

"I want to see your beautiful face when you come for me." Without giving her a chance to answer, I lift her in my arms, and walk us both to a nearby wall.

She laughs. "What's up with your aversion to beds?"

"What's the point of coming to an adult club if you're going to keep it predictable."

"Point taken."

I carry her weight with one arm, as I line up my cock at her entrance.

With a loud moan, I thrust inside her.

Since she's a little thing, this position will prevent me from breaking her.

My pace is as frantic as it was a few minutes ago, my insatiable need for her all-encompassing.

She reaches for my face and wipes away the sweat pearling my forehead. "You're fucking me so hard, you're sweating."

"Too hard?"

She shakes her head. "I don't want your heart to give up before you make me come again."

I didn't see that coming.

My nostrils flare, and my gaze burns into hers. "Is that a challenge?"

She cocks a brow.

"Challenge accepted."

I fuck her with such determination, it's as if I'm trying to pin her body to the wall.

"Dear God, I'm never going to be able to walk tomorrow," she says.

"Forget about tomorrow. You might not be able to walk all week. You asked for it."

If she doesn't respond with a wicked grin.

With that, I give her what she was itching for—a good hard fucking.

My heart pounds in my chest.

Fuck. She was right. My heart won't hold.

What a way to go.

"I'm the only one who can fuck you like this." I power inside her over and over, each thrust bringing me closer to the edge.

Her nails claw at my shoulders. "You are."

"Don't. You. Ever. Forget it." Each word is punctuated by a punishing thrust.

I've lost it.

This is insane.

The way my body responds to hers...

She's my drug.

Every time I fuck her pussy, she erodes pieces from the walls to my fortress.

Sorceress.

"You make me lose my mind," I say on a breath as my hips move at the same velocity as a piston.

I'm teetering on the edge.

I crush her body against the wall, using the only leverage I have to make her come fast. My hands firm their grip on her hips, and I angle my body so my pelvis is rubbing against her clit.

Her legs tighten around my waist.

She squeezes her eyes shut.

"No, Lily. Eyes on me."

Long, dark lashes, flutter a mile a minute. It's a struggle for her to focus on my face.

She's close.

"I want you to come hard for me." My command sounds more like a plea.

She nods in a jerky movement.

I'm too far gone to even bother asking her for words.

Her pussy grips my cock, and I choke on a growl.

Lily screams out my name.

Her muscles contract in powerful staccato pulses, ending on a hard death-grip clench.

The unexpected movement tears a growl from my throat.

My cock pulses inside her as my orgasm crashes through my body like a hurricane.

Uncontrollable.

Untamed.

Unleashed.

"Oh, God, Lily—" I come apart, staring into the hypno-tizing blue eyes of the woman who changed my strict, self-imposed rules. My head falls into the crook of her neck. It takes every ounce of energy I possess not to crumble to my knees.

My breathing is labored.

I've never wanted a woman with such unrepentant need in my life.

It's visceral.

Primal.

It's... disconcerting.

And it scares the shit out of me.

Chapter 34

Lily

Last night, Gage made up for the two days we didn't see each other.

I swear, we christened every wall in Larkin's private room.

I kept my expectations low when it was time to leave the club.

I had a hard time containing my smile when Gage announced he was spending the night in my room with me curled up in his arms.

Best. Sleep. Ever.

I figured today he would be busy doing CEO stuff and I wouldn't see him until later. He surprised me in the best possible way. He slipped out of my bed early and headed to the office to cram as much work as possible in the first hours of the day, so we can have an extended lunch.

When Mikki suggested we enjoy an afternoon French tea, I let her know I was hanging out with Gage.

She was more excited than I was.

Not that I know how that's even possible, considering, I've been counting the minutes until I see him again.

I'm being reckless with my heart. In two days, I fly back to New York, and this fairytale will surely come to a screeching halt.

Gage hasn't talked about us seeing each other or keeping in touch.

I didn't bring it up.

I refuse to stress over things I can't control. I prefer to enjoy a wonderful day with a man that knows how to rock my world. The billionaire mogul could be wheeling and dealing. Instead, he chose to play hooky with me for a few hours. He could've bought me the most expensive gift on the planet, and I wouldn't be this elated.

Spending time with him trumps everything.

The ride up Pacific Coast Highway to Malibu in Gage's German automobile was as exhilarating the second time around. This is another perfect day to enjoy a picnic outside. This time around, we're in a different resting spot than the one we were at the last time. Since it's Wednesday, there's only a smattering of people here and there, which is nice.

Instead of ordering sandwiches from the Pompadour Hotel, we dropped by one of Gage's favorite Italian eateries. The lip-smacking chicken cutlet pesto hero sandwich is one of the best things I've ever put in my mouth… other than Gage's cock.

My gaze swings in the brooding hottie's direction.

He left his suit jacket and tie in his car. Even with his white shirt unbuttoned and sans tie, he gives off the vibes of a badass CEO.

He winks.

God, I have it bad for this guy.

"I thought I was being too greedy when I couldn't decide between the cookies and cream flavor and the chocolate cookies and cream." I feign he doesn't affect me. "I'm glad I followed your advice and selected both."

"Two ice cream flavors chock-full of sandwich cream cookies outsourced from a local bakery? O'Dwyer's know what they're doing."

"I couldn't agree more," I say. "I'm a huge fan of Oreo cookies, but I must say this gourmet option is outstanding."

"You're sure you don't want me to help you with the ice cream?"

"No."

"You didn't even finish half your sandwich." Gage reaches for my dessert.

I angle my body. "Hands off, buddy." I was only able to handle a quarter of the colossal sandwich. I'm full, but I won't admit it. I narrow my eyes at him. "You knew what you were doing when you picked that sandwich place. Your plan was to get me so full, you'd end up eating my ice cream."

He finished his half pint of ice cream a while ago and he's been watching me with amusement as I struggle through mine.

He gives one of my braids an affectionate tug. "The sun is beating hard. Your ice cream is going to melt. Take one more bite and give me the rest." He attempts to grab my half pint.

I pull my ice cream away from his greedy hands. "Wash your mouth out with soap. Even when this"—I lower my eyes to the container I'm holding—"turns to the consistency of milkshake, I'll still soldier on."

"If you say so." He chuckles.

Gage is probably going to have to carry me to his Wiesmann GT MF4, but I manage to finish the last spoonful of ice cream. It's on the tip of my tongue to say, *showed you*, but I refrain.

He rummages through the freezer bag and pulls out another container of ice cream.

He bought himself two?

"Peanut buttercup ice cream." He shrugs. "I couldn't resist."

"You have quite the appetite."

On top of a chicken cutlet sandwich, a porchetta one, *and* three quarters of my sandwich, he ingested a half pint of ice cream in record time. True, he's a big guy, but come on, the man is eating for *three*.

"I fucked you hard last night numerous times and again this morning. Other than the tall latte and two almond croissants I grabbed at the Pompadour's café before hitting the road, I've been running on empty. I need sustenance."

I shake my head.

"Want a spoonful?" He extends an arm.

"No, thanks. One more bite and this flowy dress will be formfitting."

Gage nods.

As he stuffs his face with ice cream, I adjust myself on the blanket, leaning back on my hands to work on my tan.

Out of the blue, bits and pieces of the conversation I had with Dark Compulsion's owner pop into my head.

I sit up straight and cross my legs underneath my floral maxi dress. "Can I ask you a question?"

He swallows a spoonful of ice cream. "Shoot."

"Zeus-slash-Larkin said something last night I can't shake off. Maybe I'm making too much of it, but it sounded profound... like it had to do with something more than me being your date."

"What did he say?" His good mood fades.

I hesitate.

I twist my lips to the side, unsure if I have the courage to pursue this.

Remember, Lily. Curiosity killed the cat.

His eyebrows sink. "What do you want to know?"

I take in a deep breath. "Larkin said, '*Good on you for getting a tiger to change his stripes. Not an easy feat considering Lucius can be dead set in his ways. You've reformed him.*' What did he mean by that?"

His face falls.

Oh, no.

"Gage, I'm sorry—"

He lifts a hand, cutting my sentence short.

He discards the container of ice cream in a trash bag, wipes his hands with a paper napkin, and disposes of it.

"Come closer." He taps the blanket next to him.

I get on my hands and knees and crawl towards him. I sit where he indicates and adjust myself.

He cocks a brow.

"What?"

He leans in and drops a tender kiss on my lips. "Good girl. I didn't even have to ask."

I beam.

"I haven't told this story in a long time." The expression on his face is sombre. "I'm not sure how I'm going to react."

His warning scares me, but I don't let on. "I'm honored you'd be willing to share something that personal."

He responds with a slow nod.

He doesn't speak for a long beat.

"Three years ago, my mom died."

I suck in a breath.

"Even though I was the baby of the family, since I was a boy—the only boy—Dad made me promise I'd always take care of my mom and my sisters. He was most concerned about Mom because he always said she had a soft heart. He was right. Mom was always too trusting."

"Your dad loved your mom."

"He did. And she loved him right back."

If we could all be that lucky in love.

"Mom was single for many years after my dad passed away," he says. "She always proclaimed she would never love again." A cloud of sadness veils his green eyes, turning them stormy. "My sisters kept nudging her, stating you're allowed to fall in love more than once in your lifetime. Since I was never much of a romantic, I stayed out of it. Then, one day, Mom announced she had met Judson Timmons." His eyes drift in the distance for a beat. "He was in his mid-forties, so a decade younger than Mom. He was a bit player—"

"What's that?"

"It's industry talk to describe an actor who's ranked higher than a background actor, but lower than that of a supporting actor."

"I see."

"Judson had one noteworthy supporting role, but struggled to get another. His side modeling gigs were his bread and butter." He pinches his lips.

"You two didn't get along?"

"From the moment I met him, I disliked him." His eyes lower to his lap, and he curls his hands into fists. "I couldn't put my finger on it, but I didn't trust him. My sister Sara suggested I give the guy a chance."

"Did your other sisters feel the same way?"

His gaze locks onto mine. "My two older sisters were in Europe, managing international StreamTunes offices, but they flew back and forth, so they met Judson. My eldest sister Lana was Switzerland. She couldn't decide if she liked him or not. My middle sister Marika was one hundred percent team Judson. She was thrilled Mom hooked up with a hot man who was younger but still age-appropriate. She chastised me for taking the oath I took with my father too far. Mom was a grown woman and she could date—and fall in love—with whomever she wanted."

"You didn't agree?"

"It killed me to bite my tongue, but I didn't want to be labeled as the son who refused his mom's happiness. A year into their relationship, Judson proposed. I put my foot down and told Judson point blank that hell would freeze over before I ever called him stepdad. I didn't leave room for argument. Mom scolded me for using my size to threaten her soon-to-be husband. I towered over him when I explained how things were going to work between us. It's not my fault he was only five-ten. Marika wasn't impressed, but she shut up when I asked her if she intended on calling Judson stepdad."

"Your sister was rooting for him."

"She was. And she regretted standing by the idiot when we found out he was a lowlife."

Yikes.

"I accompanied Judson and a bunch of his friends to Sin City for his bachelor party. I couldn't get out of it without hurting Mom, but I wanted to be anywhere in the world except Vegas." He lets out a long breath. "There was something about the way he looked at women during the weekend that irked me. I guess my annoyance was written all over my face. His best friend approached me as I was brooding at the bar, and decided to educate me."

I tilt my head to the side. "What did he tell you?"

"Before a man gets the noose put around his neck, he's allowed to look as long as he doesn't touch."

"That's a horrible way of looking at a bachelor party. And marriage."

He shrugs. "That's what I thought. Judson might not have been touching those women, but he was undressing them with his eyes."

"Did you tell your mom?"

"I did. She parroted a line similar to Judson's best friend."

"Oh."

"Yeah." His lips twist in disdain. "Judson and Mom's first year of marriage went by without much fanfare, and life continued. During that year, Hartley Stewart and I were hooking up. She was the third assistant producer of an up-and-coming daytime talk show. It was casual. Therefore, at no point did I intend on introducing her to my mom. The universe laughed in my face about that last one—"

"In what sense?"

"Mom didn't need to work, but to keep herself busy, I hired her as a receptionist."

"She was working, but nothing too demanding."

He nods. "I was going full steam ahead, opening offices around the globe. I was out of the country for two weeks. Upon my return, Hartley and I were going out for dinner, and I was supposed to pick her up at her place, but she couldn't wait to see me. She complained about my long absence. Since she had a dermatologist appointment, she swung by my office once she was done."

"That's how Hartley met your mom?"

"That day marked the beginning of the end for my family."

My heart breaks for him.

"It so happened Judson decided to surprise Mom on the same day by dropping by at the office to take her out for drinks. I was in a meeting, and when I got back to the office, there was Hartley and Judson, enjoying coffee and desserts in the reception area, laughing their heads off like they were long-lost friends."

"They hit it off?"

"Did they ever. Flash forward four months," he says. "StreamTunes was experiencing rapid growth. I was constantly boarding a plane. I expected Hartley to bitch about my prolonged absence, but she didn't. It was a mistake on my part for not questioning her reaction. Or lack thereof."

I frown my confusion.

"She wasn't complaining because she was sleeping with someone else."

I flinch. "Did you catch her cheating on you?"

"No." He inhales a deep breath and exhales.

I can't read his expression, but I brace myself for whatever he's about to say.

"Mom was attending a friend's vow renewal ceremony in Napa Valley. Judson stayed behind, citing he had an important casting call for a supporting role in a movie directed by a blockbuster director—"

"He lied?"

"If that was his only sin," Gage says. "Mom left for Napa Valley early morning on a Thursday for her extended weekend. I was flying to Australia the next day for a week. I was burning the candle at both the ends, so when I arrived in Sydney, I crashed. I slept for twelve hours straight. When I woke up—midday Sydney time—it felt like I'd slept for a week. I was invigorated. Since it was the weekend, I made the decision to step out of the CEO role for half a day. Instead of checking different entertainment or music industry sites to catch up on the latest news, I went for a swim. An hour later, I was starved. Without a care in the world, I headed to a little eatery that served all day breakfast. Afterwards, I decided to walk around. That was a mistake."

"How so?"

"Sara was trying to get a hold of me, but she couldn't because I didn't bother checking if my battery was running low —or if it was dead." The guilt in his voice is unmistakable. "When I returned to the hotel, the concierge who had helped me when I arrived was on duty. He flagged me down and told me there was an emergency at home and I needed to call my sister in LA."

I place a hand on my chest.

"He guided me to an office where I was able to plug my phone and charge it. The second I could access my voicemail, I did. I listened to message after message of my sister begging me to call her. Sara was crying when I called her back. I thought something had happened to her husband."

"Oh my God, your mom?"

He holds my gaze for a beat. "Mom had to cut her trip short. Her and her friends took a road trip on the Friday and stopped at a Mexican restaurant to eat. The ceviche didn't agree with Mom, and she ended up sick as a dog. She was so ill, she couldn't even conceive making it through her friends' vow renewal ceremony."

"Poor thing."

"She spent most of the night hugging the toilet. The next day, she visited the drugstore for something to settle her stomach, and then flew home. She didn't call Judson to let him know. All she wanted was to curl up in her own bed."

"There's nothing worse than being sick in a strange bed."

He nods. "When she entered her home, there was a pair of women's shoes in the foyer that weren't hers. As she was kicking off her shoes, she heard people laughing somewhere in the house. Mom made her way barefoot through the house, following the sounds of laughter to the kitchen. When she got to the threshold, she froze. She had a prime view of Judson's naked butt, his arms laced around a woman—"

"Her husband was cheating on her?"

"From where Mom was standing, she couldn't tell if the woman was naked or not, but her legs were bare and she was barefoot. As her mind scrambled to make sense of what she was witnessing, Judson said, '*I can't wait to meet our baby*'."

I gasp in horror. "The woman was Hartley?"

"Yes, it was fucking Hartley."

"How could they go behind your back and your mom's back like that?"

"I wasn't emotionally invested with Hartley, so my heart wasn't broken." Gage levels me with a hard stare, curling his hands into fists. "Mom... loved Judson."

"That must've been a shock for the idiot cheaters, since they assumed your mom was at that wedding."

"Not as much of a shock as it was for Mom."

"She must've seen red."

"*What the fuck*, dropped from Mom's lips after she heard Judson's devastating revelation. When they turned to face her, Hartley was as naked as the day she was born. Her messy blonde hair and Judson's freshly fucked brown hair, telltale signs of what was as clear as day."

What a horrible way for your marriage to explode in your face. Not that there's ever a good way to find out you married a lowlife.

Gage rubs his hands over his face. The torment I read in his green eyes is heartbreaking.

I place my hand on his leg. "You don't have to continue if this is too difficult."

He places a hand on top of mine. "I want to answer your question."

"Okay."

"Mom, Judson, and Hartley got into a heated argument. It got nasty. In the end, Judson made his allegiance clear—Hartley and the baby."

"Why didn't Judson tell your mom he wanted a divorce,

instead of crushing her heart? I mean, it would've avoided so much drama." *Why do people cheat? Why? Why? Why?*

"He's a spineless piece of shit."

"And Hartley is a heartless cunt."

"Well said."

"Sorry. I interrupted you."

He picks up where he left off. "Gutted, Mom stormed out of there. She got in her car and drove for a while until she was crying so hard, she couldn't see in front of her."

Sympathy floods my system.

"She parked her car and called Sara. Through a river of tears, she filled in my sister on the dramatic scene she witnessed. Sara said she was inconsolable—"

"Which is understandable—"

"She should've never been in that fragile state of mind to begin with." Gage's nostrils flare. "Asshole Judson should've kept his dick in his pants."

I wince. "What I said, came out the wrong way."

His hand squeezes mine. "I'm not upset at you, angel."

"I get it. The emotions still consume you."

He nods.

Several beats pass.

I don't rush him.

"It took Sara a long time to calm Mom down. When our mother wasn't as frantic, she told her to drive to her place and stay the rest of the weekend." He pauses. "My sister lives in Rancho Palos Verdes—"

"Where's that?"

"Sara needs to live right by the ocean. It's in her DNA, which is why she lives in a coastal city atop the bluffs of the Palos Verdes Peninsula. It's located an hour away without traffic from Brentwood—where Mom lived. Since this is LA, there's no such thing as no traffic."

"Traffic must've been brutal on a Saturday night."

"It was," he says. "Mom called Sara at eight p.m., so she figured it would be a solid ninety minutes before she got to her place. By eleven p.m., Sara was getting worried. She texted Mom to find out if she was close. No answer. Her phone rang, but it wasn't our mother. It was Judson. The police had called him to inform him Mom had been in a fatal accident."

"Dear God." Tears prickle my eyes.

"Mom was trying to change lanes on the freeway, probably to exit, when she got hit from the back, full force by a thief who was trying to evade the police in a stolen car. From the footage, Mom was trapped in a horrific scene right out of the show *Cops*." He takes a deep breath. "She lost control of her vehicle and veered into the path of a cargo truck. She had zero chance of survival. Mom died on impact."

His revelation slays me, his pain becoming mine.

I close my eyes, as tears roll down my cheeks.

Gage wipes them with his thumb.

When I open my eyes, he's crying.

Not giving a fuck who's around us, I jump into his arms. He embraces me close to his body, his chest heaving.

There's no comparison in size.

I want to hold and protect this strong man who's been hurting for too long.

I hug the hell out of him for several breaths before I'm willing to break the embrace. When I do, he rummages through the bags for some paper napkins to wipe his face before handing me a wad of them.

I'm crying so much, I need a towel, but this will have to do.

"And you were in Australia when all this happened?" My voice cracks when I manage to speak. "You were so far way."

"Yes. I was oblivious on the other side of the planet. With

my heart broken into a million pieces, I managed to get myself back to LA."

"Did you confront Judson and Hartley?"

He shakes his head. "I couldn't deal with them."

"Was Judson at the funeral?"

"We made it clear he wasn't welcome."

"Oh, wow."

"It was either that or he would've ended up six feet under, and I would've ended up wearing an orange jumpsuit for the rest of my life."

"I understand."

"It took me a week after the funeral to confront Judson. I showed up at my mom's house with my lawyer and the police—"

"They were going to arrest Judson for your mom's death? I thought she was killed by a thief who was trying to evade the police?"

"No, Judson was squatting."

"How could he be squatting when he was married to your mom?"

"Prenup," he says. "In the event of Mom's passing, her house—and all its content and cars—reverted to me. That was part of her will. It was the proudest day of my life when I upgraded her home to an exclusive LA zip code she never thought she'd live in. It was a sad day when Judson moved in with her."

"He didn't have any claims to the house?"

"None whatsoever," Gage says. "Since he wasn't a tenant, he was a freeloader who had overstayed his welcome. The police were there to ensure things didn't get out of hand, aka I didn't force him to meet his maker." From his flared nostrils, it's clear, his bitterness towards Judson hasn't subsided. Not that I blame him.

"Did you keep the house?"

He shakes his head. "I owned a house. Renting it was an option, but that house was tainted with Judson and Hartley's betrayal. Since this is LA, and it was a fully renovated house in a coveted neighborhood, the house sold in a bidding war the minute it hit the market. I donated a large portion of the money to the single moms' shelter Mom donated money and her time to."

"That was so generous."

"Mom would've wanted that," he says. "When my half-sisters' asshole father bailed out on them, Mom didn't think she would ever be able to keep a roof over her head and food on the table, given she didn't have much of an education. She was lucky her parents accepted her back into their tiny, rented house. And she was lucky she met my father. She never took her good fortune for granted."

"Your mom, in heaven, must've been so proud of you on that day."

He closes his eyes. "I hope so."

I squeeze his hand.

Sad green eyes meet mine.

"I'm certain of it, Gage."

With his lips pinched, he offers a tight nod.

"I guess Judson saw it coming?"

"Even though he had signed an iron-clad prenup, he was irate he had to move out. He felt he should've been able to stay until he found another place to live."

I shake my head in disbelief. "Good for your mom for getting that asshole to sign a prenup."

"She didn't want to—"

"She didn't?"

"I put my foot down and I was unwilling to budge. That's one thing all my sisters and I agreed on."

"Thank God," I say. "What about Hartley?"

"I blocked her ass so she couldn't call or text. The temp who was working the phone after Mom's passing had clear instructions to tell Hartley I was unavailable until the end of time when she phoned. That didn't stop the bitch from trying harder. One day, I received a couriered envelope from her. It was a three-page hand-written letter."

"What did the letter say?"

"I don't know."

"You didn't read it?"

"No. I marched to the supply room with the letter in hand, powered up the shredder, and turned her words into confetti. Then, I grabbed the half-full plastic bag containing the shredded paper, headed towards the elevators, rode down to the building's maintenance area located in the basement, and dumped the contents of the plastic bag into the secure bin. I didn't want any part of that two-faced bitch in my surroundings."

He doesn't do things halfway.

"I made it clear to the security guards Hartley and Judson were persona non grata," he says. "Same for any parcels or letters coming from the two low-lives."

"You don't need toxic people in your life. Onward and forward."

"Not so fast," he says.

I frown.

"I'm not much of a turn the other cheek kinda guy. You hurt me or anyone I care for, you'll live to regret it."

"What did you do?" My question is cautious.

A storm whirls in his eyes. "Between my contacts, the contacts of my inner circle, and the long list of high rollers Larkin knows, I made sure Judson couldn't get a job in the entertainment industry in LA, New York, and Miami. For good measure, I extended my reach to London, Ireland, Australia, and North Hollywood—Vancouver and Toronto. Unless he was gifted with the ability to learn a new language at light speed, I had destroyed his career."

"He could've ended up being a news anchor in a small market."

"The stations in small markets from coast to coast are owned by bigger fish. I had that covered."

Don't ever get on Gage Hollingsworth's bad side.

"Did you do the same for Hartley?"

"I didn't have to. Her show got cancelled not long after Mom's death. The last I heard, she moved to Wisconsin to be with Judson. That's where he's from. As long as they were nowhere near LA, I didn't care."

A long beat passes between us.

Gage's gaze meets mine. His expression is like granite. "I regret not hiring a PI when Mom——"

"You didn't know."

"I should've listened to my gut. My instincts never failed me in business. Yet, when I needed them most, they did. There was something that irked me about the way he was so friendly with Hartley when they first met. And it had nothing to do with jealousy—I wasn't in love with Hartley and never felt territorial about her. The bachelor party was another episode that had my hackles rising. Again, I ignored my intuition. I promised Dad I'd keep Mom safe, and I failed." He furrows his brow and presses his lips into a tight line. "The warning signs were there, as bright as neon signs, but I ignored them. For years, I blamed myself for my mother's death."

An ache blooms in my chest.

I love his strength, his commitment to the oath he took with his father, and his protective nature. But he has to stop with the self-flagellation.

I bring his hands to my lips and kiss them.

The sadness in his eyes is overwhelming.

It shatters me.

I inhale a deep breath for courage. "Judson and Hartley are the guilty ones. Not you, Gage."

"My punishment for sleeping at the wheel was to cut out pleasure from my life." He keeps talking as if I didn't say anything. "So, back to your question—"

"Which one?"

"I went on for so long, you forgot the question that initiated all this rambling."

"I'm so sorry," I say. "I was so taken by your heartbreaking story."

"You asked me about the comment Larkin made at the club."

I slap my forehead with the palm of my hand. "Sorry. Yes."

"When I've visited Dark Compulsion in the past, it was either as a voyeur in one of the Peek-a-boo rooms, watching more risqué couples get down and dirty in the main party room, or hookup with an orally obsessed member."

I scrunch up my nose. "What's that entail?"

"Some female members get off giving blowjobs while taking matters into their own hands when it comes to their own pleasure."

My eyes widen. "They're nothing more than a willing mouth? Giving without receiving?"

"I was riddled with survivor guilt. I couldn't offer much more than that. I never led them on. I was always forthcoming. Since I went out of my way to avoid intimacy, I never undressed. I only pulled out my cock. And the hookups took place on the main floor."

"You mean these women were... giving you... blowjobs in the middle of the main party room?"

He shakes his head. "There are secluded spots on the first floor and in the gardens that offer privacy, without it being as intimate as reserving a room or a lounge room."

"Oh."

Jealousy prickles at my skin.

Silly Lily.

He's been with other women. Why else would he pay such an exorbitant annual fee to be part of an exclusive adult club? Still, the awareness irks me.

"I never attended theme nights," he says.

"Why not?"

"It's a mix of members and guests. Most female members knew the drill when it came to me. I wasn't in the mind space to turn down guests without coming across as rude, so I didn't show up."

"I see."

"As bad as it sounds, after Hartley, I didn't trust women, so I kept it to basic needs."

"I can understand."

"I haven't hooked up with a member or guest in an intimate way since Mom died three years ago." He taps the tip of my nose. "Not until you came along."

My smile is wide.

His phone rings.

My eyes shift to the device lying on the blanket.

He snatches it up, but not before I see a name flash on the screen.

Enid.

"I have to take this," he says.

I nod. "Sure. No problem."

My eyes shift to the horizon, pretending not to eavesdrop.

He hums and nods at whatever the other person says. "I'll see you soon." With that, he ends the call.

I plaster a forced smile on my face. "I sense you're about to put an end to our lunch."

His gaze meets mine. "The person I'm meeting arrived at her hotel. I have to go."

"Will I see you later?" I hate how desperate I sound.

He ponders my question. "I'm not sure. I might be caught up for the rest of the evening. This person traveled far to do me a solid."

Insecurity pricks at my bones.

"Playing CEO is a full-time job." I try to add levity to my voice, but fail.

"Something like that."

I wait for him to confirm this Enid chick is a business associate, but he doesn't.

My belly dives and flops.

I'm not jealous.

Nope.

Not at all.

Not even a little bit.

He's not my boyfriend.

I can totally do casual and walk away.

I'm leaving in two days.

This was supposed to be fun and lighthearted.

No strings attached.

No promises.

No expectations.

No drama.

Ba boom.

Ba boom.

Ba boom.

This stupid throbbing in my heart needs to stop. Pronto.

Chapter 35

Lily

I stand in front of the hotel and watch Gage's car drive away.

I feel foolish for getting attached to this man.

I'm such a cliché.

So what if he's my first and he makes me come so hard, I fear I'll forget my name? It doesn't mean he's going to be the father of my children.

I need to find something to do with myself for the rest of the afternoon. Obsessing over Gage isn't an option.

With a heavy sigh, I head towards the entrance.

As I enter through the glass doors, my phone rings.

Nadine.

Perfect timing.

I park myself to the side and accept the call. "Why aren't we having a video call?"

"I'm having a bad hair day."

I snort. "I've seen you at your worst."

"Consider yourself lucky I'm giving you a respite."

I frown at the phone. "So, we're not having a video call?"

"Not today."

Fine.

"*Ça va, toi?*"

Translation: *How are you?*

"*Oui, ça va. Et toi?*"

Translation: *I'm good, and you?*

"*Tout baigne dans l'huile,*" she says.

Translation: *All is good.*

"*C'est pareil pour moi,*" I say.

Translation: *Same for me.*

"*C'était comment le déjeuner avec ton Jules?*"

Translation: *How was lunch with your guy?*

I could struggle on in French, but I'm not in the mood to put in that much effort. "Lunch was great," I say. "I'm not going to complain about a picnic with a gorgeous man on a bright sunshiny day."

She lets out a dramatic sigh. "I wouldn't know."

"I wish you were here."

"Two more days and you're going back to the concrete jungle."

She ignored what I said?

She's in a weird mood today. Either that, or it was an exhausting day at the flower shop.

"I wish I could extend my trip, but I'm afraid my father will flip his lid if I do," I say. "I can't make excuses about visiting more film schools."

"What a pity your time in LA has to come to an end."

"I was getting to know Gage better…"

"That sucks."

"The man has gone through so much, Nads."

I give my best friend the highlights of the tragic story Gage shared with me.

"It baffles me how cheaters never consider the people they'll hurt with their selfishness." Her indignation is audible.

"Exactly," I say. "From the outside, Gage is a majestic oak tree, but inside, he's a fragile orchid. He's been hurting for so long, he needs to be loved by someone who's dying to give love—"

My hand flies to cover my mouth.

Fuck.

That was ridiculous and far-fetched.

What the hell is wrong with me today?

Silence greets me on the other end.

Let's hope she didn't hear that slip of the tongue.

"Play your father at his own game," Nads says after several breaths.

"I don't understand."

"Instead of an internship at a PR agency in New York, ditch the Big Apple. California dreaming, baby. You need to make it your mission to find a publicity firm in LA."

She heard me after all.

"Given what you've told me about the sisterhood, the influential people who are part of Gage's inner circle, and the brooding billionaire himself, I'm sure it would be easy for you to land a job."

Do I have the courage to pull the rug from under my father's feet?

"Gage Hollingsworth is a gorgeous, strong man who desperately needs to be loved, and you, Lily Schuyler, are the perfect woman for the job."

My heart is beating out of my chest.

Chapter 36

Lily

There's a knock at the door, and I run to it.

When I swing it open, a sexy as fuck man I haven't seen since yesterday afternoon stares down at me.

Dear God, he's devastatingly handsome.

I take him in.

His silky brown hair is mussed—probably from running his fingers through the strands—and a day's worth of scruff graces his gorgeous face.

I allow my gaze to roam up and down his tall frame.

More suit porn.

He's wearing a gray suit with a delicate checkered pattern, paired with a pale pink shirt, sans tie, with the first couple buttons undone.

I approve.

He steps into the hotel suite and closes the door behind him, causing notes of his expensive cologne to linger in the air. I'm tempted to lean into him and give him a sniff, but I resist. Barely.

"Keep looking at me like that, and we won't make it to the

Quintus Hotel without me fucking you against every wall of this suite."

I wouldn't mind making up for lost time.

I cock an eyebrow and tap a finger against my chin. "Hmmm... Decisions, decisions."

"You little tease."

I tilt my head back and laugh.

"You think that's funny?"

"What can I say?" I place a hand on his chest. "It's your fault for being such a great lover."

He laces his arm around my waist and pulls me to him, those green eyes hot and intense.

He leans into me.

The pressure of his hard cock causes my pussy to tingle.

Damn, I want him so bad.

He grazes his lips with mine, our eyelashes practically meshing together. "Flattery will get you thoroughly fucked."

I incline my chin, and his mouth is on mine.

God, I missed him.

The kiss is demanding, fervent, wet, and blazing.

I don't want to give my kisses to any other man on the planet.

Gage Hollingsworth you've ruined it for all others.

Forever more, my life is now divided into two episodes—before Gage Hollingsworth's mouth and after.

I groan as he sinks his tongue deeper into my mouth, our tongues dancing at a sensuous pace.

How will I live without this man's beautiful mouth on mine every single day of the week?

I'm not looking forward to finding out.

I pull away from him, almost out of breath. "Let's forget about dinner."

He shakes his head. "No can do, buttercup."

"Can't we push the reservation to later?"

"Nope."

I sigh. "Okay."

"Don't look so disappointed."

"It's my last night in LA..."

It went by so fast.

Too fast.

It doesn't help I lost a few days with him earlier this week when he thought things were developing too quickly between us, and yesterday again, because he spent the evening with Enid.

Damn you, Enid.

"I intend to make the most of it," he says. "Food first. Followed by a nocturnal drive up Mulholland Drive since we haven't ventured there yet. After a little sightseeing, we'll come back here, and I'll fuck you until you lose consciousness or until you have to make it to the airport tomorrow. Which ever happens first. Does that work for you?"

I giggle. "I can live with that."

"Good." He gives me a onceover. "You wore the dress."

Gage texted earlier with his fashion request, and I lost my mind laughing.

> Gage: I want you to wear that pretty dress that caused me to lose the ability to speak, leaving me no other choice but to grunt to communicate.

"I was too happy to fulfill your wish, Mr. Hollingsworth," I say in a coquettish way, from under my fluttering lashes.

He traces a languorous finger from one bare shoulder to the other. "You're more than a wish in that dress. You're my fucking fantasy come true."

I beam.

"I'll always associate pink with the first time we met."

"Is that why you picked this shirt?" I smooth down the cotton fabric.

"Yes."

I flash him a goofy smile. "From now on, when I wear this dress, I'll think of you."

"You can't wear this dress anymore."

"Why not?"

"Because I don't want another man to see how beautiful you are in it."

"So, you expect me to leave it hanging in my wardrobe?"

"Pretty much."

I expect him to tell me he's joking, but his expression suggests he's dead serious.

"Oh, you're not kidding."

"I'm as serious as a heart attack."

My heart performs the most perilous and challenging gymnastics performance ever.

"You can only pull it out when I'm in New York," he says.

"You're going to come and see me in New York?"

"Damn right."

I stare at him, dumbfounded.

"Don't you want to see me?"

Is that a tinge of insecurity in his voice? "Yes." I smile wide. "I'd like that."

"It's settled."

Does this mean we're dating? I want to ask the question, but I'm not that courageous. "What about tonight? There will be men at the restaurant."

"I don't give a damn because you're wearing the dress for *me*."

Breathe, Lily. Breathe.

His phone rings.

He fishes for it in the pocket of his suit jacket.

The conversation with whomever called is brief.

He ends the call. "We should hit the road."

"Let me grab my clutch."

I'm about to run to the bedroom, but he grabs my wrist. "What color panties are you wearing?"

"Err... soft pink."

"Hand them over."

My eyes widen in shock. "My panties?"

He extends a hand, his palm facing up. "Yes, your panties."

"You want me to remove my panties?"

"Unless there's another way for them to land in the palm of my hand, that's exactly what I want you to do."

"Do you want me to wear another color of panties?"

"I want you to go commando."

My head jerks back.

"Your pretty little pussy is mine for the evening, Lily. By going commando, you open yourself up to possibilities. Who knows? I might have the urge to eat you out in the car before we walk into the restaurant."

Chapter 37

Gage

There are four renowned restaurants at the Quintus Hotel.

Lily and I aren't eating at any of them.

After we step out of the elevator, we trail hand in hand down a maze of corridors.

"I must've been out of my mind when I agreed to your demand," Lily says in a whisper.

"You'll get a nice reward for obeying."

"I feel so exposed."

"Other than you and me, no one knows your wet panties are safely tucked inside the pocket of my suit jacket."

"There's so much wind blowing up there, I'm sure I'm walking funny."

I meet her freaked out gaze. "You're walking fine by me."

She narrows her eyes at me. "It's not fair. If I go commando, so should you."

"Who says I'm not?"

Her eyes drop to the vicinity of my cock. "Are you?"

"You pretend to be holier than thou, but your mind is as filthy as mine."

She shakes her head. "No one is as kinky as you are."

She's right. No point in arguing.

We turn a corner as the first lines of a popular song that always had the crowd dancing to exhaustion during my days as a DJ, plays.

Lily points an animated finger at the ceiling. "I love this song."

"Armand Van Helden's *My My My* is old school, but like any classic house music, it'll never die."

"It's on my LA playlist. Is there a club on the upper floors?"

"No." I keep it brief.

"Someone's having a party. And a good one at that," she says, shaking her little body to the beat of the song. "Too bad we aren't invited."

I chuckle.

As we approach the room where the music is blaring from, two waiters exit. They give us a courteous bow, before scurrying off.

"Oh, there's a party at the restaurant. Got it."

I don't correct her.

"If they keep playing this type of music all night long. Sign. Me. Up. Although, it's quite unusual for music to be playing that loud in a restaurant."

"Give me a sec." I tug on her hand to halt her dancing.

"Okay."

I pull out my phone and type a quick text with one hand.

Another popular tune blares.

She resumes dancing. "Did someone hack my playlist?"

Not quite, but close. "Wolf Story's *Waiting for You* is pure house music gold."

"I couldn't agree more." Lily is dancing as if we were at a

nightclub, hands above her head and hips shaking. "Dance with me." She takes my hands into hers.

I oblige for a few beats.

The elated expression on her face is priceless. I'd pay good money to freeze frame it forever.

"Let's go inside," I say.

"Good idea. I worked up an appetite dancing."

I open the door and extend a hand. "Ladies first."

"This is going to be a great evening," she says from over her shoulder.

You have no idea.

Lily steps inside.

"Happy Birthday! Happy Twenty-First!" A chorus of voices greets her.

She shuffles back, startled.

I catch her in my arms. "It's okay, angel. You're among friends."

She turns in my arms.

Her long, dark eyelashes are fluttering so fast, I swear she's about to take flight. "What's this?" She points a finger over her shoulder.

"A proper celebration for your twenty-first birthday."

She stares at me, unblinking.

I didn't only ask Lily to extend her trip because I wanted to spend more time with her. I wanted to celebrate her birthday. I can't make up for Fisher Edgington's shortcomings. This is the best I could do.

Her selfish, asshole father wasn't even willing to make it here today, stating Lily's birthday came and went. Granted he's on a business trip in Washington DC, and this birthday party is last minute. Still, if he wanted to be here, he would've.

I didn't bother tracking down her half-brothers. I'd rather

poke my eyes with steak knives than waste any time with those assholes.

"No one should go through a milestone birthday without it being a big fucking deal." I won't allow these lowlives, who share her DNA, to rob her from something this important.

She jumps into my arms. "You're a wonderful man."

With that, she bursts into tears.

Chapter 38

Lily

Bless Michaela König.

The makeup case containing the essentials for an emergency touch up was a godsend. Once I'm confident I no longer look like a raccoon, I step out of the bathroom.

The sisterhood is out in full force, accompanied by their sexy men.

As I take in the crowd present, I'm dizzy with emotions. I'm so elated, I feel the need to brace my arm against the pillar next to me, but I don't have time for dramatics. There's a full room of friends to greet.

I bounce from one person to another.

After too many hugs, kisses, and good wishes to count, I'm walking on sunshine. I'm so tickled pink, I don't even worry that I'm walking around people pantieless.

There are bigger fish to fry.

Like dealing with the tall man staring at me with a smug smile on his face.

I approach the culprit behind *Operation Lily's Secret Birthday Party*.

I swat his chest. "You had me fooled."

"How so?"

"You promised me dinner. This isn't dinner."

"Food will be served later."

"You know what I mean."

"You don't like birthday parties?"

"You're incorrigible." I shake my head. "You did this for me?"

"You're worth it, Lily."

With those sweet words, he claims a little bit more of my heart.

"This room is amazing." I change the subject before I melt in a puddle of lust. I turn around in a circle, taking it all in.

"The Tottenham Court is Larkin's private entertainment room. It's never up for grabs unless it's for someone in his inner circle."

I turn around and face the owner of the hotel, clamp my hands in a prayer, and bow.

He lifts his tumbler in response.

Gage—or whomever decorated the room went all out. It's over the top, but I love it. There's a huge banner that reads *Happy 21st Birthday, Lily* covering a wall—the design sparkles with rose gold, yellow gold, and diamond touches. There's a parade of helium filled rose gold and happy birthday confetti balloons hanging from the ceiling, a table weighed down with wrapped boxes, and flowers. So many beautiful flowers—

Wait a minute.

I've been so overwhelmed since I set foot in this room, it's only now I spot the type of flowers decorating the space.

"Those flowers are Yves Piaget roses."

He nods. "They are."

I frown. "They're my favorite flower."

"So I've heard."

My frown deepens. "Who told you?"

"They're stunning flowers. I can see why they're your favorites," he says. "The large headed rose is unique. It could pass as a peony, but it would be a mistake to compare the two flowers. The rose has an incredibly strong fragrance—which I can attest to—and the vibrant raspberry pink petals stand out."

My eyebrows lift to my hairline.

"How did you know I preferred Yves Piaget roses and how do you know so much about the flower?"

"A woman I know gave me a basic 101 course."

Is the woman he's referring to, Enid?

She's becoming a thorn in my side.

I hate to admit, though, she was spot on.

I'm about to drill him with more questions when he lifts a finger.

He pulls out his phone and sends off a quick text.

"Speaking of which, I invited Enid to your party."

He invited the woman he ditched me for last night to my party?

Why?

I don't even know her.

"Is Enid a friend?"

"Let me go get her."

What kind of answer is that?

He turns to the DJ and does the universal throat slashing sign to cut off the music.

Why is he making such a fuss over Enid?

And why the hell do we have to kill the music on her account? That was a great song.

Gage parts the crowd of friends on his way to the door.

I stretch my neck.

Even in my high heels, I have to stand on my tippytoes and move my head left to right to see what's going on.

A familiar brunette sporting a slick side-parted nape bob steps into the room.

I gasp, my hands flying to my face to cover my mouth.

I blink a few times to make sure my mind isn't playing tricks on me.

My best friend runs towards me.

It's not a mirage.

I shake out of my stupor and run towards her.

We jump into each other's arm, both of us crying.

We sway side to side, hugging the hell out of each other.

I pull away from her. "Nads, what are you doing here?" Tears stream down my face.

As if she was my personal assistant for the day, Mikki hands us tissues.

"Thank you."

"What are friends for?"

Her reply touches my heart.

I blow her kisses.

She blows them back.

Nadine and I wipe away our tears, giggling like silly girls.

I'm not sure why I bothered going to the bathroom to fix my face. My mascara is running again.

"Nadine Whelan, are you going to put me out of my misery and tell me what the hell you're doing here?"

"I was told someone was celebrating being twenty-one again." She winks. "I had to be here."

"Yeee!" I squeal and take her in my arms for another round of hugs.

I let her go.

She gives me a onceover. "That dress is stunning on you."

I give her a twirl.

"It's so Hollywood," she says.

"I know, right? You look fabulous, as always."

"With my demure dress, I don't fit into the LA fashion scene."

"Nonsense."

Nadine is wearing a form fitted mid-length sleeveless navy-blue dress that hits her below the knee. A delicate pattern of clusters of white flowers spots the fabric. It has a seductive V that shows off the girls nicely. Her red Mary Jane patent shoes with chunky heels have a vintage flair to them.

My eyes land on her chest, a warm smile stretching my lips. "And you're wearing the perfect accessory."

She caresses the medallion hanging around her neck I gave her for her birthday, a replica of mine.

I mimic her move, touching the one I'm wearing.

"I had to wear the necklace," she says. "First, you know how much I love, love, love it. Second, I was hoping someone from QVC might spot me and want to know the artist, so you could become famous."

This woman is the best friend a girl could ever hope for.

"Silly girl, QVC's headquarters are in Pennsylvania. Not LA."

"My bad." She smiles. "Speaking of things your father disapproves of... have you given any thought to what we talked about yesterday?"

"Yes," I say. "I'm going to put my big girl panties on—"

She shrieks.

"Shhh." I place a finger against my lips.

"Sorry." She cringes. "So, you're moving here?"

I nod.

"When?"

"The plan is for me to return to New York and set the wheels in motion. Fisher Edgington hates people who are all talk. Once I get my ducks in a row, I'll present my master plan as *a fait accompli*. Cue an evil laugh."

And she does.

I join in.

"It will all be under the pretense of gaining experience to better support Chandler's political career," I say.

She considers me for a beat, nodding.

"What?"

"This trip allowed you to find your lady balls. I like it. I like it a lot."

It's my turn to take in her words. "The trip I was dreading, turned out to be the trip of a lifetime."

"Amen to that." Nads lifts her arms over her head.

There are so many unexpected things about this evening, I can't keep up. The shock of seeing my bestie is another item on the long list. "How did you get here?"

"Airplane. Duh."

I roll my eyes. "You know what I mean."

"Gage took care of everything."

"I'm shocked he'd go to that length."

"He was willing to move mountains to make tonight happen, Lily."

Wow.

She leans into me. "In his world, nothing is impossible."

I open my arms in an attempt to encompass this room and all the amazing people in it. "I get a sense of that now."

"Between us girls, Mr. Hollingsworth is the paragon of masculinity. *Quel mec.*"

"What a man, indeed—" I laugh.

"What's so funny?"

"The playlist in my head landed on Salt-N-Pepa's *Whatta Man.*

"Good one." She laughs. "Gage fits the bill. He's the perfect Adonis." She fans herself. "He's this big, testosterone-laden hunk. Confident and in command. And he's not bad on the eyes."

That's the understatement of the century. "He's freaking gorgeous." I shift my attention to said gorgeous, testosterone-laden, perfect Adonis god.

He winks.

Be still my beating heart.

"Sexy gods hang out with other sexy gods," Nads says. "Any single guys in his inner circle?"

I scan the room. "There's Larkin."

"The owner of this amazing hotel—where I'm staying, by the way—is dangerously hot, but he scares me."

"Yeah, he's intense."

"Too intense," she says. "I'm afraid I wouldn't be able to keep up."

"Michaela"—I point to her—"is certain there isn't a woman alive capable of handling Larkin."

Nadine nods.

I keep searching the room. "What about him?" I point to Collin Dennison, leaning at the bar, involved in an animated conversation with Dominika and Rod who are sitting on stools.

"Oh, God, that man is also hot, but he comes with the same force as a Euro speed train." I laugh. "His brother Shane on the other hand... I'd leave my life in Paris behind for that fine piece of man candy." She leans in closer. "I'd even be willing to let him pop my cherry."

I stare up at her. "I doubt you'd regret it."

"A man like that would justify holding out for the right one..."

Both her mom and mine lost their virginity to married men and ended up pregnant and alone. The way we came into this world shaped us, which is why we held on tight to our V cards much longer than most girls we know.

I nudge her. "Are you going to go after him?"

"No. I'd never have the courage to approach him."

"That can be arranged—"

"I'm here for *you*. Not to get entangled with a hot guy. You know me... chicks before dicks."

With that, she sets the tone to one of our favorite games. I pick up the baton.

"Queens over peens."

"Sisters over misters."

"Breasties before testes." I keep the game going.

"Dames before dudes."

"Brains before bros."

We laugh.

"Men come and go, the sisterhood is forever," I say.

Nadine's eyes bounce around the room. "And now the sisterhood has extended to more than the two of us."

My heart swells at the mention of all the wonderful new friends I've made since arriving in LA. "It has."

"That's why when Gage concocted this last-minute birthday party idea and enlisted my help, I was on board." Gage Hollingsworth is a brooding giant of a man with an enormous heart. "I was dying to see you again and I wanted to meet the sisterhood. When he offered to fly me to LA on a private jet —nice touch, by the way—I couldn't refuse. I'm a sucker for VIP treatment. Even though my father is a former president of France, I've never experienced such luxury before. One of the downsides of being *la bâtarde* is that your father always travels with his legitimate kids and his wife. Never with his bastard daughter and her mother. Thanks to Gage, I was able to cross an item off my bucket list."

My eyes find Gage's.

He shrugs.

He knows we're talking about him.

His sixth sense is freaky.

"I'm taken aback everyone knew, except for me."

"That's the whole point of a surprise birthday party." Nads winks.

"When did you get here?"

"Yesterday afternoon while you were having a picnic with your man."

What? "So, yesterday, when I thought you were calling me from Paris, you were here in LA?"

"In my defense, you didn't ask me where I was. So, I wasn't lying."

I narrow my eyes at her. "Lying by omission is still lying."

"And I'd do it again in a heartbeat if it meant seeing you this happy."

I blush.

"You're beaming, Lily."

"You mean, my face is the color of a tomato?"

She rolls her eyes. "You're glowing. Own it."

"Okay, you're right. I haven't had a drink yet, but I'm drunk with happiness—" Realization hits me. "Are you Enid?"

A huge smile spreads her lips. "It's my code name. Enid is Nadine spelled backwards, minus the first two letters of my name. Gage didn't want to spoil the surprise. This"—she swirls a finger in the air—"was well orchestrated, down to the minute details. Same for your full day limo tour of celebrity homes and other Hollywood iconic attractions today."

The tour was a distraction?

"It wasn't by chance the driver dropped you off on Rodeo Drive." Her eyes lower to my new gold strappy heels for a beat. "After all, you can't resist a shoe sale. Gage was made aware of all of your weaknesses."

Sneaky best friend.

"I also told Gage about the songs on your playlist and

favorite cake." Nadine keeps dropping bombs on me. "And I guided him in the right direction for the flowers, so he stayed away from your no-no list. No lilies. Ever. And carnations are a copout."

God, I'd die for this woman.

My father never bothered finding out which were my favorite flowers. He'd have one of his mignons send me flowers—ninety-nine percent of the time, they were lilies—accompanied by a birthday card with the same one-liner.

Love you, Lily. Dad.

The distinctively female penmanship was a dead giveaway. It's always a blessing to receive gifts, but my father's gifts were never from him. As for the '*love you*' part, that's a big fat joke.

"Gage suggested I fly in *with* flowers that would put a huge smile on your face." She shrugs. "So, I did."

I knit my eyebrows together. "The flowers are all from Paris?"

She nods. "It took me a few days of hustling before I was able to get them from the right vendors, but I managed. Let me tell you, a private jet is quite practical when you're not traveling light."

"Unbelievable."

I'm amazed by the care and attention Gage put into planning this party.

"Gage wanted to make up for me having to close the shop for a few days."

"Wow——" I frown. "I'm leaving tomorrow for New York. Are you going to stay in LA? That would suck if we were in the same country, but on opposite coasts."

She shakes her head. "Gage is flying me out to New York tomorrow night. We won't be on the same flight, but I'll arrive in New York an hour after you. I can only stay a couple of days, but we get to spend some time together."

I'm flabbergasted. "He did all this for me?"

She reaches out and rubs up and down my arm. "He wanted to make up for Fisher being a jerk. My words. Not his."

I laugh.

"Here I thought Enid was..." I shake my head.

She elbows me. "You thought Enid was a random chick after your man?"

The DJ kicked off the music again, but I don't want my voice to carry. So, I switch to French.

"*Mais ca va pas la tête? C'est pas mon mec. On n'est pas ensemble.*"

Translation: *You're crazy. He's not my man. We're not boyfriend and girlfriend.*

Nadine stares at me like I've lost my marbles. "*T'es aveugle, ma vieille. De part ses actions, il démontre ses sentiments à ton égard. Tu es sa copine. Je n'en ai aucun doute.*"

Translation: *You're blind, dear friend. Actions speak louder than labels. You're his girlfriend. I don't doubt it for a second.*

Her eyes shift in Gage's direction before fixing onto mine. "Your father spent years hiding you. He's still not forthcoming about who you are. Case in point." She places her hands on her face, cupping her mouth. "Your Adonis didn't even know you existed because Fisher never spoke about you." She holds my gaze. "The demigod who punched your V card is flaunting you around like the prized beauty you are."

Like the beating wings of a majestic white swan, hope blooms in my chest.

Chapter 39

Lily

I've been up for a while, but I refuse to move. I only have a few hours left in LA and I want to cherish every minute spent with Gage.

I sigh, utterly content.

I'm the luckiest girl in the world.

Not only from last night's post-birthday party sex marathon, but also because yesterday will go down in history as the best birthday ever.

The only thing preventing me from giving into despair at the prospect of returning to New York is the plan to move to LA as fast as humanly possible.

I could ask Gage or the sisterhood for some help, but I want to do this on my own. And if there isn't a future between us, Gage won't feel trapped. I'd be crushed, but it's a risk I'm willing to take. I want to stand on my own two feet and distance myself from my father.

Behind me, something big and hard grinds into my ass.

I thrust my hips back, pressing myself against it.

Mmmm.

"Morning," he says in a gravelly voice.

"Morning."

Gage wraps me in his strong arms.

A wave of victory courses through me at the idea he hasn't been this intimate with a woman in years.

Michaela calls it the power of the magic pussy. It was the cure Gage needed to break the dark spell he was under. She was pretty drunk when she dropped that little nugget of wisdom in my lap last night. Nadine and I laughed so hard, we couldn't breathe. When I recovered, her revelation made me feel ten feet tall.

Could I be as good for Gage as he is for me?

"You're my safe place—" The words fly out of my mouth without my permission. I blame too many orgasms for causing my mind to short circuit. "I didn't mean to say that."

"I'm hurt," he says.

Oh, shit.

I turn in his arms.

"I didn't mean to hurt your feelings."

He kisses my forehead, my nose, and my lips. "I'm messing with you."

"Not cool." I pout.

"It's not cool when you say something and take it back."

I pull my lower lip between my teeth. "I might've said too much."

"What if you didn't?"

I search his eyes.

"It's silly of me to say things like that. I'm leaving today." I hesitate. "How can you be my safe place when a country separates us?"

"Life is a mental game, angel. Even though we'll be far apart, I can still be your safe place right here." He taps my temple.

I lower my lashes. "I like the sound of that."

"It's settled," he says. "That's how we'll play it out until I see you again in three weeks."

Three weeks? I school my expression. "You'll be gone a long time."

He brushes my messy hair away from my face.

"Traveling alone can't be fun," I say. "Who's going to keep you company? Who will you have dinner with? Who will you hang out with? Who's going to listen to you at the end of the day when you need to vent?" *Who will warm your bed?*

His eyes narrow, a sliver of green peering at me. "You want me to take you with me?"

Yes.

I flash him a goofy smile.

"Fisher is going to have my balls if you don't go back to New York."

I give him a one-shoulder shrug.

He's right.

Not to mention, how am I going to put my plans into action if I follow him?

He taps the tip of my nose. "I wish I could postpone the trip by a few days and fly with you to New York, but I can't. I have a string of publicity appearances in Sweden. Then, I fly to South Korea where I have many meetings booked. Opening a new market is demanding and requires quite a lot of negotiations."

Bummer.

"On the plus side, my extended trip will benefit you."

I frown my confusion. "How?"

"When I see you again in New York, I'll be so fucking hungry for you." He grinds his cock against me. "I'll fuck you like an animal."

"I supposed it's an acceptable consolation prize," I say with the upmost seriousness.

"Cheeky Lily."

Gage hasn't dropped the G word. The promise of seeing him again the second he's back stateside is enough for me. Like Nadine said, I shouldn't get tripped up by the girlfriend label.

He reaches for his phone. "I'm going to have to go soon."

Why can't he run his empire from my bed? "I understand."

"Nadine, you, and I are having dinner tonight with Michaela and Phoenix. Don't forget."

"I won't."

"What are you going to do all day today?"

"I received so many incredible gifts, Nadine and I have to go out later so I can buy an extra suitcase to carry them all. Then, we're going to spend the afternoon in Santa Monica and at the Pacific Park amusement park."

"You'll have fun."

"I'm looking forward to it."

"Before I go, I have one more gift for you."

My eyes widen. "Gage. No. You spoiled me enough yesterday. No more gifts."

"I didn't give you any gifts yesterday."

"Yes, you did. The incredible party. My favorite cake. Flying my best friend from Paris. My favorite flowers, straight from Paris. All those are gifts."

"I beg to differ."

You're too generous. "You're impossible."

"Sorry, angel, but the gift I got you is non-refundable. So, you have to accept it."

"Fine."

"Don't be that excited."

Who charters a private jet to fly flowers from another country? "You don't do anything in half measures."

"Why would I waste my time?"

Spoken like a high achiever.

"Can I get a little enthusiasm, please?"

I sit up in bed, pulling the sheets to cover my nakedness. "Oh my God, Gage, a gift? Yay."

He shakes his head.

He gets out of bed and rewards me with an eye-popping view of his fabulous ass.

He's back in a flash, holding an envelope.

He slides into bed next to me and hands it over.

I take it from him and stare at it. "I'm afraid to open it."

He elbows me. "Don't be a chicken."

I accept his dare.

With quick hands, I tear through the white envelope, and pull a white card in heavy stock paper from it.

When I flip the card, I stop breathing.

Three black letters inscribed on it have my heart racing.

"You should read the note inside," he says.

My hands are shaking when I open the card.

My eyes scan the words.

Holy Jesus.

My bewildered gaze finds his. "Is this for real?"

"Remember, I'm the guy who doesn't do things in half measures." He borrows my words from earlier.

"This is a dream come true."

"You won't be in front of the camera, but it'll still be a hell of an experience."

"Are you kidding me? I get to spend a day at the QVC headquarters, shadowing different producers. I'll meet the hosts and the spokespeople of the products that will be featured on the day I'm there. It doesn't get any better than this. How did you manage this tour de force?"

"Larkin had the right connections. It's an open invitation, so you'll have to coordinate things with a point person."

There are no words to describe how thrilled I am about this gift.

"You'll have to thank Larkin on my behalf."

"Consider it done. If one day, you pursue your dream and produce your signature stainless steel necklace, you'll have a foot in the door."

This man.

I open my mouth to thank him, but instead, I burst into tears.

Gage shifts on the bed so he's facing me. "Hey." He wipes away my tears with his thumb. "Why are you crying? This gift was supposed to make you happy."

"It does."

"If this is your happy face, I don't want to see your sad face."

"Mama—" I hiccup. I'm so emotional, I can't speak for several beats.

"Take your time."

"She would've lost her mind," I say. "She would've wanted to hear about every little detail, from the color of the carpet to how many cracks I could count in the asphalt in the parking lot." More hiccupping. "I won't be able to share any of that with her."

He takes my hand into his, brings it to his lips, and kisses it gently. "I get it. It took me a long time to quell the urge to call my mom to share milestones after she died." He pauses. "I don't know how it works in heaven, but I'm going to borrow a saying from my sister Sara. She always reminded me Mom was watching from up above and experiencing my milestone moments through our soul connection. It sounded woo-woo to me, but I went along with it. It helped me deal with the finality of never seen my mom again."

His beautiful words make me cry harder.

Chapter 40

Lily

I'm so different from the woman who landed at LAX.

The past eight days have gone by in a haze of orgasms, ecstasy, and sheer bliss. I've lived through so many wonderful adventures, it's hard to believe I was able to cram it all into such little time.

My grumpy bodyguard turned lover extraordinaire rolls my suitcases towards me.

It's going to be so hard leaving you, Gage Hollingsworth.

He stops in front of me. "You arrived in this city without any luggage, and now you're leaving with the contents of half the stores on Rodeo Drive stuffed into these three large suitcases."

Being the gentleman he is, he suggested I wait inside the airport while he wrestled with all my stuff. I only had to worry about my handbag and carry-on.

"In my defense, someone organized a surprise birthday party for me, and his incredible friends were quite generous."

He taps the tip of my nose. "They're *your* incredible friends, too."

"I will miss them."

"You'll be back before you know it."

That's the plan.

A beat of silence passes between us.

I flash him a lopsided smile. "It went by too quick."

Gage pulls me into his embrace. "It did," he says, before dropping a kiss on my forehead. He sighs. "I don't know if I'm going to be able to fall asleep tonight."

My eyes meet gorgeous green ones.

Soon, I'll only see them in my dreams.

Brushing off the melancholy, I play along. "Why's that?"

He twirls a lock of my hair around his finger. "I won't be wrapped around a sexy little thing with long black hair and a banging body."

This man is my kryptonite. "If it's any consolation, I'll be in the same boat."

"You'll miss being wrapped around a sexy little thing with long black hair and a banging body?"

I burst out laughing.

He chuckles.

"I've been thinking..." His words trail.

My laughter fades.

His expression transforms to something... serious.

He's no longer coming to New York to see me?

He no longer wants me to wear my pretty pink dress just for him?

Is he going to let me down gently?

Might as well rip off the Band-Aid now. "What's on your mind?"

He holds my gaze for a long uncomfortable beat.

My eyes drop to my feet.

He changed his mind.

My father was right. Gage is done with me.

I'm not good enough—

"You expect me to talk to the top of your head?"

My eyes fly up to meet his.

"Better."

I exhale a long breath.

Nads's voice rings in my ear. *"Mets tes couilles, ma vieille."*

Translation: *Find your lady balls, Lily.*

I square my shoulders, my gaze locking onto his.

"There isn't much I can do about the next three weeks. Those business trips are too important—"

"I understand." My dread is causing me to trip all over myself.

"Let me finish."

I pinch my lips.

"When I'm back stateside, I want to see more of you, Lily, and I don't want to let us living on opposite coasts to be a deterrent." He caresses my cheek with the back of his hand.

My heart bangs against my chest, beating at an infernal rate.

"I'll work as often as I can from the StreamTunes New York office, so we're in the same city. Also, I'll fly you to LA when it's mandatory for me to be here until you start film school. Your father has more than enough money to cover the flights, but let's leave him out of this. This is between you and me."

I'm about to burst from joy.

Since I'm frozen in stupor, he keeps talking.

"It's not only that I don't want any other asshole to see you in that pretty pink dress..." His nostrils flare, his lips turning up into a snarl.

And... he's Mr. Grumpy Pants again.

"I don't want any other asshole touching you. You're mine."

I'm his?

I open my mouth to speak, but nothing comes out.

He cocks a brow. "Yes? No?"

"Wh—what are you saying?" That comes out as a near whisper.

"Your film school program doesn't start for another year. That's a long fucking time to be apart."

I.

Am.

Dumbfounded.

"This morning wasn't all talk."

I can't find my voice.

"You don't feel the same way I do? If you'd rather we stop right here..."

Snap out of it, Lily. "No. I mean, yes." I shake my head, frustrated with myself. "Let me catch my breath."

"Waiting."

I laugh.

"Looks like you caught your breath."

"You're impossible."

"I'm still waiting." He has the audacity to tap his expensive watch.

Oh my God, I'm going to miss him. "I want to see you as often as possible," I say. *If I didn't have to go back to New York because my puppet master pays my way in life, I'd stay in your bed forever.* "I love the idea of coming back to LA without involving my father." I wish I were independent. "I'm so determined to forge my own way."

"You will."

It's on the tip of my tongue to share my plans, but I refrain. I want to do this on my own. It's time I stood on my own two feet.

The alarm on my phone rings.

Shit.

I rummage for it inside my handbag, and stop the ringing.

I lift my eyes towards him. "I have to check in."

He growls. "I thought we'd have more time together."

"We would've if *someone* hadn't forced me to take a second shower."

"You say that like you didn't reap the benefits."

Oh, I did. Multiple, multiple times. "And now we're cutting it close. Hence, the alarm." I flash him my phone before dropping it at the bottom of my bag.

He scowls.

Things got so hot and heavy between us at the hotel, I'm surprised the fire department wasn't called over.

His hunger for me is exhilarating. It makes me feel beautiful and cherished.

"Since we're down to the last minute, I better kiss you goodbye," he says.

Before I can respond, he pulls me to him, cups my face in his strong hands, and crushes his mouth onto mine.

My feet are no longer touching the ground.

Holy hotness.

A few people whistle around us.

I'm floating, so I don't care if all eyes are on us.

He moans into my mouth.

Needing more, I get on the tip of my toes to match his fervor, tongue stroke for tongue stroke.

How am I going to live for the next three weeks without kissing this man?

Chapter 41

Lily

Seven days later

I'm slumped over the toilet in between puking sessions.

Once I'm no longer projecting vomit from my mouth, I attempt to straighten up from where I'm crouching, but another violent wave of nausea hits me.

Oh, God.

I manage to kneel down just in time.

With my hands cupping my tummy, I empty the contents of my stomach.

That Italian sausage pizza I had a couple days ago is doing a number on me.

Was the cheese off? The sausage?

But it was a high rating pizza joint.

Unless it was the take-out lasagna I ate last night?

Message received.

I'm steering clear of Italian food for a while.

I try to get up, but I'm hit by another wave of nausea.

I angle my body and puke my guts out.

I try again to straighten up. This time I manage.

Victory.

I don't even need to check to know I'm late.

My father is going to be furious.

I need to get out of here. Fast.

I step in front of the mirror and gasp in horror.

Puke stains my shirt and some of it is clumped to my hair.

Fuck.

I brush my teeth twice for good measure.

Once my breath doesn't taste like rotten milk, I strip out of my soiled clothes, dump them on the floor in a messy pile, and jump into the shower. Fifteen minutes later, I'm clean, but I don't feel perked up. Stepping out of the shower, I tiptoe to the mirror, apprehending the face that will be reflected back at me.

Yikes.

Even with my California tan, there's a sickly tinge to my skin tone.

To avoid frightening young children, I do a five-minute face. I select a bright shade of hot pink blush to liven up my complexion.

Studying my reflection in the mirror, I sigh.

This will have to do.

Since there's no time to blow dry my curtain of hair, I pull it back in a ponytail and braid it.

I assess myself in the mirror.

I don't look like myself. Heck, I don't feel like myself.

I don't have the luxury to dwell on it for too long or else my puppet master will rip me a new one.

Go, go, go.

I rush to my bedroom and have a panic attack when I see the time on the clock sitting on the nightstand.

I sprint into my walk-in closet, slip into underwear, grab a purple maxi dress with three-quarter sleeves, and slip it on as I step into a pair of white Hermes sandals. I exit my bedroom, snatch up my bag and my phone, and run out the door. As I descend the stairs, I open the taxi app to book a ride.

Thank God, I won't have to wait too long.

I shoot my father a quick text.

His response is instantaneous.

Puppet Master: I loathe tardiness. Why can't you be on time? Go-getters show up on time.

I roll my eyes.

Lily: Sorry. Rough morning.

Puppet Master: How rough can it be when I'm footing the bill? You don't even have to show up for a goddamn job. Excuses will keep you in the same dead-end position as the average American. Being average shouldn't be your life goal.

I want to hurl my phone against the asphalt. Instead, I grunt in frustration and stomp my feet like a three-year-old. I don't care if my neighbors witness my meltdown.

Breathe.

One.

Two.

Three.

Four.

When I reach ten, I fire off a response.

Lily: See you soon.

Puppet Master: Get here before my patience runs out.

I can't wait to live on the other coast, far, far away from my puppet master.

Since returning to the Big Apple, I've been busy contacting different headhunters and temp agencies in Los Angeles. I also spent time checking out different neighborhoods where I could live. More than once, I was tempted to text Mikki, Keira, or Dom and ask them for help, but I refrained. I need to do this on my own.

Since LA's subway system is a joke compared to New York's, and distances are triple the travel time, I'll have to buy a car to get around. Gridlock traffic will be a bitch. Being closer to Gage will more than make up for it.

I lift my eyes as a taxi comes to a screeching halt in front of me.

I jump into the back seat as a text message appears on my screen.

> Puppet Master: Are you close? I don't have all day. I have a company to run.

> Lily: I texted you two minutes ago. I'm on my way. Please don't text me again. You're stressing me out.

I dump my phone at the bottom of my bag. "Fuck!"

The driver meets my gaze through the rearview mirror.

I roll my eyes.

He nods.

I'm about to rub my hands over my face, but catch myself. Smearing my makeup would only get me another verbal lynching from my puppet master.

I wish his business trip to Washington DC had extended even longer.

Sigh.

Since I have to eat—if I can hold anything down—I

intend on killing two birds with one stone. I might not be there by choice since he summoned me, but I sure as hell will leverage this face to face. The typical lunch or dinner with my father is the same old song and dance—it's me sitting there, trying hard not to roll my eyes at what comes out of his mouth.

Not today.

By the time the salad is served, I'll have informed him of my plans to move to LA.

Here goes nothing...

~

Fifteen minutes later, I arrive at Jean-Georges near Central Park—the three Michelin starred restaurant my father favors these days.

As I follow the maître d' through the elegant eatery packed with the lunchtime crowd, the different aromas hit my nostrils all at once.

I place a hand on my stomach.

I'm going to be sick.

Holy shit, what's going on with my stomach today?

I take several deep breaths, praying to God, I don't have to rush to the bathroom.

That does the trick.

When I regain my composure, I scour the restaurant, searching for my father.

Where is he?

I wouldn't put it past him if he had left.

"Mr. Edgington requested a private room," the maître d' says from over his shoulder as if he could read my thoughts.

Whatever he has to say must be important if it has to happen behind closed doors.

The maître d' arrives in front of a room, knocks three times, and opens the door. With a hand gesture, he ushers me in.

"Thank you," I say.

With a curt head bow, he scurries off.

When I enter the room, my father isn't alone.

Crap.

Two men dressed in impeccable bespoke suits rise to their feet.

"Finally," my father says. "At this rate, it'll soon be happy hour."

Asshole. I force a smile. "I'm sorry I'm late." I keep it simple. Excuses will only earn me a lecture.

"Lily, do you remember Giuseppe DeMaro?"

My eyes shift to the man with dark brown hair and coffee-colored eyes that stands a foot over my father's five-feet-nine-inch frame. His wide smile takes over his face.

"You're Dario DeMaro's son."

"Yes," he says, extending a hand.

I shake it.

"Please call me John—the English version of my Italian name. All my friends do."

We're not friends.

"I'm flattered you'd remember me." He smiles. "A stunning woman like you must meet so many men, far more memorable than me."

Giuseppe DeMaro is right. Other than his expensive tailored suit, nothing about him stands out. The same applies to his three older brothers. His younger sister is pretty in an artificial way. In my opinion, she's way too young for collagen lip injections.

I let go of his clammy hand and resist the urge to wipe my hand on my dress.

I can't find it in me to match his smile, so I don't even try.

"Your father had donated a large amount to the charity that supports the advancement of black youth from poor neighborhoods in New York's five boroughs in the technology field," I say.

"Dad is all about a good tax deduction."

So is my father. "His interest doesn't go any deeper?"

"Supporting anything black-related is big on social media, so it makes us look good. Whatever makes us look good, makes us more money. More money, more power. Power is everything."

My eyebrows hit my forehead. "Why not support a cause your dad believes in?"

"My dad believes in money. Native Americans, whites, blacks, Eskimos, Australian Aboriginals, indigenous people from the Amazon rainforest, purple people with yellow hair." He shrugs. "It doesn't matter as long as that means less money going into Uncle Sam's pockets," Giuseppe who would rather be called John says.

Alrighty then.

Gage comes to mind.

The way he helped that transition house was so selfless.

I'm sure he got a whopping tax adduction, but that wasn't his motivation. His donation had significance. He wanted to do his mom proud.

"That's why Dad is a hundred percent behind Chandler as the next mayor of New York City," Giuseppe says. "It's a great tax deduction that will help get the right man for the job in office."

I didn't expect this to be a working lunch.

Not that I had much of an appetite, but the little I had, disappears.

"This conversation is way above Lily's pay grade," my

puppet master says. "She doesn't even need to work for a living, which is why she's a half hour late."

How condescending.

It's one thing for him to put me down, but another to do it in front of a stranger.

My retort dies on my lips when there's a knock at the door.

A waiter appears, holding a bottle of champagne in one hand and a silver bucket in the other.

"Mr. Edgington you're in luck," the waiter says, "I snatched the last bottle of chilled Krug Grande Cuvee Brut."

He claps. "Excellent! This celebration calls for the best champagne."

What are we celebrating?

My father checks his seventy-five-thousand-dollar Audemar Piguet watch before returning his attention to the waiter. "Give me twenty minutes or so before opening it. Please set it on the table."

"I can come back," the waiter says. "It's best if this particular champagne is served cold."

"If it isn't too much to ask," my father says.

The waiter smiles. "Not for one of our best customers."

"Thank you." My father swings his attention to the other man in the room. "Giuseppe, do you mind stepping out so I can talk to Lily? Go have a drink at the bar. I'll get the maître d' to summon you when we're ready."

"No problem, Fisher." Giuseppe-slash-John reaches out and touches my arm.

I flinch at the contact.

Who the hell told him he could touch me?

"I'll catch you later." He winks and flashes me a seductive smile.

I hesitate. "Sure."

Giuseppe-slash-John follows after the waiter, waving at me from over his shoulder.

What the hell?

My questioning gaze traps my father's. "You didn't mention this would be lunch for three."

"It was a last-minute decision. Lucky for me, Giuseppe was available," he says. "Take a seat."

I sit, placing my handbag on the chair next to mine.

The private room is appointed in the same tasteful airy décor as the rest of the restaurant. Other than an array of colorful flowers placed in vases, white is the predominant color.

My father sits down and reaches for the bottle of red.

He's about to serve me a glass, but I stop him. "It's too early—"

"It's not that early, but if you're only rolling out of bed, it would be."

I've had enough. "For your information, yesterday or the day before—I'm not certain—I ate something that didn't agree with me and I've been sick all morning. Both were Italian meals, so it could've been the cheese. Since I barfed all over what I was wearing, I had to take a shower, wash my hair, reapply makeup, and get dressed. That's why I'm late. It's not because I think tardiness is acceptable, nor is it because I was being lazy."

A fleeting flash of embarrassment darts in his gray eyes, but the remorse evaporates in a flash.

He squares off his shoulders, sitting a little straighter in his chair. "Why didn't you say so when you texted me?"

"Would you have believed me?"

He considers me with his lips pursed.

No, you wouldn't have.

"You have a valid reason for being late—"

"Why are we having lunch with Giuseppe DeMaro?" I cut

to the chase. "You haven't bought a PR firm yet, so it's not as if my presence here is necessary if the two of you are going to talk about Chandler's political career."

"This lunch isn't about Chandler. It's about *you*. Specifically, it's about you *and* Giuseppe."

"What do you mean?"

My stomach is acting up.

Crap.

To will it to settle, I reach for the bread. Not bothering with butter, I tear off a piece and shove it into my mouth.

"Dario and I think Giuseppe and you would form a good couple."

I stop chewing.

I place a hand over my mouth. "I don't understand."

"Dario is a powerful man. We've brokered a few deals together lately and we'd love to see our alliance extend further."

"That still doesn't make any sense to me."

"The best way for you and Giuseppe to get to know each other is by dating."

I choke on my saliva. "What?"

"The DeMaros plan on being important players in Chandler's campaign. Giuseppe is single and you're single. It makes sense." This isn't a suggestion. It's a decree.

"Let me get this straight"—I lift a hand up—"you decide the trajectory of my career. You decide which film school I'm going to attend. And now, you take it upon yourself to play matchmaker? When does it end, Father? Are you going to dictate who I marry next?"

"Yes," he says. "The plan is for you and Giuseppe to get married."

My mouth drops open.

"It will be the wedding all of New York talks about."

That sets me off. "I'm not getting married to that man."

"You don't even know him." My father frowns. "He's a good guy."

"He's malleable. That's why you approve of him."

"Dario and I both grew up poor and made something of ourselves. Now that we've gained a certain amount of success, we want to make sure it's passed on to the next generation, and the one after that. The fastest way to increase your wealth is to marry into a wealthy family. Giuseppe understands that. He's willing to put the interest of his family first. He isn't selfish."

But I am?

"Good for him. I'm not dating him. Forget about marrying him."

My father's nostrils flare.

His glacial blue eyes are glaring at me, but I hold his stare. I refuse to cower.

I shove more bread in my mouth because I'm this close from being sick again. And I'm pretty sure it has nothing to do with this bug that's creating havoc on my body, but everything to do with this ridiculous arranged marriage idea.

"It's time for you to pull your weight in this family, Lily." His voice is as cold as ice when he says that. I'm surprised I don't see his frosty breath in the air.

"What the hell does that mean?"

"I've provided you with a charmed life. The best schools. A wardrobe full of designer clothes. A collection of red sole shoes."

I tear off another piece of bread, chewing on it as if I'm mad at it.

"You have an enviable collection of jewelry, even though you insist on wearing that thing all the time." He points at my medallion. "It lacks the sophistication of the pieces I've offered you." That's like a slap in the face. "When you were in Paris you lived in a multimillion-dollar apartment in one of the best arrondissements. You live in an enviable zip code in New York. You have a Black American Express card at your disposal and you don't even have to worry about paying the balance."

"Things, Father. Those are all things." I'm fuming.

"Things most people will never have."

I stuff more bread in my mouth, storing the morsels between my cheeks like a chipmunk.

"After your mother's death, you could've ended up in the system. Foster kids have it rough. Instead, you've been living in the lap of luxury."

His words have the same effect as a catastrophic earthquake.

I masticate like a cow and swallow. "Why would I have ended up as a foster kid?" He forced me here to insult me? He could've done it by phone or text. This conversation is beyond aggravating. "You're my father. When a parent dies, the other parent steps up to the plate."

"And I did. And now, it's payback time."

I blink.

"If you were to become Mrs. DeMaro, it would help further the family not only financially, but also in the political arena. Dario knows the right people."

All this vomiting must've affected my hearing. "Heading a PR company isn't my dream career." My hand cups my medallion. "I went along with your grand plan because I was hoping you'd accept me. I won't prostitute myself for the good of the family—a family that would prefer I never existed—"

"Prostitute is a strong word. It's a marriage—"

"If I was stupid enough to marry Giuseppe, I bet it still wouldn't be enough to earn your respect or your love."

My father lifts both of his brows, his attention fixed on me, his posture stiffening.

I keep offloading what's on my chest. "This craziness stops

here. I won't do it." I shake my head. "If you want to form an alliance with the DeMaros, ask one of your sons to marry Dario's daughter."

"She's a handful."

"I see." I nod. "I have to sacrifice myself, but your sons don't?"

"They're—"

"I'm seeing someone."

The evil smile stretching his lips should come as a warning. "And who is that?"

I lift a defiant chin. "Gage Hollingsworth."

"He lives on the other side of the country."

"He has an office here."

"Los Angeles is his home. Not New York. A week here and there doesn't make for much of a relationship."

"I'm going to film school next year. Speaking of which, I plan on getting a job in PR in LA, so I can cut my teeth sooner rather than later."

He levels me with a glare that could freeze an iceberg.

I soldier on. "The more experience I have under my belt, the better I'll be at my job. And that will benefit Chandler."

I sit straighter, my glare matching his.

"There's been a change of plan." He plays with his cufflinks. "You're no longer attending film school in LA."

"You've been campaigning hard, citing Los Angeles has the best film schools in the world. *'It would be a waste of time to consider any other option'*." I throw his words back at him.

"I've reconsidered. The New York Film Academy is more than suitable. No need to go across the country."

Wh—what?

My molars grind together as my hands fist. "I had my heart set on LA—"

"On LA or on being in the same city as Gage?"

"Both."

We enter a Mexican standoff for several beats.

"You may hate me now, but you'll thank me in the long run."

That sounded Greek to me.

I'm about to say as much, but he pulls his phone out of his suit jacket and checks it.

I let out of frustrated sigh.

He meets my gaze. "You're willing to give up your life and move across the country for a man you know nothing about."

I narrow my eyes at him.

"Did you know Gage is in love with another woman?"

The pain is as sharp as being stabbed in the heart with an ice pick.

"In fact, Gage and his girlfriend were spotted hand in hand entering Van Nuys Airport a couple days ago." My father continues his torture.

A couple days ago?

He was supposed to be in Sweden.

His trip was delayed?

My heart is beating so hard. "You're lying."

He smirks. "There are two ways to know someone. One, the person is truthful and forthcoming. I've been on this earth long enough to know that's rare. Two, you have them investigated."

My eyes grow wide.

My father hands me his phone. "Here's proof I'm not lying."

I reach out for it and pray my father doesn't notice how much my hand is shaking.

A paused video flashes on the screen.

My father places his weight against his folded elbow, reaches out, and presses the play button.

There's no mistaking it's Gage.

I lift my eyes. "You paid a private investigator to follow him?"

He points to the phone. "You're going to miss the good part."

Like a masochist, my attention returns to the screen.

Gage is holding a woman with black hair in his arms. I can't see her face.

The camera zooms on his mouth.

There's no sound.

He tightens his hold on the woman.

She lifts her head up at him, revealing her profile.

I squint.

She's a woman with tawny brown skin.

Is she part of the sisterhood?

I didn't meet her while I was in LA.

If her striking profile is anything to go by, she's gorgeous.

Nope, I'm not jealous of her perfect curly hair or the insane volume.

Gage wipes away her tears.

Why is she crying?

The camera zooms in on her mouth. I ignore her full lips, focusing on what she's about to say.

"*I love you.*" My heart sinks when I read her lips.

No, no, no.

This is a bad joke. It has to be.

"*I love you, too.*"

Four words that ripple out of the mouth of the man I'm so crazy about, landing in a lake like a cannon ball.

The air turns to concrete in my lungs.

I'm living a nightmare.

For several seconds, all I can do is choke on the shock of those words.

My panicked thoughts spiral.

Blood roars in my ears.

The jealousy I felt before is dwarfed in comparison to the cyclone whirling inside me.

An invisible hand wraps around my heart and squeezes hard.

Gage kisses her forehead with tenderness.

He cares for this woman.

No, Lily, he loves her.

Ba boom.

Ba boom.

Ba boom.

There's a chaotic chorus going on in my head—and in my heart. My poor heart. I fight not to bring my hand up to it to rub at the pain at my chest.

The video stops and jumps to another scene.

Gage and a short man in a suit that doesn't look as sharp as Gage's is stuffing designer luggage in the trunk of a car. The tall woman he professed his love to is standing next to him.

She doesn't travel light.

The short man closes the trunk and rushes to open the passenger door.

Gage reaches out for the woman's hand and guides her inside the vehicle. Before he closes the door, she reaches out and caresses his face.

My heart shatters in a million pieces.

The video cuts again.

The next shot shows the driver pulling out his and hers luggage from the trunk.

In the next shot, Gage embraces the woman in his arms, and together, they walk towards the entry to Van Nuys Airport. As they're about to enter, Gage drops a soft kiss on the woman's forehead.

She smiles up at him.

What.

The.

Fuck.

He said he hadn't been with a woman since his mom died three years ago.

He said he was going to Sweden and South Korea alone.

He had nothing but contempt for cheater Judson and his deceiving ex-girlfriend.

He lied?

I thought I could trust him.

I'm such a fool.

No wonder I haven't heard from him in days.

I figured between the time difference and his demanding schedule, he was overwhelmed.

Since I didn't want to come across as needy, I didn't push.

I can't breathe.

I can't fucking breathe.

I feel the weight of my father's stare on me.

My eyes lift up to meet his.

His smirk suggests he's proud of himself.

It would've been less painful had he pushed me in front of a moving train.

I will my hand to stop shaking, and give him back his phone.

He takes it, the smug expression on his face turning sinister.

A long, heavy silence passes between us before he deigns answering my question.

"You weren't receptive at the idea of going to California to check out film schools. Alder sees you in Malibu hand-in-hand with Gage, and a few days later, you inform me *after the fact,* you extended your trip. It was clear film schools weren't the reason why." The disappointment in his tone is clear and cutting. "So, I decided to do a little digging into Gage, since I had a sneaky suspicion he prompted your decision."

Manipulation comes naturally to my father, and this is further proof. Who needs a gun or a knife when backstabbing is your weapon of choice?

Conniving weasel.

"I told you to be careful with those Hollywood-slash-LA men." He shakes his head, tsking. "She's the one he loves." He points at his phone. You"—he points at me—"were nothing more than a plaything." He leans back against his seat, his gaze slithering over me. "Now, do you still want to move to LA, Lily?"

I can't speak.

"Sending you to Los Angeles was the biggest mistake." His eyes slash through me like a sword slashing through my withering pride.

Spine stiffening, I force my lips not to tremble.

Don't give him the satisfaction of letting him see how much he's destroyed you.

"Not only did you get entangled with Gage, you lost your virginity to a player."

Whoa.

How did he know I was a virgin until LA? I sure as hell never had the birds and the bees talk with him.

"On top of that stupid decision, you went and lost your phone." More venom spills from his lips. "When you bought a phone in LA instead of calling me to request a new one, I no longer had tracking software on it—"

"You had your tech guys install tracking software on my phone without my knowledge?"

"Two years ago, after you called me on the landline from the Paris apartment to let me know you had dropped your phone in the Seine River by mistake, I became suspicious.

When I sent you a new phone, I had a tracking device installed on it. Jean-Philippe's wife's waters burst at the opportune time. That baby saved your virginity."

I'm shellshocked.

"I've been tapping into your conversations and text messages ever since—"

"That's a grotesque invasion of my privacy."

He shrugs. "It was an insurance policy."

This shows how little respect he has for me.

When douchebag Jean-Philippe texted me to have sex after his wife gave birth, I was so angry, I tossed my phone in the river after I blocked his ass. I agreed to my father sending me a new one. I had no idea I was giving him a window into my life.

"Virginity is a commodity," he says.

I flinch. "Excuse me?"

"You have more value to a man if he's the one to take your virginity."

My head just exploded.

"In regards to your marriage to Giuseppe, we might have to pretend you used to be an avid rider growing up—"

I shoot to my feet. "We're done with this conversation."

The side of his mouth quirks. "Are we?"

He's amused?

Jerk.

He doesn't appreciate being told what to do, and certainly not by me.

I stick to my guns. "I don't care if Gage Hollingsworth is in love with another woman." That's a blatant lie. *I care. I fucking care.* Tears of sorrow pool in my eyes, but I blink them away. "I'm not marrying Giuseppe." I stab a finger on the table to drive my point.

"You aren't giving the guy a chance. Let's have lunch—"

"I'm not having lunch with Giuseppe."

His eyes widen. "Are you shouting at me?"

"Yes, I'm shouting!"

All I've ever wanted was my father's acceptance, attention, and love. But now that he wants to sell me off like an asset for his financial gain, disregarding my views on the matter, I wish Mama hadn't planned it so I'd end in this man's care. In his eyes, I'll never be good enough to deserve his love. I'm done keeping hope alive.

My father opens his mouth to speak, but I lift a hand. "Forget about me attending film school in New York or anywhere else on the planet. I don't want to run a PR firm." I'm riled up. "I don't want to have anything to do with Chandler's career."

"You don't get a say in the matter—"

"I'm done with you being my fucking puppet master."

My father's head jerks back.

Yeah, I'm unleashed. I point a finger at him. "I shouldn't have to bend backwards for you to love me. You've had eight years to accept me." My voice cracks. *Why is my heart not immune to the way he treats me?*

"Lily—"

"This scenario is fucked up. If you're that desperate for a merger with the DeMaros, get your current girlfriend to marry Giuseppe. You're going to dump her soon anyway and move onto another flavor. She might not be your daughter, but you treat her with far more respect than you treat me. Also, her life goal is to marry into *way, way more* money."

My father's eyes are so wide, they take over his face.

"And, she's as malleable as Giuseppe. It's a win-win—"

"In this family, the good of all, trumps the good of one."

He thinks I owe him for the fact he took care of me.

I went from being a dirty little secret to a pawn?

Fuck that.

"I'm not marrying Giuseppe." I stand my ground. "If you want to disown me, go right ahead. I'm done begging for scraps." I snatch my handbag from the seat next to me and rush towards the door.

"You need a little time to mull it over," my father says from over my shoulder. "I'm sure you'll have a change of heart by the time we all gather out East for the important party I'm throwing for Chandler. Big players will be present—including the DeMaros. You and Giuseppe can get to know each other better while you're in the Hamptons."

I halt my step and turn around. "Did you hear a word I said?"

He brushes off invisible lint from his suit jacket. "Talk is cheap, Lily. If I disown you, you'll have nothing to your name other than a degree from a Paris university. You can't even boast being bilingual since your French is broken at best."

Wow.

"You don't have any work experience. I doubt you have what it takes to survive on a minimum wage salary. If I were you, I'd think long and hard before saying anything that might come back and bite you in the ass."

His treacherous words are as murderous as bullets, even though his only weapon is his mouth.

"You're a manipulative monster."

"I've been poor and I've been rich. The latter is much better. Being flat broke in New York City is no joke." His eyes harden when he says, "You were dirt poor in a shitty town in a shitty apartment in Alabama when I sent for you. You want to live hand to mouth again? Once you cool your jets, I'm sure you'll make the right decision." That stupid smirk again.

"Go to hell, Father!" With that, I run out of the room. I slam the door behind me so hard, I'm surprised it doesn't come off its hinges.

As I rush down the corridor, my stomach revolts.

Oh God, I'm going to be sick again.

Panicked, I search around until I find the bathroom sign.

I bolt towards it, bursting through the door so hard, it crashes with a thundering bang against the wall.

I don't make it to the stall.

I bend over the sink and throw up.

For a few agonizing minutes, it's hell as my body freaks out on me.

When my stomach settles, I wash my mouth and press cold water against my cheeks. It's in vain. My face is on fire.

With a hard sniff, I push myself off the counter I'm gripping for dear life. When I catch sight of the sadness reflecting in my eyes in the mirror, I break down. My body shudders as I sob. I'm inconsolable.

Fisher Edgington is a horrible man.

And Gage Hollingsworth is a two-faced asshole.

A river of tears floods my eyes, blurring my vision, and I'm crying in earnest now, my body trembling with sobs as sorrow eats at my heart.

I was nothing more than a dumb virgin Gage could feed lies to.

I'm across the country. How was I ever going to know he was leading a double life?

My deep-seated fear of rejection that's plagued me since my mom died, rears its ugly head.

An overwhelming surge of sadness hits me, and my throat tightens up. I'm certain I'm about to throw up again, but no, it's only heartache.

I hate myself for having succumbed to Gage's charm. I'm pathetic for allowing a man to reduce me to this. I promised myself I'd never follow in Mama's footsteps and fall for a guy who was taken.

I've done it twice.

Gage was a grumpy bear from the moment I met him. I should've welcomed his cold attitude like an omen.

I should've kept it to scoping out film schools.

I should've never gone to Rhys's birthday party.

I should've never kissed him.

And I should've never slept with him.

I cry so hard, I give myself a headache.

It takes a while before my sobs quiet.

I wipe away my tears and blow my nose.

My puffy face is it telltale sign I'm having a shit day.

I need to go home and sleep for the next week. Or month.

I compose myself, breathing in and out a few times.

Don't waste your tears on that man. He doesn't deserve them.

As broken as my heart is at this moment, I need to muster up the energy to get out of here. I pull the strap of my handbag over my shoulder, and march towards the door.

I search for an exit sign, but I can't find one.

Crap.

I was hoping to avoid going through the main restaurant.

This day keeps getting better and better.

With my head hung low, I focus on putting one foot in front of the other as I trail towards the restaurant. No one pays me any attention as I pass by table after table of patrons.

I'm home free—

"Hey, Lily!"

My eyes shoot up.

Giuseppe waves. Bouncing off the barstool he's sitting on, he rushes towards me.

Dammit.

He stops in front of me, his frame tensing. His smile disappears and his eyes widen. "What happened?"

"I don't want to talk about it."

"We could go somewhere else and hang out. We don't have to talk. I want to be here for you."

Man, this guy drank some of my father's Kool-Aid. Scratch that. He probably had an immersion baptism in said Kool-Aid.

This madness has gone too far. "Listen, Giuseppe, whatever arrangement your father and my father have, I want no part of it—"

"Our fathers are dead set on this union—"

"I don't care."

"It will benefit both our families. That's how dynasties are built."

"I. Don't. Care."

He reaches out for me.

I jerk away from his touch.

A few patrons stare up from their plates, eyebrows cocked.

"Okay." He nods. "You need a little time—"

"I don't need more time to accept this preposterous idea." I'm making a scene and I don't give a damn. "I'm not dating you. I'm not marrying you." I set Giuseppe-slash-John straight. "And I don't want to see you ever again." Like a demented woman, I bolt out of the restaurant.

Chapter 42

Lily

Three days later

I nibble on a plain croissant like a kid forced to eat broccoli.

"I hope that's better," Nadine says.

I drop the croissant on the plate, my eyes shifting to the chocolate croissant I took one bite of and the bowl of latte my stomach didn't like one bit. "No. It's not much better."

"What about some plain yogurt?"

I make a face. "I'll stick to Perrier."

After that dreadful meeting with my father, I cried my eyes out all the way home in the back of the taxi. When I got to the brownstone—I video called my best friend. Once I was done telling her about the freak show that is my life, she declared I shouldn't be alone. To avoid buying a ticket with my puppet master's Black American Express card and letting him know of my whereabouts, Nadine bought me a last-minute flight to Paris.

Because she's the best friend in the world, she took the day off, letting her part-time assistant man the shop. After dropping off my suitcase at her apartment, we walked to Ladurée, located on Rue Bonaparte, in Saint Germain-des-Prés. When the shit hits the fan, you head to one of the best pastry shops in Paris.

Nadine reaches out for my hand. "So much hit you all at once. Three days ago, you got hit with a bad case of food poisoning. On the same day, your father dropped a bomb on you. And the cherry that tops the sundae, he proceeded to shatter your world with that jaw-dropping video. Add to the fact you haven't slept because you took the redeye and arrived early this morning, it's no wonder your stomach isn't cooperating. Give it a few days."

My body is out of sorts.

My life is a mess.

My heart is broken into millions of irreparable pieces.

The only thing missing is Edith Piaf's sad song '*Non, je ne regrette rien*' as a backdrop to make my misery complete.

"I dodged the bullet with one married asshole cheater, only to fall in love with——"

I clamp my hand over my mouth.

I alluded to it, but coming out and saying it, is a different thing.

"I'm not in love with him. I hate him." I go into defense mode.

I hate you, Gage Hollingsworth.

And I hate that woman you declared your love to.

I hate the thought of that woman using Gage's bicep as a pillow.

I'm envious that she'll get to wake up to sleepy green eyes blazing with desire.

And it kills me that he'll fuck her instead of me.

I'm a gullible idiot. I bought his lies about not being with anyone since his mom's death.

My best friend remains quiet, as if allowing me to process it all.

I let out an audible sigh. "Why are men such pigs?" I brush a hand in front of my face. If I don't think about him, it won't hurt as much. "I shouldn't waste brain cells on Gage, since he's the least of my problems. Finding a place to live when I get back to New York is far more pressing now that I've told my father off. I'm probably going to end up living in a tiny apartment the size of my walk-in closet, or I'll be forced to share a small and outrageously expensive apartment with God knows how many roommates if I want to stay in Manhattan."

"Your father isn't going to kick you out of the brownstone. He's not that much of a monster."

"Wanna bet?" I sneer. "He bought me the house, but it won't be mine until I celebrate my twenty-fifth birthday. Same for the apartment in Paris. The two properties are his. Not mine. The man doesn't have a heart. He'd take malicious pleasure in seeing me agree to that stupid arranged-slash-merger-marriage so I can have a roof over my head."

"*Putain.*" Nadine shakes her head.

Translation: *Fuck.*

"This isn't the 1950s," I say.

"He should've consulted you—"

"Instead of using me as a commodity to further the family fortune."

"*Précisément.*"

Translation: *Exactly.*

"Not to mention, with his wide network of wealthy connections, couldn't he have found you a guy with balls?"

"Having balls means having guts, using your brain, and being willing to stand up to the great Fisher Edgington. He hates being contradicted or challenged."

"You'll have to move to Paris and live with me. I'm not

going to let you marry Giuseppe-slash-John and I won't let your father pressure you. This is your life we're talking about."

"I know."

"Your father is trying to scare you. Don't fall for his manipulative tactics. You're smart and talented. Wherever you decide to land, you can stand on your own two feet."

Doubt trickles in. "Can I?"

"Yes, you can."

"My life has been cushy since I left Alabama." Other than respect, affection, and love, I've never had to want for anything. The irony.

"You can do this, Lily."

I bite the inside of my cheek. "I'd need to enroll in a master's degree to get a student visa to stay in Paris or anywhere in France. If I go the long stay route, I'd need a work permit, and in order to get one, an employer has to be willing to hire me... with my broken French and all—"

"Don't you dare put your father's filthy words into your mouth." She points an agitated finger at me. *"C'est un con."* She's never been shy about how little she thinks of my father.

My shoulders slump.

"I take that back," Nads says. "He isn't an asshole. He's a dick. He says things that erode your self-confidence, but you're a strong woman."

I square my shoulders and take in a fortifying breath. "You're right. He's a dick."

"Now you're talking."

Nads lifts a hand in the air.

I high five it.

"As for the work permit, you forget who my father is. My daddy outranks your daddy." She grins wide. "I'm sure he can pull some strings to find an employer willing to hire you."

I smile. "You're a good friend."

She grabs both my hands into hers. "Before the sisterhood, I was your person, and I'll always be your person. Your ride or die."

"My ride or die—" A thought slams into me and my face contorts.

"What is it? Are you feeling ill?"

"I'm sick to my stomach knowing that I won't be in contact with Michaela and the girls anymore. I love those women, but I don't want to keep in touch with them. I don't want details of Gage and the love of his life."

Her lips twist. "Men are shit."

"Yes, they are."

Nadine drops her gaze to my breakfast. "Since you don't have much of an appetite, let's go out for a walk. It'll do you some good."

"Okay."

"Do you want to take these with us for later? You might be in the mood once you get some fresh air."

High-quality pastries that will end up in the trash.

It would be sacrilege.

"Good idea," I say.

"Be right back."

Nadine rushes to the counter. She's back in a flash.

She stuffs the pastries in a box and puts them in a bag. We gather our things, and we're off.

When we step outside, the sun is shining bright.

Early June in Paris is idyllic.

For the past three days I've been living in an eclipse even though it's been sunny in New York, the images of the video of Gage and the woman he loves looping over and over in my mind.

No matter how many times I will myself to forget all about the tall, brooding man with mesmerizing green eyes who rarely smiles—but when he does, the world lights up—he invariably pops into my mind. It's like being thrust into a nightmare all over again. Shy of a lobotomy, I'm not sure how to make it stop.

It should be easy to forget him. After all, he was never going to be mine. His empty promises were as hollow as a barrel. Still, he has a hold of my heart, and I'm not sure how to forget him or the way he made me feel.

Sigh.

Nads laces her arm with mine. "What do you want to do now?"

"Nothing that requires me to be around too many people. I felt claustrophobic during the flight over. I've never felt like that before."

"All these emotions are taking a toll on your body and your mind."

"They are."

"*On flâne et on fait du lèche-vitrines?*"

Translation: *Let's walk around and do some window shopping.*

"*D'accord.* I like your suggestion."

Translation: *All right.*

We stroll together at a leisurely pace. Even though it's a little past ten o'clock in the morning, and most people are in their offices, the streets of Paris are swarming with pedestrians.

We're about to cross the street, but I pull on Nadine's arm. "Wait."

"OhmyGod, you look pale."

My vision is blurred and the world in front of my eyes is all fuzzy... even my best friend's worried face.

"Lily!"

I feel Nadine shaking me, but I'm losing my grip on reality.

Chapter 43

Lily

I attempt to open my eyes, but my eyelids weigh a ton.

"*Vous me faites signe lorsqu'elle aura repris conscience?*"

Translation: *Make sure to let me know the moment she regains consciousness.*

Who's talking?

"*Oui, docteur. Je n'y manquerai pas.*"

Translation: *I will, doctor.*

Nadine is talking to a... doctor? Why?

"*Vous n'avez qu'a demander a une infirmière a l'accueil de m'appeler.*"

Translation: *Ask one of the nurses to track me down.*

"*Merci, Docteur Cluzet,*" Nadine says.

I force my eyes to open.

"Nads—" I try to speak, but my voice comes out scratchy.

My best friend whirls around, concerned brown eyes the size of basketballs stare at me. "Lily." My name comes out in a near whisper as she rushes towards me.

I dart my eyes around the room, taking in my surroundings. "I'm in the hospital?"

Nadine takes my hand into hers. "Yes. You scared the shit out of me."

"How did I end up here?"

"You passed out."

"I passed out?"

"Yes."

"I'm never eating Italian food for the rest of my life."

Nads turns around.

The doctor standing near the door approaches the bed. *"Ah. Mademoiselle Schuyler a repris conscience."*

Translation: *Miss Schuyler regained consciousness.*

"Oui," I say.

Another place, another time, Dr. Mc Dreamy with the gorgeous hazel-brown eyes would cause me to do a double take, but given my precarious situation, I don't have time to admire how hot the French doctor is.

"Enchanté, je suis Docteur Cluzet."

Translation: *Pleased to meet you. I'm Doctor Cluzet.*

"Enchanté, docteur."

Translation: *Pleased to meet you, doctor.*

I have a million questions for the good doctor, but I'm a little too frazzled to hold a conversation in French to find out why I passed out. "What happened, Nads? How did I get here?"

Her eyes shift from mine to the doctor.

"Vous traduisez?" the doctor says to Nads.

Translation: *Will you act as my translator?*

She nods.

"D'abord, elle devra donner son consentement," the doctor says.

"D'accord." Nads nods. She returns her attention to me.

"Before the doctor answers any of your questions, he needs your approval on me acting as your translator. Since you're not fluent in French and he doesn't speak English, he enlisted my help. Protocol dictates it's close family only, but..."

"I don't have any close family and the people I'm related to aren't in Paris." *And they don't give a fuck about me.*

Nadine nods. "There's paperwork for you to sign, if you're okay with that."

"I'll sign."

"*Ça lui convient,*" Nads says to the doctor.

Translation: *She's okay with that.*

The doctor hands me an iPad, I scribble my signature, and hand back the device.

"What's the last thing you remember, Lily?"

My eyes shift to my best friend. "We were about to cross the street when things went fuzzy before it all went black."

"It was a close call," Nads says. "One more step and you would've ended up passing out in the middle of the street. A man, standing behind us at the stop light, caught you before you collapsed to the asphalt."

"This food poisoning is kicking my ass."

"It might not be food poisoning," Nads says.

"I'm dying?"

"No, you're not," she says.

"But there's something wrong with me. Why else would I be in the hospital?"

"The moment you passed out, I begged passersby to call 112 for an ambulance. When we arrived at the hospital—"

"Did they conduct tests?"

"The doctor suggested we wait until you regained consciousness—"

"He's going to conduct tests now to find out what's wrong with me?"

"The doctor has his suspicions as to why you've been this sick."

My best friend and the doctor exchange a silent conversation.

I pull on Nads's arm. "Tell me. Don't sugarcoat it."

"Let me pick up where I left off," Nads says. "When you arrived at the hospital, I wasn't about to let you out of my sight. I might not be your blood sister, but I'm all you've got."

My God, I love this woman.

"I thought it was going to be a battle—doctor patient confidentiality, and all—but Doctor Cluzet recognized my name. He felt he could trust a former president's daughter. When the doctor asked me what had happened, I told him you've been vomiting for the past four days. I let him know you suspected the cause was either the pizza or lasagna that were off. I informed him you've been having a hard time keeping any food down. Even a plain croissant. Only Perrier settles your stomach. I also told him you traveled on a redeye."

"And...?"

Nadine turns to the doctor.

His hazel-brown eyes land on me. *"Est-ce que vous vous rappelez de la date de vos dernières règles?"*

My gaze snaps to Nadine. "He wants to know when was my last period?"

She nods.

"How does that—" Realization comes crashing like a tidal wave.

"I didn't go into anything personal, but the doctor asked if you were sexually active." Nadine dances from one foot to the other. "I also told him it was your first time. I mentioned you— I mean, *he*—used a condom. But Doctor Cluzet noted they're not one-hundred percent effective. Since you weren't on any form of contraception... there's a good chance you might be pregnant. The test will confirm it."

I close my eyes.

"It's going to be okay, Lily." Nadine caresses my arm.

No, it's not going to be okay.

I swore up and down a stack of Bibles, I'd never end up in Mama's predicament—pregnant and alone.

Look at me now.

Chapter 44

Gage

Two days later

I step out of the shower and stand in front of the vanity.

I wipe away the fog from the mirror and assess the damage.

I look like shit.

I feel like shit.

This jetlag is still kicking my ass.

Two days in Stockholm and I still haven't found my footing.

It doesn't help that my days are so crammed, I can't catch my breath.

Delaying the trip caused a cluster fuck in my schedule. These back to back meetings are going to be the end of me.

Stop whining. That's what being a CEO is all about, Hollingsworth. Man up and get the job done.

I rub my hands over my face. It doesn't do much to revive me or get me moving, but the prospect of caffeine and an outstanding breakfast does.

With a towel wrapped around my waist, I step into the bedroom. As I pass the desk, I freeze.

Lily hasn't returned the last few texts I sent her.

I snatch my phone off the desk and compose another message. I'm still holding onto my phone when it rings.

My face contorts in a grimace.

It's not who I was hoping to hear from.

I'm about to let it go to voicemail, but decide against it.

Fisher could explain Lily's silence.

I accept the call. "Hey—"

"I should've never asked you to look after my daughter." He barks his greeting into the phone.

I flinch at his words. "Good morning to you too."

"I don't have time for jokes."

"It's seven o'clock in the morning here in Stockholm. If you're going to call me to chew my head off for some unknown reason, have the courtesy to do it after I've had my coffee."

"Cut the crap, Hollingsworth."

"I'm this close from hanging up on you."

"It's your fault Lily is missing."

I'm suffused with panic.

"Lily is missing?"

"Yes."

My stomach plummets to my toes. "Since when?"

"Since she walked out on me at lunch a few days ago after I showed her you're a piece of shit—"

"What the fuck is your problem, Fisher? Why are you insulting me?"

"You played my daughter for a fool, asshole."

A growl rumbles from my chest. "Whatever I shared with your daughter is between her and me. She's a grown woman. Butt out."

"You abused her innocence and put ideas in her head."

What is he talking about?

"Now she's missing, she's going to force me to back out of an arrangement because she refuses to marry someone she was betrothed to."

"Excuse me?"

"I handpicked a husband for Lily. A man who's far more suitable for her than you—"

"Lily is… supposed to get married to another man?"

"Yes!" One word that has the same impact as a slap across the face.

I thought she wasn't seeing anyone.

Was I wrong?

"You're a bastard." Fisher isn't done insulting me. "How dare you put your hands on my daughter? You fucked her—"

"Whoa, whoa, whoa." *How the hell does he know that? Lily talks about intimate matters with Fisher?* "First, you and I shouldn't be having this conversation. Second, that's none of your business—"

"It is my business when you're in love with another woman and stringing along my daughter."

"You're not making any sense."

"Come off it. I had a private investigator follow you around. I know all your dirty little secrets."

I'm about to tear him a new one, when it hit me. "I'm in love with another woman? Says who?"

"Save your breath. Don't bother lying. I have video proof."

"Fisher—"

"Here's how it's going to go down, Hollingsworth. I'm going to find my daughter. And when I bring her back to New York, where she belongs, she's going to do what I tell her to do. I need her to be a part of this family, *and* I need her to be in the

Hamptons in the next few days, *and* I need her to be invested, *and* I need her to forget all about you so she can marry the man she's betrothed to."

What in the actual fuck?

"I don't need her to be entangled with the likes of you."

"Fisher—"

"Stay the fuck away from my daughter."

Pompous jerk. "I'm not fucking staying away."

Silence.

"Fisher?"

I pull the device away from my ear.

The asshole hung up on me.

I dial Lily's number.

It goes straight to voicemail.

I try again.

Same result.

I'm going to burn Stockholm down to the ground if I don't get answers right the fuck now.

I pace back and forth like an enraged bull, my nostrils flaring, steam billowing from my ears.

I stop dead in my tracks.

Realization flashes over my head like a neon sign.

If Lily was missing, wouldn't Fisher call NYPD instead of harassing me? He might not have known I was in Sweden, but he knows I live in LA.

She isn't missing.

She doesn't want her father to know where she is.

What's going on, Lily?

Why are you running?

There's one person on this planet who knows where she is. I'm willing to bet my billions on it.

I call Nadine's number.

It goes to voicemail.

I see red.
I try again.
Nadine's cheery voice blares through the speaker.
Her voicemail. Again.
Pure white rage consumes me.

Chapter 45

Gage

Paris wasn't on the agenda today, but it shot to the top of the list real fast.

I don't appreciate getting the runaround.

After trying to get a hold of Lily and Nadine numerous times, it was clear there was only one way I was going to be able to get answers. My decision to cancel all my meetings for the rest of my trip will cost me, but not knowing where the hell Lily is will drive me out of my mind. There's no way I can concentrate until I'm certain Lily is safe.

I didn't have a private plane reserved, so I grabbed the first flight out of Stockholm. It's been years since I flew coach. I don't even fly first class anymore. The near three-hour flight was uncomfortable as fuck on my long legs.

As I was packing my stuff at the speed of light, I sent Phoenix a string of texts, explaining the situation. The time difference with LA played in my favor. By the time I rolled my suitcase near the door, he had appointed someone to help me secure a room at the Pompadour Paris. His hotel is my stomping ground, but they were fully booked, so I get to stay in his private suite. After leaving my luggage in the room, I set off on my mission.

It's two o'clock when the taxi stops in front of a tiny shop with a blue door.

I read the sign.

Blue Belle.

I pay the cabbie, mumble *merci*, and get out of the taxi.

When I step through the door, a bell chimes.

I scour the shop.

Nadine is nowhere to be seen.

Is she in the back room?

She better be.

I'm not leaving until I talk to her.

If I'm standing in her face, she can't ignore me.

I take in my surroundings, my eyes bouncing in all four corners.

It isn't big, but it's quaint.

From the little I know of Lily's best friend, the décor matches her personality.

An elegant woman of a certain age is in deep concentration as she selects flowers for the perfect bouquet. A young couple is doing the same, as the man and woman bob their heads to the beat of a jazz tune.

My eyes land on a bucket of Lily's favorite flowers, and I'm drawn towards them.

I don't have time to take a step forward.

"*Bonjour, monsieur,*" a voice says from behind me. "*Comment puis-je vous aider?*"

Other than *hello, sir* I didn't understand a word she said.

I turn around.

Lily's best friend gasps, her hands flying to cover her mouth.

"*Bonjour, Nadine.*"

"What are you doing here?" she says in way of a greeting.

I cut to the chase. "We both know what I'm doing here."

"I have a business to run. I don't have time for this." Her tone is cold and detached, her eyes emanating with fury.

I open my arms. "What's going on?"

"You're making a scene."

"Wouldn't you, if you were in my position?"

"I don't want to talk to you."

My face furrows with irritation. "Too bad. I'm here and I'm going nowhere."

She crosses her arms over her chest.

As if that's enough to shut me up. "Lily's father called to chew my head off and I have no idea what the hell he's talking about. And what's this about him having me followed?"

"Men." She sneers. "You're all alike."

I point a finger at her. "I resent that."

"You're not welcome in my shop."

"I'm not budging until you tell me where to find Lily."

"Who says I know where she is?"

I pinch my lips in a thin line.

Nadine glares at me.

The air in the shop turns icy.

The woman and the couple rush out.

There was genuine fear in their eyes.

"*Putain!*" Nadine's hands go flying in the air before landing on her thighs. "Are you happy now? You scared my customers."

"I can't get a hold of Lily and I couldn't get a hold of you—"

"Perhaps you should've clued in on the fact Lily doesn't ever want to talk to you again. Ditto for me."

"I'm tired of this cryptic conversation—"

"You're more than welcome to leave." She points to the door.

"I'm not going anywhere."

"Gage, your presence here is costing me business."

There's an easy solution for that. "Whatever you make in a day, I'll five-time it."

"You're wasting your breath." She lifts a defiant chin.

I narrow my eyes at her. "I'll five-time your month's revenue. Close the damn shop and talk to me, Nadine."

Chapter 46

Lily

I pause the show I'm binge-watching on my laptop.

I need a body break. And a bathroom one.

I stand up and stretch like a cat.

When I inhale, I take in a medley of delicious aromas.

Is that roasted chicken I smell?

The rosemary is fragrant.

I wonder if my stomach will be able to handle anything more than soup.

Fingers crossed.

Gérard pokes his head into the living room. *"Mademoiselle Lily."*

Translation: *Miss Lily.*

"Oui."

"Votre soupe de tomate sera prête dans quelques minutes." Gérard St. Aubin, the short, fifty-three-year-old housekeeper and cook with salt and pepper hair who looks after Nadine's father's property smiles at me.

Translation: Your tomato soup will be ready in a few minutes.

"*Merci,*" I say. "*Il faut tout simplement m'appeler Lily, Gérard.*"

Translation: *Thank you. Please call me, Lily, Gérard.*

"*Je promets de faire un effort, Lily.*"

Translation: *I promise, I'll try, Lily.*

Nadine's father and his wife require formality. I don't.

"*On agrémente la soupe avec une assiette de fromage et du bon pain?*"

Translation: *I'll serve the soup with a cheese plate and some hearty bread?*

"*D'accord. Merci,*" I say.

Translation: *Okay. Thank you.*

Since cheese isn't the enemy, I can eat it. Gérard suggested I avoid soft cheeses like brie, camembert, and chevre. Sharp cheddar, parmesan, and mozzarella are okay. Thank God. I can't imagine nine months without cheese.

"*Pour le dessert, je vous ai préparé une petite compote d'abricots étant donné que vous avez aimé celle aux pommes que j'ai préparé ce midi.*" Gérard keeps talking. "*Mes filles étaient friandes des compotes au tout début de leurs grossesses,*" he says with a proud smile.

Translation: *For dessert, I prepared an apricot purée since you liked the apple one I prepared for lunch. My daughters enjoyed purées in the early stages of their pregnancies.*

He has four daughters and ten grandkids. He's been pulling out tried and tested recipes to ensure I eat since I got here last night. So far, his recipes are winners.

"*Vivement,*" I say.

Translation: *I can't wait.*

"*Je vais bien m'occuper de vous pendant votre séjour ici, Lily.*"

Translation: *I'll take good care of you while you're here.*

I blush. "*Merci, Gérard.*"

I relish the attention.

I'm sure I won't get much of that in the coming months since I'll be navigating this new chapter of my life on my own.

Since the conclusive test results, Nadine has been reminding me Mama managed without much more than a high school education. There's no disputing that, but I'm still scared shitless. Gage isn't married, but he's in love with another woman. I've gone over this a million times in my head. Why would he lie about not being with anyone in three years? It doesn't make sense—

"*Ça va, Lily?*"

Translation: *Are you okay?*

My eyes meet Gérard's.

I respond with a small nod.

I quell my fear of the unknown.

For the next week or so, I intend on vegging and allowing Gérard to fuss over me. Then, I'll figure things out for baby and me.

"*Je cours à la toilette,*" I say.

Translation: *I need to run to the bathroom.*

"*Allez-y. Je serai dans la cuisine.*"

Translation: *Go right ahead. I'll be in the kitchen.*

"*D'accord.*"

Translation: *Okay.*

I rush upstairs.

Every time I visit Nadine's father's spectacular rustic villa in Corsica, I'm enchanted. Not only by the house, but by the island and the people. Being able to walk to the beach and admire the sea like I did earlier, eased my worries long enough to allow me to get out of the jumbled mess that is my head.

I climb the stairs to the top floor and make my way to my appointed guest room, complete with private bathroom.

Once I'm done taking care of business and washing my

hands, I assess my reflection in the mirror. I won't be mistaken for a woman who's on the verge of death, but I'm still unrecognizable.

Too many tears.

Too many fears.

Too many uncertainties.

I should wash up before dinner.

I get undressed and step into the shower.

I lather my body with the lavender scented products Gérard brought before washing my hair. The products are local and all natural. He suggested it might be good to avoid synthetic scents for the next few months. At this point, he has more experience with pregnancy than I do so for now, his word is gospel.

I dress in jeans, a cute black t-shirt with a slogan in gold, and black sandals. I don't bother blow drying my hair. I braid it.

I assess myself one last time in the mirror, and I step out of the bedroom, but freeze at Gérard's joyful exclamation from downstairs.

"*Veuillez entrer,*" he says.

Huh?

We have company?

Who is he inviting in?

"*Mademoiselle Nadine...* err... you in house, come," Gérard says in broken English.

Nads texted me not long ago to find out what I was up to. She never mentioned someone was coming over.

A loud clap. "*Une minute.* I... I... *mademoiselle* come."

Who would want to see me?

Other than Nads and her father, no one knows I'm in Corsica.

No way would she tell my puppet master where to find me.

And no way she would tell my former cheater lover.

"Mademoiselle Lily, vous descendez?"

Translation: *Miss Lily, can you please come down?*

"J'arrive, Gérard."

Translation: *Coming, Gérard.*

"Génial!"

Translation: *Great.*

I hurry down the stairs.

When I reach the last step, my whole world collapses.

My gaze darts everywhere. To the front door. To Gérard. To the man I'm certain is a mirage. "Wh—what are you doing here?"

Green eyes as mesmerizing as the last time I admired them land on me. "I'm here for you, angel."

My heart seizes, clamoring against my ribs at the mention of the nickname he has for me.

Don't be fooled by the smooth-talking.

He's playing you, girl.

He's playing you.

My gaze shifts to his suitcase near the door before focusing on him.

He's hot enough to get any woman pregnant on sight.

And that's how I ended up with a bun in the oven.

"You should go back to wherever you came from." My defenses are up. "You're wasting your time."

Gage's eyes burn with fury.

"I have no desire to talk to you ever again." I cross my arms over my chest.

"Ah. Je retourne de cuisine," Gérard says, his tone hesitant.

Gage frowns. "What did he say?"

"He's going back to the kitchen."

"Vous me faites signe lorsque vous aurez fini de discuter avec monsieur Hollingsworth afin que je puisses servir le repas. Soupe pour vous, et poulet rôti pour monsieur."

Translation: *Dinner will be served for you and the gentleman when you're done talking. Soup for you. Roasted chicken for the gentleman.*

So, Gérard knew Gage was coming.

Nadine is a traitor.

"Le monsieur ne restera pas pour le repas." I set Gérard straight.

Translation: *The gentleman won't stay for dinner.*

The two men look at each other, before returning their confused gazes to me.

"Ah," Gérard says, and scurries off.

Gage stares at me with questioning eyes.

Damn, those eyes...

The same pull—the same weakness—I felt for him before I found out he had played me for a fool is still burning inside me.

Focus. You hate him.

"What did you tell him, Lily?"

"I told Gérard you weren't staying for dinner."

A range of emotions flit across his gorgeous face. Disbelief. Frustration. But the last one is harder to decipher.

Determination?

"That's where you have it wrong. I'm not leaving here until you and I talk."

Betrayal.

Humiliation.

Hurt.

It all comes flooding with the force of a raging river.

"As far as I'm concerned, there isn't anything for us to discuss."

He takes a step forwards.

I lift a hand up.

He growls.

I swear, he even shows teeth like a predator.

Tough luck, buddy.

"Your father is a piece of work."

"My father opened my eyes."

Translucent green eyes turn dark and ominous. "Your father knows jack shit."

Annoyance stabs through me, fast and sharp. "My father has video proof."

"Proof of what?" He raises his voice.

"Proof you're in love with another woman and you were stringing me along, using me as a side piece." My mind still struggles to accept he's here—standing in front of me.

"That's a lie." He points an accusatory finger at me.

"I saw it with my own two eyes. And I saw you mouth the words, '*I love you, too*'. After she told you '*I love you*'." My voice breaks, but I will myself to keep it together. "So, save your sorry ass lies. I'm not in the mood."

His posture stiffens. "Nadine gave me a rundown of what you told her—"

"Nadine backstabbed me?"

"She didn't."

"Yes, she did."

"I was worried out of my fucking mind."

"I'm surprised you had time to worry about little ol' me, considering you were enjoying Stockholm with the love of your life." I bat my eyelashes to emphasize my point.

"Stop saying that."

"It's the truth."

He lets out an exasperated sigh. "Have you ever heard of the expression smoke and mirrors?"

"What does that have to do with anything?"

"That's why you and I are shouting at each other."

"No. We're shouting at each other because you should be in Sweden instead of here pestering me. I came here because I needed some alone time. Yet, here you are invading my space."

"Whatever you saw on that video clip your father showed you was smoke and mirrors."

It's a struggle to maintain the expression of indifference on my face. "I thought you were different, but you're no different than every other cheater out there. My father, included—"

"Don't you dare put me in the same bucket as Fisher Edgington."

I flinch at his tone.

He runs his hands through his thick, brown hair. "I'm not a cheater." His green eyes meet mine. "The woman—and for the record, I didn't even know what the hell tawny brown skin meant until Nadine started throwing it around like confetti—"

"That's how they say it in romance books." I wince.

His lips flatten in a thin line. "The woman in the video is my sister—"

"What do you mean she's your sister?"

"I mean exactly that."

I'm so shocked, I step back, but since I'm still standing on the stairs, I land on my ass.

Ouch.

Gage is by my side in a flash.

"Careful, angel."

"Don't touch me and stop calling me that."

"This is no way to have a conversation. Can you please put down your weapons for a minute so we can talk as opposed to talking over each other?"

I consider him for a long beat.

He extends a hand.

Conflict bats its wings inside of me.

A few seconds tick by as I stare at his hand.

I accept it.

He helps me up. "You okay?"

"I'm fine." I rub my sore elbow.

"You're sure?"

"Yes." Another lie.

Why does he even care?

I eye him warily.

"Think about it, Lily. Would Nadine tell me where to find you if she didn't trust me or thought I was a cheater?"

He has a good point, but I'm unwilling to be fooled that easily. "How can that woman be your sister?"

"Sara is my adopted sister."

"But the woman—"

"The woman with the *tawny brown skin* isn't a mixed-race beauty I'm head over heels for. In fact, she isn't mixed race. Sara Yenifer Hollingsworth, born Sara Yenifer García, is from the Dominican Republic."

My eyes widen.

"My parents adopted her when she was ten. Long story short, Mom's church supported a few churches in DR. After a brutal hurricane, hundreds of kids became orphans. Sara was one of them. She's six years older than me. And, yes, I love my sister and I have no problem telling her."

I'm speechless.

"Fisher Edgington is a sneaky motherfucker. If he hired a PI, my bet is he hired one of the best in LA. It couldn't have been that hard for the PI to figure out who the *tawny brown skinned* woman was. Sara never took her deadbeat husband's name. Her hospital badge reads Dr. Hollingsworth."

Whoa.

"Any PI worth his salt would've relayed that information. Fisher knew Sara was my sister. He used the opportunity to stir up shit so he could manipulate you. Guess what? It worked."

Chapter 47

Gage

Nadine refused to take my money, but she was willing to close her shop for an hour. We went to a nearby café and talked. She figured if I had cut my business trip short, perhaps her best friend didn't have all the facts.

She told me Fisher had me followed and I was caught on camera with a tawny brown skin woman entering Van Nuys Airport. The same woman I had professed my love to.

That's all I needed to hear.

I pulled out my phone and showed her last year's Christmas family photo of my adopted sister with the tawny brown skin, my two white half-sisters, and me. When she picked up her jaw from the floor, she revealed where Lily was hiding. It was an hour and a half flight from Charles de Gaulle Airport to Bastia Poretta Airport, Corsica. And then, a half an hour from the airport to Nadine's father's vacation house. Lily wasn't too far. If I'd had to fly to the other side of the planet in fucking economy class to track her down, I would've.

The moment Lily noticed my presence, I could see my dismissal written all over her beautiful face. No way was I leaving this island without her hearing me out. I was a man on a mission to win my girl back.

After Lily stared at me, dumbfounded for a solid minute after I made it irrefutably clear the woman her father's PI saw me with wasn't my girlfriend or lover, she agreed to sit down and talk. Gérard disappeared to his quarters, leaving us alone in the living room, promising to return the second we were ready for dinner.

Lily told me all about her lunch with her father and his attempt at playing matchmaker. The hurt in her eyes when she told me about seeing the video clip of Sara and me stabbed me in the gut.

"Your father needs to show you some respect."

"And until he does, I'm not talking to him," she says. "I'm done bending backwards. I always end up with the same results, anyway."

"Good on you for standing firm in your decision."

"When I wouldn't return his calls, he forwarded the video to remind me of the type of man you were. I received it when I woke up this morning."

The flash of sadness that glints in her eyes makes me want to slay monsters for her, even if the monster is her own father.

Asshole.

"He also made it a point to let me know he was expecting me in the Hamptons."

I shift on the couch, lifting a leg on the cushion so I can face her.

She mimics my move.

"I hope you're not going to go."

She shakes her head. "I made a firm decision before leaving New York. I even told him as much. If he wants to disown me, that's his prerogative. If he has to dictate all aspects of my life for him to feel I'm worthy, I want no part of that fucked up relationship."

She's coming into her own. Good for her.

"Not to mention, the event is taking place in three days. Even if I was tempted to give in, after finding out my father tricked me with this video"—she waves her phone—"no way am I showing my face at the little party he's having for Chandler. I need a respite from him and his undermining and manipulative ways."

"The distance might prompt your father to wake up."

"I'm not even sure a nuclear bomb would do that, but that's the only arsenal in my toolbox."

I nod.

"You said you were going to Stockholm and South Korea alone... that's why it was so easy for me to fall for my father's deception." She bites on her lower lip.

"My plans changed at the last minute when I found out my sister's husband was a cheating asshole."

"Oh."

"A few days before a business trip, Sara will drop by my place or invite me over to hers for dinner. My sister is a workaholic, but she knew I was about to leave LA for three weeks. On the day of my departure, it hit me. I hadn't heard from Sara in two days. I called her phone. No answer. Worried, I called the hospital. I was told she had been on sick leave for two days."

Lily tilts her head to the side.

"I called Sara's husband, but a woman who spoke two words of English answered. She passed the phone to a man who informed me his mom got a new phone number that morning. Why would Danny change his phone number out of the blue?" I let out a breath. "I can't tell you how panicked I was. I drove up to my sister's place and let myself into her house with the spare key. When I stepped inside, it was a war zone—"

"Did she get burglarized?"

"That's what I thought at first," I say. "The place had been ransacked. My sister is a neat freak and she has a cleaning lady come in once a week. It was so chaotic, even with a gun, I wouldn't have chanced it. I got the hell out of there. Once outside, I called the police and waited. When they showed up, they entered Sara's house and searched for the bad guys or dead bodies. There were no signs of danger. An officer called me in. Sara was in her bedroom. Her eyes were red and puffy, and her hair—the crown and glory she takes so much pride in—was like a bird's nest. She was unrecognizable. The police stepped outside until I was able to calm her down. That's when she told me the whole story."

Concerned blue eyes stare at me. "What happened?"

"Sara was in a meeting at the hospital when a receptionist paged her. Something about an urgent matter involving her husband. Since Danny was at a conference in Denver, she thought something had happened to him."

"Oh, no."

"Danny wasn't in danger," I say. "When she arrived at the welcome desk, there was a woman she didn't recognize waiting for her—"

"The other woman."

My nostrils flare. "She's a waitress from Vegas and she was holding a kid in her arms."

"Shit."

"My sister's fifty-year-old husband of ten years knocked up a twenty-year-old." I sneer. "Sara said the little boy couldn't have been more than a year and a half old, so the baby mama was only eighteen when she got pregnant."

"She was a teenager—"

"And Danny was a grown ass man," I say. "Here's the joke. He didn't want kids. He's as much of a workaholic as my sister.

Sara was okay being childless until three years ago. She tried to get Danny to reconsider his position because she desperately wanted a baby, but he wouldn't budge, reminding her he hated everything about babies."

"Only a monster could hate babies." The outrage in her voice is audible.

"I agree."

"The news must've devastated your sister."

"It did. It destroyed her."

"The other woman knew full well she was going to create drama when she showed up at your sister's hospital."

I nod. "The rug was pulled from under Sara's feet. Danny's baby mama was hoping my sister could talk to her husband because the money he was sending her wasn't enough to support her and the baby since she had to pay for someone to watch the kid while she was at work."

Lily gasps.

"And, oh, would she happen to have a couple thousand dollars kicking around to help her with rent and other essentials for Danny Jr."

"You've got to be kidding me?"

"I had the same reaction," I say. "Danny was coming back that night. I'll spare you the details, but Sara and Danny got into it and it got ugly. Danny decided to go mental on the place, destroying as much as he could, before storming out. Instead of calling me, Sara crawled into bed, heartbroken."

"Your poor sister."

"No way was I going to leave Sara behind. She needed a couple of days to be able to function. By that I mean, get out of bed, take a shower, and eat more than a protein bar."

"Dear God."

"My strong-triple-A-personality-nothing-can-stop-me sister was hurting so much, she was emotionally crippled. I had my executive assistant move all my Stockholm and South Korea appointments. After what happened to my mom after finding out her husband was a cheater and he was expecting a child with another woman, I didn't want to take any chances..."

Lily places a hand on my thigh. "Oh, Gage."

I inhale. "Other than to go to the bathroom, take a quick shower, or get some food for my sister, I didn't leave her side. I slept in her bedroom on an armchair, using the ottoman to rest my legs. I wouldn't even consider sleeping in one of the guest rooms."

"It's understandable you wouldn't want to leave your sister alone, considering your other sisters are in Europe."

"Exactly," I say. "On top of watching over Sara, I also had to take care of the colossal mess Danny left behind."

"Did you hire someone?"

"Yes. I hired a crew that could come last minute for a clean-up job. I still don't know how I managed not to chase Danny down like the rabid dog he is and beat him to a pulp. Not only did he cheat on my sister, but he tried to destroy their home instead of manning up and walking out of there with his tail between his legs."

"What a lowlife."

"I've reached out to my network to find the most ruthless divorce lawyer in LA. I want someone who'll take Danny to the cleaners. Larkin came through."

"Your sister is lucky to have you."

I nod. "When Sara was strong enough, we flew to London so she could stay with our oldest sister. She cried the whole trip. I wasn't about to get on a plane until she found her bearings."

"What about Sara's best friend? Couldn't she have stayed with her?"

"She has friends, but this is such a personal matter, Sara

was only willing to tell her best friend who now lives Down Under after marrying an Australian. Flying her to London was easier than flying to Australia."

"I see."

"Once I knew Sara had someone to watch over her, I flew to Sweden. When I landed in Stockholm, it was hectic, to say the least. Between my packed days and nights, and the jetlag that was whipping my ass, I wasn't in touch as much as I should've been. That opened the door to misinterpretation."

Lily's eyelashes bat a mile a minute, her mouth agape.

I hate Fisher Edgington's guts with a passion.

The next time I see him, I'll be sure to give him a piece of my mind, and I won't mince my words.

What a piece of shit.

Chapter 48

Lily

My father huffed and puffed Gage was playing me for a fool, when in reality, he was being himself—the puppet master.

When Gage's stomach growled, I asked Gérard to serve dinner. I still have so much to tell him. Best to do it on a full stomach.

I couldn't even manage a bite of the chicken, but I ate two bowls of tomato soup with bread and cheese.

Gage was curious as to why I wasn't eating the chicken.

I said I wanted to keep it light. When he asked why I wasn't drinking the white wine, I told him with the heat, I preferred Perrier.

Luckily, he didn't push.

I finish my apricot purée, and Gage scrapes the bottom of his crème brûlée bowl.

Do I rip off the Band-Aid now or do I wait?

"What's going on in that pretty little head of yours? From that serious expression on your face, it's as if you're trying to solve the world's most complicated equation."

Damn him for seeing right through me.

I drop my spoon on the saucer.

I sigh.

Here goes nothing.

"Those video clips broke me." My voice trembles.

He reaches out for my hand. "Hey, that's behind us."

I nod. "But I didn't know the truth when I got some big news when I was in Paris."

He frowns.

You can do this.

I tell him about my bouts of vomiting and the fact I thought it was related to food poisoning. I also tell him about passing out in the streets of Paris and my visit to the hospital.

His eyes are the size of saucers. "Did the doctor find out what was wrong with you?" I don't have a chance to answer. He keeps talking. "If not, we need to find another doctor. Can Gérard refer us to anyone? Surely, a former French president would have access to the top physicians in the country. If the French can't figure out what's wrong with you, I'll fly in a doctor from the US—"

"There's nothing wrong with me."

His brows knit together. "Why did you pass out if there isn't anything wrong with you?"

I pull my trembling lower lip between my teeth. "Um... Err... Well..." Butterflies flutter in my belly

"Tell me." His tone is bordering on annoyance.

You're delaying the inevitable. "I'm... pregnant."

Gage's gorgeous face freezes.

For a few seconds that stretch into an eternity, he stares at me.

"Even before the test, the doctor suspected that was the reason I was so sick," I say. "The test confirmed it."

He extends a hand. "Come here."

I flinch.

I'm not sure what I expected him to say, but that wasn't on the list.

He pushes his chair back. "Come here, I said."

I stand up.

He picks me up like I'm a ragdoll and drops me on his lap.

"You're pregnant..."

I expect him to elaborate, but the silence between us stretches.

I put an end to my misery. "We used protection, but protection isn't foolproof. I'm sure fatherhood wasn't part of your life goals for this year—and perhaps not for the next decade—so I understand if you don't want—"

He places two fingers against my lips, silencing me. "You're trembling and you're rambling."

"I am."

He considers me.

My heart races.

With each passing second, I grow more and more nervous. I can't read him at all. It's a good thing I'm ready to raise this baby on my own.

"I'm tempted to get on the next flight out to New York so I can track down Giuseppe—who prefers to be called John—and rearrange his face for thinking he had a chance with the woman who's carrying my child." His green eyes go dark as his words settle over me. "And the asshole tried to touch you?" He growls. He actually growls.

I'm speechless.

"You're fucking mine, Lily."

I'm astonished by his declaration.

"I told you that at the airport before you left LA. I meant every word." A muscle flexes along his jawline. "I hate that your father manipulated you and opened the door to fucking Giuseppe."

"Even when I thought you loved another woman, I shut Giuseppe down."

"Good," he says with a firm nod. "Speaking of the shit stirrer, I gather your father doesn't know?"

"Not yet. Like I said, I'm avoiding him."

He nods a few times.

He's eerily calm.

"You're not upset or mad?" *Or running for the hills?*

"I'm in shock. And you're right, fatherhood wasn't part of the list of milestones for this year. However, I'm not mad or upset."

"You're not?"

"I'm not."

A weight lifts off my shoulders. "I was afraid you might think I was trying to trap you. And after hearing what happened to your sister…"

"Once you came to LA to attend film school, I planned on convincing you to move in with me instead of renting out a place."

My eyes bulge out of my skull. "Huh?"

His mouth hitches up in a sexy smile.

It kicks the breath right out of my lungs.

He's so darn handsome.

"I own a renovated one-story mid-century-modern-style mansion, so there's plenty of room. Bonus, you'll be neighbors with Mikki since the Königs own their own renovated mansion on the same street."

As if he needed to sweeten the pot.

He caresses up and down my arm. "Are you going to give me an answer?"

"Gosh, are you sure you want me to move in with you?"

"I told you. I broke my rules for you." His eyes bore into mine. Under the light, his green irises have flecks of gold in them. "While I was waiting for my flight to Corsica, I did a search to learn how to say 'I missed you' in French."

"Tu m'as manqué."

"Even with some practice, I would've butchered that sentence."

I laugh.

"What I discovered is that the word for word translation from French to English is 'you were missing from me'... that's how I felt when you walked away from me at LAX. You were missing from me, and you hadn't even left LA."

My heart might break its way through my chest.

"This baby"—he places a large hand over my tummy—"moved things up for us."

"Oh."

"It would take me a while to transfer the headquarters to New York, but it could be done. Truth be told, I love living in LA and I want to be a part of this baby's life. It's going to be challenging when we're at opposite ends of the country."

"It would be."

"Even if I fly you back and forth, at some point, you won't be able to fly. You have a family in LA. You might not be linked to our friends by blood, but they'll show you the respect you deserve."

I love how he said *our* friends.

"I want you close to me so I can watch your belly grow with our child. I don't want to do this over video calls. The City of Angels can be your fresh start—a new beginning for the three of us."

His words touch my soul.

For the first time in three days, I shed tears of joy.

"I didn't mean to make you cry, angel," he says wiping away my tears.

"I love you so much—"

I close my eyes, clamping my hands over my mouth.

Why did I go and ruin things?

I blame the surge of emotions for making me say things I should've kept to myself.

Gage places two fingers underneath my chin, forcing my attention to him. "What was that?"

I open my eyes. "Don't mind me. Pregnancy hormones, and all."

He narrows his eyes at me.

"I'm being silly. We haven't known each other long enough—"

"I love you, too, Lily."

My eyes widen. "What?"

"I love you."

"You... love me?" My voice cracks.

"With all my heart."

Oh my God.

Oh my God.

Oh my God.

"When Fisher called me to let me know you were missing, I almost went ballistic," he says. "My gut was screaming at me. I knew you were in Paris. It was the only place you'd come to. When I couldn't get a hold of you or Nadine, I was ready to incinerate the City of Lights to find you."

I place my hand over my heart. "You would've done that for me?"

"Without hesitation." He brushes a strand of hair behind my ear. "I didn't share my feelings when I dropped you off at LAX because we hadn't known each other for long, and I thought I was half crazy. As I was playing nurse to my sister, it became clear, I had to tell you I loved you. Since we talked about me stopping by New York after my business trip, I planned on telling you then. I didn't want to tell you something that important over text, the phone, or a video call. I wanted to tell you the words in person, staring into your beautiful blue eyes."

"I love you so much, Gage."

"You're it for me, Lily. I fucking love you."

I don't have time to soak in his beautiful declaration before he crushes my lips in a ravenous kiss, so hot, it could incinerate all of LA.

I moan.

The man I love is here, claiming me.

Chapter 49

Gage

President Laurent Rocard de Villepin's sumptuous luxury Corsican villa is located not too far from the beach. There are several hundred-year-old olive trees on the property along with tall rosemary bushes, and more bougainvillea than I've seen in California. There are also tons of beautiful flowers I've never seen before. The large terrace that offers a picture-perfect panoramic view of the Mediterranean Sea is my favorite spot. The second is the large pool.

While I was swimming laps, Lily was reading on her iPad, keeping an eye on my performance. Since fucking my girl wasn't an option, I had to work off all this pent-up energy.

Nadine had one unbendable rule—I had to sleep in a separate guestroom since Gérard lives on the property. It's only one night. I can live with that. Soon, Lily will share my life and I'll be able to fuck her whenever I want.

After she shared the baby news, she video called Nadine who was waiting on tenterhooks. She erupted in a joyful cheer when Lily told her she was moving to LA.

I texted my buddies to tell them we were pregnant.

Congratulatory messages are still pouring in. Other than Mr. Bachelor-for-Life Collin Dennison who's mourning the loss of another single buddy, our friends are delighted for my girl and me. Not that I was rushing into a relationship or fatherhood, but unlike Collin, I'm not terrified of the concept.

After a shower, I make my way downstairs to the terrace where Lily is sitting.

Smiling, I approach her.

Our eyes meet.

Lily's smile could rival the brilliance of the Corsican sun.

I kiss her forehead. "What are you reading?"

"A few articles online about what to expect during the first trimester."

"I suspect *we'll* be reading a lot of those."

She offers a shy smile.

"I'm famished," I say.

"You weren't joking out there, Mr. Olympic." She drops her device on the table and lifts her eyes to meet mine. "You're an incredible swimmer. And you're fast."

I take a seat at the head of the table. "You should've joined me."

"I don't know how to swim."

"We'll have to change that when you get to LA."

"No rush."

The expression on her face is priceless.

"I have a pool on my property. You have to learn how to swim so you can teach our little one."

She grins wide. "Our little one... that's wild."

"It is."

A pummeling of emotions ricocheted through me when she dropped the baby news in my lap. I wouldn't want any other woman to carry my child.

Gérard approaches, carrying a tray.

"The breakfast," he says. Although, it comes out sounding like *De brakafast*.

"Thank you," Lily says.

"*Merci*," I say.

"Text me." He winks.

He doesn't wait for a response. He turns on his hell and heads back into the house.

Lily leans into the table. "What was that about? He's chipper than usual."

"He's happy he can communicate in English with more ease."

She gives me a thoughtful half pout. "I wish I had thought of encouraging him to use a translation app. The fact he can hear how to pronounce the words, makes a world of difference. You're pretty smart, Mr. Grumpy Pants."

"At least you know our kid will be a freaking genius."

She laughs, and laughs, and laughs.

Her laugh is a melody I've missed so fucking much.

"Our child..." she says in a soft voice.

"Yes, angel, our little boy or little girl."

"What if we have twins?"

"I'm okay with that."

She nods.

Her expression is so vulnerable, it made trekking around Europe to find her, worth it.

My stomach growls.

I gesture at the food. "Dig in before I eat everything in sight."

"I'll stick to plain bread and cheese, followed by the strawberry and rhubarb purée."

She was sick earlier this morning, but managed to hold down some fruit.

"Were you sick again?"

She nods. "While you were taking a shower."

Shit.

I wish I could do something, but I'm powerless.

I serve her.

"Thank you for taking such good care of me."

"Get used to it."

She beams at me.

I've been protective of her since day one, but after last night, something primal ripped from its dormancy.

This woman and the child she's caring are my world.

I grab the bowl of latte, load a plate with a variety of morning pastries, and a couple boiled eggs.

I finish an almond croissant in two bites.

Lily giggles.

I shrug and keep eating.

We make idle conversation over breakfast, mostly talking about how much our lives will change when we become parents.

When we're done, I grab my phone and send off a text.

"Mikki is beside herself," she says. "She can't wait for me to return to LA. She was wondering why I wasn't responding to her texts. She was unaware of the turmoil I was dealing with."

I grab her hand into mine. "It's water under the bridge now."

She nods.

"Speaking of Mikki, Phoenix texted me, telling me he's certain I knocked you up from the way I was devouring you with my eyes when we first met." I shake my head. "Idiot."

She laughs. "I'm going to have to pick Dom's brain. She understands this pregnancy thing better than me."

"You should connect with Levi Aldridge's wife. She's also pregnant."

"Thank God I don't have to go through this alone."

"No, you don't. In LA, someone will always have your back."

"What a departure from what I have with my father and half-brothers."

Best to keep my mouth shut.

As much as I'm excited about the prospect of meeting our baby when he or she gets here, I'm not excited at the prospect of having Fisher Edgington and his four sons in my life. Thank God they live on the east coast—far away, where they belong.

A grinning Gérard saunters our way with a square-shaped black box in hand.

He drops it on the table, and claps before rubbing his hands together.

"*Merci, Gérard,*" I say.

"No problem." He's still grinning like a loon.

"What's in the box?" Lily points.

"Bye-bye. I go." Gérard rushes back into the house, waving over his shoulder.

She frowns. "What's gotten into him?"

"It has to do with what's in the box."

Her frown deepens.

I hand it to her. "Open it."

Blue eyes settle on me, suspicious flashing bright.

"How else are you going to know what's in it?"

She rises perfectly shaped arched brows. "Why don't you open it?"

"Because *you* should open it."

She pulls the lid off.

Her gaze bounces from the box to me. "What are these red braided strings for?"

I grab one out of the box. "They're more than red braided strings. They're promise bracelets."

I get up, and get down on one knee.

She gasps.

"You're mine." I place a hand on her tummy. "This baby is mine. I take care of what's mine." My eyes bore into hers. "I don't want you to come back to LA with me as my girl, I want you to come back with me as my fiancée."

"OhmyGod, Gage."

"Since I didn't see the baby news coming, I'm unprepared. One of the advantages of being forced to sleep in separate rooms was that I had time to do research. In other words, I made the internet my bitch last night."

She laughs.

"Armed with a plan, this morning, I enlisted Gérard as my ally because with these big fingers"—I wiggle my digits—"I wouldn't be able to braid shit." I drop my eyes to the bracelet I'm holding before locking my gaze onto hers. "This is called the Red String of Fate. The legend goes a little like this. Forgive me for adlibbing. There's an invisible red thread that connects us to the one we're destined to meet. Regardless of the place, time, or circumstances. The thread can be stretched and sometimes tangled—as it's been in the last few days—but it will never break. It describes us to a T. I don't know when you went from being the woman I was supposed to watch over to the angel who holds my heart, but here we are. I can't promise you I'll never slip back into my grumpy-self, but I can promise you, I'll always love you. Over the past three years, I lost myself in grief over Mom's death. I was okay being single for years to come, but I found you. I like who I am when I'm around you, Lily."

"Your words touch my soul. And for the record, I don't mind a few appearances from Mr. Grumpy Pants... I know how to turn his scowls into smiles."

I shake my head.

She winks.

"I was probably too young at the time to understand the depth of my parents' love, but now, I get it," I say. "When you meet the one. That's it. Game over. Nothing else matters. The way I feel when I look at you... the way I feel when you're near me... I want this for the rest of my life."

A tear spills from Lily's eye. She wipes at it as she nods. "I want to be with you forever."

"We were fated, angel."

"We were."

"I don't have a big ring—"

"I don't need one."

"There are two bracelets. One for you." I tie the braided thread around her wrist. "And one for me." I extend my arm.

She grabs the other bracelet and ties it around my wrist. "Our thread can never be broken."

"Never," I say. "Lily Schuyler, will you do me the honor of becoming my wife?"

Her lower lip quivers. "Yes, Gage, I want to marry you. I want that more than anything in the world... other than our baby."

"You've made me the happiest man," I say before kissing her until we both run out of air. After several beats, I pull away from her, boring my eyes into hers. "We're going to have a great life together."

"The best."

My mouth claims hers in an all-encompassing kiss, chasing away years of loneliness and replacing them with my beautiful angel.

Epilogue 1
Gage

Four and a half months later

After bidding goodbye to my driver, I roll my suitcase towards the side of my Beverly Hills property. As I pass the house, I notice lights in the kitchen.

It's good to be home.

I'm back in LA after a week in Australia and another in Singapore.

I can't wait to see my girl again.

I crouch down to a low profile and rush in the direction of the pool house, carrying my suitcase, so the sound of the wheels doesn't give me away.

It's theme night at Dark Compulsion.

Lily started showing, so we've been MIA from the club. Since neither of us want to miss out on the naughty fun, we piggyback on the themes and role-play at home.

Tonight is *dirty handyman and slutty, cheating housewife.*

It should be hot as fuck.

I stand to my full height when I reach the metal gate. After unlocking it and closing it behind me, I enter the backyard. Once I check around to make sure the coast is clear, I head towards the pool house.

I don't bother turning on the lights. The glimmer from the lights on the property shining through the windows is more than enough. I traded my bespoke suit for a pair of jeans and a checkered shirt on my private jet.

I kick off my shoes and step into a pair of work boots. I don't bother lacing them. I tuck in the shoelaces so I don't trip. I grab a baseball cap and slip it on backwards.

I'm ready to get down and dirty.

Scooping down to grab the toolbox I knew would be waiting for me, I set off on my mission.

Show time.

I trail to the front door of the house and ring the bell.

The door flies open.

Fuck.

Two weeks away from her was bone-cutting agony.

"Good evening, Mrs. Robinson." My eyes drop to Lily's pouty lips painted in a vibrant hot pink shade. "You called about a problem with your pipes."

Lily's lips quiver, but she catches herself. "Good evening, Sawyer. I'm so grateful you were able to make a late-night call. Few plumbers are willing to be accommodating on a Saturday night. To answer your question, yes, it's about my pipes."

"I gather it's a different problem than the last time I was here?"

"These things are way over my head." She points a mani-cured finger at me. "You're the expert."

"Let's see what we're dealing with."

She steps to the side. "Please come in."

She locks the door. "If you'll follow me."

"I'm right behind ya, ma'am."

My eyes are on her fine ass as she sashays in front of me.

She was sexy as fuck from the first day I met her, but now, her round ass, heavy tits, and wider hips make my mouth water.

She stops near the faucet. "This is the bane of my existence." She points at the offensive object.

I drop my toolbox on the floor. "I'm sure I can take care of it."

She gives me a onceover. "I'm sure you're a *capable* man."

More than you know.

"I got home not long ago," she says. "While you do your thing, I hope you don't mind if I change into something a little more comfortable."

I take in her sexy little body draped in a white formfitting dress that hits her several inches above the ankle and the heels that match her kissable lips. The fabric clings to her body and around her growing belly.

She radiates.

My desire—and love—for her is pounding through me so hard that my cock throbs in time with it. I'm this close from dropping to my knees, shoving up the skirt of her dress, and putting an end to this role-playing.

Patience.

"Make yourself as comfortable as you want." I shrug. "It's your house."

"Can I offer you anything to drink? Juice? Soft drink? A beer? Unless you prefer something stronger?"

"Thanks, little lady, but I don't drink on the job."

"Water, perhaps?"

"You're a helluva hostess."

"You're doing me a favor. The least I can do is make sure *all* your needs are met..."

She isn't subtle.

I fucking love it.

"Careful what you wish for, Mrs. Robinson."

"Like you said, I'm being a good hostess."

I approach her, towering over her even in her fuck-me heels. "I'm sure your husband would have an issue with you being too friendly."

She makes a show of glancing around the kitchen before fixing me with her blue eyes. "Do you see my husband? Because I don't."

I cock an eyebrow. "You're one of *those* housewives."

"My husband isn't going to know how friendly I am with you."

"Why don't I check your pipes?"

She rewards me with a salacious smile. "I'll let you get to work."

With that, she turns on her heel and strides out of the kitchen, swinging her tempting hips left to right.

I walk towards the cabinets located under the sink and open them.

I squat and pretend to assess the problem. I even tap against the pipe a few times.

I stand up, lean against the counter, cross one booted foot over the other at the ankle, and wait.

Lily's heels click against the granite floor, announcing her return.

When she enters the kitchen, she's wearing a belted red mini dress. She's still wearing high heels, but she swapped the hot pink ones for a pair of open-toe slippers with a faux red fur that have a distinct 1950s vibe to them. Her hot pink lips are now fire engine red.

Fuck. Me.

Her long black hair is braided and falls over one shoulder.

Lily's hair cascading over her shoulders, down to her waist? Unquestionably sexy. Lily's hair braided? All that exquisite hair transformed into a rope that begs to be wrapped around my fist as I fuck her from behind.

It's my kryptonite, and she knows it.

Without the curtain of raven hair hiding her features, it's impossible to miss how exquisite she is. High cheekbones, an adorable pointed chin, pouty mouth, and big, blue eyes.

Damn that lethal beauty.

She pulled out all the stops.

Not only is she begging to get fucked, but she wants it rough.

I'm too happy to oblige.

My eyes travel down her body.

I always got an eyeful of her pregnant belly when she was rubbing one out on camera during our video calls while I jerked off. I want to reach out and cup it to make contact with our child, but I resist. That would be out of character.

"It's still so hot." She fans herself. "Never mind the top-of-the-line air conditioning. I can barely handle any clothes." She sashays towards me. "Were you able to fix my pipes, Sawyer?"

"It's gonna cost you."

"How much?"

"The parts I need are expensive."

She lets out an exaggerated sigh. "I don't have cash on me. Perhaps we could come to... an *arrangement*."

"I also accept credit cards."

She leans into me.

I catch a whiff of her delicate, French perfume with floral scent. A scent that followed me all the way to the other side of the planet. Even when I was far away, I could close my eyes, and I was surrounded by her smell.

"Between you and I, the problem is my fault, Sawyer."

"That's what you said the last time."

"What can I say? I'm not good in the kitchen. I wouldn't

want my husband to find out by putting the charge on his credit card." She reaches out a hand and plays with the buttons of my shirt. "Would you consider a payment plan?"

"As long as the money goes into my bank account, I'm open to considering it."

Another suffering sigh. "The last time you were far more accommodating."

"Mrs. Robinson, in the past six months, you've had a need for me to take care of your pipes on the regular. Payment is always an issue. Like a fool, I let it slide because I'm not one to let a damsel in distress fend for herself, but I'm reconsidering my position. I'm too much of a sucker. Between labor and parts, and the gas to fill my truck to drive up to your Loma Vista Drive mansion, I'm losing money when I make a house call since Beverly Hills is located on the other side of town from where I live. Not to mention, it's late." I shake my head. "At this rate, you're becoming an expensive and high maintenance client."

She takes in a deep, shivering breath. With her eyes locked onto mine, she snakes a finger under my chin.

I groan.

"But you got something in return. Every. Single. Time."

She's becoming a pro at role-playing.

I commit to memory the perfect angles of her face.

The gorgeous face I've missed seeing up close and personal for the past two weeks.

The gorgeous face I've missed waking up to.

I study her eyes as vibrant as the deep blue sea, tinged with purple. Her mouth, which I've missed kissing so fucking much, is a temptation I'm not sure I can resist much longer.

Seconds tick by.

I'm entranced by the sight of all that beauty.

The moment intensifies and becomes headier with each beat of my heart.

She sighs, like an impatient headmistress would, which isn't helping the raging lust roiling inside me in the least. "My cunt is worth it, Sawyer."

Jesus Christ.

Jerking off in the bathroom of my private jet did nothing to slake my desire for her.

I can't get enough of her.

Even after our saucy nightly video sessions, I'd jerk my cock raw, thinking of her. The satisfaction I seek always eluded me.

Before meeting Lily, jerking off dulled the ache. Since she came barging into my life, using my fist to take off the edge no longer helps. This time apart was cruel and left me throbbing in mute agony. I'm dying to have her sweet pussy wrapped around my cock.

As the days rolled on without the chance to fall asleep with her nestled in my arms after fucking her to exhaustion, I thought I was going to lose my damn mind during this business trip. Coming in the palm of my hand only made me want her to the point where I was certain my bones would crack from pent-up need.

Since having her in my bed, I've turned into a greedy man.

I run my thumb along the luscious lines of her mouth. "Your wet cunt isn't going to pay my rent, the insurance on my truck, or the gas to fill it."

"But you like my cunt because it's so dripping wet for you."

"It's still not the same as hard cash, Mrs. Robinson."

"I'll let you fuck me bare."

"That's how you got me in your spiderweb the first time."

"Tell me you didn't love it."

Did she take acting classes while I was away? "This is the last time." I shake a finger for emphasis. "Next time you have a problem with your pipes, you'll have to call another plumber. There are plenty of good ones in LA."

"You're the *only* plumber I want. The only one I *need*." The seductive voice does me in, but she takes it up by ten notches. She unties the belt around her waist, opens her robe, and exposes her heavenly body. "I bought this yesterday. What do you think? Is the color too provocative?"

She pulled out the heavy artillery.

Lily is wearing a lace, see-through chemise that hits her mid-thigh—I have French Appliqué to blame for even knowing what the heck chemise means. She paired the red-hot lingerie with a thong in the same scarlet red lipstick shade. To bring this sexy as fuck combo to ungodly levels, a red satin tie cinches underneath her breasts, leaving the lacy fabric to part over her rounded belly. The *pièce de resistance* are the two triangles covering her breasts. Since Lily's tits are growing by the day, they're spilling over.

Holy fuck.

The style is designed to bring sane men down to their knees, and I'm a hair away from dropping down to mine to worship this goddess.

She's like a present waiting to be unwrapped.

I gawk at her like a silly teenage boy in the presence of a hot girl for the first time.

"My cunt feels hollow, Sawyer. My nipples hurt so much and they're so hard from your closeness. I haven't come in a hundred years. Not since the last time you were here. I need you to fill me before I die."

My need to fuck her explodes into a throbbing ache.

Epilogue 2
Lily

How did I live without this gorgeous man for the past two weeks?

I wasn't twiddling my thumbs while my fiancé was away. I'm still adjusting to life in LA, but I missed him so much, you'd think he'd been gone for a year.

After Corsica, Gage and I flew to the Hamptons to announce all the big changes in my life. On the flight over, Gage told me he was only there for support. It was important my father heard it from me.

I summoned my lady balls.

Seeing Fisher Edgington's crestfallen expression when I called him out on his bullshit about Gage's sister was a victory. Watching his mouth gape in shock and his gray eyes take over his face when I announced I was pregnant with Gage's child was so comical, I had to suppress a smile. My half-brothers were equally stunned.

By the time I told my father I was moving in with Gage in LA, the wind had left him. The cherry on the sundae was when I put my foot down—he either treats me with respect and stops manipulating me like I'm a puppet, or he can cut me out of his life.

We didn't talk for over a month. I was fully ready for him to turn his back on me and disown me.

Two months after that showdown in the Hamptons, he flew to LA––not on a business trip––but to see me. Between my frank talk at the restaurant and in the Hamptons, my father woke up to the fact I was a grown woman.

It's about fucking time.

When I told him I had been accepted at a top school, and I was pursuing a jewelry design degree, he didn't mock me.

Baby steps...

Gage challenged me to go after what I want in life. So, I did.

I'm a self-taught jewelry designer. If I want to make my dream a reality and honor Mom's memory, I need formal training.

Between school, the sisterhood, my new friends, and living with the man I love more than anything in the world, moving to LA was the best decision.

"You want my big cock to fill your cunt?"

My lips part in a slow smile. "Yes. Yes, I do."

Sex on legs Gage Hollingsworth...

The man in a suit? Be still my beating heart.

The man dressed like a blue-collar hunk? Be still my pulsating ovaries.

Dressed up or dressed down, he exudes badassness and power.

He toys with my braid. "You're going to pay for taunting me, Mrs. Robinson."

The expression on his handsome face causes my clit to tingle.

It's dark, primal, and feral.

He moves so fast, I don't have time to blink.

He grabs me, turns me around in his arms, presses a large hand between my shoulder blades, and leans me over the countertop of the kitchen island.

I let out a long satisfying exhale when he presses his chest against my back and his massive erection rubs against my ass.

Heaven.

And there's the subtle woodsy notes of his cologne.

Masculine.

Refined.

Expensive.

The scent is heady as fuck and it drives me insane with need. More than his closeness and the bulge between his legs, that more than anything, is my demise.

"You're a fucking tease, Mrs. Robinson."

The coolness of the granite countertop should dampen the five-alarm fire burning inside me, but it doesn't. I'm this close from combusting.

I pant. "I deserve to be punished."

"Yes, you do. And I'm going to enjoy punishing you. And I'm going to relish every fucking second of it."

"Yes. Please."

"No wonder you refuse to pay me. Did you use the money you owe me to buy the cock-hardening lingerie you're wearing?" He grinds his cock against my ass. "Feel that? It's all your damn fault."

"I'm such a bad girl."

He yanks up the hem of my chemise and lets the cool air of the room caress my ass. He's breathing heavy in my ear as his finger traces the outline of my G-string.

I moan when he slides a finger under the edge of my panties and explores my needy pussy.

"Are you this soaking wet for your husband?"

"No. Only for you."

"That's because he doesn't know how to fuck a woman like you. He's prim and proper in bed, but you like it dirty."

"I do. I really do."

He bites my earlobe as he shoves my panties to the side.

The hissing sound of his zipper coming down followed by the swishing sound of his jeans makes me wetter than I am.

I moan when the demanding thickness of his cock wedges between my pussy lips.

Yes...

He's still dressed—which makes this naughty escapade even raunchier—but his shirt rides up, allowing the hard flex of his abs and hips to rub against my ass.

"You want it rough?"

"Yes. Don't hold back."

These days, he's not as unrepentant with me as he was at the beginning. My baby bump might have softened his alpha edge, but it hasn't dulled it fully. It's plenty dirty between us.

Rip.

It's like my words unleashed the beast inside him.

Without preamble or a warning, he tears off my panties.

Good God.

He snakes an arm around my waist. "Spread them wide for me." He leaves me no choice in the matter. He gives my foot a vicious kick with his own.

I whimper as I wobble a bit in my high-heeled slippers.

He firms his grip on me.

"Wider." He kicks my foot again.

I'm spread so wide, the theme night should be *hard ass cop and thief.* I'm about to get frisked. Not that I'd object.

"You okay, Mrs. Robinson?"

"I am. It's been so long."

"Don't worry. You're going to get my cock soon enough."

He slides a finger between my wet pussy lips, skating through my slickness before he penetrates me in an unhurried slide.

"That feels so good."

He pumps in and out of me in a languorous motion.

I hiss, which earns me a second finger.

A pleading grunt drops from my lips.

He growls.

He focuses on the textured spot inside me that sends a flurry of electric sensations throughout my body all at once.

I'm so wet, it's embarrassing.

He withdraws his hand.

I whimper in protest.

With my face still pressed against the countertop, I catch a glimpse of him sliding his fingers inside his mouth and sucking them clean.

"From the heady scent of your cunt and by how dripping wet you are, I'd say your husband has been neglecting you, Mrs. Robinson." His green eyes are dark when he says that.

"That's why I need your cock so badly, Sawyer. Please fuck me."

"You beg so beautifully."

Thump.

Gage drops his heavy cock onto the top of my ass.

"Oh, fuck. Your cock is bigger than I remember."

"I shouldn't be this turned on by you, Mrs. Robinson, but I want you so damn much. I'm powerless around you. You make me weak."

The searing heat of his tip flirts with my entrance.

I bite against my lower lip as he skates the head of his cock over my pussy lips, making me wet and ready for his invasion. He angles his wide crown and nudges my pussy, teasing me.

I moan.

Like a warrior on a mission, he invades.

His thick girth spreads my pussy.

My breath stutters and my fingers curl against the countertop.

He's unrepentant, driving in and out of me, tunneling through my slick pussy with force.

His cock fills a void that made me ache for two weeks that felt like a century.

He pulls out, leaving the crown nestled inside me, and with hands on my hips and a low growl, he thrusts balls deep.

If it wasn't for his hands holding me, I'd fall off my high heels.

"I bet you don't have to struggle with your husband."

I love that he keeps the game going.

"No. I don't. You're so, so much better than him and you're so much bigger. You make me come. He's never been able to, not even when I guide him."

"Your cunt was made for my cock. Not your asshole husband."

"It was. It really was."

"Does he know you're carrying my child?"

"How did you know?"

"I had my suspicions. If you were pregnant with his child, you wouldn't want me inside you bareback and you wouldn't want me to caress your belly after I fuck you senseless."

A hand brushes over my belly.

I turn my head so I can catch his gaze.

He winks.

Fuck, I love this man.

"You're so smart, Sawyer. This baby is our little secret. I've made excuses not to be with my husband for the past six months since the first time you came to fix my pipes. He thinks we had sex when he was too drunk to remember."

"Fool."

He pumps in and out of me fast and furious.

I can't imagine how debauched I look, my face pressed against the countertop, my pussy stretched by his huge cock, him fully dressed, fucking me from behind.

Gage slows his tempo.

"I need you anchored down for what I have in store for you, Mrs. Robinson." He nudges my feet back together with him still inside, and lifts my hips up. "Much better."

The height difference is—and will remain—an issue for us. Even with my high heels.

"I'm about to prove to you how much I own your pussy, your body, and every fucking part of you."

And he proves it without a shadow of a doubt.

He thrusts inside me with force.

Each time he pulls out his cock to the tip, it sends a flurry of thrills up my spine, and each shove back inside my aching pussy is a gift. He's so deep, I swear his long cock is lodged somewhere in my chest.

"Who do you belong to?"

"You. Own. Me." My words come out in staccato, matching each one of his thrusts.

"Damn right."

His fingers find my clit.

I arch and twist under his sweet assault.

I'm wild. Unleashed, even.

Slap!

Slap!

Slap!

Oh, fuck.

The sparkling pain heightens the pleasure.

I let out a shrieking gasp when his hand pulls down the top part of my chemise, causing my naked breasts to spill from the cups. As he keeps pumping in and out of me, they dangle. He gropes one breast with his strong hand.

"Fuck. Your tits are much bigger than they were the last time I fucked you." He presses his front against my back and snags my earlobe with his teeth. "Get there, Mrs. Robinson. You need to come because I won't last much longer. Unlike your good-for-nothing husband, I always make you come first."

I'm turned on beyond reason.

I open my mouth to respond, but he squeezes my nipples hard.

A choking sound leaves my lips.

I grind my face against the cold surface of the countertop, in the hopes of containing the volcano threatening to erupt. It's pointless.

I'm on fire, and there's only one way out for me.

He does it again. This time, he traps my clit between his fingers with one hand, pinching my nipple with the other.

Dear God.

I shudder and freefall.

My orgasm arrives with two weeks of need roaring behind it.

I come, and I come, and I come around his big, fat cock.

"You're such a good slut." His lip flirts with my earlobe.

God, I love role-playing.

He doesn't allow time for my feet to touch the ground.

He pushes off me, wraps my braided hair around his fist, and pulls.

"You ready for my cum?"

I'm panting so hard, I can't respond.

Slap!

"I asked you a question, Mrs. Robinson."

"Give it to me, Sawyer."

He lets loose.

He's hard as steel as his hips hammer into me, as if he's trying to nail me to this island. He fucks me like he means it.

Harder.

Faster.

More punishing.

It's so intense, I struggle to remember my name.

"I'm gonna fill you up with my cum. You're going to get a lot of it."

I squeeze my thighs together. "I want it all."

One, two, three thrusts.

"Fuck—" He releases himself inside me, emptying himself into my greedy pussy, his cum filling me up before dripping down my legs.

An explosion of pleasure detonates inside me. Against the soundtrack of my delirious cries, I clench around his cock hard and give in to my second orgasm. I wail as my pussy milks his warm release.

He growls and keeps thrusting, fucking his cum deep inside me.

Those two violent orgasms rob me of my ability to think, but I wouldn't want it any other way.

We're both wet and messy and his jeans are still around his knees, which only makes this tryst even more debauched.

Gage lays his upper body against my back, pulls me snug against him, and wraps his arms around me, his hands cupping my belly.

I love the way he does that. It makes me feel treasured.

We remain entangled, neither of us in a rush to move. His warmth seeps into me, and I have no doubt the baby relishes this closeness as much as I do.

I'm in my safe place. My happy place.

"Mine." He grunts. "And mine." He caresses my belly.

A delirious grin stretches my lips.

He's so ridiculously possessive.

It fills my heart knowing he wants this baby as much as I do.

For several long beats our ragged breaths fill the kitchen.

"Angel, I needed to be with you." His fingers reach for the red bracelet circling my left wrist.

We're back to being Gage and Lily.

"Me too."

"How the fuck did I live without you for the past two weeks?" He groans. "I've been thinking about being with you all day. You were so distracting, it was a struggle to focus on work. Visions of your sexy ass were clouding my mind."

I giggle.

"You think that's funny?"

"I like knowing I was on your mind because you were on mine."

He drops a tender kiss against my cheek.

"You're always on my mind," he says, playing with my engagement ring.

Before he left for his two-week business trip, he tricked me. I should've known I was walking into a trap considering it was the same MO as my birthday.

Behind the doors of a private room at the Quintus Hotel, our friends were waiting for us. Gage's sisters flew in from Europe with their families. Sara was there. So were Nadine and Gérard.

When I turned around, he was down on one knee. I so didn't see it coming. And I didn't see the eye-popping rock you can spot from Pluto coming either.

Gage is everything I ever wanted in a man and then some.

Even though I love the four-carat oval cut diamond ring with a pavé-set of brilliant diamonds running along the band he gave me, I couldn't stop wearing the red string bracelet. That first proposal was the most romantic proposal ever, coming from a man who professes to not having a romantic bone in his body.

Gage made sure my father and half-brothers showed up at our engagement party. They weren't all smiles, but nothing offensive spewed from their mouths. I considered that a win.

"I love you so much, angel."

My heart flips over like it always does when the L word drops from his beautiful lips.

"I love you with all my heart—" I take in a shaky breath.

"What's wrong?"

"Nothing." I shake my head.

"Don't bullshit me."

"It's just..."

"Tell me."

"I've never felt truly loved before," I say. "It just hit me." Another shaky breath. "I mean, Mama loved me and Nads loves me, but it's different. The way you love me is..."

"The way I love you is everything, Lily. My love for you redefines who I am as a man." He holds me in his warm embrace for several breaths.

When he pulls out of me, I moan my disapproval. "Why can't we stay like this forever?"

"Because..."

He helps me up and adjusts my chemise.

I turn to face him. "Are you going to finish your thought?"

He cups my face and pulls me into a fierce, hard kiss that takes my breath away.

My spent, weary body melts against his strong one.

This man...

He breaks our heated embrace. "Because I missed your mouth on mine and because I need to get my sexy fiancée upstairs for round two."

"I haven't caught my breath yet."

"I have to make up for the last two weeks."

Giddiness fizzes through me, but I pretend to be unaffected. "You don't have to do it all in one evening, Hollingsworth."

"Tu m'as beaucoup manqué, mon ange," he says. "You were missing from me, angel."

He prefers the word for word translation from French to English.

So do I.

"Tu m'as beaucoup manqué, mon amour," I say.

Translation: *I missed you so much, my love.*

"I'm glad we're on the same page. Now, let's go upstairs so you can correct the error of your ways."

I frown. "What do you mean?"

"When you came, you called out God's name. He's great and all, but I want to hear you scream out *my* name at the top of your lungs."

I laugh, and laugh, and laugh.

He joins me.

Of all the wonderful things about my husband-to-be, his laugh is my greatest gift.

"Let's go, soon-to-be Mrs. Hollingsworth. I need to be inside you again."

I take the hand he extends.

I love this man so much, I'd follow him to the ends of the earth.

The Next Book Boyfriend
Roderick

Reader's note: The Moguls series is a spin-off of the It Was Always You series. Although Rod's and Dominika's heartbreaking friends to lovers story is book number two in the series, it's the first book I wrote. Like Gage, Rod is an emotionally scarred hero. And like Rod, he's fiercely protective. Enjoy the excerpt.

Things have been pretty weird between my best friend and I lately. It seems like everything about me irritates the hell out of her. The problem is, I don't know why. Maybe it's a natural progression when people have been this close for this long. I've been tiptoeing through it like I'm walking on glass, careful not to make matters worse. I can't afford to lose her as my best friend. She means too much to me. Whatever it is that's caused this friction between us, I hope her time away will have mellowed her out. Eager to hear all about her trip and catch up, I dial her up. She answers on the first ring.

"Hey, Dom, you're back."

"Rod, how are you?"

"Good. Did I wake you up?"

"No, I've been up for a while. I got your text message. I was going to answer after coffee."

"No problem. I'm sure you're still a little tired."

"That's the understatement of the century. I'm so jetlagged, I don't even know what planet I'm on. Is this Pluto or Mars?"

I laugh. "I hear you. When I came back from Australia two months ago, I thought I woke up on Jupiter. Are you going to be able to stay awake until tonight?"

"I might have to take a nap if I want to make it to Zoe's birthday party. I wasn't planning on going since I just landed, but she insists. She also invited me to dinner along with her best friend before we head out to her party. Something about thanking me."

"It makes sense. You're responsible for her big break."

"It was an introduction. Nothing more," she says.

"It's much more than that and you know it."

Thanks to Dom, Zoe secured a phenomenal job at my brothers' TV production company. Dom would never take credit where credit's due. She's so self-effacing.

"Will you stop by Zoe's party?" She changes the subject.

"I'll head there the second Eddie's yacht docks."

"I don't understand."

"Remember how Eddie proposed to the so-called love of his life after a three-day sex marathon?"

"Don't tell me. It wasn't love ever after."

"It was a quickie Vegas wedding that lasted seven days. The six-month waiting period has elapsed and his divorce was finalized on Monday. Since she's loaded, she didn't ask for a dime, so it ended up being a smooth divorce. Eddie says her father is relieved."

"I don't blame the man. At least she isn't pregnant."

"Yeah, I don't see Eddie as the father type. The guy isn't wired for commitment."

"One could say the same about you, Rod."

"I never professed otherwise, Dom," I say. "Anyway, back to the divorce. Eddie invited a bunch of us to celebrate his newfound freedom by chartering a yacht."

"The usual suspects will be present?"

"No doubt."

"Kudos to Eddie. Nothing like getting back on the horse," she says.

"Yeah, well, Eddie loves women—"

"As much as you do."

It's not like I can deny it, but her snarky tone annoys me. She's been throwing these digs at me since before she left. I thought we were past that.

I let it slide. "How was the training?"

"There are no words to describe how amazing it was. I'm now armed with even more cutting-edge skills. My head is filled with ideas. I can't wait to put them all into practice. Thanks again for pushing me to apply." She clears her throat. "And... thanks for helping me get there."

I detect a touch of shyness in her voice. Even after all these years, Dom doesn't accept gifts easily.

"It would've been a shame if you'd missed out," I say.

"Yeah, well, it cost an arm and a leg."

I paid for it.

I didn't care how many times she protested. She was going to be part of that group of eight.

"It was worth it?"

"It was so much more than I expected."

"That's all that matters."

"Thanks again."

Dom is so freaking talented, it's ridiculous. She makes good money, but she's still a freelancer and she doesn't have a previous multi-millionaire career to fall on. When the opportunity came for a handful of professionals to be part of an advanced month-long video production program offered by Pepperdine University's Communication Division, I pushed her to apply. Since the training started in LA—New York was next—and ended in London, I nudged her to stay in Europe and play tourist. She didn't fight me.

"How was it seeing your mom and cousins?"

We've been relying on texting since she left because the time difference was challenging. I've also been catching the highlights of her trip on social media, but it doesn't compare to hearing all the details from her.

She lets out a long sigh. "I don't miss living an ocean apart from my mom." No chances my mother would've ever won a Mother of The Year award. Neither would Dom's. "Seeing my paternal grandparents is always weird. Are they still family when your father abandoned you as a kid?" It's a rhetorical question. "It was awkward. The language barrier doesn't make communicating easy since my German is rusty. And how many times are they going to apologize for my father's behavior? Their only son and he turns out to be a disappointment."

"Parents aren't always biological, Dom. You and I both know it."

"Isn't that the truth," she says.

Despite all the rotten and shitty things she's gone through in her childhood, she's always managed to maintain a cheerful facade. She knows how to keep her pain buried deep.

I, on the other hand, was a hellion growing up.

Some called me the devil's child. With good reason. I wore my anger on my chest like armor. It scared the shit out of most people.

Not Dom.

She's always accepted every part of me and she always knew how to turn my foul moods around. Until recently, that is. Lately, our bickering gets me all riled up.

"You turned out great," I say.

"Thanks to you. And so did you."

"Damn right I did."

"Roderick Wolfe. Always Mr. Humble."

"I'm a former rock star. I don't even know how to spell the word."

"No, you don't," she says with a laugh.

I love it when she's lighthearted like this.

Maybe we're back to being Dom and Rod.

"Other than family reunions, what kind of wild and reckless adventures were you on? European men must be grieving your departure."

Don't ask me why I'd dig my own grave by poking into her love life. It's not like I want to know she's been with other guys.

"Reckless adventures? As in vacation flings?"

"Yeah."

She laughs.

"What's so funny, Dom?"

She hasn't been in a relationship in so long.

The last idiot was a dickless mama's boy. I guess, in many ways, I should be grateful because I don't have to worry about some jerk disrespecting her or treating her badly. She's yet to date a guy worthy of her.

Shame.

Dom is gorgeous. Her jet-black hair and blue eyes against her luminous complexion is every man's dream. Her full lips could drive a guy wild. Other than for a dye job, she's all-natural. She wears a minimum amount of makeup. And in a sea of silicone, her tits are real. Bonus, she never uses her body as if it were her only asset. She doesn't have to.

She's super smart, too—in high school, she could solve complex math equations that stumped some of her teachers. To this day, she's still a math whiz. She's also vivacious and fiercely loyal. She's the whole package. Not that I'll ever tell her, but I've harbored a secret longing for my best friend for a while now. However, I have no intention of screwing up what we share with sex. Crossing that line could potentially be lethal.

"That's your department, Rod," she says.

I guess I spoke too soon. She still has a bee in her bonnet.

"After all, you're the self-indulgent bad boy who still—after retiring—gets women to drop their panties on command. I'm a good girl. Thank God I don't have a dick between my legs *dictating* my every thought."

What can I say? There's an abundance of gorgeous and willing women in LA. Add the former rock star factor and getting pussy is a joke. That's why I subscribe to the 'once and done' school of thought. It's best that way. Women can put too many expectations on a relationship, and that screws everyone up. Mom was a prime example. But coming from Dom? It slices.

"Is that your way of saying you got zero action in Europe? Because it sounds like you're still a bundle of nerves."

If she wants to go there, I'm game.

"Fuck off, Rod."

I let out a strangled laugh laced with irritation.

"Is that any way to talk to your best friend?"

"That's low even for you," she says.

I jam a hand through my hair in frustration.

"I was hoping you would've worked out some of the tension you've been carrying so you can stop being so short with me. I guess I was wrong."

Silence.

She shuts me out. Again.

"Dom?"

Nothing.

"For God's sake. Are you still on the other end?"

"I am. No need to shout, Rod."

That's it?

I don't get the woman. I swear I don't.

One minute hot. The other cold as ice.

I didn't think anyone could be worse than my mother, but for the past few months, Dom's erratic moodiness is putting Mom to shame.

I let out an impatient exhale. "Why don't I let you go? I'm sure you have a million things to do. I'll see you at Zoe's party."

"All right," she says.

Two fucking words?

"I won't stay too long because the guys will be waiting for me at the Quintus—"

"You mean Dark Compulsion?"

"No, Dom. I mean the Quintus Hotel."

"Surely, you'll stop by the private adult club that caters to Hollywood's Who's Who since it's annexed to the Quintus. After all, membership has its perks. Unless you hook up with a girl on the yacht."

"What kind of statement is that?" Now, I'm pissed off.

"Just sayin'."

I let out a loud exhale. "Are we fighting again, Dom?"

"We aren't fighting," she says. "Why don't you just come out and say it?"

"Say what?"

"After Eddie's party you'll find an eager fuck buddy for the night—like you always do—which is why you'll only pop in and out of Zoe's birthday party."

Her bitter tone jabs at my heart.

"This conversation is heading south. Fast. I called to find

out how you were doing after an extended absence from LA"—*and because I missed you*—"I didn't call for us to be at it like cats and dogs. I thought our time apart would cool things off between us. Not that I know why the sight of me—or the sound of my voice—repulses you so much, but it does. I'll catch you later."

With that, I hang up.

What the fuck?

~

Bonus Scene

For a bonus scene about Gage and Lily (Gage and Lily Seven years later), subscribe to my newsletter.
www.MyRomanceAddiction.com

Who's The Next Book Boyfriend in This Scorching Hot Series?

Drum roll...

Larkin Gallagher

Coming Soon.

In the meantime, binge read Rod's book and the entire It Was Always You series. The Moguls are part of that binge-worthy world.

The series is so unputdownable, you'll lose sleep over it. And no, I'm not sorry.

Each book in the **It Was Always You** series can be read as a standalone, but why miss out on a copious amount of sauciness by not starting at the beginning?

Always You (Levi and Jules) kicks off the series with a naughty ball that's so hot, it comes _with_ a warning.

★★★★★ "Wonderful writing! I love a Cinderella story that pulls you in and invests you in the emotions of the characters. I felt Jules' pain and anger with her family situation and Levi's immediate need for her. Just wow! Can't wait to read number two." – Kelli S.

Reviews are like a cherry on a sundae–they make all the difference.

It only takes a few minutes to leave a review, which makes a huge difference for an indie author like myself.

**Here's the link to leave a review for:
Damaged Mogul**

Scarlett's Book Banter

Dear Sexy Reader,

Gage + Lily = MAGIC!

Even though those two are opposites in every way and they live on opposite sides of the country, they were meant for each other. Lily's desperate need to be loved and to love makes her the only woman who could've melted Gage's hard shell. Her innocence heals this big, gruff man from the guilt he's been carrying surrounding his mother's death.

Lily may have found herself in the same precarious position as her mother—an unplanned pregnancy at a young age, but unlike her callous-and-incapable-of-showing-human-emotions father, Gage would scorch the Earth to embers to keep her and her baby safe. Every girl dreams of that kind of over the top alpha protectiveness.

The week Lily spent in LA allowed her to stand her ground and blossom into a woman. I'm not just talking about her losing her cherry. Gage pushed her to fully embrace the fact she was born to be a jewelry designer, and not her puppet master's pawn. I love that kind of 'stand by your woman' vibe.

LA also allowed her to let the massive amount of love she had to give flow out, and Gage Hollingsworth got to bask in it.

Make sure to read the bonus scene because we get to visit the couple seven years in the future and find out if they had a boy or a girl and we get a sneak peek into their lives as parents.

Now, let's talk about the spice.

Since Lily is a virgin, I wanted to keep that innocence, but I didn't want her to be a Pollyanna. For three years, Gage has been suppressing so many of his raunchy, sexual needs—and his desire for Lily is so potent—I had to make it dirty in a way that hits just right.

I'll be honest, I hesitated about that scene in the car, but in the end, I thought, this is fiction and book boyfriends push you pass your comfort zone. Mr. Hollingsworth delivered in spades. He's the perfect lover and teacher for her.

The scene at Dark Compulsion was a hoot to write because the point was what can I throw at Lily to shock her. Also, after writing that scene, I too want my own pair of Victoria's Secret wings.

The translations

There was a lot of French in this book and I wanted to make sure you didn't miss a beat. Also, it was pretty cool to have both languages. Lilly's father may think she can't speak French, but girlfriend can hold her own.

For those who read French, I wanted to point out something so it doesn't come across as an error. In French, there's a space between the words and an exclamation mark or a question mark.

So, "*Mademoiselle Lily, vous descendez ?*"

My editor suggested my anglophone readers would think it was a mistake, which is why we eliminated the space.

Now that you're all wrapped up in Gage's alpha deliciousness, what next?

If you haven't binge read Always You, you should totally devour the pages of that book. If you've already fallen in love with Levi and

Jules's story and the five other couples in that series, don't worry. I've got you covered.

If your cat nip is a grumpy hero, Bryce Van Der Linden (Forever You) is about to become your next book boyfriend hangover.

If you love a grumpy hero that melts for the woman who brings him down to his knees, you won't be able to turn the pages fast enough. The brusque CEO never expected to fall for the *Pretty Woman* he hired for an evening at first sight. Bryce and Sofia's love story isn't smooth sailing. The drama and unexpected twists, will keep you reading well past your bedtime.

Forever You is an angsty romance between a jaded billionaire who has written off love after being betrayed one too many times and a selfless soul with a fighting spirit.

★★★★★ "First time reader of Scarlett Avery and I will definitely be reading more. Loved Bryce and Sofia's story! Kept you glued to the pages of all the twists and turns. Couldn't wait for my grandson to take a nap so I could finish this novel in two days." – Barbara

★★★★★ "Her books are nothing but fan-your-whole-body steamy and on-fire hot. She never fails to get you worked up." –Amazon Customer

★★★★★ "Oh my goodness! This book is so good and keeps you reading until the last page!" –Patsy

★★★★★ "I love this book! I don't read these types of books. But once I started reading this one, I couldn't put it down." –Stitchinggma

Binge-read now: Forever You

That's it for me.

Back to writing.

Much love,

Scarlett Avery

P.S. Reviews warm my heart as much as a bright sunny summer day.

P.P.S. I keep writing because of your hunger for my stories. Thank you for your fervor, love, and loyalty. I'm humbled and incredibly grateful. Without you, there's little reason to keep coming up with new stories.

P.P.P.S. For access to the Bonus Scene, go to:

www.MyRomanceAddiction.com

If you've already signed up to my list from previous books, you can visit the same page to download the Bonus Scene and/or Storyboard for this romance.

$$\sim$$

Welcome to the City of Angels where sparks fly and ignite into burning love. The beaming California sun pales in comparison to the wattage of passion in this series and the series it originated from. Framed by the Pacific Ocean, palm trees, an abundance of colorful flowers, and breathtaking views, Los Angeles is the city these commanding billionaires call home. These movers and shakers might be bone fide forever bachelors, but they'll risk their hearts for the women who bring them down to their knees.

The Moguls Series

These commanding CEOs and COOs go after the women who steal their hearts with guns blazing.

Bossy Mogul (Beckett and Arianne)

Off Limits Mogul (Rhys and Keira)

Ruthless Mogul (Phoenix and Michaela)

Damaged Mogul (Gage and Lily)

Roark Wolfe's grumpy/sunshine romance coming soon

The Moguls series is part of the It Was Always You world.

It Was Always You Series

These sexy as sin tattooed billionaires are notorious forever bachelors... that's until they cross paths with the women who bring them to their knees. And when they fall, they fall hard.

Always You (Levi and Jules)

Always Mine (Roderick and Dominika)

Always Destined (Lochlan and Kyla)

Always Forever (Holt and Everly)

Always Us (Jace and Eliana)

Always Love (Jagger and Stasia)

You'll find **all my books** and **reading order** on my site:
www.ScarlettAvery.com

About Scarlett Avery

Two-time *USA TODAY* and Amazon TOP 21 bestselling author Scarlett Avery unapologetically brings book boyfriends to their knees. Only smart, sassy, and vulnerable heroines are brave enough to unravel these heroes.

Scarlett's love stories are intense and passionate, emotional and steamy, layered with some delicious angsty scenes that always leave you begging for more.

She writes romance because with every story, she goes through the beautiful adventure of falling in love.

On a personal note...

Scarlett lives in the North Pole (aka Canada).

The Thomas Crown Affair (1999) is her favorite love story.

Love Actually is her all-time favorite Christmas movie.

She's a polyglot who'll gladly listen to the same audiobook in multiple languages when it's available.

She could live off elaborate cheese boards accompanied by

French or Portuguese bread and a fantastic glass of white wine.
Same goes for a mezze platter with Greek pita bread.

She has a serious love affair with Italian gelato and ice cream.
During summer months, you're sure to catch her sipping on an
Aperol spritz because, OMG those are so amazing.

Made in the USA
Columbia, SC
29 September 2025